WOLF

Patti Corbello Archer

Copyright

When one text changes everything...

WOLF

PROLOGUE
South of Marrakesh, Morocco

Covert operative Jax Carrington lay in the dark. Alert. And the small desert camp lay eerily silent on a chilly Wednesday night in October 4,000 miles from home.

Wind whipped his tent like a canvas windchime. Firepit flames danced in reflection against the walls. The shadow of a scorpion crawled along the outside of his tent looking for a way inside, eager to snuggle against his warmth. And not far away, bells jingled on camels. Six of them. The only transportation in this dry world of sunset-colored sand and wind.

Jax tensed suddenly. Something was wrong in the darkness. Not that he heard anything, but he sensed danger coming. It's stealth. A wolf howled in the distance and that was the last prompt he needed.

Avoiding the firelit entrance, he sliced through the back wall of his tent and slipped out. Kneeling behind Blaze's tent, he whispered, "Abort."

Without a word, Blaze's knife pierced the wall of his tent. Camels stirred beyond the firelight - grunting in alarm. Bells loud now.

Jax said, "Trouble's here. Hurry—"

A hail of automatic gunfire shattered the night from the far side of the camp. The Moroccan guides' screams were abruptly silenced as bullets tore through their tents. Jax and Blaze ducked low and ran toward the darkest shadows in the sand dunes. Gunfire continued to tear the night apart.

Jax stumbled but kept going as a searing pain hit his arm. Then another burn sliced across the side of his head just as he reached the edge. With a grimace of silent pain, he pitched himself forward, rolling down the backside of the dune into blackness.

He had barely stopped when Blaze slammed into him. Silent. Not moving.

Breathing hard, Jax drug Blaze with him until he couldn't see the light of the campfire in the sky anymore. Then dropping to his knees by a cluster of prickly desert shrubs, he grabbed a small flashlight and turned to his partner.

Three bloody holes in Blaze's torso explained why his blue eyes were open. Unblinking. Jax checked for a pulse. Not expecting one. Not finding it. With a tightening of his jaw, he did what he was trained to do and dug a shallow grave. Removed all identification off Blaze and took a picture of him with the satellite phone. Proof of death.

Then Jax sent two texts.

One to the only man he could trust now.

And the other to his sister.

Afterwards, he buried his partner. Then buried the satellite phone so the body could be located by GPS. And finally, he bandaged the wound on his head and arm. Once he was done, he pulled out a compass. A mental map of their location flashed in his mind.

He knew where he was.

Pulling night vision goggles over eyes that were hard and lethal now, he grabbed all the backpacks and weapons. And in seconds, disappeared into blowing sand.

The night had just begun.

Chapter 1
Same time: North of Dallas, Texas

The click of a bolt was loud in the cottage filled with late afternoon sun rays. The door from the garage into the kitchen opened, and auburn-haired beauty, Velvet Carrington, stepped inside with the phone to her ear.

Shutting the door, she said, "Exactly which wild animals should I be prepared to encounter while I'm there?"

The realtor said, "Black bears, coyotes, bobcats, deer, and even mountain lions. And believe it or not, even bison and elk have been seen. We advise you to admire everything from afar. You might want to bring bear spray as a deterrent."

"No problem. How close is the nearest cabin to mine?"

"Not close at all. You will see rooftops dotted throughout the mountain ranges, but privacy is a given. The trails are fabulous and the creek beautiful. You will enjoy your stay. And since you are prepaid for the month, come and go as you please. It's yours."

"Where can you leave the key since I won't arrive until well after midnight?"

"On the back deck, third post to your right of the steps. The security code is set for you. Velvet numerically is 835838."

Velvet smiled as she dropped her purse and keys onto the table. "I shouldn't forget that. Again, thank you for everything."

Disconnecting the call, Velvet's high heels clicked smartly on wood floors as she passed through the den and headed down the hall. Flipping on the bronze candlelight chandelier in her bedroom, she settled her phone into the speaker and turned on her playlist.

Sighing in relief, she kicked off the heels she'd worn all day as one of the curators at the Dallas Museum of Art. Music filled her room and she unzipped the classic black dress. Mid-thigh. Sleeveless. V-neck. Classy and elegant. She tossed it on the bed. And did a little freedom dance.

Since receiving her history degree from Tulane in New Orleans over four years ago, her in-depth knowledge of world exhibits, art, civilizations, documents, maps and excavations had transported her into a realm filled with the past. And all this time it had been exciting. Thrilling even. But it was still the past.

A place where her secrets lived too.

So, today was her last day at the museum and the next step into all her tomorrows. Of a future yet unknown. No longer living in remnants of years gone by. But rather, determined to find the adventure she'd hungered for since leaving Louisiana…and the pain she'd left behind.

She was ready to experience a life she'd only dreamed about. With thrills she could feel. And with someone that made memories worth having. Memories that would still give her a rush in fifty years. A mental movie in old skin that still remembered how it felt.

Forever extraordinary.

Heading toward the closet she pulled the clip from her hair. A cloud of dark auburn waves with streaks of brown and gold tumbled down her back, stopping just above her waist. The color, an accurate depiction of the fire inside her.

She slipped on faded jeans with expensive rips and frays. Soft and sexy. And they rode her narrow hips tight, reminding her of the firm hands of her dreams. Not yet known but believing for.

Next, she reached for a moss green turtleneck covered with embroidered flowers. It was thin, silky, and vibrant, leaving her waist bare. Much sexier than her usual clothes, it proved freedom - and was one of her favorite purchases for the trip.

And last, her boots. Knee high painted leather. A boho cowboy design with a touch of fringe. Fun and sassy. Bold. Slipping them on, she headed to the mirror to touch up her makeup.

Extra eyeliner and mascara turned her green eyes sultry. Burgandy lipstick covered her full lips. And a spray of perfume was the finishing touch. She was done. Laughing, she spun in the mirror, auburn hair flying.

Gone was the calm classic beauty.

The enchantress was loose.

Ten minutes later she wheeled her luggage into the garage. She loaded the hatchback of her bronze Jeep with everything she would need for a month. Two suitcases. A duffel bag. Hiking gear. Yeti cooler. Pillow and quilt. Her briefcase, computer, and backpack. She tossed her leather jacket on the back seat and climbed in the front.

Watching the garage door rise in the rearview mirror, Velvet smiled. A month's vacation on her own. She had a month to decide what her next move would be.

∗∗∗

The traffic was crazy as Velvet headed back into Dallas to the Warwick Melrose hotel. Not that the hotel was her intended destination - The Library inside of it was. And not a traditional library, but an opulent hotel-based lounge with live music, cocktails, and delicious food. Leather furniture. Gorgeous lighting. Impressive dining tables. Beautiful wood everywhere. Including bookshelves filled with books for a warm, study-style atmosphere designed with great seating for a group or privacy.

Not far from the museum where she'd worked, it had always been the perfect place for after-work socializing. Like tonight. Her friends had insisted on celebrating her last work night with her. And Indigo, her best friend since college, was already there. Waiting. And based on her texts, impatient.

The phone rang.

Indigo's name flashed. Velvet smiled as she answered, "Come on, Indigo. I'm almost there."

Indigo huffed, "What have you been doing? I'm dying here."

Laughing, Velvet said, "You just want to put me through an inquisition. You can't stand not knowing what I'm up to."

"What do you expect? You are just like your brother. Secrets. Hints. Innuendos. And more secrets. I'm forced to be a detective."

"It's called nosey."

"It's more than that. It's my job as a best friend and I am excellent at it - if I say so myself."

Smiling as she turned into the hotel drive, Velvet said, "You are. And I'm here. I'm pulling up to valet. Are you at the bar or a table?"

"At the bar on my third margarita."

Laughing, Velvet hung up. Indigo rarely drank.

Dusk was slipping into ebony as Velvet handed off her Jeep to the valet who tried hard to keep his eyes off her body – surprised at her unusual sexy appearance.

She smiled at his effort, and said, "Good evening, Chad."

The college senior who was always tipped well for his excellent…and wise…service to well-connected and lovely clientele responded, "Welcome, Ms. Velvet. It's always a pleasure to see you."

With a smile and nod, Velvet climbed the steps into the boutique hotel, a far cry from ancient exhibits and art she spent her day with. Turning left, she entered The Library and scanned the occupied gold leather bar stools across the room. She easily found Indigo in animated conversation with a man seated next to her and one standing nearby.

Indigo was intelligent and beautiful. Single. Petite with long layered black hair. Tawny skin. And dark brown eyes with a sexy but mischievous grin. Their gazes met and Velvet laughed at the jaw-dropping surprise on Indigo's face as she did a double take.

Halting her conversation with a raised hand, Indigo slid off the stool. Dressed in black slacks, fabulous high heels and a deep V top, she met Velvet in the middle of the room. She said, "You are sex in boots. And look at the shocking amount of skin you've got on display. Are you high, Velvet?"

Velvet burst out laughing. "Hardly. But thank you – I think."

As they walked toward their reserved table in the corner, Indigo said, "Out with it. What's going on?"

Settling onto a thickly padded leather chair, Velvet laid her fringed bag on the table. She crossed her legs.

Playing the game, Indigo laid her phone down and leaned back in her chair and waited for answers.

Velvet said, "I'm leaving tonight for a month. My Jeep is loaded. I'm headed to the Kiamichi Mountains in Oklahoma. I've rented a getaway perched on a bluff high above Eagle Fork Creek. It's beautiful with great hiking. This change has been coming. I need adventure. I want this."

"Don't lie to me. You need a man."

Velvet's phone vibrated with a call. She slipped it out of her purse and checked. Anger flared at the name on the screen. She killed the call and looked back at Indigo.

Indigo continued with her comment, "You never date. Tell me you don't need a man. I've seen you look at Crazy Horse's statue as you work his exhibit all touchy feely. I'm not blind. You have the hots for a man that will be hard for eternity."

They laughed until they were breathless. Though Velvet knew the comment wasn't totally in left field. Then her phone vibrated again – demanding her attention. She saw the same name and killed the call. Again. She was not answering it.

Velvet glanced at Indigo and said, "You miss the point entirely with Crazy Horse. Let me ask you a question. What type of man are you attracted to?"

Indigo's cheeks flushed. She side-stepped the question and countered, "Be more specific."

Velvet said, "Ok. Do you like a man with long hair or short? Skin that's tan or fair? Great eye action? Sex appeal? Great body? I mean, what turns you on?"

"Well, it seems you've been busier than I thought in the recesses of the museum."

"Answer my question, Indigo. But then… I already know the answer, don't I? I know your type. My brother."

Indigo frowned. "Fat lot of good that does me. It's been Jax since college. Not that he cares. He considers me another sister. Speaking of, have you talked to him lately? He's been silent for a couple of weeks. Oh…wait. Save that for another conversation. Get back to you…and your Crazy Horse point. What is it about him that turns you on?"

Velvet smiled wistfully. "The concept of a true alpha male. Hero and protector. Rugged. Wild. Beautiful, with an obvious passion you can taste before he even touches you."

Indigo whistled softly. "Shit. I get you. And I sure can't think of anyone around here that fits that description. So, you aren't looking for a city boy."

"No."

"So that's why you've only group dated since you've been in Dallas. No wonder you're heading to the mountains. How long has it been since you've even kissed someone?"

Velvet's phone vibrated again. Irritated visibly, she checked the caller, killed the call, and glanced at Indigo who was frowning – finally grasping that something was wrong with the calls.

Sliding the phone across the table to show Indigo the caller ID, Velvet said, "I haven't kissed anyone since I divorced him."

Indigo's gasp was loud with pure shock. Including the gasps coming from the crowd that had just walked up behind Velvet. Ignoring their friends, Indigo picked up the phone and read the name: Detective Dillon Black.

She looked at Velvet. "Just when did you get yourself a husband?"

Everyone waited for Velvet's response. No one moved. Not their friends behind Velvet. Or the waiter who'd gotten caught in the middle of the unveiling. Suddenly amused at the situation, Velvet bit her lip trying not to

7

laugh. She glanced at the shocked faces around her and shrugged. "A public proclamation wasn't how I would have chosen to share this. But… Everyone, get seated and I'll explain after we order."

Blonde museum co-worker, friend, and all-around sweetie, Miranda, sat next to Indigo.

River, Indigo's hot cowboy brother, sat next to Miranda – his fiancé.

And charming, handsome Dominic, photographer, and fellow member of their hiking team, sat next to Velvet.

And in a minute, the waiter was on his way back to the bar, relieved to escape the drama.

Dominic bumped against Velvet's shoulder. "I love the new look. You are fabulous. Do you have any idea what striking pictures I could take of you? Throw your other clothes in the trash. You have found the defining you. Too bad your ex-husband didn't see you like this. What's the idiot's name again?"

Everyone laughed, and humor found its way back into the unveiling conversation. Indigo stared at the name on Velvet's screen and said, "Detective Dillon Black." Glancing at Velvet she said, "I know that name. Wasn't he the detective investigating the shooting the night we graduated from Tulane?"

Velvet nodded. "He was." She paused. "After you moved back to Texas, he and I connected throughout the months waiting on the trial. And then after the trial, we dated, skipped my master's graduation and got married in Vegas. Then divorced. All in a shockingly short period of time."

River asked, "Damn. How shocking?"

"The marriage…a little over two months. I moved to Dallas just before the divorce was final. And I haven't talked to him since. I don't know why he is calling, and I don't want to know."

Indigo fought hurt and said, "I can't believe you didn't tell me. Why the secrecy?"

That answer was a nightmare that Velvet had no intention of sharing. With anyone. Ever. She said, "I know and I'm truly sorry. It was a rash decision that went downhill quickly. No one knew. Not even Jax. I didn't want to talk about it then, much less now. So… Let's forget it."

Indigo narrowed her gaze as she pondered the explanation and eyed Velvet. She said, "Everyone figures Jax is a spy with all his disappearances. So, for you to hide it from him tells me that there is a tremendous amount of something

8

crucial that you aren't saying. Or did you think Jax would hide the detective's body in a Louisiana swamp?"

The phone vibrated in Indigo's hand. It was Dillon. She handed the phone back to Velvet to see what she would do. Velvet killed the call and blocked the number. There would be no more calls.

She smiled and said, "Now, where were we? Does anyone want to know about your Oklahoma hiking invitation?"

✳✳✳

Two hours later, they called it a night since Velvet needed to get on the road to Oklahoma. River and Miranda left first - after River insisted that she tell Jax about Dillon. The Louisiana swamp idea was always an option.

After a fist bump in agreement with River, Dominic coaxed Velvet toward the music for a short dance. His expression turned serious as he drew her close. He scanned her face. She smiled, knowing what was coming.

He tucked a stray auburn strand behind her ear and said, "Dillon hurt you. A lot. You should have said something. Secrets have a way of sinking in their claws to stay hidden…and painful. Look…now you've quit your job and are running off alone."

"Not for what you think. I need adventure. You know, spread my wings and explore life."

"He is why you and I didn't become a WE."

"Dominic, stop it. You have women fawning over you and your blonde ponytail. But I need the friend you are to me. A lifelong friend." She touched his face. "I've never been the one for you, and you know it."

She glanced toward the beautiful blonde singer who watched them with pained eyes. "Chantel is the one for you."

He glanced at the singer and winked. Chantel smiled. Relieved. He pulled Velvet's hair. "I hate it when you're right."

"Which is often."

He laughed, then sobered. "Be careful, Velvet. You are a gorgeous woman. Protect yourself. Douse any man with bear spray out on the trail. They're all wild animals."

She laughed. "You would know. Now, go sit and listen to Chantel. I need to talk to Indigo. See you soon."

He kissed her on both cheeks as Indigo motioned for her to hurry up.

9

In the hotel lobby, Indigo said, "It's pitiful. Dominic does love you."

Velvet said, "And I love him. A male friend is a special bond. But affection and friendship don't mean he's in love with me. At least not by my definition. I would never waste what he means to me on a fling."

She shrugged. "Especially since I don't have flings. I want him to have everything he deserves. And that's not me. It's Chantel."

Indigo nodded. "I agree. So now, let's get back to the man you're looking for in the mountains."

"No. Let's talk about Jax."

Indigo glanced away with a look of pain. "What's to talk about? Your brother will never see me the way I see him. I've never seen passion or attraction in his eyes. Ever. I'm 29 and wasting my time. A worse pitiful than Dominic."

"Then make a move on Jax. Shake him loose. Challenge him. Tease him. Give it your best shot and walk away. See if he lets the beast loose. Personally, I think he's hooked and holding back. He deserves a taste of the siren in you. Then…make him work for it."

Indigo smiled, dark eyes flashing. "That sounds delicious."

"Exactly."

The valet stepped inside and motioned Indigo that her car was ready. Velvet hugged her and said, "Go. Don't wait for me. I'm going to run to the restroom before I leave. I'll keep in touch."

As she walked away, Indigo called over her shoulder, "You better… I will find you."

***

A short time later, Velvet walked out of the restroom headed to valet when she heard a text on her phone. She pulled it out of her purse. It was an unknown number from a satellite phone. Jax had called and messaged her like this before.

She opened the text.

Velvet, someone is trying to kill us.
You have got to run. Hide. And don't tell a soul.
Forget your normal life and get out of there.
Get your go-bag like we practiced.
Wear your disguise and take the next Amtrak to Denver.

Nothing else matters.
Just get to Denver.
Jax

Velvet froze in the middle of the hall and read it again, oblivious to the people around her. She believed every word Jax had typed. And just like that, everything changed. Taking a deep breath, her mind clicked into survival mode. She used a hotel phone to call a taxi and slipped out a side door onto Dickason Avenue.

And vanished in the shadows of Dallas.

Chapter 2

It was dark in the country with only sporadic porch lights as Velvet followed the road that would lead to the back of her property. She listened to every sound, watching for movement as she walked in the grass. Making sure to stay near trees if she could. She was nervous, not knowing what she might find at home. And she had to go home.

That was where her go-bag was.

She was almost there.

A few owls hooted. There was a cat fight in the distance. A limb fell in the woods. And a couple of dogs barked, but no owners came outside to check. Nearing her neighbor's barn garage combo, she turned and followed alongside his building. Walking slowly, she checked out her yard, patio, and back of her cottage. The soft glow of the fairy lights helped to see, but the plants and furniture on the patio hid most of the back door. She knelt beside an oak tree and watched. Five minutes. Ten.

Then moving swiftly, she slid along the back of the house into the plants. She ducked by the kitchen door and keyed in the security code for entrance without lights - then slipped inside.

She stood still and listened. Looked around. Nothing screamed danger. So, taking off her boots and carrying them, she quietly made her way to her room. And with only filtered moonlight from shaded windowpanes, she pulled her go-bag backpack and a large box out of the closet.

Working fast, she stripped, leaving her new clothes in a pile and opened the box. She pulled on a black warm up suit and nondescript tennis shoes. Then grabbing a zipper bag from the box, she headed to the bathroom.

With only the nightlight to go by, Velvet braided her hair and wound it around her head. Then washed off her makeup and applied a darker, unflattering shade of foundation – adding dark rings around her eyes.

Unzipping a smaller bag, she pulled on a salt and pepper wig styled in a shoulder length bob with bangs. And last of all, slipped on a pair of black framed eyeglasses.

Velvet stared in the mirror.

In the space of a few minutes, she had aged 40 years - maybe 50.

Now, the final step. She sighed. Some of what she needed was in the Jeep at the hotel. But it was totally inaccessible now. She would have to make do with what she had here. Denver would be freezing. Snowy. Windy. She pulled out enough winter clothes for two, maybe three days. Jeans. Leggings. Sweatshirts. Hiking boots and thick socks. A hooded parka, hat and gloves. She stuffed it in a duffel bag and set it by the window.

She locked her purse and phone in her closet safe and opened the backpack. She verified the contents:

- 9MM pistol and ammo
- Flashlight
- Hunting knife
- Burner phone with chargers
- First aid kit
- Protein bars
- Two thousand dollars cash with a fake driver's license and credit card
- And Jax's storage building key

She added her makeup kit, toiletries, and wet wipes. Zipping it up, she heard a car on the road in front of her house. She stopped, listening. A dog barked. Hurriedly, she unlocked the window facing the back yard and raised it, dropping the duffel bag and backpack outside. Quickly pulling on a hoodie, she slid one leg over the windowsill.

Glass shattered somewhere in the house. They were here.

In a second, Velvet was out of the window grabbing the bags. Then she smelled gas and ran. She was almost off her property when the house exploded.

The blast threw her forward and she landed face down. Debris rained down with bits of fire still attached. Catching her breath, she brushed embers and pieces of her house off as she glanced back at the inferno.

Scrambling to her feet, she raced for the woods.

Velvet sat hidden in the trees watching her house burn. Too scared to cry. People were everywhere. Neighbors. Cops. Firemen. And maybe the one that tried to kill her.

She leaned her head against the tree, aware that she couldn't wait long before running. Once they didn't find a body inside, the killer would be after her again.

✳✳✳

It was after 3 a.m. when the yellow taxi dropped Velvet down the road from a self-storage facility not far from Amtrak Union Station in Dallas. Fifteen minutes later, she unlocked the padlock on Jax's temperature-controlled room. Locking it from the inside, she leaned back against the concrete wall.

Adrenaline began to fade as she listened to herself breathe in the dark. Exhaustion rose. She was safe for the first time since she'd gotten the text from Jax… She looked at her burner phone for the time.

Six hours ago.

She flipped the light on and looked around the storage safe room her brother had set up for her to use for exactly a moment like this. Eleven years older than her, and protective, Jax traveled continually with a government job he never discussed. And the two of them were the only immediate family that remained. Their parents, much older, passed away during the Covid pandemic.

So, Jax prepared this room. Trained her how to shoot. Set up her go-bag. And told her if anything ever happened to do exactly what he told her. No deviation. And now here she was, where she never thought she'd be. Which meant, Jax was a lot more than an overprotective brother.

Danger had been a real possibility.

She headed down the hall between moving boxes and furniture to the back of the unit. There was an area with a desk and chair. A twin bed with a small vanity. And a portable toilet.

Sighing, she sat on the chair. Living in a storage unit wasn't legal. But this wasn't living, it was staying alive. As it was, she would have to sleep with her gun and the burner phone. What if someone followed her?

She'd shoot them. She really would.

After cleaning up as much as she could, she got into bed and leaned against the small headboard. Pulling her knees against her chest, she wrapped her arms around them as tremors of fear played havoc with her senses.

She couldn't relax even though she was exhausted. Her mind was frantic. The news would broadcast about her house explosion. The hotel would claim she was missing because of her unclaimed Jeep. The Fire Department wouldn't find her body.

And what about the attempted killer? Indigo and her friends? And where was Jax? Was he even alive? Tears trickled down her cheeks.

She glanced at the gun and at the shadows in the room. She had done all she could. Even Amtrak reservations were made. But what would happen when she arrived in Denver?

She had no idea at all.

Chapter 3
Colorado 4 a.m.

Northwest of Denver, secluded deep in the Rocky Mountains, Remington Wolf sat at his computer watching a GPS grid. The tracker he'd been monitoring went live before midnight and stopped in downtown Dallas thirty minutes ago. It was on but not moving much.

That meant she'd made it to the safehouse.

Relieved, he leaned back in his chair and ran a hand through his shoulder length brown hair, then stretched. He rose to his six-foot three-inch, lean, tough frame wearing faded jeans. A pistol. Hiking boots. And an unbuttoned turquoise flannel shirt exactly the color of his eyes. He headed upstairs for a fresh mug of coffee.

He'd never met Jax's little sister. Time, military ops, and responsibilities always interfered – though Jax kept trying to set it up. And now he would meet her, but he was damn sure it would not be the way she preferred.

So, in preparation for that, research was necessary. In depth. He needed to know her behavior. Her movements. Expressions. And any dangerous history in her life. Which meant, he would need to know more about her than she would ever want him to know.

Everyone held things back. Be it privacy or secrets. But these were extenuating circumstances, and he didn't even know what she looked like…yet. All Jax said was that she was beautiful and smart. But none of that mattered - only keeping her safe. Jax's sister would be treated like family. Even if he had to die doing it.

A few minutes later, zipping up a coat, he walked outside on the porch. A wolf howled close by. Wind whipped. Snow flurries twisted and turned. Fanciful. Nothing heavy. Not yet. The blizzard wouldn't arrive until the day after tomorrow. Friday. Which would be a challenge.

Velvet's Amtrak trip to Denver would leave Dallas in 11 hours. Tomorrow…well, today at exactly 3:38 in the afternoon. And she would arrive at 7:30 on Friday morning. A 17-hour trip. His goal was to follow her tracker. Take her. And have her here by the time the blizzard hit the mountains.

Looking just beyond the edge of the porch light, he whistled. A few minutes later a pair of eyes moved from the dark grove of trees. Remington cracked open the massive door behind him and waited. A four-footed shadow walked toward him.

Stepping inside, he stayed silent as a large male wolf with a hip scar climbed the steps and entered the log cabin. With silent communication, they both settled by the fireplace. Remington with his coffee. The wolf with his bowl of coffee milk - wolf cappuccino.

Their connection was obvious. The wolf had been viciously hurt a few years ago by a mountain lion. He'd taken it to a vet, got supplies, and nursed it back to health. The massive animal visited from time to time...without doglike affection...but with trust in abundance. An honored gift.

In the stillness, Remington thought through his rescue plan for Jax's sister. Time passed as the wolf dozed. The fire crackled. But still he focused on the plan. His eyes, intense.

In an hour the wolf was gone. Then he headed downstairs to meet Velvet Carrington. He typed her name into a search engine that made Google look like a toy...and hacked her.

Chapter 4
Thursday: The Trip

It was afternoon when Velvet arrived at Eddie Bernice Johnson Union Station in disguise. It was a relief to blend into the Dallas crowd with all the commotion. Who would notice an elderly woman in black sweats with gray hair and a couple of bags?

Exactly. No one.

She had left the original sweatsuit and hoodie behind. The explosion left them smelling like smoke and peppered with dozens of small holes from burning debris. She'd dug through a box of Jax's old workout clothes in the storage room and found a sweatsuit and hoodie that would work – though baggy.

Heading to the waiting area specific to Amtrak, she settled in a corner and picked up a magazine. She watched over the top for anyone focused on her. And slowly, she relaxed. Everyone was either looking at their phone, tickets, or corralling kids.

The train arrived at 3:15. A few passengers exited the train, then new passengers were allowed to board. Velvet entered her assigned sleeper car. She'd reserved accommodation for a private bedroom and bathroom and didn't intend to leave it until she'd reached Denver.

And it was well worth the money she charged on the credit card in the name Sarah Thomas. Hopefully the charge went to some fund, somewhere, in an agency allotted for this type of emergency. She couldn't handle getting arrested for theft.

She followed her friendly first-class attendant, Randy, as he carried her bags to the room. He was fair with short hair. Probably early twenties. And he talked the whole way.

"Ms. Thomas, welcome aboard Amtrak! We hope that your trip is wonderful. Be sure to press the call button if you need me for anything." He stopped at an open doorway for sleeper number 28C and motioned her in.

18

After showing her the amenities in her room, he pointed to the menu and said, "Room service is provided if you prefer not to visit the café or dining car. I can bring you anything at any time. And just let me know when you are ready for me to set up your bed."

He touched the call button. "If you need a snack or coffee, let me know — and enjoy your ride."

Smiling slightly, Velvet said, "Thank you, Randy. I appreciate it. I'm tired and will probably just stay in my room. I'll let you know if I need anything."

Saluting, he smiled and shut the door behind him.

She locked it. And stood there for a minute with her eyes closed. Acclimating. Then turning, faced the large windows overlooking Dallas. The conductor announced over the intercom that the train would be departing the station in ten minutes.

Before long, the train rocked smoothly as Velvet sat on the sofa in disguise. Gun near her right hand. She was weary, desperately needing the next 17 hours to be relatively safe. She refused to consider whether anyone had followed her aboard the train.

Pulling out her burner phone, she searched Dallas news for updates on the explosion. Nothing new besides the original reporting. Indigo, Dominic, River and Miranda had to be tripping. Panicked. Or maybe they didn't even know yet. For all they knew, she was in Oklahoma looking for adventure.

She wiped tears off cheeks caked with mottled makeup four shades darker than her young skin.

Adventure had found her instead.

∗∗∗

Fifteen hours later, Amtrak pulled to a stop in Colorado Springs. Dawn was still an hour away. Several people disembarked onto a platform lit by bright lights and hurried inside the station. It was cold. Windy. And snow flurries danced about.

Several passengers waited to board. About 20. Two groups of skiers. Several businessmen and women with briefcases. A young family. And three lone men. Before long the passenger exchange was made.

Velvet heard men's voices on the other side of the wall as she climbed out of the shower. The door shut in the room next to hers as she dried off. They would be in Denver in less than two hours. She pulled on a black sports bra and bikini underwear. And because it was getting colder, added a luxuriously soft long sleeve cotton undershirt with a pair of flannel lined leggings and heavy socks.

Then as the train left the station, she removed the towel from her hair. Wet auburn locks tumbled around her. Glancing in the mirror, she gave a small smile. It gave her a little bit of comfort seeing herself again.

Except for the new cuts and bruises.

And thirty-five minutes later her hair was dried, braided and hidden under the gray wig. Her face had aged again. And she was dressed in baggy warmup pants, a hoodie and hiking boots. Adding the fake glasses, she pressed the button for the attendant.

In moments, Randy knocked on her door. "Morning, Ms. Thomas. I hope you slept well. May I help you?"

Unlatching the door to slide it open, Velvet said, "Morning, Randy. And yes. Please." She handed him a note and said, "That's a list for a bottle of water, a large coffee with cream and sugar on the side, two breakfast burritos, and fresh fruit. And if you need to change it, that's fine. Whatever they have. I do appreciate it."

"Absolutely! I will be back as quick as I can."

Shutting and latching the door, she began to straighten the covers on the bed. A knock sounded on the door. Randy must have a question. Smiling as she unlocked the door, all she saw was a broad chest and bright blue eyes.

Before she could do more than register shock, the man was in her room. And in one fluid movement, her feet left the floor as he spun, covering her mouth with one hand while locking the door with the other. A second later, she was pressed face first against the wall pinned in arms of steel as she struggled, trying to scream.

A deep voice said, "Easy, Velvet. Jax sent me."

She blinked, thinking... What?

He said, "I'm sorry for the scare but I couldn't let you scream. If you promise to be quiet, I'll remove my hand. We can't afford a commotion. I don't know if anyone hunting you is on the train."

Velvet nodded. He moved his hand a little, testing her.

Heart racing, Velvet said, "Who are you?"

"Remington."

Her mind raced to place it, but it landed nowhere. She hissed, "Jax hasn't ever mentioned a Remington to me. Your name means nothing. Who the hell are you?"

Behind her, his lip twitched. "I'm Wolf. Remington Wolf."

Immediately, she twisted, trying to turn. Expecting her response, he let her go. She spun, meeting his gaze. "Prove it."

"We don't have time for this, Velvet. I don't have my license on me."

"Then if you're Wolf, you have a tattoo."

Without hesitation, he unsnapped his jeans - and that was proof enough for her. She grabbed fistfuls of his shirt. Breathless, she said, "Where is Jax, Wolf? Is he hurt? What hap—"

Wolf silenced her, covering her lips with his fingers. "All I can tell you is that he is working with a problem. Keeping you safe is my mission. Just you and me. So, when this train stops, I've got to get you to my truck and then to my cabin. That is all that matters right now. Including your obedience – unless you know how to survive in mountains, snow, and wilderness all by yourself."

"I know next to nothing about snow and mountains except for two skiing trips. I know how to hike and shoot. That's it."

"That's more than most people know that come to Colorado."

Something occurred to her. She frowned. "You recognized me through the disguise."

He knew what was coming. "Yep."

Her eyes narrowed. "Jax told me you had skills. Are you a hacker?"

"Sort of. Among other things."

Looking away, knowing what he probably knew, she said, "That doesn't mean I want to talk about anything you discovered."

Turning her back to face him, he said, "What you want isn't going to matter. We will have to discuss Dillon at some point."

She shrugged him off. "I'll think about it. How did you find me?"

"When you activated your burner phone, I tracked you."

A knock sounded on the door. Randy called, "Ms. Thomas? I have your order."

Wolf stepped into the bathroom and pulled his gun. He pointed at the door. Eyes wide, Velvet grabbed the hundred-dollar bill off her table and opened the door. Not giving Randy time for conversation, she handed him the money, took the basket, and shut the door.

Wolf pointed to her two bags on the floor. "Is that all you brought, or do you have any checked luggage?"

"Two bags are all I had time for. My house blew up before I'd barely reached the edge of my yard."

He tensed. They'd already tried to kill her. He growled, "Damn it. Are you hurt?"

"A few cuts and bruises on my head and back. I was half out of my window when I heard someone break into the house. I smelled gas and ran. After the explosion, I hid in the woods for hours. I thought the guy might still be around."

Looping her bags on his shoulder, he said, "We can't stay in this room. They might know the number. Let's go." And with a quick glance in the hallway, they went to the room next door.

The rooms were the same of course. Velvet noticed a cowboy style hat, a thick jacket, and well-worn leather gloves. She faced him.

Noting the time, he pointed toward the sofa. "We have almost an hour. Have a seat and eat your breakfast."

She wrinkled her nose. "My stomach is fighting off adrenaline. I'll just drink the coffee and let them fight it out."

She took a sip and glanced at him, fighting a sudden urge to giggle.

Leaning against the wall by the door, Wolf narrowed his gaze. "Say it. You're about to explode."

With a straight face she said, "One room over. We didn't go very far."

"Nope."

"So, you came aboard in Colorado Springs. I heard you when I was in the shower."

"Yep. I heard you."

"Soooo, what if you're the only one hunting me on the train?"

He sighed. She was certainly Jax's sister.

Velvet checked him out. He was taller than average. Not that anything about him was average. And he was sexy and gorgeous in jeans and a chocolate-colored turtleneck. Brown hair to his shoulders. And those blue eyes… It was amazing that she knew this man. Well, not know him, know him. But she felt safe, closer to Jax, and cocky.

She picked up his hat. It was sturdy. Kind of a wool, felt, oily mix with little flaps you could pull down over the ears. It reminded her a little of Indiana Jones. But it was heavier than she expected.

Innocently, she met his gaze. "Do you have a horse too?"

"A comedian. Aren't I lucky?"

"And I look old. If anyone saw us, they'd feel sorry for you. The cougar and the mountain hottie."

22

He shook his head. Beautiful, witty, and fine. He'd felt the body under those clothes. He said, "It's been a long time since I've been called a hottie."

She rolled her eyes. "Liar. You just ignore them. Jax told me about the women who want you. Everywhere... And all the times he saw—"

Dryly, he interrupted, "Jax should keep his mouth shut." And deciding to give a little back, he looked her over and said, "Besides, don't forget that I know exactly what you look like under that disguise. And from the top of your head to the soles of your feet, you are mouthwatering. I especially like the outfit you had on the other night – like a cowgirl gypsy all wild and free. I could smell you just looking at the picture."

Velvet took a deep breath as her face went red under the makeup. He winked and said, "And FYI, the blonde guy...Dominic...wants you."

"Ok, I get it. We're even."

He shifted and shoved a hand in his pocket. "Maybe I'm not satisfied with even. Tell me about the Native American Indian statue in most, and I repeat, most of your pictures. That's certainly an unsatisfying infatuation."

"That's my business. I love the Crazy Horse exhibit. He's taught me a lot about myself."

Now that was unexpected, and he said, "Do tell."

"Today was supposed to be day two of my month-long vacation all by myself in the Oklahoma mountains. I wanted to change my life. Hike the trails. Get out from behind a desk...from behind other people's lives in the museum. And embrace adventure, freedom, something wild and—"

His sexy smile flashed as she stopped. "Come on, Velvet. We both know you're looking for more than simple adventure. You want a man. Anyone special in mind?"

"That is none of your business, Wolf. And you sound like Indigo."

"I know that name."

"I'm not surprised. She's been after Jax since we were roommates in college. He won't bite the bait she dangles, but I know he's hungry."

Wolf nodded without saying anything in response – knowing a whole lot more than she did. And watching her, he thought about Dillon. Fury stirred at what he'd learned.

Velvet studied him. "What do you want me to call you? Remington or Wolf?"

He enjoyed the way she put pieces together. Feisty. Confident. She wasn't afraid of speaking her mind. He shrugged. "Whatever fits your mood."

Seriously, she said, "Thank you for coming, Wolf."

"Anytime, green eyes."

"Am I in serious danger?"

"Yes."

"Jax too?"

"Yes."

"You?"

"No. This isn't about me. I'm all about you, Velvet."

Worried about what her and Jax were tangled up in, she looked out the window and watched the sky lighten into a snowy Friday morning. Miles clicked by. Time. And picturesque Colorado filled the window. She was quiet as she prayed. Solemn. A lot of things could happen after they stepped off the train. A bodyguard redefined adventure. What did she really know about a man like him?

Wolf watched her. He hadn't lied. He could smell what a hot fire they'd make. But later. For now, life was going to be like a pinball machine with them avoiding what came at them. He touched his gun. No problem. He was the best at doing this. A pilot responded like electricity. In a flash.

The conductor announced over the intercom, "The train will be arriving in Denver in fifteen minutes."

Blue eyes met green ones.

Here we go.

Chapter 5

In north Maryland, a black Mercedes turned off Foxville Road and headed north on Park Central. Ignoring the beautiful scenery of Catoctin Mountain Park, the silver-haired driver stared straight ahead. Jaw tense. Hands kneading the steering wheel. Revenge stoking the flame inside of him.

Denver was on his mind.

He smiled, a hard one, and checked the time. He was satisfied. It wouldn't be long now. Speeding up for a few minutes, he saw the Visitor Center sign come into view. Then waited impatiently as a huge motorhome, hauling a truck and off-road vehicle, struggled to turn the massive convoy into the driveway.

The owner waved an apology, but rudely, the Mercedes sped to a secluded corner. He unbuckled, leaving the car running for the heater, and settled back to wait. Deadly focused, he watched the time.

Two minutes later his phone rang.

He answered, "Where's the train, Ziva?"

A female voice answered softly through her hidden microphone, "It's rolling in."

"Are you ready?"

"When am I not ready, Boss?"

"Good. You know what you're looking for. Take her out and disappear."

"Ten-four."

"How's the weather there?"

She said, "Winter with a snowstorm ramping up." There was a rustling sound, and she whispered, "Hang on... It's time. The train stopped. I've got to get moving."

"I'm listening. Make sure you keep me on the line."

Young athletic Ziva looked like a blonde college snow bunny. Ponytail, sports parka, snow boots, and rolling a suitcase with a snowboard strapped to it. She stood with other new passengers watching offloading passengers exit Amtrak. She eyed the platform for Velvet's particulars. A lone woman. Height and size first. Then face.

25

Professionally, her eyes scanned the women as they headed inside, checking only the ones who could identify with the picture in her head. Mentally she checked each one off as they entered the station.

No.

No.

No. Pause...

No.

No.

And after nine women, that was it.

She walked away with a frown, watching them stroll through the station. She turned to the others who disembarked. Couples. Groups of people. A pregnant woman. Three old women. Two tall ungainly women and a couple of chunky ones.

She heard Boss in her ear. Impatient. She glanced at the old women. One was limping with an old man. Another was ushered along by family. And one was escorted by maybe her son. A hot one. Or maybe he wasn't a son...

Ziva said softly, "I've got one old gray-haired woman with a man that could be security. He's got eyes like an eagle and is fit. And if he's not packing, I'm a mermaid. I'm going to follow them to the parking lot."

"Don't you dare lose them."

She ignored him and left her suitcase and snowboard by a chair. Eyes locked on the suspicious couple she followed them through the crowd.

✳✳✳

Wolf felt it. Eyes on them. He hadn't seen anything suspicious as they left the train. But now...

He steered Velvet to a rack of tourist information and turned to scan the crowd behind them...looking at each face.

Picking up on his intensity, Velvet glanced up. "What's wrong?"

"Give me a minute. Check out the brochures."

Trying not to be nervous, she snuggled into her hooded parka and faked reading. Edging a little closer to him.

Wolf watched a couple argue. An old man hurried to the bathroom. And a blonde woman with a ponytail suddenly put a lip lock on the man beside her. Several people laughed. He sighed. Nothing jumped out at him.

Turning back to Velvet, he slipped an arm around her. Pulling down the brim of his hat, he said, "Let's head out to my truck. We've got a good way to go. I've got you…"

They headed into the snow.

✳✳✳

Ziva stepped back and looked at the shocked, but eager skier she'd just kissed. He was still growing into the handsome man he'd be. But now, he was maybe 20. She winked. His group howled.

In seconds, she disappeared through the front doors.

Catching sight of the man's hat, she ducked low and followed behind a line of vehicles. Unzipping her jacket, she put her hand on the gun. He started a jagged path through the parking lot which kept her busy, preventing her from getting too close.

His hand moved under his jacket, and she smiled. A gun. Then he started to jog, pulling the woman with him. And it was confirmed. She knew there was no way an old woman could move like that. It had to be Velvet.

Target dead ahead.

When they were about a hundred yards from the train station, the man took a sharp right and vanished around a concrete wall into another parking lot.

Ziva ran.

Wolf clicked the key fob to his high-lift black F-150 king cab with snow tires, and literally chunked Velvet into the passenger seat. "Get down."

As she slid down, half in the seat, half on the floor, he ran to the driver's side and tossed her bags in the back seat. He started the truck as he climbed in – and put it in gear. Velvet squealed as she slid around – hanging on.

Ziva stood near the concrete wall. Pistol with silencer pointed at a family that had climbed out of their vehicle…right between her and the speeding truck. She scowled and they stared at her. Frozen with fear. Ziva turned and ran - updating Boss that they got away, but she was going after them.

He started cussing about the time she saw a big guy, 300 pounds or better, getting out of a souped-up blue king cab Ram pickup. She glanced around the area and smiled. Perfect.

Dropping the call with Boss, she quietly stepped up behind the man as he gathered his travel bags. She cleared her throat to get his attention.

He turned. Then seeing the little woman with the big gun, he froze.

Ziva said, "Get in the back seat."

He hesitated, then opened his mouth to say something. She interrupted and said, "This won't go well for you if you don't."

She watched him debate tangling with her for only a second, then he climbed in the back. And with two quick puffs of air, she shot him twice. Shoving him over on the seat, she took his keys, and in a minute, drove after the black truck.

She'd seen the direction he turned.

✳✳✳

Wolf gunned the truck to put distance between them and Amtrak. Glancing at Velvet, he said, "Sorry, that got intense. Go ahead and buckle up. You good?"

She nodded yes and settled safely in the seat. A few moments passed and she said, "I didn't see anyone."

"I didn't either, but that doesn't mean he wasn't there. I felt him."

"Would you have shot him?"

He gave her a direct look, and she nodded. Understood.

He yielded onto Interstate 70 west and said, "I'm going to travel northwest out of the mountains for a while. It will give us a faster trip since it's snowing – and it gives me time to see if we picked up a tail."

She nodded again and he met her gaze before continuing, "We are looking at two hours or better before we reach my place. Do you need anything before the snow gets worse?"

Velvet unzipped her coat. "Only permission to take off the top half of my disguise."

"Sure. My windows are tinted. Do you need your bags?"

"I do."

After passing her bags over the console, he watched the traffic behind them in the rearview mirror. He wanted to have a clear memory of which vehicles were there. Later, he changed lanes, merging with Highway 72 which would later take them into the mountains.

28

Wolf noticed Velvet toss the wig in the duffel bag and glanced at her. She unwound two long thick auburn braids. They dropped down well past her shoulders like ropes of fire. The glasses had already vanished.

She laid her head back and sighed. "Relief. I'm almost free." He chuckled.

Producing a wet wipe, she looked in the visor mirror and began to wipe makeup off her face. Fair, rosy skin began to emerge with each wipe until a pile of dirty rags filled her lap. She did a little seat dance.

He smiled and said, "You look 16."

The look she turned on him was not 16. And the spark that kicked off a flame in his gut resonated lower. He groaned silently. She had hair like fire. Sultry, heavy-lidded emerald eyes. And full lips. Damn it.

She waved a hand. "Sixteen was a long, long, time ago. I've earned every bit of the 28 I turned a few weeks ago. I'm expecting adventure this year. It looks like I got it."

"It looks like it."

"Thank you for what you're doing, Wolf – but my vacation hasn't turned out the way I planned." She cleaned wet wipes off her lap and continued to chat as she tossed her bags behind the seat. "Are you the same age as Jax?"

"Give or take a few months."

She smiled. "Thirty-nine, and oozing power and sex appeal. Your eyes are killer. Are you dating?"

He winked. "I could be. Are you offering?"

Teasing, she smiled. "It's a thought. But then again, I haven't dated in a long time."

Watching a truck pass them, he asked, "How long is long?"

"Since a real date? Since Dillon. But then again, he hardly counts."

Their eyes met. She saw the same look in them as when she asked about him shooting the guy at Amtrak. He grunted and fell silent.

Snow fell faster and heavier once they were entering the mountains. Wolf noticed a handful of familiar vehicles still following them. He'd have to lose all of them before he got near his turnoff. Looking up ahead he could barely see the mountains through the snow. And heavier snow was coming.

Things were about to become super challenging.

An hour later, Velvet frowned and glanced at Wolf. How was he driving in this? It was worse than trying to see through a wall of Louisiana fog and hope you didn't dive into the murky waters of a moss-covered bayou. This was like driving through a world of white that hid cliffs, rails, trees, and rock walls reaching into the sky.

She could see a few shadows beyond the truck - and that was it. Though his green GPS monitor on the dash helped her stay grounded. He even had a compass mounted under it.

Velvet said, "I'm surprised the GPS works."

Without taking his eyes off Highway 7, Wolf said, "It comes and goes most times, but it seems to be hanging in there today. And just to be prepared in case the weather gets worse, go ahead and put your parka back on. And grab your gloves and cap in case we need to get out. Just remember…cover as much as you can and do exactly what I say."

As Velvet nervously put on her winter gear, Wolf frowned in the side mirror. He knew there were two trucks behind them. A red one and a blue one farther back. He tapped the steering wheel…he was running out of time. Suddenly, a blinker came on. The red truck turned left and was gone.

***

Ziva watched the red truck turn off the road as her phone rang.

She answered through her headpiece, "Boss."

"Why in the hell haven't you called me back. I'm almost to Camp David."

"I'm in a snowstorm in the mountains. I'm tailing them through a wall of white. But it's almost time. A truck turned off and I'm finally directly behind them."

"What's your plan?"

"I'm winging it. And I can't talk so you'll just have to listen." And with no further explanation, she dropped the headpiece on the console.

Ziva could barely see black paint around the truck's red taillights. Calculating, she figured she was 60 to 75 feet behind them. Glancing at the GPS app on her phone, she groaned. She'd lost signal again. And all she knew was that they were on Highway 7.

The rough outline of a plan ran through her mind.

***

Wolf glanced at the GPS, setting their location in his mind. He knew that he had to make a move to evade the truck behind him now. And then he heard it. A quick glance in the rearview mirror confirmed it. The blue truck was heading straight for them.

30

"Cover your face," Wolf yelled at Velvet. "He's going to ram us!"

The sound of a screaming truck engine was loud. Velvet screamed as Wolf veered right at the same time a herd of elk appeared out of nowhere. One slammed into his window. Another jumped on the hood, cracking the windshield. And the other truck slammed into the back of them.

The world spun.

Wolf pressed Velvet back against the seat as she screamed.

***

The silence was cold when Wolf opened his eyes. It was snowing on him. He was hanging sideways over the console with his right arm tangled around a limp Velvet. The truck was lying on its passenger side. The windshield was shattered and bloody on the outside. He saw fur. Turning his head back toward the snow, his window had a gaping hole.

Ignoring the taste of blood in his mouth, he pulled Velvet up toward him. Blood was smeared across her face from a cut lip and eyebrow. Several scrapes. And a bruise on her forehead. Placing fingers on her neck, he found a pulse.

Not sure of her injuries, he squeezed her gently and said, "Velvet."

She didn't respond. Touching her face, he said it again, "Velvet."

Moving, she frowned with a low moan. He coaxed, "Come on, green eyes. Talk to me."

Her eyelids flickered as she mumbled, "Ouch."

Relieved at any response, he asked, "Are you hurt? Can you move?"

Her eyes met his...trying to focus as she gingerly raised her hand. "Something...is pulling my hair."

He saw the problem. And in a moment, untangled her long braid from his arm, her coat, and the seatbelt.

Velvet zeroed in on the blood on his face as she rubbed her head. He had several cuts. On his lip. Cheek. In his hairline. And a bunch of scrapes. Then his frown registered. And as if in a dream, she noticed snow falling in the truck. Blood on the windshield. And that they were hanging...not sitting. She gasped as panic shoved her into reality.

Wolf said, "Easy...just listen to me. We are alive with minor injuries. But I need to get out of the truck to see where the other truck is. We aren't safe until I know that."

"Don't leave me."

31

"I'm not leaving you. I've got to assess our situation to get you out of here. That means I need to get out of the truck."

Horrified that he would even consider it, Velvet shook her head. "Don't."

He continued, "I am going to undo my seatbelt and climb out. But I need you to stay in the truck. I don't know where we landed, so we need to avoid jostling the truck. Give me a minute and I'll tell you when to release your seatbelt. And after I clear the area, I'll get you out."

She shivered. Cold and scared. "Hurry."

Nodding, he pulled the compass off the dash and dropped it in his pocket. Checked his gun and pulled on his hat and gloves. Then with a nod to Velvet, he pushed his door up halfway – and got a face full of snow.

He reached behind the seats and grabbed their bags. One at a time, he chunked them out the door. They couldn't survive without them on the mountain. Then holding the doorframe, he unclasped his seatbelt and pulled himself up to balance on the side of the console. And stood, pushing the door open. Gun drawn.

The first thing he saw was a glimpse of blue through the snow directly in front of him. Maybe 30 feet away. It looked like the other truck nosedived into a stand of trees. He didn't see the driver or footprints. Just several dead elk and a lot of blood.

Looking down at Velvet getting snowed on through the open door, he said, "The other truck hit a tree. I doubt he survived. It's not far so I'm going to check and come back. Now, unbuckle and stand on your door."

Trying not to make extra movement, Velvet released her seatbelt, which left her lying against the door. She stood. Eyes wide on Wolf and very still. Except for random shivers laced with tremors of fear.

Meeting her gaze, he promised, "I'll be right back." And balancing on the running boards, he lowered the door a bit to block most of the snow for Velvet, then jumped.

He made a quick pass in the knee-deep snow around his truck. Everything seemed stable and he headed to the blue truck.

Wolf stared at the gruesome scene. The driver was dead. Killed either by the elk that went through the windshield or the tree. He was surprised to see that it was a young blonde woman with a ponytail.

A picture flashed in his mind. The last time he'd seen her at Amtrak she was kissing a man.

32

Hurrying back toward Velvet, he noticed fresh sliding tracks behind his truck. It had moved. Not much, but it had slid forward at least a foot. Maybe the heat of the engine melted the snow under the hood.

And then he thought back to the GPS map before the crash. His stomach tanked. The pond.

He rushed to the truck, calling, "Velvet, get out! Now!"

Reaching up to grab the steering wheel, Velvet put a boot on the console to climb, and yelled, "What's wrong?"

He climbed up and balanced on the running boards, grabbing the door. "The truck is sliding into a pond!"

"*It's doing what?*"

And as he swung open the door, the truck slid forward almost knocking him off. Velvet screamed as she slipped, landing flat on her back as water poured in. She gasped, unable to breathe as the coldest water she'd ever felt in her life engulfed her.

And in a flash, she went airborne as Wolf snatched her out of the water.

She couldn't even scream.

Chapter 6
The Blizzard

Velvet couldn't think as Wolf stood her in the snow. All she could fathom was cold. Ice in her veins, cold. It was hard to stand, and she wobbled.

Pulling her close, Wolf met her shocked, wet gaze as he ripped her coat off. "I have got to strip you. Just look at my face. This part will be over in a second."

She couldn't answer as she heard her wet coat splat on the ground. The sopping hoodie followed. And her once warm shirt.

Leaving on her bra, Wolf cussed as he moved fast. Her shivering was shocking. And then her knees gave out. Catching her, he ripped off his coat and wrapped it around her nearly naked upper body. Scooping her up, he headed to the blue truck, leaving a trail of wet boots, pants, leggings and socks. Her body was crazy cold. Her eyelashes, freezing spikes around green eyes.

Tucking her tightly in his arms, he reached the back door of the blue truck. Yanking it open, he wasn't even shocked at the body of a dead man in the backseat. The blonde's kill, no doubt. He shoved the big guy over and climbed in. With Velvet on his lap, he slammed the door.

He pulled off his sweatshirt and wrapped it around her butt and legs tightly curled in his coat. Grabbing a duffel bag off the floor, he noticed a blanket under it. He wrapped Velvet in a cocoon. Face and all. And held her against his now shivering body as he continued to dig through luggage.

He found a gold mine. Thick jackets. Sweats. Socks. Thermals. Gloves. Snow hats, goggles, and a snow suit. A big one - at least a size 3X. He took a deep breath and sat back holding Velvet as a survival plan fell into place.

Opening the trembling blanket bundle, Wolf touched Velvet's cold cheek. Her eyes opened. Teeth chattering, she tried to talk, "I'm…so…cold."

"You need body heat. I have a plan."

She saw him shiver and noticed his bare shoulders. "You…gave me…your…clothes."

"I have more. In fact, I'm going to leave you safe right here, and go get our bags out of the snow. Stay bundled up – face too. Got it?"

"Is…there…a pond…under this truck…too?"

He tweaked her cold nose. In a few hours, she'd be feisty again. And away from the icy fingers of death.

After Wolf dressed again, Velvet felt the blast of frigid air when the door opened. And then he was gone. She sniffed. Something smelly hovered in the cold air. An odd mixture of things…and her stomach lurched realizing that the dead driver was in the truck. She covered her nose and tried to think of something else as she shivered. She couldn't.

And then she heard a noise. A voice.

Out in the blizzard, Wolf combined his and Velvet's bags into two, leaving an empty one for her wet clothes. He would dry them once they got to his cabin. He tucked her gun in his jeans and grabbed a couple of power bars and a frozen bottle of water.

Wishing he had a snowboard or sleigh to haul their bags on, he made do with a waterproof cover he kept in his truck. And after adding a few other items from his stock to the pile, he pulled it to the blue truck.

He called her name to warn her that he was coming in, shook off the snow, and slipped back inside.

Velvet whispered through the blanket as he lifted her back on his lap, "I hear…a…voice."

Wolf froze. "Where?"

"In here."

Opening the blanket to see her, he covered her lips and listened. Far away he heard a man's voice. Setting Velvet aside, he wrapped her with another coat, and began looking for a phone, radio, or some type of transmission device. He leaned across the console and found a Bluetooth headpiece under the crashed dash. He put it on while looking for the phone it connected to.

A man yelled, "Ziva! Where the hell are you? I'm almost at the turn off to Camp David. I need to know. Did you take care of Velvet? I repeat. Did you complete the mission?"

Wolf's eyes went hard. Jax was right. This went all the way to the White House.

The man continued. "I've got a bead on your location. I'll send Jagger after you. Just hang tight." The call ended.

Tossing the headpiece, Wolf searched Ziva's body for the phone. He found it under her. A high-class burner phone. It was still on because the call had just ended. He pulled up her phone call list and snapped a picture. He did the same with her text list and emails. And the only picture was of Velvet. He left the phone. It was too risky taking it. They could be tracked, and they had enough trouble as it was.

He checked Ziva's pockets. Nothing useful. Then checked for weapons - and found a gun. It was probably the murder weapon for the poor guy in the back. He left it. Then pulling some paper out of the glove box, he dipped Ziva's finger in her own blood and took a DNA fingerprint. Better than a license.

Sitting down in the backseat, Wolf opened a peep hole in the blanket. Velvet's teeth still chattered, "Did you…find it?"

"Yeah. She's a mercenary. Which means, we can't stay long. They'll come looking for her. Let's warm you up."

"She?"

"A young blonde. Forget about her. Now…I am going to pull on a snow suit. And you are going to get in it with me skin to skin. That's all we can do. And in thirty minutes, we need to get the hell out of here. We have got to disappear."

Her eyes grew huge. "Naked? On…a…mountain?"

"You, almost. I'll have jeans on. Now, I've got to get in the snow suit."

Still shocked, Velvet watched him take off the sweater and coat he had on. His body was tan, toned, hard, and sexy as hell. Even with bruises. Even when she was nearly frozen. Silent, she watched him step into what had to be an arctic snow suit. White one-piece. Zipper up the front. Pockets. Loops for attaching things and an elastic waist.

Before long, he was sitting next to her in the suit with the zipper undone all the way to his lap. Bare chested. His eyes met hers. "We need to do this fast. It won't be pleasant. I'll help you straddle me and zip us up. Belly to belly will give you the best heat. Ready?"

She nodded. Never in a million years had this occurred to her.

He said, "Let's do it."

Velvet gasped as Wolf pulled her from the partially warm cocoon into freezing air. She struggled to function as he guided her shivering body astride him in the suit. Pulling her chest and belly tight against him, he arched giving her room to hook her feet behind him.

36

Wolf shivered uncontrollably. Her skin was like ice as her arms and legs wrapped his body. He quickly zipped them up from the inside leaving enough of a gap for her to get air.

Velvet sighed at his heat and moaned, scooting closer. Clutching. Shivering. Forgetting that she was in a bra and panties that covered next to nothing. Because the only thing that mattered was the heat of his body.

Wolf looked at the ceiling and clenched his jaw, trying to warm up and forget the image of her straddling him. Even freezing, she was killer breathtaking. Built for love. Now it would take all his control to ignore where she sat.

Wrapping her in his bare arms inside the suit, he began to massage and warm her. The time on the truck's dash caught his eye. It wasn't even noon yet.

Twenty minutes later, Velvet's shivers had lessened. Her teeth chattered less. And goosebumps were fading as Wolf's hands continued to knead and warm her shoulders, back, hip and thighs. She was getting closer to the edges of warmth, like when you stretch your hands out to the campfire. The killing cold behind you - but not consuming you anymore.

And she knew this changed things. Wolf had crossed the invisible line from Jax's friend, to bodyguard, to intimate hero all in the space of a few hours. She inhaled a deep breath that no longer hurt and listened to his heart. Now what?

Wolf felt Velvet relaxing more, and more as cold and fear eased. He thought of Jax in the desert of Africa while his sister fought to survive a blizzard. Who, high enough on the totem pole in Washington D.C., hated this brother and sister enough to annihilate them?

It was unfathomable. Jax had told him to keep Velvet safe and give him four days to find the traitor. Then Wolf could enlist his forces. Not until then.

Velvet said from inside the suit, "Do you think Jax had this in mind?"

Wolf smiled though she couldn't see it. "You, half naked on my lap. I doubt it."

"Almost naked is a more apt description. "

"Don't remind me. How do you feel?"

"Like a piece of frozen meat that got left out on the counter to thaw."

He laughed.

She said, "How much longer do we have?"

"Five minutes."

"What now?"

"I'll carry you to my safe spot a few hours away over the mountain. The blizzard should end by nightfall. We'll sleep there."

"You can't carry me all that way."

"I'm used to this, and I can take breaks. The most important thing is for me to get us away from this wreck and to my cabin - without us being seen by anyone. I need you invisible. My body heat is the safest option."

"That sounds like a line."

He pulled her hair. "I don't need a line, sassy. Stay focused. My mission is to keep you alive."

She knew she shouldn't say it, but did anyway, "And if you didn't have a mission?"

He caressed her fine butt and thighs. "You damn sure wouldn't be cold."

Against his chest, she gasped. That was the hottest pass ever.

Smiling to himself, he said, "Do you need anything before we leave? To use the bathroom? Food? Water?"

"I don't ever want to see water again."

"Copy that. Let's get situated for the hike." He unzipped the suit several inches below his neck and said, "I need you to wrap your arms around my neck to hang on. Your face will be partially exposed – with a mask. And then I'll wrap a belt around my waist to make a pouch for you to sit in – to rest your thighs from being wrapped around me."

Before she could snap a sarcastic response, he cupped her butt, lifting her until her face popped out the zipper by his jawline. She locked her arms around his neck inside the suit.

Their eyes met.

She said, "You're enjoying this."

"It's definitely an unexpected perk."

And then she saw the dead man right next to them on the seat. Bloody holes in his chest. His eyes open. Velvet looked at Wolf in horror, wanting to gag.

Shoving his arms through the snow suit sleeves and putting on gloves, he said, "Breathe. Just breathe. Look somewhere else." She swiveled to the front and squealed at the bloody woman tangled with an equally bloody elk.

He jostled her to get her attention. "Reality, Velvet. She shot him, and the wreck killed her. You might see or do a lot of things you would rather not, but we are the ones trying to survive. Look outside. That's where we are going. You can do this. Say it."

She snapped, "I get it."

"Good. Now, I'm filling a duffel bag with the big guy's clothes. We might need them. In two minutes, we are heading north." He pulled a furry mask with an eye window over her head. Then goggles. He did the same for himself and zipped the bag. Lastly, he pulled the big guy's belt off, cut in several more notches, and buckled it around the waist of the snow suit.

"Prepare yourself," he warned Velvet. And opened the door.

Chapter 7
Friday in Dallas

Indigo locked her office at the museum. Tired. It had been an extremely busy day. With Velvet gone, several other curators in their department had divided up her projects until the replacement curator arrived. So, extra work. Exciting work, but still extra.

She heard footsteps and glanced up as Raymond, the director, rounded the corner with two men in suits. He looked upset. This didn't appear to be a social call. She turned to face them, a question in her eyes.

Flustered, Raymond said, "I'm glad I caught you, Indigo. These two detectives are from the Dallas Police Department. They need…"

His voice faded as he swept his arm to the detectives, not sure what to say. So, the black-haired detective picked up the conversation, "Ms. Shay, I'm Detective Allen. We are investigating a missing person. Velvet Carrington. We believe you might be able to help us."

Indigo didn't hear the last sentence. Shock and fear made her weak. She reached for the wall. Both detectives stepped forward to assist and she held up a hand to stop them. Voice tight with emotion, she said, "There…must be a mistake. Velvet is on vacation. I was with her just before she left Wednesday night. Did someone report her missing? Did you talk to her brother?"

The detectives glanced briefly at each other, and the blonde one said, "I'm Detective Lassiter, and it's complicated. Would you like to step into your office and have a seat?"

A few solemn moments later, they faced each other across her desk. Lassiter asked, "Do you recall the house explosion Wednesday night north of Dallas?" At her hesitant nod, he said, "It was Velvet's house that exploded."

She gasped. "Thank God she wasn't there—"

"You are correct. The Fire Department cleared the building and no bodies were found. However, no one has been able to locate her, or her brother Jax. Nothing. Then today, the Warwick Melrose hotel called the police department.

Velvet's Jeep, fully packed for a trip, was still sitting in the valet parking lot. It seems, Ms. Shay, that she vanished Wednesday night. In fact, you might have been the last one to see her."

Indigo covered her mouth to stop the sob. It couldn't be. No. No. No.

But tears fell anyway.

Chapter 8

Five hours later, still breathing heavy in the thin, frigid air of the Rocky Mountains, Wolf stopped inside a cluster of trees and sat on a small boulder. Grateful for the wind and snow break, he stared up the ridge. It had taken longer than he expected, but at least they were almost there. He checked the compass, and they were right on course. He stretched his back, one arm around Velvet, and tried to catch his breath.

Skin to skin inside the suit, Velvet felt his muscles flex. Every inhale. And even his heartbeat. She heard his groans and felt the strain as he held her and pulled their bags with a rope tied to his belt. Uphill. Literally in the snow.

Her face, burrowed against his neck, was cold but not freezing. The rest of her was well protected. Humbled and respectful at the sheer power of his strength, she touched his chest and tried to speak over the wind, "Wolf…"

He squeezed her against him and lowered his face to say, "Hey. Are you cold?"

"No. I quit shivering a while back. I'm almost hot."

He gave a breathless chuckle. "I'm doing something right."

Worried, she said, "You can't keep up this pace. Your heart is pounding and you're sweating."

"The air is thin. But once I cross the ridge we don't have far to travel."

"Where are we going?"

"A small cave."

She groaned. "What about bears?"

"There wasn't one last week."

"Bats?"

"Now you're getting picky. Do you need to pee?"

She flushed. "I don't want to have this conversation."

He laughed. "Right. Now…let's be quiet. I need to breathe."

Thirty minutes later, after several slips, Velvet's screams, and the full force of the blizzard, Wolf topped the ridge…now giving them a much-needed wind break. He headed downward at an angle toward an outcropping of trees and rocks.

Before long, he said over the wind, "We're here. I need to check the cave for visitors so hang on tight, I'll need both hands."

Tightening her thigh muscles and posture, Velvet hung snug against Wolf, giving him more room to work. She heard rocks tumble, and limbs crack.

Wolf panted as he dug out a snow-covered path, then cleaned off the camouflage netting hiding the mouth of the cave. So far, nothing looked disturbed by man or beast. Pulling his pistol, he stood to the side and slowly lifted the net, shining the flashlight next to the gun. He scanned the cave.

About 12 x 12, the rock room made a terrific safe place during a storm or when hunting. He'd found it a few springs ago when a snarling badger darted out behind the brush that hid it. Since then, he kept a few supplies stocked and worked on making it more hospitable. Most mountain visitors treated it respectfully. Repaying in some way anything they used. Basically, the way of the land.

He said, "It's clear. I'm going in, so hang on. The door is shorter than me and I need to bend over." And with a short squeal, Velvet went backward and then straight up again.

Wolf said, "Home sweet home," and turned so she could see it.

Velvet was amazed. In the back left corner was a wooden platform with short legs. Clearly a bed. Centered on the back wall were three wooden stumps. Two were stools. The taller one, a table. A firepit was in the middle of the room. And a large pile of wood was stacked in the back right corner.

Next to the bed was a waterproof crate of supplies. Bottled water under the bed. And on one side of the door, a large limb with branch stubs made do as a clothes rack. On the other side of the door was an empty bucket. No explanation necessary.

She said, "This is great, Wolf. Did you put all this together?"

He took off his goggles and hood. Red faced and icy from the weather, he said, "Yeah. I ride the horse up every summer, restock, and add new things."

Then taking off her goggles and hood for her, he said, "Do you think you can hang on to me for a while longer so I can light a fire? I can't separate us until it is well above freezing in here. Your body absolutely can't tolerate any extreme cold temperatures yet. It won't take long to bring the temperature up."

"I'm in no hurry to be intimate with cold again."

"Why don't you watch what I do. You never know when you might need to make a fire. Rocky Mountain winters at this elevation can last six to eight months. And this storm was early."

Velvet watched his fire building technique as she contemplated living in this environment for long periods of time. Even when civilization wasn't far away. Why had a man with his looks and skills chosen this isolation? And what was the exact connection between him and her brother?

The flash of a match and quick smell of sulfur drew her attention. Fire licked the dry kindling and climbed the logs. Flames began to flicker on the walls.

Sitting on the bed, Wolf settled her on his lap. "If you turn around and sit facing the front, we can watch the fire while we wait. I'm sure you are tired of watching my neck."

She slowly maneuvered the turn with sore thighs and leaned back against his stomach and chest; her bare legs hanging down next to his jean-clad ones. She sighed, grateful for the new position, and said, "I don't know if I'll ever be able to close my legs again."

He laughed. Long and hard.

She sighed. "You enjoyed that a little too much. It wasn't that funny."

"Oh Velvet, it was. Though, I don't think I'll share that comment with Jax."

"Yeah, well, I guess not."

They sat quietly for a while watching the fire. She asked, "Are your hands cold, Wolf?"

His hands were bitterly cold but not freezing. He played it off. "It's not bad. Nothing to worry about."

"There's no way they're not cold. Pull them back inside the suit so they can warm up."

"I would love to, but I don't think that's a good idea. My hands touching a naked freezing woman is one thing. A naked hot one would be something else. Unless something else is what you have in mind."

Dryly, she said, "Funny man."

He chuckled and she asked, "Do you have a sister?"

"No. But I have six nieces that have me wrapped around their fingers."

Smiling, she said, "No boys?"

"Three wild nephews. And I'm always voted the cool uncle."

"No doubt. Do they ever see you this way?"

"This way?"

"A hair from wild. Tough. Rugged. Blunt. A smoking hot warrior with secrets."

44

"Are you trying to make me put my hands back in there?"

She ignored the question. Not sure if he was teasing - and not sure if she was doing what he claimed. She changed the subject. "Where are you from? I hear a hint of a drawl at times."

He said, "North Carolina. My formal education didn't quite eliminate the accent entirely. And you... Your Louisiana accent is sexy with that husky tone. A man could get used to that."

"Maybe you should check the room temperature. I think it's time for clothes."

He smiled and pulled off a glove. He raised his hand. It was warmer above his head but way too cold at their level. He said, "How about we lay back and take a short nap while it warms up. We both need the rest." She nodded. Sleep sounded wonderful.

They lay on their left side facing the fire – her head on his arm, her legs stretched out with his. After two nights of little sleep, being wrapped in his arms was heaven. She was out in seconds.

Wolf felt when her body relaxed. Heard her even breathing. He pulled out his gun and laid it within easy reach. Keeping his eyes on the cave entrance, he wondered how long it would be before a new set of mercenaries came for them.

An hour later, Wolf was hot in the snow suit. His phone showed the cave had reached a temperature of 47 degrees by the rock floor. Which meant that it was probably 60 or more at head level. Perfect without a snow suit. And the fire needed wood.

He shifted to look down at Velvet, and said quietly, "Hey, Green Eyes."

Her eyes opened with a touch of alarm – finding his. He said, "Nothing is wrong. We just need to get out of this suit so I can add wood to the fire. We should be comfortable dressed in regular clothes now."

Velvet nodded and held onto his thighs as he moved them to a seated position. She said, "I feel the warmth on my face. It's almost comfortable in here."

"Compared to outside, yes." Dragging her bag closer, he said, "If you put a shirt on, we can stand, and I'll get out of the snow suit so we can finish dressing. Then I'll step outside to look around and…" He pointed to the metal bucket. "I'm sure you need some privacy."

Appreciating Wolf's non-specific remark, she answered, "Sure."

He rustled around in her clothes and pulled out a turtleneck and jeans. She nodded. "Perfect."

45

They stood. He unzipped the snow suit to her waist. And in seconds, she pulled the shirt over her head as he kicked off his boots. Then without commenting on her nearly bare bottom half, he slid the suit down and stepped out of it.

As Velvet pulled on jeans, Wolf added wood to the fire and headed to the entrance. He turned and said, "I won't be far. Just call." And he was gone.

Velvet watched the netting fall back into place after only a brief glimpse of white. It was still snowing but not as heavy. She hurriedly drew on thick socks and her furry snow boots. Well, slipper boots really. Which meant they wouldn't be of much help outside. But they were perfect for inside comfort. And this cave was exactly that until tomorrow.

Pulling colorful leg warmers over her boots and leggings, she wiggled her toes. Warm and toasty. And lastly, she added a Dallas Cowboy hoodie and sighed. She'd been almost naked and cold for... She thought about the clock on the truck dash. It had been almost 10 a.m. before the crash. What time was it now?

But she couldn't find her burner phone.

Outside, Wolf stood on the shelf above the cave in jeans, snow boots, and a parka checking his phone. No new messages from Jax. He pulled up the security grid around the cabin. Twelve cameras watched. No alarms had been tripped. Next, he searched internet media in Dallas and Denver.

Velvet was all over the news in Dallas. Details of her house explosion. Her abandoned Jeep. And her disappearance. Even Indigo was mentioned. He looked out into the world of white around him. The commotion was bound to happen.

But only the one paying for the hit would know why the death of Jax and Velvet was necessary. He frowned. Hopefully, none of this would identify him – and make Velvet vulnerable at his cabin.

He closed his phone. There had been no mention in Colorado about two wrecked trucks on Highway 7 this morning. He was sure someone made all that disappear. That's why he kept pictures of the man in the backseat, his driver's license and license plate. As well as Ziva's DNA fingerprint.

They weren't forgotten. Just put on hold. He heard Velvet moan inside the cave. Jumping down in front of the entrance, he said, "I'm coming in."

He found her standing by the fire looking in a small mirror. Shock on her bloody, bruised face. She looked up. "I look like someone beat me. And my hair is a nightmare."

46

He tilted her chin up, checking her injuries for the dozenth time. "They were trying to kill you…and failed. This is victory. We'll warm up some water and clean up. And in the spirit of honesty, Velvet, your body is covered in bruises. You're going to be sore in the morning – unless the freezing water worked as well as ice packs."

He pointed at the stool for her to sit and hung up his parka.

As she sat, she said, "You look worse."

"I had a little contact with the window. It's minor. Just messy."

She offered, "Jax packed me a first aid kit."

"I saw that. Let's use yours."

As she grabbed the kit, Wolf pulled out a tin pot with a lid and poured two bottles of melted water inside. He set it on a rock at the edge of the fire.

Velvet said, "I have wet wipes too. The only thing I can't find is my burner phone."

"I have it."

Surprised, and annoyed, she said, "Why?"

"I've carried you naked, and your burner phone offends you?"

"Why did you take it?"

"So, you wouldn't use it."

"Again, why?"

"I live in a secure area."

"Who are you exactly?"

He checked the water in the pot. "Exactly who I am will have to wait until tomorrow."

Velvet narrowed her eyes and watched him. Scenarios ran through her mind.

Wolf easily read her expression and shrugged. "Things are rarely what they seem. But if you don't trust me now, you never will." He put the pot on the table.

She asked thoughtfully, "When did Jax decide I might need a bodyguard?"

"A few years ago."

"About the time he changed jobs."

He lowered his face very close to hers. Their eyes met. Breath mingled. And he said softly, "Change the subject and open the wet wipes."

Velvet let it pass, mainly because she'd lost her train of thought at the nearness of his mouth. She bit her lip, suddenly remembering what it felt like to want to get consumed in a kiss.

Wolf felt the awareness flare. Saw it in her eyes. And satisfied knowing that, he dipped the rag in warm water. Twenty minutes later she was clean.

47

Disinfected. And had medical glue in her eyebrow cut. He handed her the mirror and said, "The bruises and scrapes will fade. Your lip cut is minor. And you'll only be left with a nearly invisible eyebrow scar."

She nodded as she looked in the mirror. "Thanks, Wolf. The blood made everything look so much worse. Let me do you now."

"I'll do it. I'd rather we talk about Dillon."

She gave him a sharp look. "I'd rather not." She stood, pointing at the stool. "Your turn, bodyguard."

He sat, running his hand through his hair, and said, "I'll glue my cut when you are done."

She nodded and stepped between his legs. Brushing his hair back, she touched his face. Magnificently masculine. Good looking. And bronze like he spent a lot of time on the water. His very aware blue eyes locked with hers.

She said, "You have more raw places than I do."

"Just wipe, Green Eyes. Don't worry. I'd be rougher than you."

She did…and only hesitated when she reached his mouth.

He said, "I don't bite."

Meeting his gaze, she said, "I'm not sure I believe that."

He ran a finger down her thigh. "Or, should I say it wouldn't hurt if I did."

At that, she realized he liked the game. The hunt. And she realized even more. She wanted this game with him. She just needed the rules. The safety zone. Because she didn't know what or how much she was ready for. But for now…a kick-off would work.

And she touched his lips.

Before long, the blizzard stopped, and dusk drew close. Wolf heated Velvet's frozen breakfast burritos from the train and made coffee. Velvet cut up an apple and a peanut butter power bar. They ate, then sat by the fire.

A wolf howled and Velvet looked at the cave entrance cover. "Will that keep them out?"

"Not if they want in. But they don't like fire as a rule. Much less bullets and humans."

"How far away can they smell our food?"

"A mile or two – like a black bear."

"What about a grizzly?"

"They can smell for up to 20 miles." As her eyes widened, he said, "But there haven't been any grizzlies sighted in Colorado in decades. Black bears live here."

"Shouldn't they be hibernating?"

"Some, maybe. Most start in November. That's why I'll hang the food away from here."

"How far?"

"A hundred feet or so." He stood and glanced at his watch. "I'll go now. And we need to get to sleep soon. I want to leave at dawn. We're only two or three hours from the cabin...depending on what the blizzard left behind."

Wolf pulled on his parka and gloves. And after packing all the food in a thick black bear bag, he said, "I won't be long, or far away. Stay by your gun. And remember that I can hear everything in this silence. Just call."

She saluted. With a grin, he took off.

Velvet tucked the gun in her waistband and checked her clothes drenched from the pond. Wolf had hung them on the rustic clothes rack and put her hiking boots by the fire. Everything thawed but was still wet. She sighed. With only boot slippers, tennis shoes, and her dress boots dry, that meant tomorrow would be another day unable to walk in the snow. Shit.

Grabbing her vanity bag, she pulled out a brush and mirror. She had to tackle her hair before bed. And began to undo the braids.

Wolf tied off the knot in the tree. The bag of food hung at least 15 feet in the air on a branch that stuck out at least 10 feet from the trunk of the tree. He turned to head back to the cave and paused. He heard rustling.

A big bull elk stepped into the colorful dusk sky just beginning to emerge from the tail end of storm clouds. His rack was impressive. Thick, with a good spread. Six points on each side. One fine animal.

About that time, a wolf howled not too far in the distance. The elk bolted. Another wolf howled way too close. Pulling his gun, Wolf hurried to the cave. As he reached it, he glanced back toward the woods. A pair of eyes gleamed. Wolf whistled.

Velvet heard Wolf's footsteps outside. Before she could call out, he stepped inside, leaving a small gap in the flap.

He covered his lips for silence and headed straight for her. He whispered, "Be very quiet. Don't scream. I have someone I want you to meet." He pointed at the entrance and pulled her to his side.

Velvet glanced from his face to the entrance. A moment later, glowing eyes came through the darkness. A form began to emerge in the firelight as a wolf entered the cave. Velvet forgot to breathe at the sheer size of the animal as he looked around. And then he looked at her. Really looked at her. Intimidation crawled all over her.

Then Wolf sat, drawing Velvet down on his lap by the fire. The male wolf still watched Velvet. Wolf whispered in her ear, "Easy. I know him."

The wolf took a few steps closer and sat next to them. Wolf took Velvet's hand in his and put it on his leg. The wolf smelled their hands…and Velvet's hair. And leaning closer, he smelled her. Then slowly walked to the other side of the fire and lay down, head on his paws. Watching them. And then his eyes closed.

Velvet looked at Wolf. Amazed and fascinated. Fear evaporating. Wolf ran a finger over her lips and whispered, "Welcome to adventure. Now, lean forward so I can help with your hair. You still have a few things caught in it. Where's your brush?"

"You're kidding."

"Hardly. My nieces trained me well."

Wolf fanned the hair across her back, almost to her waist. It was thick. Wavy. And rich with the colors of auburn, brown, and gold. He untangled a few strands then pulled out small debris. Then slowly brushed the silken curtain from top to bottom. Over, and over. Then massaged her scalp until she swayed, completely relaxed and drowsy.

Grabbing a hair band off the table, he braided it into one loose braid. Then spread his coat by the fire and said, "Lay here. I'll fix the bed."

Velvet didn't argue. She was so sleepy. Curling up on the coat that smelled like him, she glanced across the fire at the other wolf. This was incredible…and her eyes fluttered closed.

Wolf unzipped the sleeping bag and laid it out on the platform, bundling jackets for pillows. Then he scooped her off the ground, laying her in the bag. She reached down sleepily to take off her slippers. Wolf eased her back down and took them off.

After adding more wood to the fire, he poured water in a dish and placed it near the wolf. Somewhat surprised that the animal seemed content to stay right where he was. Which he was glad about. The wolf would hear and smell danger long before he could.

Taking off his snow boots and positioning his gun close, Wolf pulled Velvet in his arms and zipped the sleeping bag. He fell asleep watching the wolf. The fire. And feeling her.

Chapter 9
Saturday Morning

Before dawn, Wolf woke. His warm breath blew clouds in cold air. He knew it would be colder this morning because he had only added wood twice last night. He didn't want to leave a fire behind.

Velvet stirred, snuggling into him. Her leg sliding along his, touching what certainly wanted to be touched. He shifted. Ignoring, but making room for the arousal that eagerly responded to her. Hopefully, she wouldn't wake up for a few minutes.

No such luck.

She rolled to her back, and he watched her eyes open in the firelight. With a tiny moan, she stretched, arching her back. Literally making his problem much harder. Which meant he had to get up before he had any more ideas than he already had.

He said, "Hey."

She turned to face him and smiled sleepily. "Hey. What time is it?"

Propping on his elbow, he saw the wolf slip outside, and said, "Almost dawn. But I need to get up so I can tend to a few things before we leave. Why don't you stay under the covers where it's warm. I'll cross over you."

In no hurry to be cold, she nodded and stayed still, watching him reach across until he straddled her - all six foot three inches of him. Their eyes met. And then his eyes dropped to her mouth. He lowered his body on hers as his lips found her neck.

Velvet inhaled, lost in a whirlwind of sensations at the heat and pressure of him. She clutched his shirt. Breathless, she whispered, "Wolf…"

"Thirty seconds," he said, as his mouth moved up her neck. "Let me taste you for just thirty seconds." And his mouth closed over hers. Velvet didn't remember opening her lips to him. Nor did she expect the lightning bolt that scorched her. All she knew was that he was pure fire.

And then he stopped. Wolf groaned looking down at her, then nudged her cheek with his lips. "Thirty seconds is just a start. One hot moment at a time. It makes you wonder what it'll feel like later."

He saw her anger at his presumption. She said, "And how do you know they'll be a later, Remington Wolf?"

Smiling, he got out from under the blanket and stood. His tight pants hiding nothing. "Because you want me too. Play it any way you want. I can nibble for a long time."

"Or starve."

"Not with the chemistry we've got. I'm what you went on vacation to find. Your search is over."

She threw back the covers and got up, daring her body to show weakness and shiver in the cold. She lied and snapped, "You wish. That was a 30-second kiss. Nothing more, so get over it. Now, who's making coffee?"

He was amused at her avoidance of the bulge in his pants, and said, "I will. You bring the sugar."

She flushed. "Shut up."

He laughed.

A few minutes later Wolf handed Velvet a cup of coffee and winked. She rolled her eyes – but despite herself, gave the tiniest grin as she focused on the fire. What else had she expected from a lone mountain man? And wanted herself...

He took a sip and said, "The terrain today will be heavily wooded and have several cliffs, boulder beds, and creeks. I checked, and your hiking boots are dry. I have an idea for you to be able to walk."

She smiled. "Snowshoes?"

"Yes. I wish I had another pair for you, but I'll make some out of small bushy branches. It's rustic, but it'll keep you above the snow - and dry. And I'll link you to me with a rope, so there won't be any danger of falling or getting separated."

She nodded. "Will it be as cold?"

"Temperature wise it will. But it won't feel like it. The sun will be out, and the wind won't be as strong. You'll even get to enjoy the scenery."

"Understood. Adventure day two. Without killers, please."

"Exactly."

"Did the wolf leave for good?"

"He'll probably be around as we head home. I've seen him up here before."

"Where did he get the scar?"

"I found him in a fight with a mountain lion. With the help of a vet, I nursed him back to health and released him. He's usually not far from the cabin. If I see him, I whistle. He visits…though he's never stayed the whole night before."

"What's his name?"

He shrugged. "No name."

"That's challenging. Man-Wolf, or the wolf?"

He chuckled, dumping coffee grounds on the fire. "I can see that. Pick one. Now, let's load up."

In a short time, the firepit's remnant was a thin trail of smoke.

Layered in snow gear, Velvet was warm and eager for the trip even though her breath made cloud puffs. Wolf strapped her boots to spruce branches, then checked to make sure their backpacks were secure. At his nod, they pulled on masks and goggles.

He glanced at her. "You ready for this?"

"Ready."

He pushed open the flap and said, "Let's go…"

Watching her feet as she walked clumsily with the snowshoes, she followed him out of the cave through the path he'd dug. When he stopped, she glanced up and gasped.

The glow of dawn lit the east with pink and gold as it climbed a far mountain ridge. The snow-covered world around her was pure majesty. Lush green trees draped in white. The rocky ridges. And the valley below.

"This is…simply incredible, Wolf. The raw wildness and crisp beauty. I've seen mountains and snow…but a ski resort can't touch this. It feels… I don't know. Like another world."

"It certainly is." Pointing northwest, he said, "We are headed there. See the ridge in the distance?" She nodded. "The cabin is on the other side. But for now…"

He indicated a diagonal direction down the ridge they were on. "We'll travel at an angle. It's not steep here but it will make it easier for you with the tricky landscape. And our snowshoes are less likely to leave a blatant human trail. Now, let me know if you need to stop. And if you fall, just hang on to the rope. I've got you."

He started walking.

And before long, Wolf saw the wolf in the tree line. Velvet was right. He did need a name.

An hour later, a bloody patch disturbed the pristine whiteness of the snow ahead of them. They stopped, and Velvet turned away. The attack had been brutal. And very little was left of the bobcat. Wolf's eyes followed the trail the predators made. The smaller tracks indicated coyotes. Two. Maybe three.

As they continued toward a group of trees, Velvet sighed. "That puts things terrifyingly into perspective."

Wolf said, "The wilderness is beautiful but dangerous. There's always something lower on the food chain."

Minutes later, a distant sound broke the silence. Wolf spun, looking up. He unclipped them and ran back down the trail behind her yelling, "Get to the trees! Now! I'll be there in a minute!"

Velvet didn't argue as the sound grew louder. But she didn't get very far when a running Wolf came from behind, picked her up, and dove into the trees. Landing under a low branch, he rolled behind the trunk with her and saw it.

A helicopter topped the ridge they'd just descended. Pushing her behind him, he pulled his binoculars. It was black. No name or identification on the sides. Three men. Two with long guns. He growled out a hot string of cusswords. The man named Jagger, and his mercenaries were looking for them.

The helicopter passed by, low and loud. Rotors swirled the snow. Then they made a sharp turn and made a second, slower pass. Wolf knew what caught their eye. That's what he'd planned on. And he knew they'd bought his ruse, when they headed for the next ridge to the north. Leaning against the tree, he drew Velvet up. She wiped off snow.

He glanced at the disappearing helicopter with a frown. She said, "I take it you recognize the sound of a helicopter."

"In my sleep."

"Were they—"

He cut her off, "Mercenaries. The bad kind. Not all are bad. But those are undoubtedly comrades with Ziva."

"Ziva? Is that the woman in the truck?"

"The voice you heard in the truck said he was sending Jagger to her. No doubt, one of the men in the helicopter would be Jagger."

"You mean they're going to track us?"

"If they want to get paid, they will."

"So, what now?"

"We get out of here. Staying hidden as much as possible."

Velvet shuddered. "It's crazy knowing someone wants me dead."

Gaze intense, he said, "But they're not going to get what they want."

"You have to tell me about Jax, Wolf."

"Soon."

As they got up, she said, "Why did they make two passes? Did they see us?"

"They might have been curious about our tracks. But I made sure they only paid attention to the two large blood patches in the snow."

"Two? We only saw one."

"I squirted a pouch of fake blood."

Velvet blinked in stunned silence, contemplating the comment. He tugged her arm and led the way through the woods. She followed…trying to fathom the kind of mind that packed fake blood for a trip. Or even considered it.

It got cold quickly among snow-covered trees as Wolf listened to the sound of the helicopter. Closer at times. In the distance at others. He knew it would sweep through the peaks and valleys until they were relatively sure they hadn't missed anything. The rotors faded slowly until only the silence of the mountains remained.

Meeting her gaze, he said, "They're gone. At least for a while. Let's get out of the shade."

Eagerly walking out of the trees, Velvet sighed in relief. The warmth of the sun touched her body with sweet heat, like sitting by the fire. She appreciated it and promised aloud, "I'll never complain about sweating in the Dallas heat again. Thank you, God."

Wolf glanced back with a chuckle and slowed for her. She caught up as he said, "Don't lie to God, Velvet Carrington."

"That wasn't a lie. He knew I meant when I was in air conditioning."

He laughed, then sobered. "Just how cold are you?"

"My face and fingers are part tingly part numb. It's easing off already in the sun."

He knelt with one knee up. "Sit here."

"Wolf—"

"Sit."

She sat. For a few minutes he rubbed her hands briskly. Then unzipping the top of his parka, he said, "Take off your mask and goggles." She did…shivering at the added cold. Pulling her close, he said, "Bury your face in my neck and chest as I cover you. Your face will warm up in no time."

Velvet's eyes closed as her face connected with his skin. And she knew it wasn't just because of the warmth. She remembered his kiss this morning. And him getting out of bed…visibly all man. She adjusted her face to where her lips touched his skin.

Wolf felt the shift in her…and the change in her touch. He knew that she was remembering earlier…just like he was. He lifted her chin as his face lowered. Their eyes met just before their lips.

Flames rose like they had tossed gas on a fire. Velvet's arms wrapped his neck as he lifted her higher into him. One hand clutched her butt. The other, the back of her neck. And his throaty growl expressed the depth of his hunger.

Wolf wanted what he couldn't have. Not here. Or certainly under these circumstances. But he wanted her. He lifted his head, replacing his mouth with his thumb. Caressing her moist lips, he dipped inside. So hot…

He met her gaze. Her cheeks, pink. The cold, long forgotten. Their breath mingled with cold air. He said, "We'll pick this up later."

She pulled back, acting way cooler than she felt, "If I feel like it, mountain man. We only met… What, 24 hours ago?"

"Twenty-five. But our meeting has been a long time coming. We don't count as strangers. Besides…I insist."

"I just bet you do."

"Then it's settled."

She pulled on her mask as they stood. "It's hardly settled." The look she gave him was way more challenging than she intended. "And you'd have to catch me first."

He pulled her close. His eyes and body saying way more than his words, "I dare you to run. Just see how fast I catch you."

Almost two hours later, they topped the last rocky ridge.

Impatient, Velvet said, "Are we there yet? I would love a shower and a real toilet. Though I will miss the view when I'm trying not to sit on something with teeth, or a jagged edge."

Wolf shook his head. "Jax did not exaggerate your penchant for sassy when pressed."

She rolled her eyes. "Or your testosterone."

"My point is now proven. I'll just let you pee outside for a while longer. So… Are you ready to rappel down a small cliff?"

"How small is small?"

"Sixty feet or so."

"That's not small."

"Velvet… Compared to a mountain, it is small."

"Well, I've climbed a rock wall in the gym and a few 20-foot walls on hikes. Small stuff. But I've never rappelled down."

"You'll do fine. You'll be attached to me regardless. Come on... We're not far from the cabin."

Fifteen minutes later, Velvel looked over the edge of a cliff that she hadn't seen from a distance. At the bottom was a rocky, fast-moving stream that flowed in and out of holes in snow headed down the incline. She looked at Wolf as he rigged her harness.

His lip twitched. "I thought adventure was your middle name." She hit him on the arm. He laughed and said, "We'll rappel down, side-by-side on this rope. All the bags are on your side to counterbalance us. We'll be on the ground before you know it. Now, let's go over the instructions. Just hold the main line and brace your feet like mine... And follow my direct—"

A deep-throated grunt and growl came from behind them.

Wolf pulled his pistol, as he spun. The muzzle of his Desert Eagle 50 AE now beaded on the head of an unusually flustered black bear. Medium sized. Young male. Something had it all stirred up since they were not aggressive as a rule.

Without turning from the bear that was 40 feet away and closing, Wolf said roughly, "We are hooked up and ready to descend. I need you to go over the side and hang as far down as the rope will reach. Do it now."

"But you—"

"Now, woman."

Velvet dropped to her knees, eyes focused on the metal hook attached to the cliff and to the rope around them. She could smell the bear in the breeze. As she went over the side, a flash of snarling wolf headed off the bear. She screamed as she dropped into nothing but air.

Wolf braced, knees bent, as the weight of Velvet and the bags pulled on him. His pistol stayed steady on the bear as both animals prepared for battle. Snapping teeth. Snarling. Claws swiping. Charging. Retreating. Spittle flying.

It was his wolf.

Then he noticed the snow turning red under the bear. It was injured. Probably crazed. He whistled to call off the wolf so he could shoot the bear. The wolf wouldn't stop. Cussing, he dropped partially over the side of the cliff. His elbows were propped on the edge with his gun as Velvet hung below.

Suddenly the animals met in a flurry of teeth, and twisting fury. The fight spun toward the edge like a fur tornado.

57

Wolf dropped about three feet and covered Velvet against the rock wall. Making them as flat as possible. They smelled and felt the brush of the bear as it went over. Hearing scrambling above, Wolf looked up. The wolf was lying on the edge with its foot caught between the rope and the hook. Pulling himself up to take weight off the rope, he released him.

And the wolf was gone.

Wolf lowered to Velvet. She was trembling. Eyes shut. Both hands against the rock wall. He pulled her close. "It's over. You did everything perfect."

"Was... Was that your wolf?"

"Yes. He's alive."

She moaned. "I heard the bear land—"

"Try not to think about it. And don't look at him, we're going down."

Velvet sighed. "Have you considered having an apartment in town?"

He smiled as she waited for an answer she already knew. No.

In a surprisingly short amount of time, Velvet followed Wolf down a path closer to where the trees clustered on a plateau. A perfectly secluded location. And it was beautiful. Lush. Wild. Decorated with snow, a blue sky and warm sun. She could still hear the trickle of the stream as it continued around another rocky cliff farther to the right.

Wolf veered to a break in the trees and stopped. He pointed and said, "You can barely see the top of a green roof and chimney."

She did a little dance, and he grinned.

She took off and said, "Well, hurry!"

He caught her arm. "Give me a minute. I need to check a few things before we barge in. It won't take but a second."

Pulling his phone, he tapped an app. A map opened. Locations were noted. Listed below the map, alarm and camera locations were listed – and all were lit green. No human or machine had entered the secure 20-acre area. Putting his phone away, he said, "All clear. Let's go. Who gets the master bathroom first?"

Velvet laughed and ran ahead of him.

Breathless minutes later, she paused and took in the two-story log cabin. Rich dark wood. Obviously sturdy. Large porch. Shuttered windows. Massive door. Giant chimney. And she knew without a doubt that this was not some random cabin in the wilderness.

A barn stood in the back right and there was another roof to the back left. She didn't see a garage or vehicles anywhere.

He pointed left and said, "That's a guest cottage."

She repeated. "A guest cottage. I don't picture you having social gatherings out here. Where's the garage?"

"Connected to the back of the cabin."

She looked around. "This is truly beautiful…and private. A fortress if I'm not mistaken. And as a historian, I've seen, been in, and studied many around the world."

Wolf offered his elbow. "Then welcome to my fortress. And you'll love the shower."

Velvet whistled as they walked up the porch steps. The door had to be over four feet wide. Maybe eight feet tall and curved at the top. And there was no actual keyhole or normal handle. Instead, there was an antique iron ring where the door handle should be. She stepped closer and touched it. It was very old. Maybe 14th century and very valuable.

She glanced at Wolf. "A step back in time, my Lord?"

He said, "Don't be deceived, my Lady." Then pressing a button on a gas lamp, an electronic panel slid out. He keyed in a five-digit code, and two metallic clicks later, he pulled open the door.

Velvet just stood there. Everything inside was on. Fireplace. Lamps. And heat. Like he'd never been gone. Waving her in, he stacked their bags inside. Velvet removed her winter gear as she picked up the nuances of the room.

It appeared traditionally rustic with a real mountain feel. Leather furniture. Rugs. Blankets. And everything seemed to be built from wood. The snack bar and stools. Cabinets. Tables. Rafters above. The floor. Stairs. And a huge balcony with a carved railing that overlooked the first floor.

Yet… There was no firewood stacked close-by. No smell of burning logs or fireplace tools. She walked toward the kitchen. There was a commercial sized refrigerator freezer and an enormous stove with a gas grill and oven. And a nice DeLonghi coffee maker with grinder and carafe.

She was wrong. Wolf evidently did have guests with this setup. Men, she guessed. She didn't get a feminine vibe at all.

Wolf watched her. Questions would begin soon. He offered, "There's a mudroom down the hall to the garage. A restroom as well. The master bath and bedroom are upstairs."

She said, "No other bedrooms?"

"At the cottage. It's more a cozy bunkhouse really. It can get busy here at times."

"I see. Doing what?"

59

He ignored the question. "Head upstairs. The shower is incredible. I'll follow you up with your bags and then shower down here."

She didn't move…only said one thing. "Tell me."

He knew what she meant. Brushing hair from her face, he said, "We will talk. I'll give you all the answers I can."

"That you can?"

"That's what I said."

"About Jax?"

"And anything connected."

She nodded, believing him, and headed upstairs.

Wolf led the way in the bathroom. He set her bags on a massive rock vanity and said, "The bedroom doesn't provide privacy. You'll probably want to dress in here."

He smiled as she walked in the shower. It was like a cave. No door. And the walls, floor and ceiling were made of rock. A three-tiered waterfall took the place of a showerhead. And there was even a window seat. Velvet looked out at the mountains where she'd spent more than 24 hours.

She glanced at Wolf. "You're right. This is incredible."

"Nature has its luxury."

She caught her wild reflection in the mirror and moaned. "I look—"

He interrupted. "Like a woman who survived. Take your shower. You'll look like yourself soon enough. Meet me downstairs by the fireplace. I'll be the one with the coffee."

"Thank you, Wolf. Have I said that?"

"Every time you clung to me. And you're welcome."

She watched the door close behind him.

In moments, she stripped and unbraided her hair. She still looked wild and bruised, but less filthy. Grabbing the shampoo, she headed to the waterfall. And then it was bliss. The power of the water massaged. Cleansed, washing everything away. And the sudden tears surprised her. Had she cried yet? She couldn't remember. Time had no meaning.

How long had it even been… Jax's message and the explosion, Wednesday night. The Amtrak trip, Thursday. Denver and Wolf, yesterday. So, today was Saturday. Maybe midday.

Almost three full days had passed. Where was Jax in all this?

She had so many questions.

And then there was Wolf.

60

Later, finding clean clothes to wear in her bags turned out to be a challenge. Most felt damp. The others smelled musty, a cross between moisture and dirt. She checked her new boots. Dry. And smiling, she drew out the new jeans she'd shoved down inside them. She sniffed. They would do. At least they smelled more like leather than dirt.

Her driest shirt was a black long sleeve undershirt. Super thin and soft. V-neck. But no clean bra or underwear. Making a face, she debated her options as she dressed. Jeans first. Boots. And holding the shirt up to her, she looked in the mirror. Shit. There was no hiding her overflowing C cup, especially without a bra. But then again, it's not like Wolf hadn't already seen and felt them.

She pulled the shirt over her head.

Now for makeup. Her makeup, not the disguise stuff. But just enough to accent her face instead of her wounds. She passed on perfume. And after partially drying her hair, she left it loose. The fireplace would finish it. Then packing all the clothes that needed washing in the duffel, she headed for the stairs.

Wolf heard the door upstairs as he walked out of the kitchen with coffee. He glanced up just in time to see Velvet at the top of the stairs. And he almost missed the full duffel bag she carried because of the rest of her.

Sexy emerald eyes. Long auburn waves. Jeans that cupped her in all the right places. And those breasts... He groaned silently. Damn. He was going to ache.

Smiling as she descended, Velvet said. "The shower was wonderful. I needed that."

Setting the cups down, he said, "Hang on, let me get that bag."

As he headed up to take it from her, she said, "Please tell me you have a washing machine. This is literally all I had left to put on."

He stopped next to her. Intentionally close as he looked down at her. "Lucky me."

Her dark lashes fanned up as their eyes met. She said, "You're not a subtle man."

"It's the mountain air." He motioned with his free arm. "After you. I'll put this in the mudroom for now. Have a seat by the fire."

Picking up the two cups of coffee at the base of the stairs, Velvet walked toward the enormous fireplace. It centered below the balcony and jutted two stories high before breaking through the roof. It had a wide base for seating, so she settled on a plaid cushion with her back to the fire. She sipped perfect coffee. Rich, with plenty of cream and sugar.

Wolf rounded the corner running a hand through his own partially dried hair. Brown layers brushed his shoulders. His blue eyes focused on her as his long strides crossed the room.

Velvet's eyes scanned the tight black T-shirt gripping his lean hard body. She quipped, "We match."

He sat next to her and picked up his coffee. With a sexy grin, he said, "Shirt colors maybe. Not the rest of us, which makes everything else much more interesting."

Awareness of the passionate kind sizzled between them, until it slowly slid into awareness of the reality kind. It was time to talk.

Wolf watched her expression and asked, "You ready for this?"

"Past ready."

He nodded. "Come with me."

He stood and walked toward a bookcase lining the wall left of the fireplace. Dark wood. Row after row of books, maps, pictures, and statues. He lifted a thick brown book with a gold spine, then pressed his thumb against the wall.

Velvet inhaled sharply as a whole section of the bookcase simply opened. A hidden door. She glimpsed a stairway. Gas lights. And a mysterious space beyond that beckoned.

She met his gaze. "Just who are you, Remington Wolf?"

Chapter 10

One hundred twenty miles to the northeast, rotors were loud as the helicopter lowered to land. Deep in the middle of nowhere, just shy of the Colorado Wyoming border.

Jagger's phone rang. He yelled in the mic of his headpiece, "We're landing, Boss. Give me a minute — I can't hear you."

Ignoring the angry response, Jagger unbuckled and climbed out of the bird with his rifle. Ducking to run under the blades, he headed toward a building nestled with several others.

Tucking the phone by his ear, he said, "I'm back."

A terse tone said, "Give me an update."

"We didn't find anything suspicious in the mountains behind the wreck. The blizzard wiped out any trace of them. Even around the few sporadic houses in the area after the sun came up. There weren't any tracks. Everyone was snowed in."

"That is not helpful. The woman did not just disappear." He paused. "Ziva suspected the guy with her on the train was a professional. Accurately it seems. Apparently, they survived. Did you clean up the wreck?"

"That's a yes. The tow truck left with both trucks before daylight. Consider them vanished."

Callously dismissing Ziva, Boss said, "And the bodies?"

"They'll vanish too."

"Did you find anything useful?"

"I got some blood off the man's window. No identification. And grabbed a cup for fingerprints along with his license plate. We'll find out who he is."

"You better. Ziva left two messes. One in Dallas and one here. Get your evidence to the office and lay low. Once we get answers, they're all yours."

***

Outside Langley, Virginia, Boss disconnected the call. He raked his hand through silver hair and growled in fury. None of this was going as planned. It had been two simple hits in two secluded locations. And they failed. Now they were both on the run.

He thought of Trevor and hated knowing he'd failed him. For the moment anyway.

Jax Carrington would still pay with interest.

And Velvet was the interest.

Trevor would be avenged.

Chapter 11

In Dallas, Indigo researched fights leaving tomorrow night from Dallas to Langley, Virginia. Arriving late. She scrolled through the flights and finally booked one landing at Ronald Reagan Washington National Airport after midnight. Then she booked a car. And last, a hotel. She was done.

Closing her laptop, she walked to the apartment window and looked out across the city. It had been three full days already. Three. And her shock had morphed into raging determination. Even her brother, River, couldn't dissuade her plan of action.

No one had any answers about Velvet. And Jax was unavailable. What the hell was that? His sister was missing. Hell, unavailable probably meant he was missing as well. And the detectives wouldn't speculate. But they had tried to assure her that all the bases had been covered. No stone left unturned. And even Jax's employer, the CIA, was on it.

Indigo smiled. She might not know how to find the others, but she knew how to find the CIA.

Chapter 12

At the cabin, Wolf answered Velvet, "I am Lieutenant Colonel Remington Wolf with the United States Air Force. Pilot and headquarters commander of the Peregrines." Seeing the expected surprise on her face, he motioned toward the stairs. "Follow me. We'll talk."

As they descended the staircase, she tried to assimilate hot, wild Wolf as being Air Force. Nothing made sense.

Reaching the bottom, they stepped into a room that was a bunker of sorts. Only it had none of the woodsy warmth of the house. Instead, the room was concrete, she guessed. Covered with a texture that gave it almost a rock-like appearance.

But the focal point of the room was undoubtedly intelligence, based on the monitors, equipment, maps, and weapons on three walls. Totally military. She faced Wolf. "What do Jax, and I have to do with the Air Force?"

"Nothing directly. Yet. You are indeed here solely because of Jax. Our relationship as professionals and friends is entirely true. The bodyguard part, wanting us to meet, all of it. My assignment here is with the Peregrines. Jax and I do not work for the same people."

Velvet took in his rugged good looks. "You don't look Air Force."

"Agreed, for the moment. It's a special assignment. Off grid. I would stick out in my uniform."

She pressed. "Who do you work for?"

"Next question, Green Eyes."

She continued, "Ok. So… Peregrines… As in the falcon?"

"Exactly."

She put it together. Air Force. And peregrines. That falcon breed boasted the fastest creature on the entire planet. Stealthy. And dove 200 plus mph if she remembered her biology.

She said, "So, this is a secret military air command of some kind. Ok. I get that. Now… Where is my brother?"

Wolf pointed to an electronic world map on the wall. "Unfortunately, his location is classified. All I can tell you is that he was approximately 4,000 miles from where we stand now when he sent our texts Wednesday night."

"Can I read the text he sent you?"

"No. Though I can tell you that he was ok and dealing with a complication. Besides activating my mission with you, he insisted that I allow him four days before I got involved. I agreed."

"Involved how?"

"It's Saturday. We'll know specifics Sunday at midnight. That's all I can give you. I know it's hard - but we wait."

She glanced at the large wall clock; her face flushed in anger. "No. That's 36 hours, Wolf. Unacceptable. What if he—"

He held up a hand. "I get it, Velvet. But Jax is powerful and skilled at what he does. His concern is not himself, but because they threatened you. But now that he knows that I have you, he is focused on completing his mission. I need you to work with me."

"Seriously? By waiting?"

"Among other things."

"Like what?"

"We investigate your past for any possible link to all this."

She knew what he wanted and walked away, looking at the equipment. Monitors. A world weather station. Airports. Some type of ongoing chat. Multiple news channels. The map with flashing lights at different locations. And lots of security cameras watching everything outside.

She said, "And why do we need me to bare my soul about my ex-husband? Dillon is not trying to kill me – or Jax."

"That convinces me of absolutely nothing. Just talk to me and I'll know what's relevant. And then this part is over." He turned her to face him. "I hate to make you relive your secret for even a moment, but we have got to do this. Today. Besides, you need to practice telling your brother anyway. Don't you?"

In moments they were back in the den.

Velvet gathered her thoughts as she stared at the washing machine. Her stomach churned as she watched the same thing happen to her clothes. Relating as they tumbled behind the glass door. Drowning. She closed her eyes. She didn't want to think about Dillon...or the night everything ended. She'd worked too damn hard to forget it.

In the kitchen, Wolf heated a container of chili he'd thawed out. Not TV dinner chili. His freezer was full of homemade meals. He didn't cook often, but when he did, it was for stocking the freezer. Chili. Spaghetti. Taco meat for burritos. Soup. Stew. He also prepared and froze marinated steaks for skillet grilling.

But he didn't bake. He ordered butter crusted cornbread, fluffy biscuits, and jalapeno hush puppies from the bakery in town, packed and ready for freezing.

Not hearing any sound from Velvet, he glanced around the corner. She just stood in front of the washer. Still. Silent. Lost in memories no doubt. Concerned, he called down the hall, "Do you want cornbread or hushpuppies with your chili?"

Startled back to the present, she smelled chili and headed to the kitchen. With a quick glance at him, she climbed on a bar stool and said, "Either. No, both. I'm starving and it smells wonderful – and homemade. You cook?"

He saw the shadows fading from her eyes, and answered, "Yeah. I usually stick to one-pot meals loaded with meat, with plenty of leftovers to fill the freezer so I don't have to do it often. Do you cook?"

"A Louisiana girl? My grandmother insisted I learn the Cajun basics. With those, you can throw anything in the pot, and it smells and tastes delicious. She taught me to:

- One, keep onions, garlic, celery, and bell pepper on hand - with a jar of Cajun seasoning.
- Two, how to sear meat in an iron skillet to make a rich natural gravy with drippings.
- Three, how to make chicken and sausage gumbo with roux.
- And four, how to cook rice, measuring with my finger and not a cup."

She smiled. "Of course, I don't cook all that for me, but the knowledge is there. Does that count?"

With a chuckle, he said, "I can smell it already. You bet it does."

Wolf spooned steaming chili into clay bowls then popped the bread in the microwave. It whirred, then beeped. He grabbed the butter.

Velvet said, "I didn't see electrical lines outside. Or chopped wood for that matter. What is your power source here?"

"Propane. There are two large tanks in the garage. It takes the work out of winter for one person. I'll show you around later if the area is secure."

She frowned. "Do you think they'll find us?"

"They'd have to find out who I am first. And it would take one hell of a breach in protocol for that to happen." He slid her food across. "But we are wise to presume it is a possibility. So, we stay alert."

And at that, they ate their first cooked meal in 30 hours.

There was no conversation. Just pleasure-filled moans, groans, and one-word remarks as they filled their bellies. Before long, Velvet pushed her bowl back, taking one last hush puppy to nibble on. She leaned back with a satisfied sigh.

Already on his second helping, Wolf said, "You didn't eat much."

"I'm nowhere near your size. Besides, there was enough meat in my bowl for three meals. But I loved it. For the most part, I try to eat light. I tend to get…"

And she paused, realizing too late the focus her comment would draw.

Wolf looked up. "You tend to what?"

She waved it away. "Oh, nothing. I was rambling. Hey…what extra ingredient did you use? I tasted an extra creaminess not usually in chili."

He put his spoon down. "You tend to what?"

She shrugged casually, groaning inwardly. Faking nonchalant, she said, "No big deal. I love hiking and staying in shape. That makes me careful with what I eat. I tend to get top heavy if I gain weight, so I avoid…"

Her voice faltered as his gaze dropped to her high, full breasts. She refused to cover them – knowing it would make everything worse. But her nipples betrayed her, bringing worse to an even higher level. Along with the sharp bite of awareness now sizzling in the room.

She got up and carried her dishes to the sink. Maybe he would let it pass. Hearing his stool rake across the floor, she turned on the water and busily rinsed her dishes. Wolf pressed behind her…his body pinning her in.

He reached over and turned off the water. Then, moved her hair aside. His breath sent tingles everywhere as he kissed her shoulder and trailed his lips up her neck.

He said, "Turn around."

Her eyes closed. They were alone. Familiar with each other's bare skin and playing house in the wilderness. Unavoidable true…but things already flared hot…way too fast with them. She wanted him. Hell, truth be told, she had wanted him before she ever left Dallas. She just hadn't met him yet.

She laid her head back against his chest and said hoarsely, "But Wolf…"

"Quit thinking. Dance with me."

Velvet felt the wildness as he turned her. Their eyes met and desire was exposed. Wolf growled softly, pulling her close, raising her arms to his shoulders.

She whispered, "There's no music."

"I don't need music."

69

And he lifted her.

Their mouths were close as her legs locked around his hips. Their lips hot from breath - but not from touching. Just breathing each other in. Watching. Tasting the intimacy. Anticipating.

Pulling her tight, his lips captured hers.

And he began to dance.

Velvet's arms wrapped his neck, fingers in his hair, as his whole body moved along with the rhythm of his mouth. Deep. Sensual. Graceful. Yet hungrier with each spin as he pressed her against him. Body friction now stoking the flames hotter with each second that passed. Until she lost count.

And too fast it seemed, Wolf dropped to his knees in front of the fire and took one more long drink of her...then stopped. His gaze met hers, then slid to her lips. Her breasts. And her open thighs against him.

Letting out a long sigh, he sat back on his feet. "Stopping is hard, Green Eyes."

Brushing her hair back, she asked breathlessly, "What happened to the 30-second rule, mountain man?"

"I upped it to five minutes when we reached the cabin. Thirty seconds wasn't near enough. Hell, neither is five minutes, but it'll have to do."

She touched his face. "You assume your clock will keep me in check?"

He bit her finger softly. "I don't want to keep you in check. But we get five minutes and my zipper stays up."

"And my zipper?"

He touched it, sliding his finger along the tiny metal teeth as she gasped, covering his hand with hers.

He said, "Oh, I'll touch you. But your pants stay up. For now. But we both know...I will take you."

She stared into blue eyes she could drown in. "I don't do hook ups, Wolf. Affairs. Or casual sex of any kind. But this..." She struggled for the right words. "In reality, we barely know each other...but then we do. What is this?"

Wolf knew without a doubt exactly what it was. He'd been waiting forever to find it. He said, "Our reality is that we've lived a lifetime in just 30 hours. So, don't let time fool you, Velvet. It sure as hell hasn't fooled me. This is something that's been a long time coming."

He turned with her, and they snuggled before the fire. Hidden from villains. Passion at peace as words and questions faded. Till silence and heartbeats were the only sound they heard.

Thirty minutes passed.

Forty maybe, before Velvet shifted. Turning so they sat across from each other. Auburn waves draped her shoulders. Eyes solemn. And Wolf knew that it was time. He leaned back against a chunky footstool and waited.

Velvet watched him for a minute. His casual posture didn't hide the power always coiled in him. The fire in his eyes. His depth. Or even the gentleness his muscles hid. She glanced back at the fire. She could bare her soul to him. If he was going to have the rest of her, why leave that out?

After a moment, she turned back to him and gave the tiniest shrug. "It's not a long story. Just a short end to a would-be beginning. A painful bleep of time. Tell me what you want to know."

He remembered his research, understanding at least partially, the bleakness of her words. Then he asked what he didn't know, "Tell me how you met Dillon."

And surprising him, she smiled. "It started out as a great night in New Orleans. Indigo and I had been roommates through college, and it was graduation night for Tulane. She graduated with a master's degree in history. And me, with a bachelor's degree in the same. I still had another year to go to complete my master's.

"Jax was supposed to have been there but hadn't been able to make it. He was out of the country working on yet another assignment he couldn't talk about. He'd been intense when he called - upset and not himself at all. I told him not to worry – that Indigo's family made it in from Texas and made reservations to take us out to dinner.

"And dinner was fabulous. We went to Coquette. A charming two-story restaurant on Magazine Street in the Garden District not far from the Mississippi River. It was late when we arrived - and after closing by the time we left."

She paused for a moment, remembering. "The sidewalk was busy when we got outside. Which wasn't unusual for New Orleans. River left to get the vehicle while we chatted, dodging people, and looking forward to moving on to the Fat Catz Music Club on Bourbon Street for dancing.

"That's when several vehicles pulled to a stop along the sidewalk in front of us. A taxi first. And River behind it in the suburban. Then a gray truck pulled alongside them on the street side. And out of nowhere, a man in a suit ran through the crowd on the sidewalk, shoving people out of the way as he tried to reach the taxi.

"At the same time a man in black darted from the truck blocking them and shot the guy. Twice. In shock, I met the shooter's gaze as the victim fell back into me – and we fell. Screams surrounded us, including mine.

"And then the shooter raised his gun at me. I briefly wondered why. He was covered from head to toe in black and all I could see were light eyes. Unusually light. Almost silver. And then I realized that I recognized those eyes.

"When I heard the gunshot, I flinched, thinking I got hit. But the gunman fell instead as River ran toward us, gun drawn. And then the men around us overtook the gunman. Disarmed him and pulled off his mask. His eyes were still on me. In disbelief, I stared at a guy I went to high school with. And dated."

She brushed her hand down her chest remembering the blood. "I didn't find out for several minutes that the blood on me wasn't mine. And it was crazy after that. Surreal. Police. First responders. Reporters. And River and I were ushered into separate police cars to wait for the detectives.

"And that's when Detective Dillon Black arrived."

Wolf watched as she got to her feet and began to walk as she talked. Her tension building. He stood. Not missing a single gesture or expression she made.

She said, "He was smooth. Efficient. And professional. Kind of an intense moody good-looking. And quite a bit younger than the other detective. He walked me through everything, and in the wee hours of the morning, delivered me home.

"And then life changed. Indigo moved back to Texas. And since we'd been roommates, I moved to a smaller apartment closer to school. And dove into my master studies.

"Dillon would call or show up to check on me during the next year. He was always professional and focused on the court date quickly approaching. But I knew he had other ideas...and I didn't mind knowing that. I'd spent years on the fast track for my master's - immersed in my studies. No time for relationships and barely time for socializing."

Velvet opened the refrigerator and stared – seeing nothing. Just needing a moment to hide from Wolf. To gather herself for the necessary invasion of privacy. Taking a Dr. Pepper, she turned, offering him one silently. Propped against the wall, he watched. A slight shake of his head indicated no. She grabbed a glass. Ice. And listened to the sound of the drink pop and fizz as she slowly poured it, buying more time.

After drinking half, she carried it to the den. All the window shutters were still closed. She asked, "Do you ever open the shutters?"

Understanding the evasion, he said, "Most of the time, yes. The glass is bulletproof against average ammo, but I don't want anyone to see you."

"Wouldn't your security system let you know if someone was close?"

"It takes more defense than that. A military scope or drone can see for long distances. Now, tell me…what was the shooter's name?"

She answered, "Brody Jon Grant," as she climbed and sat about halfway up the stairs. She explained, "And the guy he shot survived. So, Brody was charged with second-degree attempted murder. The list of charges was long, but that was the big one. The prosecutors hoped he would get the maximum sentence of 15 years."

She shook her head. "But that didn't happen. He was a first-time offender. His uncle was a judge in Mississippi. And it was a vigilante crime he committed – which made the jury sympathetic. He was only sentenced to seven years.

"But everyone knew that it would be a long seven years in Angola – a prison wrapped by swamp and the Mississippi River. And tales of horror. Brody would have been terrified. I still can't believe he shot someone."

Wolf said, "And would have shot you."

"And there's that."

She hesitated to continue, and Wolf prompted, "How long did it take Dillon to make a move on you after the trial?"

"Not long. The same week. And he didn't have to work hard. Then after two months of dating, I skipped my Tulane graduation, and we flew to Las Vegas and got married."

She laughed without humor. "I never told anyone about him. Not a single person. I didn't want the backlash I knew would come from Jax and Indigo. I wanted what I wanted."

Wolf got it. Who didn't.

She took a deep breath. "Two short weeks later, I knew I was in way, way, way, over my head. He was more than moody - he'd hidden that he drank. Not a get drunk type of drinking. But something else. I guess it was the job…or the pressure he couldn't shake. He got broody. Dark. I mean soul dark and intimidating…"

She paused, then said it. "Particularly in the bedroom. And…before long, I couldn't find the man I married. And love had morphed into something ugly. Creepy even."

She leaned against the wall, staring across the room. "It got worse, and we teetered on the edge of an abyss I wanted no part of. And I knew I had to get out.

"So, after being his wife for less than two months, I planned to leave. I wasn't afraid of him. Not exactly…it was just like having an animal in the house. He was a predator. And smart. I mean, he was a cop. All his friends were cops. And I hadn't told a single soul about him. I had completely set myself up to be the perfect victim.

"Then I got a break. A big case came up. Which meant, for days he would be gone more than he would be home. I made plane reservations, got money together and packed. The last thing I remember was heading out of the bedroom with my luggage."

She swallowed hard. "I woke up on the floor. Alone. Terrified. And less than two hours later, the doctor confirmed I was pregnant."

The silence was loud after that. Wolf watched as she dropped her head in her hands for one minute. Two. And tear tracks spoke of pain when she lifted her face.

She said, "I knew then that Dillon wouldn't let me go easily. Not pregnant. But I also knew that I could never let my child grow up in that dark place. So, I decided not to tell him. Not forever – just not yet.

"I made it home from the doctor and Dillon's car wasn't there. I ran upstairs for my bags." After a long pause, she said, "I should have known it wouldn't be that easy. He was sitting on the bed next to my luggage. Drink in hand. He took a sip as we stared at each other. And I wasn't sure how it would play out, but I was leaving even if I had to call 911 to do it.

"Without a word I grabbed my bags. I'd almost made it to the second-floor landing when he yanked the bags away and shoved me against the wall with an angry kiss. And in the fight that followed, I'm not exactly sure what happened. I remember the sound of my shirt ripping and his elbow catching me in the head. And then falling.

"I woke up in the hospital."

She glanced at Wolf. "I know you found the hospital report. You know about the concussion. Stitches. Broken arm. And the miscarriage." Her breath caught. Locked with a sob for a second.

She whispered, "Did you know they can determine the sex of a baby with testing?"

Wolf walked up the stairs, his eyes never leaving hers as he said softly, "I'm so sorry, Velvet." A tear rolled down her face as he sat and put his arm around her.

She said softly, "It was a girl."

He laced his fingers with hers and squeezed. Taking a deep breath, she continued, ready to get it over with, "And as far as Dillon, he was devastated. Or, more shocked at the horror of what he had set into motion. Between the fight, the fall, finding out about the pregnancy and the loss of our daughter, I finally saw a glimpse again of the man I'd married. But it was way too late.

"I called an attorney to find out my options for a speedy divorce. Six months was the usual minimum, unless there was a fault-based divorce for adultery or abuse, etc. So, I bribed Dillon. More like traded him really. The police wanted my statement, and his future hinged on my statement matching his. I demanded that he lie and admit to adultery, or I would tell them the truth about all the rest. He agreed.

"We used the same attorney. And after two visits to her, we signed papers. I never saw or spoke to him again. That was the deal. Six weeks later, my body was healed, and I was on an airplane to Dallas to start over."

She met his gaze and said, "So, mountain man, I committed perjury. What say you?"

"Not to the real judge you didn't."

She smiled softly. "You can't lie to Him."

"That's the point. Now, how about a break?"

As they walked downstairs, she asked, "So, when are you going to tell me what you put in the chili to make it creamy?"

"Right after I tell you that top heavy works for me, Green Eyes. All day. Every day."

After cleaning the kitchen and tending to clothes, they bundled up in winter gear and headed to the back door. Wolf entered a code, and the metal panel slid sideways into the wall.

Taking her arm as the door slid shut behind them, he pointed down and said, "Always check the steps for ice. Even in the garage. Drafts and condensation can lay a trap anywhere."

Velvet stopped at the bottom and looked around the cold, but not freezing building. A large heater vent blew from the house into the room. The building itself was about the size of a four-car garage. Concrete and wood. No windows. Three large hydraulic doors were on one wall. Two propane tanks were locked and surrounded by metal fencing on another. Outdoor equipment and tools hung neatly everywhere else.

Vehicles sat in the middle. Another black truck like the one they'd wrecked was in the first stall. Next to it was a Ford Bronco Raptor. Red. Impressively decked out for off road. Then two snowmobiles. And...

She said, "Is that a dog sled?"

"Originally. Anything can pull it now."

"I want to drive all of these...and ride in the sled."

He chuckled. "You will, but not yet. Put these snowshoes on and let's take a walk. You need to get familiar with your surroundings."

Later, Wolf glanced at Velvet's breath clouds and red cheeks after the trek to check out the snowed-in bunk cottage. She pointed toward the barn. "Those walls are two foot deep in snow. You mentioned a horse at the cave, I presume you don't have any animals in there now."

"Wild cats and anything seeking shelter. Most summers, I borrow a couple of horses from a ranch in Oklahoma."

"Anything else?"

"My two German shepherds adopted my nephews in North Carolina. So, for now just the wolf. You?"

"My neighbor has a golden retriever that I adore. We play a lot."

They walked between snow drifts toward the front of the cabin. Velvet said, "Tell me about your place in North Carolina."

"It's a beach house. An old two story that I fixed up. It's secluded with a board walk through the dunes."

"That's where you get the bronze tan. But why always the seclusion? You don't like socializing?"

He grunted and waited for her to catch up. "I don't have a choice. I juggle tons of socializing since my family is involved in politics. And that includes activities on way too many levels to even mention. But I like privacy at home. Besides, I swim nude."

Their gaze met and that image rose in Velvet's mind. Vividly. She said, "No tan lines."

He winked, "Not a single one. Just the tattoo." He drew her close. "But you'll see that long before you see the ocean."

Their mouths met and hunger flared. Impatient for more, Wolf lifted her for a much deeper taste as he carried her toward the front. The porch hit him thigh level, and he laid her back. Her legs opened as he pressed in, their kiss wild in the intimate position. Flaring out of control.

And before long, frustration flared.

Wolf groaned as he looked at her face flushed with desire and said, "It's a good thing we have all these clothes on."

"Wolf...it can't have been five minutes yet."

He slid his hand between her legs. "I want to take you right here, right now, so time has got to be up - five minutes or not."

Pulling her with him, they sat on the porch and waited for the fire to simmer down. Velvet focused on their surroundings again. The trees. Snow. Sound of the breeze. And the cold. She realized that she still clutched his parka in her fist...and opened her hand on his thigh.

He looked at her hand. "We have serious chemistry, Velvet. I've felt you since I met you."

She swallowed, feeling things all the way to her toes. "You're going to heat things up again."

He covered her hand with his. "It doesn't take much. Does it?"

"No, What now?"

"We take one kiss at a time."

"That was more than a kiss, Remington."

Helping her up to go inside, he said, "Not by my definition."

After darkness fell, they went back outside for a safety test. Only the gas lamp lit the porch, reaching out with shadow fingers into the yard.

Wolf said, "Walk out to where the lamp light fades and tell me what you remember about the terrain you've seen. Including the direction. Be as specific as you can. Because if you need to run in the future, you need to be able to make the right choice for escape. Now think. One. Two. Three. Go."

Velvet walked into the yard, her back to him. Snow crunched under her boots. The moon was full. The breeze light. An owl hooted. But it was much colder. Facing the darkness, she pointed. That's east. The way we got here. There's a stream by a large cliff."

"What else is there?"

"A rope and hooks at the cliff. And a dead bear, so possibly, other animals feeding."

"Good. Go on."

She pointed. That's west. The barn is southwest. The road out is northwest. She pointed behind her. "South. The shop is behind the house, and I can only enter through a single secure door."

She pointed straight ahead. "That's north. Through the trees is a smaller cliff. The same stream passes there. But no rope. Or hooks. There's a path to climb down."

77

"Excellent. Tomorrow, you'll begin to wear your gun."

A wolf howled in the distance. Another answered from farther away. Wolf said, "That reminds me, did you pick out a name for the wolf?"

"I thought of Brave. For when he fought the bear for us."

"Cool name. Good choice."

Walking out to meet her he said, "I'm going to code you into the security system for all the doors. And get you familiar with carrying a gun and being outside."

She shivered. Hopefully from the cold but his words bordered on ominous. "That's alarming, I hope it's overkill."

"Me too. But until we know more, overkill is the way to go. Now, let's head to the bunker. We have work to do."

His phone vibrated as he keyed in the door code.

Wolf ushered Velvet inside and glanced at the caller. His uncle. Perfect timing. He answered, "Hey, Ace. It's been a while."

Ace laughed at the coded name. "You're not alone."

"Nope. But good timing. I was going to call you for a favor later. What's going on?"

Serious now, Ace asked, "I'm hearing some back-alley whispering. Have you heard from Jax recently?"

Wolf headed to the kitchen and began making coffee. "In a manner of speaking. Who's whispering?"

"Remington, just tell me what you know."

Coding his answer, he replied, "I might be able to get the bird up by early Monday. You'll be the first one I call. But until then, I need that favor."

"Shoot. What do you need?"

"I'm having a little trouble closer to home. I have a DNA fingerprint. Can you call in an anonymous favor for me at the Denver FBI? I'm trying to find out where on the totem pole this trouble is connected. I need you to handle it…like a ghost."

"That blows casual favor all to hell. Explain."

"I can't yet. I'll know more by Monday. Hopefully. Message me when I'm clear to send my drone with the package."

"I will. And Remington, I'll give you till Monday, then we're coming."

"Looks like Monday is going to be a busy day."

"Keep in touch."

Wolf turned as he slipped the phone in his pocket.

Velvet had leaned against the wall, listening. Curious at the first contact she'd seen him have with anyone. She asked, "Who's Ace?"

"An uncle on my mother's side."

"Interesting that he's got connections with the FBI."

"Not really. A lot of people know someone in a government job."

"Ace is his real name?"

"It's his callsign. He's a pilot too."

"What bird are you getting Monday?"

He smiled. "You're enjoying the interrogation."

"It's only fair."

"A bird is a helicopter."

"You have a helicopter."

"I'm a pilot. I have a few things that fly." The coffee finished dripping. He said, "I'll fix us a thermos. It's time to head to the bunker."

"Where is your drone?"

"I can tell you're a pro at research."

"And I can tell you do intelligence."

When they reached the bunker, Wolf said, "Give me half an hour to get up to date on my message feeds. Then we'll work."

Velvet sipped coffee and watched Wolf at the large workstation. His chair rolled between three computer stations and a couple of printers. For such a big guy, he moved and keyed fast, watching various screens flip at his instructions. He made notes and pulled documents off the printer. At one point, he rolled his chair back and just watched the world map. He zoomed in on Europe and Africa and made more notes.

And then he checked his phone. Glancing back at her, he said, "FBI is a go. You ready to see a drone?"

"Absolutely."

Pulling a large black case off a shelf, he laid it on the counter. Unlocking it, he lifted out a drone. Black and thin. Eighteen inches wide. Velvet was surprised. She had expected something that looked like a helicopter spider – this looked like a miniature stealth bomber.

As he opened a door on its back, she stepped closer to watch. Slipping on gloves, he pressed a plastic bag inside and snapped it shut. Then taking a long slender case out of a box labeled long range batteries, he slid it in a two-inch opening.

A green light blinked on the drone.

Carrying it to a small door in the wall, Wolf opened it to reveal a metal closet of some kind. He said, "This is a mini elevator, like a dumbwaiter, it rises to the roof. I launch the drone from there."

"What was in the plastic bag?"

He glanced at her. "Ziva's bloody fingerprint."

She winced at the awful image of the woman that popped in her mind. "How long will it take it to fly to Denver?"

"Twenty minutes in this weather. Not a cloud in the sky. Light wind."

"Unbelievable. How fast does it fly?"

Smiling, he said, "A little over 200 mph." He pointed toward a rolling chair. "Do you want to take a trip with me?"

Excited, she sat as he pulled up the drone on a large screen. She could see metal walls and a tall dark chute.

Wolf texted Ace: Leaving now. ETA 18 minutes.

Velvet heard the mini elevator rise, then watched the screen. In moments, all she could see were treetops…then stars. And it shot into the sky.

Chapter 13
Same Time, Across the Ocean

Jax could smell salt in the night breeze on the wharf at the Tangier port in Morocco. Wind whipped his hair and shirt, as well as the safari hat in his hand. Two duffel bags sat at his feet. He glanced at his watch and calculated.

It was 3 a.m. here. That meant it was 8 p.m. at Wolf's. And he knew without a doubt that Velvet was at Wolf's. One, because he knew Wolf. And two, because she was all over the news as missing in Dallas.

He inhaled the ocean breeze trying to rid himself of three days of the smell, taste, and feel of sand, sweat, and blood. It had taken nearly a full day for him to catch up with the mercenary that killed everyone but him. And after that, it had taken a painful convincing before the merc gave up the information he insisted on.

It had taken another day to get back to civilization.

And then, most of today, to meet up with his contact. And this was still far from over. The one that hired the merc still had to pay. Because now he knew who it was.

A reckoning was coming.

Nico, his contact, joined him on the wharf and said, "The ferry leaves for Tarifa, Spain in less than two hours. And it takes an hour to cross the Strait of Gibraltar. A car will meet you at the port there by 6 a.m. She will be your driver for the last leg of the trip."

Jax nodded. "Who is she?"

"Blanca. Lovely, but deadly. And more than capable of distracting any questioning police or military. The trip to Seville Airport will take a little over two hours. Do you have a flight back to the States?"

Jax held up a new burner phone. "As soon as I leave Africa, I'll work on that." They shook hands and he said, "I owe you, Nico."

Nico said, "You owe me nothing. I wouldn't have Farah or my kids if not for your help years ago." He handed him a bag. "Now, here. Eat while you wait. And take care of those wounds."

As he walked away, Jax said, "What wounds?"

And it was almost true. He barely noticed them. Fury was all he felt.

Chapter 14
Saturday Night

Wolf lowered the drone's altitude coming out of the mountains. The uncontrolled airspace for drones was a maximum of 400 feet, so he stayed close to that boundary but wasn't overly concerned. He certainly had no intention of announcing his presence to anyone, much less the airport. Undetected was the goal. Except for the FBI agent waiting on him. He decreased speed and headed for the lights of Denver.

Velvet watched Wolf's hand eye coordination on the drone controller versus the fluid movement visible on the screen. And it was incredible. He was an exceptional pilot, not that she was surprised.

She said, "How long would it take me to learn to fly that?"

He glanced at her. "Do you want to try now?"

"Maybe not. How much does the drone cost?"

"Not as much as a spaceship."

"Right. So, the comp and collision on my Jeep wouldn't cover it?"

He chuckled and scooted back in his chair, spreading his legs. "Come sit in front of me. I'll let you get the feel of it."

"Seriously?"

He tugged her out of the chair. "Come on. Sit. We need to land in a minute."

Settling between his thighs, Velvet's eyes were glued to the screen. They didn't seem to be going as fast as they were in the mountains, but it was still fast. And in a flash, they were over the city.

Then the drone seemed to be lowering closer to the buildings. Really close. Until she could see through windows and thought they were going to crash. She gripped his legs. But then it slowed. Then slower still. Until she could make out a man on the roof ahead. His suit jacket fluttering in the wind.

Wolf said, "Here we go. I'm switching to hover." And in seconds, he gently landed the small aircraft in front of the agent who now looked like a giant.

Flipping on speaker, Wolf said to the man, "The drone will be hot. Wait for the panel to open."

The agent squatted and said, "Now this is impressive." The hatch popped open.

Wolf said, "Technology makes life a video game. Go ahead. Take the bag. And I appreciate the cloak and dagger."

"No problem. Some nights it's boring, and others, a stealth drone shows up. You never know. I'll take care of it personally since it looks like we know some of the same people."

"Looks like it. Hope to get that answer yesterday."

"Understood."

And they were gone again.

Velvet found herself leaning back against Wolf as he flew the drone up and out toward the mountains, higher, and higher. Faster, and faster. She caught herself holding her breath just like they were inside it.

Wolf smiled. "You like the rush."

"It's like a roller coaster times a million."

Quickly leveling off to 200 mph, Wolf said, "You make this a hard act to follow for a regular guy."

She laughed. "But then we know you aren't a regular guy."

He nuzzled her hair, smelling his own shampoo. That alone was stimulating. But with her nestled between his legs and her hands on his thighs, everything she touched got hot. Taking a deep breath at the firm appreciation growing, he knew she would be feeling that about now.

Velvet closed her eyes at the feel of Wolf's desire boldly against her back. Dominant. Masculine. And exciting. She slid her hands along his thighs, caressing his muscles - feeling them tense in response.

He squeezed her between his legs and promised, "This damn sure isn't over when we land."

She looked back at him and whispered, "And until then?"

His blue eyes seared her. "Do what you want. You have less than ten minutes before I land this plane."

"What about your five-minute time limit?"

"Forget the clock."

Velvet smiled and pressed back into him. Teasing. Sensual. Rhythmic. Her back and head caressed his chest. Her hands caressed his thighs. And her hips rotated against his groin. Basically, giving him a lap dance over the Rockies.

Wolf growled, "Damn it, Velvet, I'm about to let the drone crash." He bit her arm as he pressed into her. Aching. Knowing he couldn't get any harder.

Velvet arched against him in response, then reached behind her and finally touched the bulge in his jeans. Wolf jerked, sweat beading at his temples. And it took every ounce of his control to multi focus on the drone…her body…and her hands. A quick glance at the monitor told him the drone was a mile or so from the cabin.

He quickly initiated the hover command and dropped the controller. His hands were free.

Velvet saw the controller fall and looked up as his mouth covered hers. He grabbed her hips, turning her. In a voice tight with raw passion, he said, "You're not on birth control," and it clearly wasn't a question.

Breathless, Velvet felt the fire consuming them, and shook her head no. Then Wolf's hand was in her jeans…her panties…and her. He growled, kissing her, drawing her wildly to the edge until she screamed his name. And still, he didn't stop. She screamed a second time.

Then he stood with her - aching at the panting beauty in his arms – and knew they'd never make it to the bedroom. But before he took the first step up the bunker stairs, his phone rang.

Then the fax machine.

Their eyes met with the same thought. No. Wolf growled at the timing from hell, as Velvet groaned, "Wolf… Please…"

He gritted out, "Son of a… I can't ignore it." Lowering her, he grabbed his phone to see caller ID.

He kissed her fast and hard. "Give me a few hours." And turning, he answered the ringing phone sharply, "Wolf."

Up in the den, Velvet lay by the fireplace wrapped in a blanket. She'd go to bed in a little while. For now, her body was still in the afterglow of Wolf's touch. And she wanted to remember all of it. His passion and his charismatic sensuality. She'd been shocked at her wildness – and at the strength of his self-control. He was unbelievable.

She hadn't thought of birth control…well, in years. Hadn't needed it. She closed her eyes wondering when she had ovulated…and realized, she really didn't care.

She wanted Wolf.

An hour later, Wolf went upstairs for coffee and found Velvet by the fireplace. He had a few minutes…

He slipped under the blanket next to her and watched her sleep. Soft and warm. Satisfied. Dark eyelashes fanned against her cheek. Lips parted. Firelight flickered against auburn hair pooled around her.

He slid a hand down her body, covering her hip. Possessive. She was his. His touch had made sure of that even if he hadn't taken her yet. She leaned closer in her sleep. A sweet surrender.

He glanced at the fire. He'd never believed in love at first sight. Or even in a day. Or a week for that matter. But to find their kind of powerful connection in less than a single day?

Hell, yes, he believed.

Pulling back the blanket, he scooped her off the rug. She needed to sleep in a real bed. She'd slept on the run in a storage unit. On a train. In a cave. And on the floor.

Velvet's eyes opened sleepily as she looped arms around his neck. "Where are we going?"

He kissed her forehead. "To bed."

"I forgot what a real bed is like."

"My point exactly. But I can't stay. I'm still working. I'll join you when I can."

"Do you ever get tired of carrying me?"

"No."

"I can walk."

He shushed her. "You're going to wake up if you keep talking. You need rest."

In a minute she was tucked in his bed. King size. Soft. Coffee-colored sheets. Matching down comforter and pillows. And a gorgeous fur blanket at the foot of the bed. He kissed her and she snuggled in, almost disappearing.

Back downstairs, Wolf checked the doors. Security. And brewed a fresh carafe of coffee. Before long, he heard his fax ringing again. It was spitting out paper when he stepped in the bunker. Two flashing lights blinked on the world map in Jamaica. A rescue mission was underway.

After midnight, Wolf climbed the steps to the bedroom. Velvet didn't even look like she had moved. She was sound asleep.

He turned on the shower.

The sound of rain woke Velvet. Rolling over, she burrowed into the covers again, loving to sleep to the sound of rain. Her eyes opened. It didn't rain in mountain winters.

She sat up. It was the shower. And then she wasn't going back to sleep. Sliding out of bed, she walked silently into the bathroom leaving her clothes behind.

Wolf was magnificently naked in the rock shower. Hands against the wall...face up, as water cascaded down his bronze, lean hard body. His hair much longer wet. And the large wolf tattoo was exposed in full detail from his hip to his thigh. He was manhood at its best.

Wolf felt her presence rather than heard her. His turquoise eyes locked on her through the water as he turned and gave her the full view of him. He drank in her nakedness as his body hardened.

Velvet said huskily, "I heard water."

He walked toward her. Bold intent in every inch of him. He scooped her up and licked her from abdomen to neck. "You know I'm going to get you pregnant. Is that what you want?"

Her heavy-lidded eyes met his. "Yes."

And Remington Wolf let go.

He carried her through the waterfall and pressed her against the wall. He took her mouth, and her, at the same time. He tasted his name on her lips. Felt her fire. And they rode hard. Wild. And fast.

Hearts racing toward each other.

Over, and over.

***

The smell of his coffee alarm woke Wolf just before dawn. He smiled. Velvet was stretched out on her belly right next to him, arms under the pillow. Legs spread. He kissed her shoulder and said, "Good morning."

She stirred, turning toward him with a sleepy smile, "Morning, Remington Wolf."

Pulling her close with a chuckle, he said, "We've passed formality at this point, Velvet Carrington." He kissed her. "Maybe we should talk about that."

She looked at his chest instead of his eyes. "Or maybe not."

He lifted her chin, forcing her to look at him. "Pregnancy is not something you can overlook. And that's just the first one."

"You want children."

"As many as I can make with you. Which means—"

She pushed away. "I don't want to talk about the M word, Wolf. Vows don't mean anything. I've tried it."

87

He drew her back. "Point one, marriage isn't evil, Velvet. That was Dillon. And point two, there's your brother. Can you imagine Jax's reaction to me getting you pregnant without the honor and commitment?"

"I don't want to talk about Dillon or Jax while I'm in bed with you."

"Then let's talk about the L word. That's appropriate with you in bed with me. Especially since it's where you're staying."

She said stubbornly, "It's too soon for all of that."

"Time has nothing to do with it."

"Yes, it does."

He said it anyway. "I lo—"

She covered his mouth. "Don't say the word! I don't trust it. I really don't. It's you I trust."

His heart hurt at the deep disillusionment and betrayal that she'd suffered. He moved her hand and kissed it. "Easy, Velvet. I can do that." He held her face. "Because we already know it's there whether we say it or not."

She kissed him. "Then we understand each other perfectly."

He rolled with her, landing on top, and loved her all over again.

Later, they sipped coffee as bakery biscuits heated in the oven. Butter and blackberry preserve containers sat close by. And the smell of breakfast sausage filled the air.

Velvet's gun and holster lay on the counter. He glanced at her. "I need you to get as familiar with your weapon as you are driving your car."

She sighed. "I miss my Jeep. But…I sure like your Bronco. Can I get as familiar with it as I am my Jeep?"

He grinned but didn't waiver his focus. "The point is your gun. I need you safe, Velvet. There are just the two of us here. Anything can happen. It could be another 24 hours before we have any answers."

"Are you trying to scare me?"

"More to force you to be prepared. It's the fastest way for you to stay alive."

She frowned. "For both of us you mean."

"I repeat… I need you to stay alive. If trouble comes, and it might, you'll know what to do if I prepare you."

Velvet paled. Getting it.

Later, they stood at the base of the small cliff north of the cabin. Wolf screwed a small silencer on the end of her pistol and handed it back to her. He said, "Always check that the safety is on, and holster it. Every time."

She did, and asked, "Do you always use a silencer out here?"

"Not necessarily. I just don't want anyone to know we're here. But if attacked, it doesn't matter. Just shoot to kill."

"You sound like Jax."

"We have the same plan in mind. You. Now, for the sake of an exercise, let's say you are out here by yourself. What would alert you that you might not be alone? Sometimes even your instinct kicks in and you feel that you are being watched. Everything counts."

Velvet said, "If I heard movement, like breaking branches or rocks getting tumbled."

"Exactly. Listening. Maybe even noticing startled birds or scattering animals. They run from humans or predators."

"I know the bear didn't give us much warning."

"That's the nature of the beast sometimes. Literally. If a suspicious noise is at a distance, duck for cover or flee. If you identify lethal danger near you, pull your weapon and fire. Don't stop until it drops. Then get to safety. And now, one more time, how many rounds are in your pistol?"

"Nine."

"How many reloads are on your belt?"

"Two."

"Last question, what is the best option for you – if you have one?"

"Hide."

"How would they follow you?"

"My tracks - try not to leave any. And don't stand out in my surroundings." She pointed at her auburn hair under a cap.

He smiled. "Excellent. You ready? Let's practice some movement with you shooting."

Wolf stood at the top of the cliff watching Velvet swivel and shoot at a target he'd set up. She was growing more fluid. Less hesitation. More confidence. He could tell that she'd quit thinking about him watching her and focused on her task. Getting the feel of the gun. Trusting it.

He took a deep breath and looked out over her. Eight hundred private acres was his. Not impressive by Colorado standards, but more than enough. And the cabin, Peregrines headquarters, was a secure 20 acres. Nothing should be close to it in any direction. Legally, that is. But he knew breaking the law wouldn't stop the ones after Velvet.

She called up, "I'm out of bullets!"

He followed the path down and said, "How did it feel?"

89

"Awkward at first. Then I found my rhythm. I feel pretty good. It's like the gun and I understand each other now."

He joined her with a kiss. "I'm impressed. It wouldn't take long, and you'd be a very formidable frontierswoman." He slapped her on the butt. "Now come on, let's check your target, Annie Oakley."

"Seriously? You're going to grade me?"

He pulled her with him. "You need to know your skill level, so you don't get cocky. You don't want to aim at a bear's eye if you can't hit his ass."

She closed her mouth as she followed him. Oh. That made sense. A few minutes later, she frowned at the target in dismay. "I only hit it 15 times."

Wolf said, "Take in the big picture. How many bullets did you have?"

"Twenty-seven."

"How many did you miss?"

The look she gave him spoke volumes. She snapped, "I can count, Wolf. Twelve."

He choked back a laugh and said, "Easy, hot stuff. I'm making a point. How many men do you think can walk around with 15 bullets in them?"

She blinked as it registered.

He winked. "So, for your first field test, I give you a well-deserved C+. Congratulations."

She narrowed her eyes and spun on her heel, heading toward the cliff path. "Kiss it, mountain man. I have never made a C in my life."

Wolf laughed, which made it worse. He heard a string of rowdy cuss words as she climbed. He waited till she reached the top, then chased her. Caught her. And slung her over his shoulder.

He made love to her bent over the porch rail.

Both, as wild as the land they were in.

They washed up in the bathroom.

Wolf zipped his pants. Velvet braided her hair and glanced at him in the mirror. "I'm jealous. Men don't even have to drop their pants."

He twirled a piece of auburn hair around his finger. "That's what a zipper is for. Your pants on the other hand…are in the way."

"Speaking of hands…" She held up a finger. "I have a splinter."

He nuzzled her neck and whispered, "Yet you still came three times." He sucked her finger. "I'll take care of this - and get those rails wrapped."

Before noon they were side by side at computers in the bunker.

Wolf handed her ear buds and explained, "I've set you up on a read-only internet app. You can't enter passcodes to access your personal sites or respond to anything at all. All you can do is click on websites and read.

"When we were at the cave, I checked Dallas news. You've caused a bit of a stir as a missing person. More as a vanished one really. And even though you've been on a technical blackout so no one can find you - you do need to be aware of what's happening there."

"Why are you just now telling me?"

"When we were on the run, I needed you focused on staying alive. That was enough of a challenge. After we arrived at the cabin yesterday, I planned a research session after we finished with the drone last night."

He turned his chair to face her. "Only...something else came up instead."

Velvet fluttered her eyelashes. "I forgive you then."

"I believe you. Now... Work on searches of the explosion, the hotel, the police, your Jeep, your friends, or anything that relates to you. Make a list of what we need to discuss. I'm going to research Brody, as well as see what Dillon has been up to."

"Hack them you mean. Why Dillon?"

"If the legal agreement in your divorce was no contact, why did he keep trying to call you Wednesday night?"

"I didn't care."

"And he didn't leave a message."

"No, I ended the calls. When he kept calling back, I blocked him. I have no idea what he wanted."

"Based on your description of him, I picture a cool and calculated guy. Didn't that seem out of character for him?"

She thought for a second. "Now that you mention it. But we had nothing to talk about. Not a single legal or personal thing."

Wolf could have argued the point but didn't. He said, "Got it. Let's get to work. Ask away if you need anything." He paused. "And you need to be prepared. Seeing what happened in Dallas may upset you."

Velvet put the ear buds in and laid her hands on the keyboard. She considered Wolf's comment and thought of the usual dramatic effect of the news. She sighed and simply keyed her name in the search bar: Velvet Carrington Dallas Texas. Looking at the screen, she hit enter.

Videos popped up. A house on fire. Firetrucks. Police. Reporters. Her neighborhood with debris everywhere. She watched them all. Then read the news articles. One from the hotel with the valet. Pictures of her Jeep being towed. Then updates from the fire marshal proclaiming arson. And lots of pictures. Indigo, River, Miranda and Dominic at the police station…and at her house. Indigo talking to reporters in tears, holding up a newspaper headline: Where is Velvet?

She turned the sound down and closed her eyes. The house burning wasn't new. She'd watched it for hours from the woods. But the rest…was difficult. Gradually the images faded in her head. Except the pain across her friends' faces. A tear trickled down her cheek. And another. She promised herself that she would call Indigo the second she could.

She inhaled slowly, trying to breathe in peace with reality. Jax was supposed to contact them tonight. And maybe Ace or the FBI by tomorrow. Surely, hope was near, and the danger would end.

Then she thought about Wolf. What about his family? How did they deal with all this cloak and dagger lifestyle? She put her cursor in the search bar and keyed in: Lieutenant Colonel Remington Wolf North Carolina. If they were political, she might recognize some of them.

She hit enter.

It took Wolf a while to hack through all the firewalls in the Louisiana State Penitentiary's server. It wasn't that he was a great hacker - he simply had access to the skills of a great hacker. Thornwell. A very grateful Thornwell who hadn't lost his legs in a freak accident with Wolf's team. Afterwards, appreciative, but with a touch of humor, Thornwell created a custom hacker app as a thank you. Its cover was a video game. The title: *Callsign Wolf.*

And five minutes later, using the app, Wolf hacked into Angola prison's database. He made his way through over 6,500 inmates looking for Brody Jon Grant. Page after page until finally, he found his name.

He frowned at the recent notation: Paroled. Current address, Baton Rouge.

Wolf thought about Dillon. Had there been a threat at the trial? He backed out of Angola's server and hacked the personnel files at the New Orleans Police Department for Detective Dillon Black.

In a second, he sat back. What the hell? Dillon's file was documented: Detective Black missing. Suspicious circumstances. Under investigation.

Wolf backed out of the NOPD server and searched the internet: Detective Dillon Black missing New Orleans.

Velvet mouthed the word, WOW, as all the pictures with Remington popped up. He was crazy handsome in formal pictures. In his Air Force uniform. In a tux. At weddings. At formal dinners. Receiving awards. At political functions. Family functions. And so very hot with lots of beautiful women. No surprise there.

She stopped at the next picture, then scrolled back to a few others. She started reading the names and putting the people together. She looked down absentmindedly as her finger tapped the keyboard. Thinking.

Why were the President and First Lady in so many of the pictures? And wasn't there a marked resemblance between Wolf and the First Lady?

She turned to Wolf.

Catching her movement, he met her gaze. Her very intense gaze. Then he glanced at the pictures on her monitor.

Velvet said, "What is Ace's real name?"

Impressed, he said, "Very good, Green Eyes."

"Your uncle is Zack Madden, the President of the United States."

"See, you already know Ace's real name. You are a hell of a researcher."

"A historian researches. And I remember some of his speeches. He's a pilot."

"Come work with me."

"But you work for the President."

"In the Air Force, yes. The rest is more complicated. You know you're interested."

"You just want more sex on the porch rail."

He laughed. "I want a lot more sex on the porch rail. But I want more than that and you know it."

"I'll think about it." She turned back to the pictures. "You come from beautiful people, Wolf. You are a hot Remington in these."

"You have a thing about my name."

"I know. It's just that I can see Wolf making love to me on the porch like a wild man. What would the sophisticated Remington do?"

He pulled her chair between his legs. "I'd still make you come three times. Who cares what I wear." He kissed her. "Let's take a walk. I have something I need to show you."

"You haven't told me what you found out yet."

"We need a break. The news can wait."

He followed her out of the bunker thinking... Damn. He wasn't looking forward to telling her what he'd learned. Not at all.

Chapter 15
Sunday: High Noon

Velvet followed Wolf single file up the forest path behind the house. The trees were close together, keeping the snow shallow and easy to walk on wearing hiking boots. She heard squirrels, or maybe chipmunks, chattering above them. She noticed tracks from other animals. Gratefully, small tracks.

The incline rose as they continued. She glanced up. The sky was a crisp clear blue, and the trees smelled just like Christmas. Minus the baking.

Wolf stopped where the trail widened and turned to her. He drew her close and pointed diagonally to a taller cluster of trees up ahead. He said, "That's where we are going. From there, you'll be able to see the roof of the cabin and around our niche of the mountain. And we'll still be in the secure zone."

They started walking again. Velvet said, "How big is your niche of the mountain?"

"Eight hundred acres. I inherited most and bought the rest when we started Peregrines."

"When was that?"

"When I left Air Force One."

She grabbed his arm. "You flew Air Force One."

He chuckled, pulling her along. "Each President chooses their personal pilot. Ace chose me."

"Then why did you leave? He's still in office."

"For his second term. He had two missions for me this term – and gave me the choice."

"You chose Peregrines."

He nodded and began to weave in and out of the trees before stopping at the base of the largest one, then pointed up. Velvet glanced up. Above them, a manmade enclosure wrapped the tree. It blended in, making it almost undetectable. Same colors. Same overall shape. She followed the line of the trunk down and noticed foot rods for climbing.

She said, "You made a treehouse."

"Close. It's more a disguised lookout. But I added a few features and could stay the night if necessary. It's also another hiding spot for you. Go on up."

She started climbing. He followed. As they neared the top, he said, "Let me reach above you. The hatch opens inward." He pressed what Velvet thought was a screw. A panel began to slide up and over, opening a two-foot-wide gap.

Wolf said, "That's it. Go on in."

In a minute they were inside, and the door was closing. The room darkened. He bolted the hatch and said, "Stay still and I'll work around you. It won't take but a second to open it up."

A light came on revealing a room around the natural trunk of the tree. The ceiling, floor, and part of the walls were made of thick sturdy wood. She could smell it. Six stools were mounted around the room, including a full bench with a blanket and pillow. And a cabinet-style table that apparently folded up and down.

Wolf clicked a switch. And with a soft hum, shutters rose from the outside, slowly revealing windows from thigh level almost to the roof of the entire enclosure. Velvet gasped, touching the glass, looking out across the Rocky Mountains. Branches above the windows and below. She almost felt like part of the tree. Incredible.

Wolf lit a tabletop propane heater and smiled at Velvet. "Beautiful, isn't it."

"It's spectacular. Just spectacular. How is it powered?"

"The windows are solar panels. Very effective. And speaking of windows, I know things look different from the air. Can you tell where you are?"

She glanced up the ridge. She knew they were behind the cabin, higher, and a little to the right. "South, up the ridge with a nudge west."

"Excellent. Can you find the cabin roof?"

She knew they'd climbed uphill, so she looked downhill. Just before a clearing she saw most of the roof coming through the trees. The chimney. And...

She said, "You can land a helicopter on your roof?"

"Sure. This is Peregrines headquarters. But I don't keep the bird here unless I've got a few missions going on. It's tucked up nice and warm at the airport."

He took his coat off and hung it on a rack carved in the tree. "You'll find it warms up quick in here. Feel free to get comfortable."

Velvet could already feel the heat. She hung her jacket, and taking off her cap, shook her hair loose. Facing the window, Wolf drew her in front of him, his arms around her waist as they gazed across the panoramic view. It was peaceful. Truly glorious, and time passed in silent togetherness.

Five minutes.

95

Ten.

A little more…

Wolf inhaled her scent. A hint of jasmine and gardenia laced with his shampoo. He kissed her head and laced his fingers with hers, hiding a frown. The last thing he wanted to do was bring up Dillon at a time like this.

Sensing something, Velvet looked up at him. His eyes met hers with a mixture of concern and the L word. A tiny frown touched her brow. Gentleness was his response, and the softest whisper of a kiss.

She knew he was keeping something from her and turned, facing him. Touching his chest she said, "Tell me it isn't Jax."

"It isn't."

"Then just say it."

Sliding his hands in her hair, he tilted her face. Voice husky, he said, "Not yet." And his face rubbed hers. Sensual. Cheek to cheek. Their breath, soft and warm. He kissed her ear. Her eyes. And open-mouthed, his lips covered hers, without closing over them or diving inside. Just feeling her. Breathing her. Slow. Soft. No rush.

As Velvet's hands wove through his hair, his hands slid up her shirt. Growling at her bare skin. He pulled her turtleneck off and his shirt quickly followed. Then he picked her straight up, his lips finding her breasts. Velvet's legs locked around him as her head dropped back. Long hair brushing her back. His name, on her lips.

But Wolf took it slow.

Real slow.

Making love to her one hot second at a time. Until finally, he took her to the hilt of him – and stopped. Holding them together. Staring at each other without movement. But with a great deal of burn. Intensity. And emotion.

Saying so many things without a single word.

And then he lit her up.

***

On a ridge three quarters of a mile away, Jagger growled as he watched through his scope as the wild sex in the treehouse came to a crescendo. The crosshair he had locked on the woman's back didn't stop the fierce throbbing in his groin. He took his finger off the trigger and shifted his hips as hot relief shot into his insulated pants.

As pleasure faded in the noon day sun, he laughed. This sure as hell hadn't been on his agenda today. But catching that flash of red in the trees had rocked his world. He'd watched it all. Hell, he'd felt it. Smelled and tasted her too. He licked dry lips and knew it wouldn't be the last time.

Everything had just changed.

The next man inside her, would be him.

He glanced at his watch and shifted his scope aim to the far left of the treehouse. Two big burly men topped the ridge across from him. They were right on time. Jagger followed their path down the slope, well out of range of Wolf's security.

It hadn't been easy to find out who the mystery man with Jax's sister had been. His team had been locked out of literally every fingerprint database they'd entered his print in. Which told them the guy was an important somebody. Well protected.

So, he'd called Boss.

And now Jagger was intrigued. Excited even. He'd personally been a mercenary for hire for years – legally having worked for several since he'd left the marines. Private military agencies (PMAs) worked fast and got paid well around the globe. Who didn't mind paying a private army or soldier to take the chances that political or military channels couldn't? Publicly anyway. Covert was a different story.

And then there were PMAs that crossed ethical and professional lines for special clients. Like he did for his Boss on this mission. But Boss had to get his hands dirty on this one. Making a wreck in the Colorado mountains disappear was a doable thing. Even blowing up a house in Dallas.

But finding out that the guy with Velvet was Wolf was a big deal. First, because he knew Wolf. Back in the day, they'd worked on a couple of the same missions. With respect. Integrity. Though Wolf had known him by a different name – before he'd had to change it and disappear into a shadow of what the soldier code used to be.

The second big deal was because he knew that taking out an Air Force officer related to the President of the United States on domestic soil - with a female civilian - was a bad idea. A case of C4 waiting to go off in your life type of bad idea. Though…you might get away with a hit on two CIA operatives in Morocco.

All Jagger knew at this point was that if he went down, Boss was damn sure coming with him. But until then, Velvet would be his bonus for treason. Hot

97

and alive. And hell, tangling with Wolf over his woman would be badass on every level.

Oorah, fly boy.

***

An hour later, Wolf sealed the treehouse and climbed down behind Velvet. He hooked the top button of her parka for her, and said, "I can tell what you've been doing."

Velvet pursed her lips. "They're puffy."

"And you have whisker burns."

She took his arm as he led down the trail, and said, "Well, I know where you have half-moon shaped fingernail indentions."

He slapped her butt. "And I remember why."

She grinned. Then it faded as she remembered his secret. Without looking at him, she said, "Tell me, Wolf. I know you don't want to but do it anyway."

He stopped and met her gaze. And laid it out there. "They found Dillon's body in the Mississippi River this morning."

Shock washed over her. Then a strange numbness. "I…can't believe it. What do you mean? What happened to him?"

"He was murdered. It's being investigated."

She closed her eyes remembering the calls. No. No. No. She forced herself to ask, "When?"

Knowing what would come next, he said, "They think Wednesday night."

She gagged, and turning, threw up. Tears found their way from under tightly clenched eyelids as she heaved. Wolf supported her, grabbing a rag from his pocket to wipe her face, saying, "Oh, baby. I'm so sorry."

Her knees buckled and he knelt with her. She drew a deep breath and said, "That's why he called me." A sob broke free. "I should have known something was wrong when he kept calling…" She moaned. "I didn't even care."

She turned to Wolf with a look of torment. "What kind of person does that to someone they were married to? What's wrong with me?"

"Don't you even go there. It's not your fault. And it's not that simple, Velvet. Your pain and loss were real. The victimization was bad. Dillon knew that. I think he called because something scared him. That leads me to a question. Did Brody ever threaten you or Dillon during his arrest or trial? Maybe something that you overlooked and didn't take seriously?"

98

Wolf watched the truth cross her face. Her words stumbled clumsily, "But...people say all kinds of things in the heat of the moment. I didn't think... I just...blew his threats off. Dillon stressed about it—" She frowned. "But wait. Brody is in—"

"He was paroled last week."

She blinked, trying to grasp everything. Then confused, said, "But he wasn't mad at Dillon."

Wolf said, "Right. But I think...as detective on the case, Dillon was informed when Brody made parole. He tried to warn you. Brody probably found out about your marriage – and maybe the divorce. Then he went after Dillon to find you."

She paled. "Dillon died because of me."

"No. Dillon died because of Brody. But Dillon chose to make up for what he had done to his wife and child. That's my guess. Proof will have to come later."

She looked through the trees. Still and silent. Kneeling in the snow, she began to feel the cold again. The breeze. And clarity. She glanced at Wolf. "Where is Brody?"

"In the wind. But my guess is, Dallas, since I'm sure he found out that everyone there is already looking for you."

His alarm vibrated.

Opening the security grid on his phone, he saw that something large had just breached the secure zone. He glanced up the slope, but at this angle couldn't see anything. Looking back at the grid on his phone, the heat source shifted to two shapes instead of one - with increased speed toward their general direction.

Someone was coming.

Wolf pulled Velvet by the arm and jogged back up the trail to the treehouse. "Two men are coming. When we get to the break in the trail, I'll stay behind. Get to the lookout and hide."

She glanced uphill and saw the tree. Heart pounding, she said, "Come with me, Wolf. You can't—"

They reached the split in the trail. He said sharply, "Get up that tree and bolt the hatch. If you see anyone's face but mine, unload your gun in them. Do you understand me?"

Scared now, she nodded quickly.

He pushed her, "Go!"

And she ran.

99

Wolf checked the grid again, watching the movement of the men for a moment. They were splitting up to trap him. He ran into the trees toward them, already knowing the best spot to confront them. He'd have to kill one to be able to fight the other.

He couldn't let them find the trail to Velvet.

A short time later, he stepped into a twisted tangle of dead trees. The result of a back-to-back lightning strike. Climbing inside it for the best angle, he pulled the shotgun off his shoulder and laid it across a branch, then tucked his pistol in his pants. He watched and listened.

He heard noise first.

Then saw movement.

One man was straight ahead. The other to his right – a little farther back. They were big guys. And the closer they got, the more familiar they became. He sighed. It was those damn poachers he'd run into several times. Even in town.

Wolf fired in the air and watched both men disappear in large puffs of snow as they dove for cover. He called out, "Willie, what in the hell are you doing here again? How many times are we going to have this debate? You are trespassing. I almost shot you. I still might."

Willie yelled, "Aw, come on, Wolf. You don't need all the elk. You're skinny. We're big boys. We need the food."

"Quit whining, Willie. You eat too much anyway. Which brother is with you?"

Tom answered for Willie, "Kiss my ass, Wolf. We have the right to be up on this ridge."

"Nope," Wolf said. "You're not on the ridge. You passed onto private land, and you know it. Both of you get out here where I can see you. Now, with hands in the air."

They didn't move. Wolf said, "I'm going to say it one more time. Get out here."

The brothers still didn't move. Or answer. But he heard them talking back and forth. Wolf got a tingle up his spine. These brothers weren't above taking illegal jobs – and were no stranger to a jail cell. He figured they would do anything for a buck.

And then Wolf thought about Jagger. It was entirely possible he hired some poacher thugs. To test his theory, he tossed his cap to the end of a log where it could be seen. Both men shot it.

100

Wolf looked at the holes in his hat and aimed his shotgun at Tom's location. He was the hothead and more apt to make the first move. Wolf said loudly as he staired down the scope, "So, you boys decided to switch from poaching to murder."

Tom shot twice in answer. The third shot that split the mountain air was from Wolf's gun. Tom didn't shoot again.

Willie screamed, running from behind a tree firing toward Wolf and slinging snow. "I'm going to kill you! You killed my brother!"

Wolf shot him twice in the chest.

Willie flew back, feet in the air and dropped like a stone, blood splattering the snow. Wolf walked toward him, shotgun in hand. He looked down at the big man, who was at most, 30 years old. Blood flowed from two holes.

Wolf met Willie's quickly fading gaze.

Willie gasped. "The…guy…paid a lot…for the girl."

Nodding as his suspicions were confirmed, Wolf said, "Too bad you'll never spend it."

Willie gagged, then went silent at the sudden gush of blood.

✳✳✳

Huddled in the dark lookout, Velvet was a nervous wreck. How many shots had that been? Nine? Or ten? Giving Wolf time to get back, she counted to 60 four times. Four minutes. She started to count again, then jerked at the sound of a growl outside - almost shooting a hole in the wall in panic.

Wolf called out, "Velvet, I'm here. It seems like you have two bodyguards. Brave's standing at the base of the tree."

Velvet laughed and cried at the same time. And in a minute, the hatch opened, and Wolf had her.

Brave was gone before they reached the ground.

Wolf checked her out. "Are you okay?"

"Forget me! What about you? That was a lot of shooting. What—"

He cut off her conversation as he hurried her down the trail. "I'm not hurt, and we'll talk later. I've got to get you back to the cabin. The mercenaries have found us."

Chapter 16
Fortress

Velvet gasped as Wolf pushed her into the cabin in front of him. A loud thud confirmed the massive door shut behind them. A bolt clicked into place. She turned as he lowered a large metal bar behind the door. It clanged as it landed in the latch, metal on metal. A steel bar. Her mind flashed to castles, moats, armor, and enemies trying to breach city walls.

She met Wolf's intense blue eyes and couldn't imagine anyone coming through that door and facing his wrath.

He held her face. "We're going to be busy locking down the cabin. Then we'll talk about what happened. For now, get out of your snow gear but keep your boots on...in case we need a quick exit."

That reminded her of the blood she'd seen on his boots...and in his footprints on the trail. She nodded, and they removed snow gear. Wolf pulled on a different pair of boots without comment.

Heading to a wooden gun case built into the wall on the right side of the fireplace, Wolf said, "We are going to put weapons and ammo around the house. Follow me."

With little conversation, he handed boxes of shotgun shells to Velvet for the six shotguns he gathered. And in minutes, the weapons were in place. Then he opened the bunker door, and they disappeared down the stairs.

Velvet tried not to think about the battle he prepared for and focused on the activity instead. She watched Wolf enlarge all the security camera views, as well as the security grid. And then he flipped a large red lever with a lightning bolt sticker. Electricity.

Finally finished, he faced her and said, "For now, I will leave the bunker door open for quick access. When our security zone is breached, and it will be, the alarm will sound through the house. Loud. And at that point, your responsibility is to get to this bunker. You are to stay down here no matter what I do or how scared you are. For me to fight, you have got to be safely out of the way."

He pointed to the camera views. "But you will be able to see what the cameras see outside and even hear some of it. But you are not to have any physical participation.

"And when I determine the threat is too great, I will lock you in here and destroy the entrance so no one can reach you."

Her eyes widened in alarm, welling with tears. "Then how would I get out? And what if you need something? You seriously expect me to watch and do nothing? Well, forget it." She tried to walk away.

He drew her back and kissed her. "Listen to me, Velvet. Jax and Ace are not going to leave us here. Help will come. But until then, we do whatever we need to. Did you see the red lever I flipped?"

She wiped tears off her cheeks. "Yes."

"Consider it our force field. It's a stun-lethal net border. Sheer and nearly invisible. And it now borders the entire cabin and garage about a foot off the ground. It also covers the external side of the doors and windows.

"One touch of it gives off a shock that makes someone wish they were dead. With a second touch, they are dead. High-security prisons use it as a fence. So, we are not helpless."

Velvet breathed a sigh of relief. "So, they can't actually reach us."

"I didn't say that."

"Then how—"

"A bomb. Or fire. Massive artillery even. I didn't say we were impregnable, though the bunker is close to it. Call us a well-armed fortress until the army arrives."

"So, how would I get out of the bunker once I'm locked in?"

"Basically, we get to you. But you'll have everything you need. Air. Food. Water. Bed. Bathroom. Radio. Visual access outside. And you'll have my phone. But don't make any calls...just answer it if it rings."

"Why can't I call for help?"

"Because help will already be on the way."

He led her to the ammo locker. Handing her a tactical shotgun with a box magazine attached like the ones upstairs, he said, "Have you ever shot one of these?"

She said, "No," as she touched the barrel.

He showed her how to turn the safety on and off. "You aim and pull the trigger. If you hit what you aimed at, they're critical, if not dead. But the kick is hard. I don't foresee any actual face-to-face confrontation for you - and you have your pistol. But if you see a face you don't know, fire."

103

He laid two handheld radios on the counter, then checked batteries. "Once the bunker is sealed, I can talk to you through the TV monitor in the den or with these. Just listen and watch. Now, do you have any questions?"

She looked around the room and saw the drone case. "Will you use a drone?"

He opened the mini elevator door and looked up the three-story chute to the roof. He considered his options then shook his head. "I wish I could, but no. I need my eyes on the cameras and my hands on the guns."

He motioned to the stairs and said, "Let's go up and take a break. It's time to talk about what happened on the trail earlier."

Velvet climbed ahead of him, thinking… Ziva was dead. The big man in the backseat of the truck was dead. And two people by the lookout. She took a deep breath as she stepped into the den, two questions running through her mind.

Had anyone else died in this nightmare?

And what in the world was happening to Jax?

Wolf opened the fridge and held up a coke. Velvet nodded and listened to the clink of ice in the glasses, and the fizz. They sat facing each other at the snack bar.

Wolf dove right in. "I ended up recognizing the two men that breached security on the ridge. Two brothers, poachers, that I'd had issues with before. So, I warned them to lay their guns down. They ignored me – which was unusual. And that brought the mercenaries to mind. I knew they wouldn't be beyond hiring locals to give them a hand.

"So, I tested my theory and baited them. They fired first. I fired last. And found out that Jagger had hired them. Now, I'm not making light of the fact that two brothers bled out in the woods. That's a tragedy. But they chose to become hitmen and died for it. That's how it works."

Velvet nodded. Sad. And scared. She said, "That's four."

He knew what she meant. "That we know of, plus a house and a wreck. And whatever your brother is dealing with."

She was silent for a second, then said, "So this Jagger knows where we are."

"Yes."

"Do you think he'll come personally?"

"Yes. There is not a doubt in my mind. But hopefully not till morning."

She looked at the clock on the front of the microwave. Five o'clock Sunday afternoon. She said, "In 12 hours."

"Something like that. But I expect to hear from Ace and Jax before midnight. And then it will all come to a head."

She repeated, "By morning."

"That is the best scenario."

She winced. "What's the worst?"

"If Jagger comes at night. But then again, it makes it a challenge for him too."

Velvet nodded, her mind jumping to Dillon's body in the Mississippi River. She looked at her hand and refused to touch where her wedding ring had been. It was long gone. She'd tossed it in the same river before she left New Orleans. And now he was dead. And she'd refused his call. And Brody was hunting her.

She met Wolf's gaze and said, "And then there's Brody."

His jaw tightened, but he stayed calm. "Brody's already dead, he just doesn't know it yet. Way too many people want him. He'll never touch you."

"But are Indigo and the others safe?"

Wolf couldn't guarantee that and thought of covert options to help her friends. After a moment, he said, "I've got something in mind."

"Tell me."

He pulled out his phone and opened an app. A few busy minutes later, he keyed in a number and tapped the speaker. Velvet listened to a phone ring and glanced at Wolf when no one answered.

Then a gruff irritated voice said, "New Orleans Police Department. How may I help you?"

Wolf said, "I need to talk to Detective Black's partner."

Alert now, the man said, "Who's calling?"

"It's a tip. Just get the detective."

Wolf and Velvet waited, imagining the scrambling to get the detective on the line.

A minute later, a breathless man answered, "Well, you've got me. What do you know?"

Wolf said bluntly, "Did you know that Detective Black's ex-wife is missing in Dallas? And that her testimony put Brody Jon Grant away? Well, he's out on parole, and I'll bet Brody killed Black for her. Maybe Brody's in Dallas right now…stalking her friends for information. Why don't you get out of Louisiana and find him. Or do you want him to kill another detective?"

Wolf ended the call.

Ace called a couple of hours later. Seven o'clock sharp.

Velvet heard one side of the conversation as Wolf answered, "Ace, please tell me you found a name."

"Yes. I have a name. But I'm concerned as to the name's possible connections. I need more information."

"It's too soon to involve you officially. I have no verification of the source of the problem. That's why I need fingerprint information."

"Then talk to me as your uncle. I demand to know."

Wolf growled. "Any holdup is critical. I have two dead hitmen in the woods behind my house."

"Shit. Why are they after you?"

Wolf looked at Velvet and didn't answer.

Ace snapped, "What the hell… I'm not supposed to be out of any loop, Remington. I out rank you – especially with two dead men in your yard."

Wolf said, "Plus two more bodies on Highway 7. Hence the fingerprint. That's why I'm desperately waiting for a phone call. I know very little - and I need to know what you found out."

Ace said, "Not until you tell me who's calling you - and why."

Wolf paused. It's not like he could refuse an order. "I'm waiting on a call from Jax by midnight."

"Jax? What's the deal?"

"I have his sister."

A loud silence followed. Then Ace said, "I don't like the way that sounded. Explain."

"Damn it, Ace. I made a commitment to Jax because of his job. I promised to be her bodyguard anytime. Anywhere. And someone has put out a hit on them. He messaged me to get her. Now give me the information." He stopped. Then said respectfully, "Sir."

Without hesitation, Ace said, "I found out from the fingerprint that Ziva Ballard worked for three years with a U.S. paramilitary group called the TRF. Team Raw Force. CIA Special Operations has used them a couple of times for small things since they are new.

"You may remember missions with them back when they were previously named HBD. Honor Brigade on Deck. The CIA used them more back then. But HBD restructured after internal trouble with soldiers going rogue and losing sight of the already narrow line.

"So, give me a little time and I'll send you a list of names and pictures of TRF's current operation officers. Let me know if anyone looks like trouble. It's not like I can alert the CIA."

106

Wolf got it. "So, you think there's a CIA leak. That is the back-alley whispering you mentioned regarding Jax. That's traitor territory."

"Afraid so."

"Who is it?"

"Like you, I'm gathering info. But I can tell you that Ziva shortens the list substantially."

"That's a shitty list."

"It is. And be ready. We're coming to get both of you out of there at dawn. We don't need a mercenary war in the Rockies for a reason we don't even know yet."

Velvet watched Wolf lay the phone down and said casually, "You cussed at the President of the United States."

He raised his eyebrow. "It's not the first time. Or the last."

She tilted her head with a quizzical frown. "And... I didn't hear you mention to Ace about Jagger or the battle we're waiting on."

He said, "I don't have verification of the one funding the hit to include the United States on the front end of this. But he is sending someone to get us at dawn."

"I doubt he cares about verification."

He pulled her in his arms. "It's too soon. I don't know who's calling the shots. It could be close to him or make matters worse."

"Wolf, he's going to be so pissed at you."

"Again, it won't be the first time. Now, let's eat. I'm starving."

✳✳✳

At 8 p.m. Denver time, Jax was flying over the Atlantic Ocean at 690 mph in a Gulfstream G700. His private contacts in Spain had hooked him up with a U.S. paramilitary company stationed in Spain for a very wealthy unnamed person. And the unnamed person had been thrilled at the idea of a U.S. rescue mission. So, he loaned Jax a three-man team and his jet.

A fine jet. With white leather recliners and all the comforts luxury could buy. But the nine-hour trip from Spain was winding down to a close, and tension was building. Jax studied the Colorado map.

A previous Navy Seal named Cuda, short for barracuda, swiveled his seat to face Jax. "How long is the flight from South Carolina to the cabin?"

Jax glanced up at the tough guy. Smart and skilled. He was lucky to have him on the mission. He answered, "Five hours. The weather report looks good. But by mid-morning snow moves in over the mountains. We should be long gone by then."

Sting, the pilot on the rescue team, walked over and perched on the arm of the sofa. "Tell me about the bird and helipad."

Turning his chair to encompass all three soldiers, Jax said, "It's a Black MH-6 Little Bird helicopter. Thirty-three feet long. It seats six. Night vision equipment is on board. The only weapons will be ours.

"The helipad on the cabin is 50-foot square, built like a helideck on an oil rig. It's located on the north quadrant on the second story roof giving us a clear landing near the front of the house. On the ground, there's a porch and a decent sized open area where the road comes in. Around it will be a couple of buildings, trees, cliffs, and a big southside mountain ridge."

Steel, a Green Beret. Rugged. And decked out in camo, rubbed his stubble beard. He drawled in a deep Texan accent, "What mercs are we tangling with?"

Jax shook his head. Frustrated. "I don't have that intel yet. I'm sure Wolf is working on it. I'll message him when we get to the States."

Sting asked, "What about Wolf's uncle?"

Jax knew they'd heard of Wolf and knew about Ace – and who he really was. He said, "I can't tell Ace. Not yet. We'll call him once we're on the way to D.C. That means we've got to be prepared for trouble and get Wolf and Velvet out of there. I don't care how many mercs we leave dead."

Cuda twisted the top on a energy drink and said, "You sure know how to show a soldier a good time, Jax. Fine ride, the big dogs, and a gorgeous woman. Hooyah!"

Amid the laughter, the pilot announced, "Buckle up boys, we're beginning descent. Touchdown in 30."

***

In Texas, Indigo made it through security at Dallas Fort Worth International and hurried to American Airlines. She grimaced when a quick glance at her phone showed that it was 9 p.m. She'd cut it close.

Two minutes later she was the last one in line for boarding.

Fifteen minutes later she was seated. Her phone vibrated. It was her brother.

River texted: Tell me you did not get on that plane.

Indigo: You know I did.

River: This trip is not a good idea. What if you disappear?

Indigo: Then you know I was on to something.

River: This is a big deal, Indigo.

Indigo: I know. That's the point. Jax should be here for Velvet. Something is terribly wrong. I feel it.

River sighed: Please don't make me put my ranch up for bond to get you out of jail.

Indigo: I'm not committing a crime…yet.

River: Confronting the CIA surely falls into that category.

Indigo: Stop it. And now I've got to get off the phone - they're taxiing. Don't tell Mom and Dad.

River: You owe me.

Indigo: You wish.

Indigo took a deep breath and looked out the window.

Her eyes welled with tears. She was filled with questions…and grief. Where was Velvet? Was she hurt? Terrified? Who blew up her house? Why did she leave her Jeep? And what if the calls from Detective Black that night had something to do with everything?

And what about Jax? She wasn't sure whether to be scared for him or furious that he was ignoring her. A government employee doesn't just disappear. Or a brother. Surely someone with the CIA would tell him about his sister.

Her heart ached for them. Velvet was more than her best friend. She was her chosen sister. And she wanted them to be old grandmothers one day doing dance moves on TikTok or getting massages at the spa by well hung body builders.

She swallowed a sob. Jax…damn him. She loved every inch of that mysterious beautiful man. Had for years. And even though they'd always been a threesome with Velvet when he visited - he had to know how she felt. There's no way she'd hid it that well. Not from someone like him.

But he'd shown no interest. Ever. No looks. No flirtatious accidental bumps into her. And not once even an almost kiss. Not a single sensual move of any kind. Anger flared. He deserved it if she married some hot jock that kept her blissfully sore from wild sex and orgasms. Hell, two or three times a day. And he cleaned the house and cooked too!

Tears rolled down her cheeks as she looked into the dark sky.

But she wanted it to be Jax.

Closing her eyes, she forced herself to refocus. She'd arrive there by midnight. The Central Intelligence Agency opened officially at 9:30 in the morning in Langley, Virginia. Somebody there was going to listen to her, or she was going to the media.

$$***$$

Back in the mountains, Velvet drew slender lines across Wolf's thigh. Erased. And drew again, joining the brush strokes of fur along the wolf's neck and shoulder. Then she stopped and stared at the look in the wolf's eyes in amazement. How had the tattoo artist matched the animal's eyes to Wolf's? That was a personal touch with extreme skill.

Sliding her hand along the drawing, she contemplated just how close Wolf's naked manhood would have been during all those hours of inkwork. She glanced at him working at the computer. Typing. Watching the monitors. Making a few brief calls. Then she glanced down at the image coming to life on copy paper.

His arousal would have been unavoidable. Which meant, the tattoo artist had to have been a woman. She contemplated Wolf again – and he turned, startling her. "Hey, Green Eyes, are you busy?"

She felt a flare of heat up her neck and straightened the papers with a smile. "Not at all. Can I help? I was just occupying myself."

"Would you do some current news research for me on the link I set up for you? I need to know what's happening in Dallas and New Orleans on you, Dillon, and Brody. Add your friends too since I made the anonymous call to the cops."

She sat in the chair next to him and said, "I'm on it." And opened the search link.

He stretched and stood. "I'll be right back. Do you want anything?"

Without looking, she said, "I had a coke. I'm good. Thanks."

Wolf touched her cheek, then checked the clock and thought about their timeline.

It was almost 9 p.m. and everything was quiet. Only three hours till midnight. Jax had better call. He didn't want to call Ace without the answers he was demanding.

Frowning, he jogged upstairs thinking... Nine hours till dawn. This night could explode at any point. He switched the wall-mounted television in the den to computer and all the security cameras popped up. No movement was visible. He heard a wolf howl in the distance. Just once. Then silence. Nothing was happening.

Noting the flicker in the fireplace, he turned off the fuel, killing the flames. Then pulled a lever barely noticeable around the corner. A metallic click echoed from above. An open hole in the middle of the ceiling was never a good idea in a fortress on lockdown.

Heading to the kitchen, he thought about dinner. He had seared a pound-sized ribeye. He could still smell it - and was still full. But Velvet had only nibbled on a few pieces of that and a baked potato. Not surprising really. A lot had happened to her in 24 hours.

The worst was bad, but the best was better – and had happened six times already. And he had long been ready for seven. He adjusted his focus to every nook and cranny in the night ahead. He couldn't miss a single thing even though he'd rather curl up by a bonfire with Velvet, open a beer, and dive deep into her till the wolves howled...or they did.

Damn, he loved her. And it changed everything. He just had to keep her safe and get them through the night. He wanted babies with her. A future. The laughter. Adventure. Fights. Love. And for damn sure, the sex. Even when he got old and couldn't get it up anymore. He would always want her body by his, the look in her eyes, and the touch of her lips.

Sighing, he checked the doors, the weapons, and looked around. Everything was ready, and he headed back to the bunker.

Velvet heard Wolf coming downstairs and called out, "Hey! I found a news report about Brody skipping out on parole. They've called in the U.S. Marshalls and the FBI because... Someone called in a tip! It worked! You rock, Wolf."

"No mention of your connection to him?"

"Not yet."

He passed the table and stopped. Then stepped back and picked up a drawing in progress. It was him, naked in the shower. He took a good long look. Velvet had caught the expression on his face that he'd felt when he saw her. Wet eyelashes. Water rivulets on the contours of his muscles and masculine lines. Even the tattoo on his hip and thigh - positioned just so, not to be erotic but extraordinary.

111

His eyes met hers. She shrugged just a bit. "I have a knack for it. I studied in college because it helped to sketch exhibits. And... Like you, somethings are art."

He pulled her in his arms. "I wish I could draw what I saw that night. You are burned into my memory. And your work is incredible. That's quite a gift."

She slid her hand down his hip where the tattoo was. "Your tattoo artist was incredible too, wasn't she? There's no way you let a man ink you intimately for hours. Not with all those details."

His hand slid over hers as his mouth lowered, "The tattoo was never about her. It was always for you."

And his kiss was hot...and getting hotter when the phone rang. Wolf reached for it and glanced at caller ID. Unknown number.

It was Jax.

Chapter 17
Tangled Web

Velvet choked up as Wolf answered the call on speaker, and said, "Jax."

They only heard wind. Raising his voice, Wolf said, "Jax! Can you hear me?"

He heard bits and pieces until the call cleared, then Jax said loudly, "Wolf!"

"I'm here, and Velvet's listening. Are you in the States?"

Jax said, "Yes, I made good time. And Velvet... I'm so sorry. I'm on my way to get you, and all of this will be over soon. Just listen to Wolf. And Wolf - man, knowing that you had her was the only thing that's kept me sane. But I can't talk long. Four of us are climbing into an MH-6 Little Bird to head your way."

Wolf calculated the trip in his head. "You'll be here early morning by 2:30 or 3:00."

"Copy that. Have you had any trouble?"

"Yes. Who's with you?"

"A borrowed U.S. paramilitary team on mission with a source in Spain. I've got a Seal. A Beret. And Sting is a pilot. They are ready to jump in this fight."

"What the hell is going on, Jax? Who did you get tangled up with? I've got four dead people here in Colorado. Someone is seriously after Velvet. We're in lockdown now. And from DNA results, all I know is that the mercs seem to be a U.S. group – the TRF. The guy after us is someone called Jagger. But I don't know who the money man is."

"I know the SOB. It's a CIA senior-level supervisor in the Special Activities Center. And you know him. It's Hal Beckett, damn him. He sent me and Blaze to Morocco on a bogus mission. Blaze got killed. And I won't tell you with Velvet listening what I had to do to get Hal's name out of the guy."

Wolf was floored at the name and thought about Trevor. He said, "We have to tell Ace."

"We can't. Not yet. We don't know how close the leak is to Ace. Or who is working with Hal. No one in the States even knows I'm alive – and it's got to stay that way. Once we pick you up, we'll head straight to D.C. Then I'll tell the President myself."

"I get that, Jax. But you need to know that he'd already gotten wind of something. He ordered me to tell him about the hit just to give me FBI results. And even before knowing it was Hal, he expected a CIA connection. He is sending someone to get us at dawn."

Jax said, "I'll have you out of there long before dawn. And Hal Beckett is in a shitload of trouble. I'm still trying to wrap my head around the concept of him being a traitor."

Someone hollered in the background at Jax. A helicopter started up and everything got loud. Jax yelled in the phone, "Gotta go… I'm coming… And I'll call before I get there."

The line went dead.

Velvet met Wolf's gaze. Her eyes wide. She said, "That was like eavesdropping in a war room."

"It was."

"I heard the name Hal Beckett. Why does he want Jax and I dead?"

Wolf ran his hand through his hair, his heart heavy. "I can tell you about the trauma that links him and Jax together, but I can't tell you why it came to this. I doubt Jax knows why yet." He paused. "But then again, it has to be about Trevor."

The name seemed familiar to Velvet from a long time ago, but she couldn't quite place it. "Who's Trevor?"

"Hal's son and Jax's friend. They trained early on and worked together for years as partners. And then there was an…accident. I can't discuss anything specific about the classified nature of the incident. But I can tell you that Trevor sacrificed everything to save four men – including his leader, Jax. He took five bullets and earned a Purple Heart."

Velvet covered her mouth, mind in a whirl. Horror filled. What a terrible burden for Jax to bear. She asked Wolf, "When did Trevor die?"

Wolf shook his head and said, "That's the double trauma. He didn't. He's been in a coma for well over four years."

Wincing, Velvet thought back to the time of her and Indigo's graduation. Was that why Jax hadn't been able to come? She said, "Was it around the time Brody shot the man in New Orleans?"

"The week before."

With a heavy sigh, she said, "What a tragedy. That explains so many things about Jax." She frowned. "Wait… He didn't have trouble with Trevor's family when it happened?"

"No. Everyone grieved. Family. Friends. The team. The agency. Oh hell, the whole intelligence community did. But this… This hit came out of nowhere. And it's hard to imagine the Hal that I know making this choice."

"So, what now? What will happen when we get to D.C.?"

"A firestorm."

His phone dinged with a text. He read it and said, "I've been waiting on this attachment from Ace. I'll have to work for a while."

"I'll go shower."

Not wanting her two stories away from him, he said, "Why don't you grab your stuff and shower down here. I'd rather keep you close. Trouble isn't far."

Velvet nodded and glanced at the world map, zeroing in on Washington D.C., as she walked toward the stairs. She wondered…

Do traitors at this level get the death penalty?

Or are they just forgotten at Guantanamo till they die?

***

East of Langley, Virginia, a black Mercedes rolled to a stop in front of a two-story teal Victorian house with gray and white trim. Hal Beckett left the car running. It was late. Getting close to eleven o'clock. But he needed a few minutes of false peace.

His eyes followed the line of fancy gas light posts that bordered the brick path to his front door. The flames flickered warmly. Welcoming. Promising a haven to those that entered.

But it was all a lie.

Turning from the house, he watched leaves tumble across the driveway. Running from winter. A graceful race, true. But Hal knew they could never outrun it. Nature had forbidden from the beginning that they would be fast enough to beat the frigid air. Or wind. Their brief colorful glory would soon be over. Crushed into pieces under the soles of men's feet. Children tumbling. Or animal paws.

Broken like Trevor. To be remembered only in pictures with smiling faces on someone's desk, or a mantle. A flash of time long passed. He sighed with pain for the millionth time. You couldn't stop some things no matter what you did.

So, he sat in the middle of reality. Drenched in it. Drowning. Dying like his son.

Where in the hell, had honor gone?

His phone rang. It was Jagger.

He answered, "Tell me what I want to know."

Jagger said, "It's set. We'll hit them in three hours. Thirty minutes max is all we need to complete the mission."

"It had better be. Nothing has gone according to plan since this started. Have you heard from your guy in Morocco? It's been silence from Jax and Blaze. I know nothing."

"I haven't heard a word." Jagger said. "Maybe they all killed each other. Which works. Besides, if Jax or Blaze were alive, wouldn't they message you?"

"Blaze would. Jax, I'm not so sure. If he caught a whiff of trouble, he'd follow the trail like a rabid Rambo. So, be damn sure tonight works. Kill Velvet and send me a picture. I want proof. I don't care what else happens. Your money depends on it."

Jagger rolled his lying eyes as he blew out a thick stream of cigarette smoke. "Got it, Boss. One dead woman coming up. I'll call you when it's done."

Hal ended the call and got out of the car.

In minutes, he walked quietly down the hall in Trevor's private wing of the house. The hospice nurse looked up as he entered the room.

She said somberly, "Evening, Mr. Beckett."

He nodded, "Evening, Grace. Go ahead and take a break. Give me a few minutes with him."

In a second, she was gone.

Hal softly touched Trevor's foot. He'd long ago stopped praying for a response. Now, just touching him was enough to know that he was alive. But not for much longer. Turning, he walked around the room looking at pictures – the life Trevor once lived. Memories danced in his mind from birth till the day of the call.

He sighed. Five bullets had riddled his son. They'd gotten the bullets out, but he wasn't responding to anyone or anything. Lost in a coma. A different type of enemy.

Turning from the pictures, Hal's gaze landed on two Purple Hearts on the bedside table. His and Trevor's, side by side. Proof of injury. Valor. Honor. And of fighting for one's country no matter what the cost.

116

He swiped them into the trashcan where they clattered loudly. Metal on metal. They meant nothing anymore.

Trevor's body was giving up the fight. Systems failing. They'd found out a month ago. There would be no more solace by touch or walks down memory lane with his brilliant, powerful son. The room would turn dark. Empty. Itself, doomed to a lifetime coma.

That's when resentment began to eat at him. Thoughts of revenge. Jax was alive. Living Trevor's life. He would get a wife. Have children. Receive awards. Save lives on missions. Feel the searing heat of honor. And one day, watch his hair turn gray and have grandchildren. Something real and tangible. A future.

Jax wouldn't be just a picture in a frame or in a memory locked on rewind.

Hal picked up a family photo and stared at his wife. Trevor's mother. Strong, beautiful, Dr. Angela Beckett, Psychologist. He smiled. Trevor was so much like her. They were both resilient to the core.

And with her skills, she'd been able to recover from the ravages of grief and find her new normal in just over a year – taking each day with Trevor one at a time. But he'd buried himself in work and shut her out. He'd refused her attempts at bringing him back to life with her.

He hated the new normal.

And now, he was pretty sure she'd found someone else to take his place. With his intelligence skills, he just knew it. Sometimes it was the smell of a man. And sometimes, it was the look of satisfaction on her face. Now both her and Trevor would be gone.

So, Jax's debt doubled.

Two losses for two losses.

That had been the plan. But now there was a big chance Jax was still alive, and just as big a chance that Jagger would fail tonight. Hal was aware that he had a 95 percent chance of getting caught in this web he'd woven.

Which meant, he'd step into loss three. Or had he lost himself long ago? He leaned over and kissed the face that looked like his.

***

Back in the bunker, Wolf went through each page of the printout from Ace. He studied the names, skills, and faces of each paramilitary operator in detail. Some he knew and some he'd heard of. The rest were strangers. He did a quick search on each one. But none so far seemed to be anything other than who they appeared to be. A soldier with a job.

117

He heard movement behind him and glanced at Velvet. She had pulled the blanket over her on the bunk bed. Her sleepy green eyes met his blue ones. He smiled and said, "Go ahead and doze off. When I finish here, we'll go up to bed for a couple of hours."

She blew him a kiss and closed her eyes.

He turned back to the papers and flipped to page three and began to review. He was about halfway down when he got to the name Jagger Dean and looked at the picture. He did a doubletake.

What the hell? Was it a typo? The name said Jagger. But the picture was Razor Chance. And he knew Razor. Knew him well. And there was no way in hell Razor didn't know who was protecting Velvet. So, why had he taken the job? Money, sure. But Razor was about more than money.

Wolf turned a grim face toward Velvet.

He had a pretty good idea what Razor was after.

Chapter 18
Monday 2 a.m.

After a quick shower before midnight, Wolf dozed lightly upstairs. He was dressed, leaning against the headboard. Velvet was dressed too and slept fitfully with her head on his thigh. He listened. Waiting. He expected Jax by 2:30, or 3 at the latest. And as far as Jagger, he had no idea when he would show.

Sometime later in the darkness, Wolf's eyes opened. A quick glance at the clock showed almost two in the morning. And then he heard it. Rotors. As he jumped out of bed waking Velvet, the alarm blared through the house. Security had been breached.

Velvet screamed, scrambling out of bed.

Wolf yelled, "Get to the bunker! Jagger came in a helicopter! Run!"

The sound of the helicopter grew louder as they ran downstairs. Really loud - like it was on top of them. When Wolf heard it land on the helipad, he growled. Damn it to hell. Leave it to them to make a grand entrance.

The only good thing about a roof landing was that the ladder was hidden, which meant, the men would have to rappel over the side of the house. The electric net might take out some of them.

Running down the bunker stairs behind Wolf, Velvet yelled over the noise, "How do you know it isn't Jax?"

Reaching the bunker, he said, "Jax said he would call – and he damn sure wouldn't set off the alarm. This is Jagger - but we know that Jax isn't far behind."

Filled with adrenaline, they watched the house on security cameras. It was lit up in all directions. Bright like day. And a dark gray helicopter sat on the roof helipad. Four men dressed in black poured from the doors with ropes, bags, and guns as the rotors slowed to a stop.

Wolf laid his phone in front of Velvet. "Answer it if it rings." Then he flipped on both handheld radios – one for each of them. And when the noise faded on the roof, Wolf turned on the speaker so they could listen and watch.

Handsome with long blonde hair, Jagger ordered the men, "Secure the perimeter. Jackson, you take south."

The man with red hair nodded.

"Thompson, you take west." The shortest one nodded.

"Miller, take east after you leave the equipment with me." The muscled black man with a big bag nodded.

Jagger couldn't find a ladder and looked over the edge of the roof. "I'll take the front. And all of you better remember I want the woman alive. You forget, you die."

Eyes glued to the cameras in the bunker, Wolf and Velvet watched large hooks secured along the roof edge. Then all three men rappelled down the east side of the two-story cabin. Kitchen side.

Wolf watched their progress and said, "You better cover your eyes, Velvet."

And moments later, the short man's foot moved from the log wall to the electrified window resulting in a loud pop, sizzle, and flash. As the other men yelled in alarm, covering their faces, the now smoking man dropped silently to the ground. And suffered the same fate again. Pop, sizzle, and flash. Fire licked where he lay on the net.

Wolf glanced at a shocked, wide-eyed Velvet, and said, "One down."

Hanging from the rope, Jagger yelled to the other two, "Don't touch the damn windows! They're wired – that crazy ass, Wolf. Something is on the ground too – so, swing wide and jump! Now!"

Powerfully, the three men pushed to get momentum going, and shoved off the wall letting go of the rope. Flying into the yard, Jagger landed first. Right on a pile of wood. He felt the burn of splitting skin and blood trickled down his face. He let loose a string of raw profanity and jumped to his feet.

Red-haired Jackson hit a tree with a grunt, and winded, dropped to the ground in a small pile of something vile. Gagging at the odor, he scrubbed it off with snow.

Miller's deep voice broke the silence with a harsh, "Jagger."

Jagger turned, saying, "What." But saw the problem. Miller, carrying the 100-pound bag of weapons, didn't fly far. He lay a couple of inches, if that, from a short net sticking out of the ground. He was as close to frying as you could get. And they all knew that the fuel he carried would go up like a bomb.

Jagger said, "We're coming, Miller. Jackson, get over here and help me."

Both men grabbed the parts of Miller closest to the wire, and Jagger said, "On three, pull. One. Two. Three!"

And the flurry of movement found all three men stumbling back in a tangle. Getting his balance, Jagger took a deep, focusing breath. They were down, but one short.

He picked up the heavy bag himself, and said with a sharp edge, "Search the perimeter. Radio me if you find anything. Move!"

He carried the large bag toward the front of the house.

In the bunker, Velvet frowned at the vicious look on the pretty blonde man's face. She said, "I gather the blonde is the one you know?"

"That's him, Jagger, a/k/a Razor. He was a damn fine soldier at one time."

"What do you think happened to turn him into a killer?"

Wolf watched the three men search the perimeter while the fourth one still smoked and sizzled. He said, "Talk has it that his weakness is women. Not getting them – but satisfying them. Abundant libido doesn't do him much good with small equipment. He's been in some rough fights that have gotten him in a world of hurt. All I can figure is that he finally must have hit the wrong man."

Cringing at a sudden thought, she asked, "Do you think he is here for more than money?"

He met her gaze. "He's here for every inch of you is my guess. But that doesn't mean I'll let him live to get you. Just be aware that his motive may be different than the one he's being paid for."

She looked at the man on the camera, and suddenly being killed didn't sound like a worse option. Her stomach churned. "Why didn't you tell me?"

"This is me telling you."

Turning back to the cameras, they watched as the red head and the black man met back up with Jagger after the perimeter check. Pulling machine guns out of the bag, all three men advanced on the house.

Wolf kissed her hard. "I love you, Green Eyes." And he was gone. Running up the stairs pulling on a bulletproof vest and calling behind him, "Keep the phone and radio on you!"

The bunker door slammed shut to the sound of Velvet screaming his name.

Velvet's heart raced as she watched the cameras. The men outside split up. One in front of the house. And one on each side. Wolf had told her that the house was bullet proof. Maybe he only wore the vest to be extra careful.

She watched Wolf in the kitchen. He slid the refrigerator over then strained to open something on the wall. In a second, a small square beam of light lit up the corner he was in. He looked through the opening. Velvet glanced at an outside camera on that side of the house. The guy with red hair raised his gun.

And all hell broke loose at the sound of automatic gunfire. She screamed.

Wolf ignored the sounds of war and focused on the man that would soon be in his line of sight. He slid the shotgun barrel to the opening – not threw it - and waited for the sounds to draw closer.

Ready.

Ready.

And then he fired three times, sending the body of the red-haired man flying back toward the trees.

He spun to look at the security cameras on the TV in the den. The other two men had taken cover – knowing the sound of a shotgun when they heard it. And then he heard a wolf howl.

Brave was close. They better not shoot his wolf.

Jagger radioed Miller. "Get to the east side of the house and find out where those shots came from. If there's an opening, find it."

"Copy that."

Staying in cover of the trees, Miller ran around the back of the house. Behind the large shop, the cottage, and slowed as he neared the east side. Carefully. Trying to steer clear of the flood lights.

He growled at the scene. It was a blood bath. Blood sprayed the snow from where Jackson first got hit, to the tree line. He glanced at the house. No opening was visible from this angle. He edged deeper into the timber and headed for Jackson.

Velvet watched the guy move through the trees toward Wolf's side of the house.

Wolf watched from the TV cameras in the den.

And Jagger watched from the trees in front of the house.

All eyes waited on the black man headed to the blood splattered snow.

Miller made it to the timber behind Jackson and began to edge forward.

Sliding the steel plate over the opening in the wall, Wolf left just a crack. If he could get a shot, he'd take it. But a big gap in the wood would be visible in bright light for someone looking for it.

Miller squatted on the backside of the tree closest to the dead man. The smell of blood was strong. Revulsive. And he began to look for an opening on the cabin wall. But before long, he was distracted by a whiff of something other than blood. A foul earthy odor. Musky…animal like. And then he heard breathing.

Slowly he looked behind him.

The wolf was nearly on top of him. A big one. Their predator eyes met, and the animal bared his teeth. Silently. Long vicious fangs threatening. A deep throaty growl filled the air. Miller moved his hand ever so slightly toward his pistol, and the wolf lunged.

Miller never had time to scream as Brave's fangs ripped his throat, dragging him into the open. Growling and ripping into the man. Mixing one man's blood with another for all of them to see.

Velvet covered her face.

Wolf sealed the opening and glanced at the cameras again. Three men down. Two to go. Way to go, Brave.

Jagger turned from the carnage and leaned back against the tree. He was the only live man on the ground with a wolf. He radioed the pilot, "Billy, if you don't get your ass out of that bird and be useful, I'm going to shoot you myself. There's a wolf eating Miller to your right. Shoot the damn thing. NOW!"

Velvet was shocked to see a man exit the helicopter. She'd forgotten about the roof, the helicopter, and the pilot. The guy was maybe six feet and bald with a rifle hanging from his shoulder and a pistol in his hand. He was headed to the east side where death was piling up.

She gasped, realizing that he was going to kill Brave.

Wolf saw it too. But he hadn't forgotten the pilot. So, he slid the wall plate open and shot twice in the air. Brave vanished. And the shots startled the pilot so much he almost fell off the roof – and dropped his pistol in the process. One gun down.

Jagger quickly considered his options.

Killing Velvet had been the money plan. That would have been easy. He could have just blown up the house. Over and done without even landing. Except he wanted her alive. And breaching the cabin was not going to work. Not with Wolf.

He smiled. Having witnessed sex between the two of them - he had allowed for a contingency plan. If he couldn't get in the fortress, he'd get Wolf to come out. He just needed to threaten Velvet.

Running toward the weapons, he pulled out his threat of choice. A flamethrower. Quiet. Deadly, and terrifying. And he had two fuel canisters. Which meant, he could make this fortress a Rocky Mountain bonfire in minutes. Not that he intended to, but Wolf wouldn't take the chance. He'd bet his life on it.

Jagger buckled on the flamethrower and radioed Billy on the roof. "Stand down. Plan two."

"I see that big match you're wearing. I don't plan on being up here when that helicopter blows."

"It's just a threat. Keep a bead on him when he comes out, but don't shoot him. He's mine."

"Copy."

Wolf watched the camera. He knew what Jagger had on, and Velvet's danger level just increased 100-fold with the threat of fire. Smoke. Loss of oxygen. And explosions from all the fuel in the shop. Plus, the helicopter full of fuel on the roof. Surely Jagger wouldn't blow up his only way out.

Unless he had another one.

Wolf removed his bullet proof vest. He wouldn't play Russian roulette with Velvet in the balance. There wasn't a chance in hell – and Jagger knew that. Which meant, he wanted Wolf to come out.

He sheathed his hunting knife. Stuck his gun in his pants and walked toward the front door with his shotgun.

Jagger yelled from outside, "Get out here, Wolf. You've got two minutes or I'm going to torch this place."

Wolf looked directly at the camera in the den. "Turn off the electric net, Green Eyes."

Velvet grabbed the radio, "No! Don't go out there! What does he have on?"

124

"Something we don't want him to use. Now, turn it off."

"Wolf—"

"Now, Velvet. I'm going out... But I'll be back."

Tears rolled down her face as she forced herself to flip the large red lever with the lightning bolt sticker.

Wolf nodded as the power flickered. The net was off. He said, "Just listen on your radio so you can hear what's going on. And remember, Jax is coming. This is almost over."

Then facing the door, Wolf yelled, "I'm armed, but I'm coming out!"

He unbarred the door. Unlatched and opened it. Standing on the threshold, cocky, he said, "What's up, Razor?"

Chapter 19
Face to Face

Razor laughed, lowering the end of the flamethrower. "Damn, it's been a while. You're such a cool ass dude. You knew it was me."

Hand on his holster, Wolf walked out on the porch. "Surely you knew I'd find out."

Razor spit on the ground. "Ziva?"

"Yep. Hal ranted over Ziva's headset after the wreck and said your new name. But I had Ziva's fingerprint. I found you with TRF."

Razor nodded. "So, you think you have all the answers."

"I know you are in a shitload of trouble for breaching Peregrines headquarters, taking on the President, the CIA – plus me and Jax. You want Velvet that bad?"

Razor smiled. "You ought to know. I watched you today in your treehouse through the crosshairs of my scope. I was going to kill her, but instead, we all came. So, yeah. You might say that. I'm damn sure not done with that piece of ass. Hell, I haven't even started yet."

Wolf wanted to kill him out of pure rage – and hated knowing Velvet heard all this. But he also knew that it was the fuel he needed to keep Razor off balance. Grabbing his crotch, Wolf said, "My dick's twice the size of yours before its even hard. Yours is a waste of time, pretty boy. You know you can't make her scream like I can."

Enraged, Razor went for his pistol.

Shocked out of her mind, Velvet panicked in the bunker as raw testosterone raged like an animal out there. She looked around the room for something…anything to help Wolf.

Outside, Wolf laughed. "Come on, Razor. Surely you have balls to take me on. Show me what you can do. I'll lay my pistol down first. You're next." He laid it on the porch and kicked it aside.

The desire for the fight raging out of control, Razor literally threw his pistol.

Wolf slid his shotgun across the floor and held his hands to the side. Empty.

Razor was already unbuckling the flamethrower.

In the bunker, Velvet opened the door to the drone chute. She knew it was the only way out. Making her decision, she thought of weapons. She tucked a pistol in her jeans. Then considering the sexual element outside, took off her shirt and let her hair down. Jeans, a red bra, and wild hair. That should distract Razor and buy Wolf extra time.

Slipping on Wolf's fur-lined bomber jacket, she tucked the phone in one pocket and the radio in the other. Then grabbed gloves and a flashlight. She climbed into the narrow metal chute and looked three stories up. Trying not to think about anything but Wolf, she punched the green button with the toe of her boot. And listened to what was happening over the radio as she rose in the cold.

Wolf walked down the steps.

Hand-to-hand combat was a revered skill among men, and Wolf knew they were close to being evenly matched. Both had a single weapon - knives at their hips. And neither offered to take them off. One, or both would die today.

Twenty feet apart they circled each other. Slowly narrowing the ring. Not bouncy like boxers. But crouched, arms in a defensive position. Stance wide. Muscles tight. Eyes hard.

They circled once.

Twice, as tension thickened. There were no sounds. Just a frigid breeze and the pilot on the roof. Rifle aimed at Wolf.

Wolf saw the man move, adjusting his stance on the angled roof near the helipad. He nodded up at the roof and said, "I thought you laid all your weapons down, or does a little dick mean a liar too?"

Razor lunged with a scream of rage.

Velvet heard the battle going on outside as the roof hatch opened. She saw stars and trees, then quickly squatted as the platform reached the top. Silently she slid onto the roof and knelt. The helipad was close. The pilot's door was open not far from her. And the pilot was standing on the slanted roof with a rifle. There was no doubt it was aimed at Wolf. None.

She raised her gun. Aimed. And fired.

127

Wolf felt blood run down his face as he flipped Razor over his back, landing with him in a chokehold. Razor struggled, getting lightheaded and elbowed Wolf in the stomach twice, then rolled with him. Both men scrambled for the upper hand in a tangled mess of twists and turns - with fists the size of sledgehammer heads.

Sending a back-kick into Razor's gut, Wolf followed with a knee – then fist slammed both sides of Razor's head. Razor hit his knees, head ringing and face dripping blood. He pulled out his knife.

Wolf jumped back, pulling his blade from the sheath.

A muffled cry split the night.

Wolf and Razor swiveled as the pilot's body fell, slammed onto the porch roof, then rolled off, landing face first on the ground. Four bloody holes in his back. He didn't move.

In unison, Wolf and Razor looked up.

Velvet stood on the edge of the roof holding a gun. In jeans, boots, and a jacket wide open showing lots of skin in an overflowing red bra. She raised the gun at Razor. Then screamed at the speed in which both men ran for the climbing ropes. Wild. Slashing at each other.

Wolf yelled as he climbed, "Get in the helicopter, Velvet!"

Velvet climbed onto the helipad and ran to the open helicopter door. The sounds of the fight were quickly drawing closer to the roof with groans. Yells. And boots kicking against the cabin wall. Lots of cussing.

She glanced toward the noise. Torn against helping Wolf and—

Wolf's hands and head topped the roof. With one glance at her, he yelled, "Get your ass in that bird!"

Velvet jumped into the pilot's seat and slammed the door, then panicked. There was no lock. But she noticed the latch slid over and bolted all the doors just as both men climbed on the roof.

Razor ran for the helicopter. Wolf tripped him, knocking them both off balance. Velvet screamed as they slid toward the edge of the roof. Wolf grabbed the helipad. Razor rammed his knife into the roof as his feet neared the edge.

The phone rang in Velvet's pocket, scaring her. She answered it screaming, "Jax! Hurry! They're going to kill each other."

Jax yelled at his pilot, "We're out of time – get us there!" Then he said, "Where are you?"

128

Velvet yelled, "On the roof! We're all on the roof. I'm locked in the helicopter and they're fighting with knives—"

"How many men?"

"Only Wolf and Razor are left alive. And the wolf. Don't kill the wolf." She choked on a sob. "Jax—"

"We're almost there. You should hear us. I see the lights. And don't get out of that helicopter. Stay on the line…"

Dropping the active call in his pocket, Jax joined the other two men. With ropes and weapons, they slid open the helicopter door. The wind and rotors were loud.

Jax yelled, "We're landing on the roof. Steel, guard Velvet. Cuda, we keep Wolf alive – and I don't care what happens to the merc."

On the roof, shoving away from Razor, Wolf swung and hit him with a bloody right hook just as Jax and two men lowered from the helicopter.

Wolf yelled at Razor over the noise, "You're a dead man!"

Razor snarled and lunged at him. They fell, and Wolf rammed his knife deep in Razor's thigh, hearing the blonde man's scream of pain over the rotors. And then they slipped, sliding toward the edge again.

Velvet screamed and tried to get out of the helicopter. Steel ignored the half-naked woman with a gun and slammed it closed. He said, "Stay!"

She shot him the bird - and lurched toward the glass, watching. Praying. Crying. Locked in a glass cage.

On his back, Wolf caught the brace of the helipad as he slid by. Straining. Growling. Slipping. The metal digging into his hand with the added weight of Razor hanging onto his hips…slowly dragging him off the roof too.

Cuda reached down and grabbed Wolf's left arm and belt, taking the full weight of both big men. He groaned, locked in position.

Jax grabbed Wolf's belt on the right side, then pulled his gun to finish it.

Wolf growled, "Give it to me…"

Without hesitation, Jax handed Wolf the gun. Aiming, Wolf leaned forward meeting Razor's gaze.

And pulled the trigger.

In seconds, Wolf was standing, getting his balance. He was bloody and sweaty in the freezing air. But after a hard handshake with Jax and Cuda, he headed straight for Velvet - wild and fabulous climbing out of the helicopter.

She ran and leapt in his arms. Their lips met as adrenaline raged, and fear faded.

Razor was dead.

Wolf held her tight and glanced at Jax. No words were necessary. Everyone knew he was more than her bodyguard. He glanced down at her exposed chest and said, "We definitely need to talk, Velvet."

She pulled her jacket together. "It was a distraction tactic."

"I'll say. It still is."

The other men, not looking, but overhearing, chuckled. Wolf lowered her and she zipped it. Flushed, she turned to her brother.

Jax was tall. Six foot two. Dark hair. Hazel eyes. A little shorter than Wolf. And leaner after his mission from hell. With bruises. Cuts. And stress, still on his face. Now Velvet understood the heaviness she'd always wondered about since her graduation. It was all there. And all about Trevor.

And he didn't even know about Dillon yet.

She burst into tears.

Jax grabbed her up in a bear hug, her feet dangling, and said, "Oh, honey, don't cry. It's almost over. Let's get off this roof…we need to get out of here."

He motioned the helicopter. Grabbing one of the rappel lines hanging from the open door, he carried her to the ground.

Wolf was on another line.

And Cuda the last.

Steel rappelled down the side of the cabin.

The helicopter landed and killed the engine. As the rotors stopped, there was silence again on the mountain. And a lot of blood.

Jax turned Velvet around, inspecting her for injuries – while at the same time, stunned at the changes in her.

He said, "I've never seen you like this. And is that gun loaded?"

Velvet nodded. "It's missing five rounds. I shot the pilot, but I missed once." She motioned to the dead man by the porch. It's been a crazy five days, Jax." She moaned. "And I've seen so many dead people—"

"Back up. You killed the pilot?"

She winced. "That sounds horrible. But yes. Wolf made me practice. That's why I went to the roof. The pilot had his rifle aimed at Wolf. I was not going to stand by and do nothing."

She looked him over. "And you've been hurt."

He shrugged. "It goes with the territory. Just a few scorpion stings and that type of thing. It happens."

"Please tell me this won't happen often."

Jax glanced at Wolf, who was watching them. "I don't think so. You have your own personal bodyguard now."

He motioned Wolf over and said, "I need to call Ace and then we've got to get out of here. Hal could have a backup team."

Wolf and Jax led the way to the house, Velvet between them. The rest of the team guarded the perimeter.

Jax said, "Later we can have the other talk, Wolf."

Wolf drawled, "Talk all you want. She's mine. Deal with it."

Jax laughed and said, "Finally, fly boy. About damn time."

Inside the cabin, Wolf made the call and handed the phone to Jax.

Jax answered, "Mr. President…" and walked away.

✳✳✳

Upstairs, Wolf kissed Velvet as he pressed her against the bathroom wall and slowly unzipped her jacket. Spreading it open, he said, "Tell me again how you got to the roof?"

She felt the sensual rise of heat as his eyes focused on her breasts. She whispered, "But…I didn't tell you."

His blue eyes met hers. "Exactly. You went up the chute without telling me." He kissed her. "Do you have any idea of all the things that could have happened to you in there?"

Distracted at his handling, she said, "I tried not to think…of that. I just didn't want the pilot to kill you."

He unsnapped her bra. "When did you make that plan?"

She groaned, "Wolf…who cares—"

He bit her ear. "Tell me."

"When you were outside enraging Razor about the size of your—"

Lifting her around his waist, he pressed that very part of him as close as he could. "Speaking of the size of this… This is as close as we'll be since we'll be in the public eye now. Are you ready to wait?"

"But why—"

He rotated his hips. "Because privacy matters to me, and we're not married. Yet. I live a very public life away from here and won't have you smeared across the internet. I love you. It's as simple as that. So, you better do some fast soul searching. Our baby's growing in you."

131

Jax hollered upstairs. "We're out of here in ten minutes. The Marines will be here in half an hour for security and patrol. The FBI from Denver is on the way to handle the crime scene. So, suck up whatever you're doing and get moving."

They hadn't moved away from the wall.

Velvet teased Wolf. "So, that means you won't be bending me over a porch rail anytime soon?"

Wolf felt sure his expression matched the fire between his legs. He said, "Dammit, Velvet."

She glanced down at his ache and said, "You started it."

He popped her on the butt. "Get dressed and pack a small bag."

Thirteen minutes later, at three-forty in the morning, they buckled up in the helicopter. Cuda sat with the pilot. Wolf, Jax, Velvet, and Steel sat in the back. Velvet looked out the window as the helicopter rose. Before long, the cabin disappeared in darkness.

She looked across where Steel sat.

He smiled and saluted her.

She yelled over the noise, "I'm sorry!"

He laughed. "No problem!"

Wolf asked loudly, "Sorry for what?"

She returned loudly, "I was rude when he wouldn't let me out of the helicopter."

Jax got in on the conversation when Steel laughed, and asked, "What did you do to him, Velvet?"

"I shot him the bird!"

Jax frowned over the noise, "What?"

Annoyed, she shot Jax the bird. And the howls of laughter that followed were louder than the noise. For a good while.

***

As the adrenaline of the night faded, Velvet dozed fitfully on the long trip to D.C. She nodded off, then inevitably jerked awake from the wind. Turbulence. Radio communications. And the hard seat. At some point Wolf buckled her in with him, and she crashed as he held her.

Jax chuckled at tough Lieutenant Colonel Remington Wolf. Bad to the bone and captured by his little sister. Wolf shot Jax birds with both hands - and the guys laughed.

They stopped twice for fuel on the six-hour trip. Once in Missouri. And now, as dawn touched West Virginia.

Velvet took a bathroom break and flinched at her reflection. Survival, and roughing it with the men had wreaked havoc on her hair and skin. She freshened up and put on the only attractive shirt she had. The green embroidered turtleneck she'd bought for vacation. Then she made a quick single braid and added a touch of mascara and lip gloss. She sighed. That was the absolute best she could do without a shopping trip, nail salon, beautician, shower, and spa.

In the commissary, Wolf and Jax filled several thermos' with coffee and grabbed food. Biscuits loaded with tons of protein, along with a bag of fruit and power bars.

As Jax signed off on the voucher, Velvet joined Wolf. He put his arm around her. "Hey, beautiful."

She smiled. "I saw myself in the mirror. I don't know about that…but one does the best one can when trying to survive."

He whispered, "I could eat you alive."

Her knee touched the inside of his thigh as she whispered back, "You are starting something you can't finish again."

Jax walked up. "I bet a few horny snipers are catching your PDA. Don't you remember what it was like being couped up without a—"

Wolf said, "Back off, Jax. I've been in the woods too long to be civil this soon."

Jax laughed. "I hear that. How long does it take you to acclimate to civilization?"

"Long enough. I hope I'm closer to it when we reach Camp David."

Velvet said, "Wait… What? Camp David in Maryland? As in—"

Wolf said, "That's the one."

As they walked out to the helicopter, she said, "But I thought we were going to D.C."

Wolf said, "We are at some point. But for now, Camp David is your new safe house."

She stopped. "You're kidding."

"Not even a little. A storm is coming today, Green Eyes. Prepare yourself."

Chapter 20
Washington D.C.

Ace walked out of the Oval Office. Secret Service followed at a respectful, but lethal distance. Ace removed a new burner phone from his pocket and scrolled to the private cell number he'd just saved. And tapped call.

It rang. Once. Twice.

Outside Langley, Virginia, Sebastian Kane waited impatiently for the coffee to drip at home. He'd gone to bed extra late last night because of a have-to-attend dinner party he hadn't wanted to go to. Which meant he passed on his usual morning run. And that was a crappy, lazy start to a busy Monday at the CIA. He looked outside and rhythmically tapped his fingers on the marble counter, impressive in shades of blue with silver shimmer.

Not that he cared.

His wife rounded the corner and smiled. She slipped her arms around his thickening middle in a gray shirt and tie. "Don't be fussy."

He grunted. "You owe me."

"Add it to my list."

"It's already long."

"Then throw it away and start a new one. That's what I do."

He looked sideways at her and couldn't help but smile as she batted her eyelashes. He said, "That's not how a list works."

She kissed his back. "You have too many lists. Try it."

One of his cell phones on the counter rang. The private one. He looked at the ceiling in frustration and said, "It's the day that keeps on pissing me off."

She laughed and it rang again.

Sebastian picked it up. Unknown number. He answered, "This had better be good. I haven't had my coffee yet."

And he knew the laugh that followed. Shit. He scrambled out an apology, "Mr. President...my apologies—"

Still chuckling, President Madden said, "Shut up, Sebastian. I couldn't have said it better myself. And keep it informal. Are you alone?"

Without looking at his wife, Sebastian said, "No, sir."

"Get alone."

"Sure, let me check the files in my office…" And heading across the house, he shut the door and said, "Go ahead, Zack."

"We've got a traitor in the CIA, Sebastian. High up. He put out a hit. People are dead. Meet me at the White House. And don't repeat it to anyone – just get here."

The Director of the CIA said, "Son of a—" Then he cut it off. "I'm on my way."

And he ran.

Wide awake now.

***

Two and a half hours later Velvet was more than ready to get out of the helicopter. She turned from the window and reached for Wolf's watch, then sighed.

Wolf typed on his phone for privacy and showed it to her: Only thirty minutes to go.

She held out her hand for his phone, then typed: I want a phone. And handed it back.

Wolf: I'll give you your burner phone today. Hang in there.

Velvet wrote in caps: I WANT AN IPHONE.

Wolf laughed: Of course you do.

Velvet: I prefer typing to screaming. I've been couped up with Rambo's for six hours in a wind tunnel 6,000 feet off the ground.

Wolf: What's on your mind, Green Eyes?

Velvet paused briefly: I killed a man less than seven hours ago. Am I a murderer?

Wolf quickly typed: No. It was self-defense. Home invasion.

Velvet: But he didn't see me.

Wolf: They were all there for you. Same thing. And you did it to save my life. That's what I call *I love you* in action. Can you say it yet?

Velvet felt it. Knew it. And could taste it on her tongue. But she couldn't say it. She typed instead: No, but have I mentioned that I don't have panties on?

Wolf's eyes followed the line of her body down. He stared at her V until she squirmed. And then his eyes met hers. He typed: I'm going to check the first chance I get. And I'll take that as another *I love you* for now. He winked.

Velvet held up her fingers shaped like an L and handed him his phone. He hugged her, loving her.

Before much longer, the pilot yelled, "We're 10 minutes out. Prepare to land."

✳✳✳

In Langley, Virginia, a taxi stopped before reaching Gate No. 1 at the Central Intelligence Agency. It was the south entrance closest to Route 123.

The elderly taxi driver turned. "Lady, this is a secure location. I mean, really secure with lots of guns. If you don't have authorization, you're not getting in. And I'm not getting involved. I don't want to move to Guantanamo permanently or pay legal bills till I die. Please, rethink this. Surely some young man down in Texas is waiting for a beautiful woman like you to come home."

Indigo handed the driver two hundred dollars then gathered her purse and briefcase. She said, "My man is missing. So is his sister. And he works for the CIA. The answers that I seek are here. If they arrest me, so be it. Somebody is going to talk to me because I'm not leaving."

He handed the money back. Concern all over his face. "You keep it. You're going to need it. And I'm going to pray for you." He made the sign of the cross, fretting like he was leaving his granddaughter at hell's gate.

Velvet saw the rosary hanging in the front and touched his arm. "Thank you. I need it. I'm literally all prayed out."

She opened the door and stepped onto the pavement.

And he was gone.

Walking toward the gate she played the script in her mind. Her plan was extreme – and risky - but it was her last option. She stopped and pulled her phone out, but it rang - startling her so much that she almost dropped it.

Then she winced. It was River. She killed the call with love and scrolled to NBC4 - an NBC affiliate she hoped would give her the leverage she needed.

And hit call.

A professional female voice answered, "Thank you for calling NBC4, how may I help you today?"

"This is Indigo Shay from Dallas, Texas. I'm outside Gate No.1 at the CIA. I'm trying to reach one of their employees because his sister is missing. And someone blew up her house. The brother is not responding, nor is the CIA. So, I'm here for answers and need news support. Can you give me the national voice I need to get help?"

The woman said, "Stay on the line. Give me a minute."

Less than a minute later, Indigo heard a couple of clicks and then a different woman came on the line. "This is Leah Lawrence, a news correspondent with NBC4. Are you still at Gate 1?"

Indigo said, "I am."

"Who's missing?"

"Velvet Carrington is missing from Dallas, Texas. It's all over the news there. And I think her brother is missing too. He works for the CIA, and I can't find him."

"What's his job?"

"I don't know. But surely a brother needs to know his sister is missing. No one will help me. It's a dead end everywhere I go."

Leah motioned her cameraman. "We're on the way. Wait for us."

"No. I'm tired waiting. Find me."

At the gate, security personnel watched the beautiful brunette in a gray suit wait in line behind a navy-blue BMW. She was calm. Professional. The two guards glanced at each other.

Larry said, "She looks smart enough to know you can't just stroll into the CIA."

The older one, Travis, said, "These days everyone thinks they're entitled." He sighed. "I'll handle her. Call the gate supervisor if it turns into a problem."

"Got it."

The blue BMW in front of Indigo flashed a badge at security and entered the gate.

She stepped up and nodded at security. "I'm Indigo Shay. I've been unable to reach a CIA employee. Jax Carrington. His sister, Velvet, is missing in Dallas, Texas. It's a possible kidnapping. Would you please contact Human Resources for me?"

Travis frowned. This was unusual, which gave him pause on how to proceed. He said, "That's not how things work. We aren't the switchboard. Have you left a message?"

"Several. But I've not received a response. This is an urgent situation."

"It sounds like it. But this is not a public facility. And the people behind you need to get to work. I need you to please step aside."

She sighed. "I waited my turn. Why can't you just call Human Resources? It could be the simplest solution to both of our problems."

He considered the next best step. "Step out of line and I'll make a call."

As the woman moved aside to let the next car up, Larry said, "What are you doing, Travis?"

"Just call the supervisor. This might involve an employee. Let him decide what to tell her."

The next car was waved through. And the next. Then the younger officer, Larry, finished the call and walked out to talk to the brunette. "My supervisor suggested that you go to the local police department for assistance. This is not the place to address such issues."

Indigo frowned as her patience squeezed thin. Her tone sharper, she said, "Your boss might want to know that I've called NBC4. A news correspondent is on the way for a live interview. This non-public facility is about to be plastered all over the news because of two missing United States citizens connected to it."

Behind Larry, Travis said, "Shit."

Handed authority by his supervisor, Larry held his ground with Indigo and said, "You need to leave the premises. You are on federal property without authorization."

Cars in line were rolling down their windows. Phones recording the commotion. And then NBC4 arrived.

Indigo pointed at the news crew headed their way and warned Larry, "You better call your boss. I'm not going anywhere."

Larry pulled out his handcuffs. "Have it your way."

And NBC4 caught it all while running toward the gate.

***

Velvet watched as Camp David came into view in the middle of the woods. In seconds, the helicopter hovered over the helipad and lowered. Shortly, the noise faded away.

As they were unbuckling, Velvet glanced at Wolf. "We are in the middle of nowhere again."

The men laughed and Wolf said, "We're only 30 minutes from D.C. And there is plenty to do here."

139

"In the woods."

Jax said, "At the safe house." He slid open the door as four Marines arrived. "Let's get out of this bird. Our friends from across the ocean have a long way to travel back home."

Outside the helicopter, they shook hands with the team from Spain.

Wolf said, "I owe you. Call me anytime."

Cuda grinned. "It doesn't hurt to have the private number to a CIA operative and callsign Wolf."

Velvet held out her hand. "Thank you, Sting, Cuda, and Steel. I don't have a secret number, but I'll remember what you did. Always."

Sting shook her hand.

Cuda too.

Steel raised it to his lips and kissed it. "My pleasure."

Wolf grunted good naturedly and said, "Easy, Casanova."

Everyone laughed. Jax said, "You guys really need sleep. I can get you a cabin to rest."

Sting said, "Thank you, Jax. But we need to get back to the plane. We'll sleep then. Appreciate your offer though. We'll just take a break and head out."

Nodding, Wolf turned toward the Marines and said, "Morning, Captain."

The captain saluted Wolf. "Morning, Colonel. As always, welcome to Camp David."

Wolf casually saluted in response. "Wolf is fine. I'm not official this trip." He motioned to Jax and Velvet. "Do you have the safe house we're assigned to?"

"The President assigned you to Aspen Lodge."

"That's his."

"Yes, sir."

"He is stubborn."

"Shall I pass that on to him, sir?"

"I already have. Many times."

"Understood. Then I won't repeat it."

Wolf grinned. "Jax and I may need flights to D.C. soon. Velvet will most likely stay here."

"No problem at all. We're her protection for the duration of your stay." The captain glanced at Velvet and nodded. "Ma'am."

She smiled. "I'll try not to cause too much trouble."

The captain's lip twitched. "Don't take the fun out of it."

They laughed and he pointed toward two military jeeps.

A short time later, Wolf showed them around Aspen Lodge. A kitchen. Living room. Dining room. Four bedrooms. Multiple bathrooms, and five fireplaces. He stopped by two bedrooms.

He told Jax and Velvet, "Take your pick."

Jax pointed to one and said, "This is good. It doesn't matter to me."

Velvet looked at Wolf. A question in her eyes. Wolf glanced at Jax. "I'm not leaving her even if I stay in the hall for proprieties sake. There's more that you don't know. A lot more. Her danger isn't over."

Jax frowned at Wolf, then turned to Velvet. "What the hell does that mean?"

Velvet opened her mouth to answer just as Jax's phone rang. Jax recognized the number and answered, "Director..." as he disappeared around the corner. His voice trailing behind him, "What? Excuse me, say that again, sir..."

Wolf opened Velvet's bedroom door and motioned her in. She walked past him and snapped, "A little warning would have been appropriate, Colonel. Ambush wasn't necessary. I know I need to tell Jax about Dillon."

He smiled at her temper, arms crossed, as she explored the room. It was attractive. Cozy, rustic and roomy, with all the amenities.

She dropped her bag on an easy chair, and said sarcastically, "A shower would have been nice first. Or a sudsy bath. Even a coke with ice or a white chocolate cappuccino." She threw her arms in the air. "But no... Colonel Wolf made the decision for me."

She spun to face him. "Didn't—"

He was already there - and kissed her. Walking her backwards. Hands holding her face to his, drinking her in. For a second.

Jax interrupted from the doorway, "We've been summoned to the CIA. All of us. We need to leave."

Wolf lifted his lips, meeting Velvet's shocked gaze. He turned to Jax. "For a briefing already?"

"Not quite." Jax glanced at Velvet. "It seems Indigo has been detained. She was handcuffed and locked in a holding room at headquarters a short time ago."

Velvet gasped. "Our Indigo? At the CIA?"

"So, it seems. And all I have to say is, this is the first interview I've looked forward to in a long, long time."

Velvet was confused. "What was she doing at the CIA?"

"Causing a scene. Refusing to leave. And looking for me."

✳✳✳

In the Oval Office, President Madden stood behind his desk. Director Kane of the CIA stood in front of the desk. They both listened to the details of what was found at Peregrines headquarters in the Rocky Mountains.

The President's FBI contact from Denver explained, "It's exactly like Colonel Wolf said. Two dead men were found up in the timber behind the cabin. Shot. Three more dead men were found on the east side of the cabin. Two by the trees. One was killed by shotgun. The other was attacked by an animal. Undoubtedly the wolf he mentioned. And the third was burnt – electrocuted to a crisp near the cabin.

"There are two dead men in front of the house. One is missing most of his head. The other was shot in the back and fell from the roof. As for weapons and equipment, there is a helicopter on the roof helipad. There are casings everywhere. Machine guns. A flamethrower. Pistols. Shotguns. A rifle. And knives.

"None of the deceased had identification on them. But I found TRF stickers and paperwork inside the helicopter. Fingerprints and pictures are headed your way."

The President asked, "Was the building damaged?"

"It wasn't breached. But the outside logs are riddled with machine gun fire – though it did not penetrate. The structure is secure, but the electric fence and the bunker access panel is damaged."

Director Kane said, "Who was in the bunker?"

"Velvet Carrington."

The President frowned. "Then how did she get to the roof to shoot the pilot?"

The FBI agent smiled to himself and said, "She rode up the drone chute."

The President said, "That's impressive. And Wolf killed Razor."

"With Jax's gun."

"That's fitting. Any word on the missing wreck from Highway 7 and the two bodies?"

"The tow truck has been confiscated and the driver brought in for questioning. I hope to have that information for you soon."

"And the status on the TRF operation?"

"It's been overrun by the FBI and is under investigation."

"And Velvet's house explosion?"

"Dallas agents are gathering the evidence as we speak."

"Excellent job. Keep me up to date on the progress."

As the call ended, the CIA Director sighed. Heaviness in his voice as he said, "A team is on the way to retrieve Blaze's body in Morrocco."

Both men paused for a moment of silence for the fallen CIA paramilitary operator – and his family. There would be no worthy compensation, though they would do their best.

The President said, "I want to be at the airport when they bring him home. And I want you to find out who the three desert guides were that lost their lives. Make sure all their family's needs are taken care of."

"Yes, sir."

"And what about the hitman Jax interrogated in Africa?"

"He'll never be found."

The President nodded. "That's it then. We're ready. Bring Hal Beckett to me."

Chapter 21
Central Intelligence Agency

Velvet buckled up in the Marine helicopter. This one was much larger and quieter than the one she'd arrived on earlier. It was kind of like a military taxi. She scratched at a spot of dried dirt and blood on her jeans in nervousness.

She laid her head back and looked out the window. Her mind, spinning with fear for Indigo. She must have been out of her mind with worry to literally storm the gates of the CIA.

Did they hurt her? Did she fight? Velvet knew Indigo could be an imposing force. Bold. Insistent. Confident. And stubborn. Would she go to prison over this? And does anyone in Dallas even know this has happened to her? What about River?

She turned to Jax. "Tell me Indigo won't go to prison."

He shook his head. "I don't see that happening. My intervention will override most issues. Besides, it's not like Ace wouldn't step in. I think the CIA intentionally scared her. Something happened that they didn't like. We know Indigo can be a wildcat."

Wolf drawled, "And we know you like wildcats."

Jax gave him a warning glare.

Wolf said, "I'm sure it was a desperate measure for Indigo. They should have the gate video."

"It will be ready when we get there. Then I'll go see her. Alone."

Velvet thought about that. And Indigo's feelings for Jax. She hedged, "Don't be rough, Jax. Give her some leeway. This had to be traumatic."

"I don't need a pep talk, Velvet. I know Indigo."

She snapped, "You know what she wanted you to know. Which means, based on what I've seen, you're clueless."

"I know more than you think I do. You forget, this is what I do."

"For a living. True. But this is personal. And nothing about you and Indigo is on a personal level."

144

***

Black-haired Indigo ignored the two-way mirror behind her and sat facing the wall. Her gray jacket lay on the table. No longer pristine but smudged with dirt. Her white lace tank top, now stained with blood. Three drops. Her long legs were crossed with dried blood from scraped knees coming through her slacks. And her high heels were ruined from raking concrete.

She'd stared at nothing for the last half hour. Her expression switching back and forth between fear and anger – like her thoughts. And she still didn't have answers.

On the backside of the mirror, Jax entered the observation room alone. Furious already. And without looking at Indigo, went straight to the computer and hit play on the gate video. He wanted the rest of the facts since he'd already read the security report.

In moments, he saw where security lost control of the situation. The argument. NBC4 arriving. Phones recording the commotion. Handcuffs. The struggle when security got rough. When he smashed her against the wall. When she tripped. And when she was hauled off as the news crew filmed the contents of her briefcase scattered all over the ground.

He turned to the mirror and stepped closer. He took in Indigo's rigid, unapproachable posture and his muscles tightened. Damn them.

There was no doubt as to her state of mind.

He left the room.

Indigo heard the door open and close. She heard heavy footsteps and sighed. Another man.

Looking the opposite way, she said, "I'm done talking."

Jax didn't crowd her. He leaned against the wall giving her space. And time. After a few moments, he said softly, "Indigo."

Her head spun, black hair flying. Eyes wide in disbelief as she stared at him. Incredulous, she whispered, "Jax," as she stood. Instant tears rolled down her cheeks. She wiped them away, choking up – and all she could manage was, "Velvet is—"

He stepped in front of her.

Even a mess, she was shockingly beautiful. Her dark eyes like liquid chocolate swimming in tears. Very upset. Weary and wounded. He touched bloody skin near her lip. "She's safe, Indy. I have her. And I'm sorry…this should never have happened to you."

She blinked as his words registered. What? She said, "You have Velvet."

"Yes, we picked her up in Colorado a few hours ago."

She frowned, quickly recouping her thought processes. "Wait. Where? And who's we?"

"My team. We snatched her off a rooftop in the Rocky Mountains."

Taking a step back, she gave Jax a once over, beyond the fine hunk with black hair and hazel eyes. His answer was not a normal answer. And finally, she noticed the black cargo pants and shirt. Boots. Tough. Military. Along with bruises. Healing cuts and scrapes. And a deep cut in his hairline. Not counting the tension in his frown.

And it dawned on her. She said, "Velvet wasn't missing. You knew where she was."

Jax saw her anger stirring. "It's not anywhere that simple. But yes."

She crossed her arms. "And they don't have phones in the Rocky Mountains? Or news to see that a whole city was looking for her?"

"Ease up, Indy. We'll have that conversation, but this is not the time. I'm here for you."

She hit him on the arm. Hard. "Don't call me Indy, it doesn't fit me."

"It fits you perfectly. Always has."

She stepped closer to him. "You don't know me as a woman, Jax. So don't give me that. Hell, you even ignored my calls." She stopped for a moment and met his gaze. "I needed you, Jax. I was so scared trying to find both of you."

He pulled her against him. Man-woman tight. This was billowing over into something beyond Velvet missing. Not that he was surprised. "I get that, Indigo. It was unavoidable. And you'll get your answers once I get you out of here. And the personal part of this conversation for damn sure isn't over."

She pushed away. "Personal? There is no personal between us."

And that's when she noticed blood running down his bicep from where she'd hit him. Shocked, she reached for the edge of his shirt to see what it was.

He stopped her. "It's just bleeding through the bandage."

The mystery crashed around her again, and she said, "What happened?"

"It's not the first time I've been shot."

He caught her as she wobbled from the blow of truth, then pulled out a chair for her. She sat. Weary. Shaken and ashamed. She said solemnly, "I'm so sorry, Jax. I pride myself on professional control, yet I've handled today badly—"

He smiled. "I don't know. You got what you wanted. I'd say your mission was successful. I'm here."

She said, "Does your arm hurt?"

"Not as much as the scorpion stings."

She winced. "You're serious."

"Unfortunately. But… Now I need to get you released. Stay here. Behave yourself and don't hit anyone else."

She flushed.

He smiled. "Don't be embarrassed. I'm impressed."

And he was gone.

✳✳✳

Velvet paced by the window in the plain office. "This is taking too long, Wolf. Something's wrong."

Behind her, he slipped his arms soothingly around her. "I'm sure it was a shocking meeting for Indigo. Jax can handle one beautiful wildcat."

"But I feel so guilty."

"Green Eyes, none of us had a choice. Seeing you will make all the difference to her."

"She holds a grudge."

"Stop it. She loves you."

"And she loves him. But it won't stop her wrath. It's reflexive."

He laughed, turning her around. "What's she going to do in the CIA?"

The door opened.

Jax walked in with blood dripping down his arm. He said, "Come on, I'll bring you to Indigo. Wolf, stay with them. I need to run to another building before we leave."

Shocked, Velvet said, "What happened to your arm?"

He shrugged. "She hit me, not realizing I'd been shot. It's nothing."

Velvet's face lost all color. "Shot! When?"

"The night I texted both of you. Now let's go. I've got a feeling that everything's coming to a head this morning. We need to get out of here."

Seven hallways later, Jax stopped at a closed door. Two leather chairs sat in the hall. He said, "Indigo's been on an emotional rollercoaster ride. And she had a physical run in with the security officer. Her lip is busted, her knees scraped—"

Velvet yelled, "What!" and barged through the door.

Jax walked away, calling over his shoulder, "They're yours, Wolf. I won't be long."

***

Two buildings away, Jax ignored the receptionist. The officers in front of him. And a man that took one look at his security badge, angry face, and bloody arm and decided not to question him. Jax turned left down the second hall. And in ten angry strides, found the office suite he wanted. He walked in without knocking.

The door slammed against the wall.

Two women and three men in uniform looked up. Startled. Jax scanned the men's faces, then headed for the middle one - who backed up. The security supervisor had no trouble recognizing fury. And even less trouble recognizing Jax Carrington.

He held up a hand and said, "Let me—"

Jax grabbed the supervisor's arm, spun him, and slammed him against the wall. In seconds he cuffed him. Tight, as the man yelled.

Jax growled, "If I ever hear of you instructing security to use violence against an employee's family or friend without contacting the director, I will find you. And when I'm done with you, I'll drop what's left in a nest of vipers in India." He paused. "Is that clear?"

The supervisor grunted a painful, "Yes...dammit. You're breaking my arm."

And Jax walked out.

***

In the holding room, Velvet and Indigo wiped tears away and finally sat facing each other.

Velvet said, "I can't believe you came to the CIA. That's insane, Indigo. No, not insane - brave. I can't believe that River let—"

Indigo said, "Forget about me. You were the one that vanished! And I have so many questions. First, what were you doing on a roof in Colorado? Why did

148

your house blow up? Why did you leave your Jeep? Why was Jax shot? And why are you all bruised up…and here with Jax?"

Wolf knocked as he opened the door. "Time's up, Velvet, we've got to go. We're meeting Jax out front. And Indigo, grab your things. You're coming with us."

Indigo looked at the bossy hunk with turquoise eyes, then at Velvet. She said, "Who is he?"

Velvet smiled as Wolf rushed them down the hall. "Wolf, meet Indigo, my best friend. And Indigo, meet Wolf…my…uh, bodyguard."

Wolf laughed and pulled Velvet close. "Don't lie to her. I'm a hell of a lot more than that, Green Eyes." And he kissed her.

And for the first time in a long, long time, Indigo was speechless.

Jax pulled to a stop in front of the building as Wolf ushered the women outside.

Velvet climbed in the back of the military jeep and said, "What's the hurry, Jax?"

Indigo struggled to climb in her high heels and asked, "And where are you taking me?"

Jax turned to Indigo. "Did you bring any other shoes? You've already fell once."

"That was not my fault."

Wolf reached in the back and snatched the shoes off her as she squealed in disbelief. He dropped them in her lap, turned around, and said, "Let's go."

The jeep roared away.

Velvet explained over the wind, "Give them a break, Indigo. There's a lot going on, and now you're in the middle of it. Just hang in there."

Sarcastically, Indigo said, "With no shoes."

Velvet shrugged. "I've only had three changes of clothes for five days. It is what it is. We'll find you some. Besides, your toenails look great."

"Oh, shut up, Velvet."

Wolf laughed.

Jax shook his head. It was like their college days all over again.

Six sharp turns later, they neared the helipad.

Wolf's phone dinged. He checked the text: Get to the Oval Office. He typed back: Be there in 10.

Wolf met Jax's gaze. "White House."

With a nod, Jax floored it to the helicopter. Wolf turned to Velvet and Indigo. "We have to get to D.C., so you're coming with us."

He stopped, thinking of something. "And Indigo, be sure that you don't use your phone or computer. It's off limits for the moment."

Indigo frowned. "Why?"

"Just don't use them."

"Like my shoes?"

Jax laughed.

Velvet nudged Indigo. "Stop arguing. You don't understand what you're up against. Hell, I've even killed a man. Now promise him. We're trying to stay alive."

In shock, Indigo nodded at Wolf. And then glanced at the helicopter in front of them. It was a huge military helicopter. Loud and terrifying. With soldiers. And for a moment she thought she would throw up. But she refused and instead allowed Jax to usher her underneath massive whirling blades and be buckled up inside the beast. Barefoot. Next to him. She met his gaze.

He saw the confusion, fear, and annoyance on her face. She was not used to being bossed around. He yelled over the noise, "I'll make this up to you, Indy."

She yelled back, "Kiss my ass, Jax."

Everyone laughed but Indigo. She kicked Velvet and stubbed her bare toe.

Eight minutes later, the helicopter lowered to land on the White House lawn where a lot of people in suits waited.

Jax pointed to Indigo's shoes in her lap. "Can you run in those?"

"Probably not."

As everyone unbuckled, he said, "Then carry them. We've got to run."

Chapter 22
Monday 9:48 a.m.

Hal Beckett stood next to the bed and touched his son's hand. Warm, but lifeless. The smell of sickness around him, strong.

Trevor's fever broke half an hour ago and now he was resting - not that he had been aware of anything. But the hospice nurse was exhausted. He was too. Only the pictures around the room smiled.

Last night had been a close call. Too close. Death had left, satisfied with leaving despair behind. But Hal knew death would return. Trevor's time was short.

His too.

Jagger never called last night. No victory message. No texted picture of a dead Velvet. And the helicopter never returned to TRF. Silence screamed failure. There hadn't even been any calls from work this morning. That was telling. He normally had half a dozen calls by now.

He could imagine the commotion stirring at the CIA. The calls through the city. The whispers. The meetings. Facts lining up. The mission coming to light. The bodies. And now the tidal wave of fury building. There would be no mercy for him.

And he didn't give a shit.

Revenge ravaged his insides. Bring it on.

And the doorbell rang.

Hal listened to it ring once. Twice. And casually cracked his neck as he tapped his gun. It was time to see how it played out.

He opened the door on the fourth ring.

Four FBI agents stood there. Tense. Alert. And ready for war. Multiple black SUVs lined the street. And his well-trained eye caught the sniper on the rooftop across from him. One agent stepped forward sliding his jacket aside to reveal his badge and gun. "Hal Beckett. You need to come with us. Step outside and prepare for a pat down."

Wordlessly, Hal complied. They took both of his guns. The one at his waist, the other at his ankle. And they took his phone.

The ride was fast and silent.

Fifteen minutes later, the White House came into view.

Ten minutes later he was escorted into the Oval Office.

President Madden didn't look up, just said, "Everyone step out and leave me with Hal. And turn the cameras off."

The room cleared out.

Hal stood in front of the President's desk and felt the first twinge of shame. Like he'd spit on the man he'd always respected. Regret mingled with revenge tasted foul.

The President looked up. "You set all this into motion, Hal, so you know why you're here." He stood and walked around where they stood face to face. They were near the same height. Same size. In their 60s.

The President continued, "And I have got to tell you, the disgust and fury I feel right now is as great as any I've known. And nothing you say can change that."

His voice raised in anger, "Your actions left one CIA operative dead. Four Africans. Three Colorado civilians. And six TRF paramilitary employees. Fourteen people! Plus, the attempted murder of Jax Carrington, his sister, Velvet, and Colonel Wolf."

The President stepped closer. "You do recall Colonel Wolf is my nephew."

Hal didn't answer. The question was rhetorical. Of course he knew.

The President's tone softened. A clear warning to anyone that knew him. He said, "Do you know what enrages me the most, Hal?"

Again, Hal didn't answer.

The President swung a right hook. Hal flew back, tripped and knocked a table over as he landed on the ground. And as all the doors flew open, the President's words traveled loudly down the halls, "You spit on the honor of your own son's sacrifice. Trevor chose to protect Jax and the team on that mission. In bravery. Honor. "But you...for whatever warped motive you fed to fruition all these years...decided Jax and his sister had a debt to pay."

He straightened. "But you forget. I am the Commander in Chief. The buck stops with me."

The President walked behind his desk running a hand through his hair. He motioned at all the waiting faces in the doorways, "Get everyone in here and let's get this over with. And get up, Hal. It's time to be exposed for the damn traitor you are."

152

Secret Service entered. The FBI Director and agents, CIA Director and Deputy Director, National Security Advisor, and the Chief of Staff of the Air Force.

The President sat on the edge of his desk as everyone quickly settled.

Hal stood alone. Bleeding from his left eyebrow and chin. Rumpled from the tangle with the table. But rigid. Eyes hard.

The President glanced at Hal. "If you've got anything to say, this is your moment. You have us all in one place and it's all about you. You will never get this chance again. And feel free to say what you will. You can't get in any more trouble than you're already in."

Hal said, "Where's Carrington?"

The President said to no one in particular. "Get Jax."

Jax entered, bruised, cut, still dirty and dressed from the battle in Colorado. Fury not hidden, his eyes locked with Hal's. Tension increased exponentially in the room and the Secret Service moved closer. The President waved them back.

Hal looked Jax over. Hate emanating from him. He said, "What'd you do, sacrifice Blaze too?"

Jax felt the ripple of rage travel his spine, but responded cool, lethally, "Not me. You did that all on your own. I felt trouble coming so we were pulling out. A minute too late it turns out."

He took a step closer to Hal. "I got hit twice but managed to get us out of there." He paused. "And then I hunted your merc down and made him sing like a girl spitting blood and saying your name."

The rawness of that truth rose sharp in the room.

Hal shrugged. "He was paid. His choice."

"True, but Blaze was following orders. Yours. If this was revenge, he had no business being there. You killed your own man you son of a—"

Hal snapped, "You were questioning the validity of the mission. Adding Blaze shut you up and got you on the plane."

It was a blow to Jax's gut. It all made sense in a serial killer sort of way. Sick. Twisted. But it was still inexcusable. Jax said, "Why now? Why not then?"

Hal sneered, "Because you're still alive and Trevor's body is shutting down. He has days to live. I can't stand the thought of you breathing air when he's gone."

153

Jax swallowed pain for a moment. Pain for Trevor – not for himself. Or Hal. Then said, "And what did Velvet ever do to you?"

"Simply be someone you loved. If you had been married, I'd have killed your wife. If you'd had kids, I'd have killed them. But all you had was Velvet. She won the lottery ticket."

Jax side-kicked Hal in the stomach sending him sliding across the floor.

The President touched Jax, stopping him. "Easy everybody. Someone, bring in Colonel Wolf and Velvet Carrington."

Wide-eyed and sitting in between Wolf and Indigo on a bench in the hall, Velvet watched as a seriously intimidating man in a suit walked out of the Oval Office. He pointed at her and Wolf. "Come with me."

Velvet shook her head, no, but Wolf pulled her with him and said, "You've got this."

Indigo groaned for Velvet as they disappeared in the room where everyone was mad. But she was grateful she was left in the hall. Maybe everyone would just forget about her. Please, God. Please.

Velvet tried not to faint as she entered the Oval Office. All eyes turned toward her and Wolf as they joined Jax by the President. And a man who was having a really bad day stood not far away. Bloody. Messy. But evil. She saw it in his eyes.

Hal Beckett in the flesh.

She looked up at Wolf. He touched her back to assure her everything was alright, but she knew he wanted to kill Hal. She'd seen that look on him before.

Wolf nodded at the President. "Yes, sir," and then he glanced at Jax and Hal Beckett. It looked like he'd been missing all the fun.

The President said, "Wolf, for the sake of the record, introduce yourself."

"Lieutenant Colonel Remington Wolf with the U.S. Air Force." He didn't mention the family connection.

And then all eyes focused on the auburn beauty next to him, noting the battle wounds and blood on her pants.

The President said, "Velvet, forgive me for putting you on the spot, but would you please introduce yourself."

"I am Velvet Carrington. Jax's sister."

He motioned to all the people in the room and said, "Everyone here is either in intelligence, military, or politics. I wonder if you would be willing to share from your point of view a glimpse of the danger you've been involved in these last few days."

Surprised, and nervous, she said, "Of course."

"When did it begin?"

"Wednesday night when I got a text from Jax."

"Then let's start there."

She scanned the faces watching her and said, "Jax texted that someone was trying to kill us. That I needed to run, hide, not tell anyone, and take Amtrak to Denver." She held her hands open and explained, "He'd prepared me a few years ago with a go-bag, so I knew what he meant. So, I dropped everything and made my way home.

"I put on my disguise and gathered my bags. Then I heard someone break into the house as I climbed out of my back window. The house blew up as I ran across the yard. I stayed hidden in the woods until all the commotion was over. Then went to Jax's storage unit in Dallas – hiding there until Amtrak left the next afternoon.

"I boarded in disguise and stayed in my room for the 17-hour trip." She glanced at Wolf. "And the first direct contact I had with anyone was when Wolf forced his way in my room Friday morning between Colorado Springs and Denver."

The President repeated, "Forced his way in."

"Well, yes, sir. He was a stranger to me. We'd never met. I guess he knew I wouldn't let him in."

"What happened?"

She shrugged. "It certainly wasn't much of a fight."

Jax raised an eyebrow at Wolf. Several men smiled at the only humor in the room.

Velvet said, "But then he told me that Jax had sent him."

"You believed him?"

"Not at first. I'd never heard the name Remington from Jax."

The President nodded. "You only knew the name Wolf."

"Yes. And about the tattoo."

Wolf gave Jax a look. Several men choked back smiles, including the President, who asked, "Then what happened?"

"All Wolf would tell me was that there would be trouble when we reached Denver, and he had to get me to his place in the mountains."

"And was there trouble?"

"Yes. Someone chased us out of the parking lot onto the highway. Later their truck ended up behind us in a blizzard in the mountains. It rammed us in the back at the same time a herd of elk crossed the road. It was a terrifying wreck.

"Wolf woke me with our truck laying on the passenger side. It was snowing through the busted window. He climbed out to find the guy that hit us. And found a dead woman in the driver's seat instead - with a dead man in the back."

She grimaced. "But on his way back to me, his truck began to slide into a pond, breaking through the ice. And before he could get me out, I was dunked in freezing water."

Meeting Wolf's gaze, she was grateful all over again and said, "And he kept me from freezing to death while gathering evidence on the mercenaries at the wreck. Then he carried me inside his snow suit until my body temperature returned to normal. Off grid. In the mountains. During a blizzard. For hours."

Silent for a second, Velvet looked at everyone waiting for the next part of the story. She said, "I never knew that you could be that cold and survive. But I did know that I'd never trust anyone as much as I trusted Wolf.

"That night we slept in a cave with his pet wolf. And the next morning we were on our trek to his cabin when a helicopter showed up. I didn't hear it coming. But Wolf did and we hid in the woods as they circled the area – low and loud looking for us. Blowing snow everywhere. But not finding us, they left.

"And by the time we reached Wolf's place before noon, we'd survived 24 hours in the Rocky Mountains on foot."

Wolf slid his hand down her back, and their eyes met.

Aware that a lot of their story would never be shared, Velvet continued, "And once we were in his secure area, I finally got a few answers to some of the secrets. I found out who Wolf was. I found out a little bit about Jax. About Peregrines headquarters."

She looked at the President. "And about Ace."

The President smiled and several chuckles were heard.

She continued, "We didn't see another soul for close to 24 hours. Not until Sunday." She held up a hand in apology. "Sorry. Sunday was yesterday. So, yesterday we were hiking back from Wolf's lookout when someone breached security. Wolf sent me back to the lookout to hide with instructions to shoot anyone that wasn't him."

She winced. "There were a lot of shots as I huddled with my gun, not knowing what had happened. Until I finally heard Wolf's voice."

She shook her head. "As I know you've heard, the mercenary hired two local poachers to kill us. But instead, they died on the mountain. And after that, we went on lockdown at the cabin. And last night, after four days of not knowing how Jax was, he finally called. He'd reached the United States and was on his way to get us. And...he had learned who wanted us dead."

Velvet looked at Hal. "But Jax still had to work in secret. He couldn't tell anyone that he was still alive because the man that caused all this was in the CIA. Someone he knew. Someone he trusted. And he couldn't tell anyone until he got us out of there."

She stopped. "And that's when I learned about Trevor."

Hal flinched at Trevor's name.

Velvet looked at the President and pointed toward Hal. "May I?"

He nodded. "Absolutely."

Wolf followed behind her as she neared Hal and stopped. She said, "Jax was set to arrive last night about 2:30 in the morning. But your team got their first. And since they're all dead, I'll tell you what happened.

"The helicopter landed on the roof with Jagger and four other men. Wolf and I headed to the bunker. The first of Jagger's men to die was electrocuted as he rappelled off the roof. The remaining three on the ground opened fire with machine guns as I watched by security cameras.

"Wolf shot one man's face off through a hole in the wall. Then Wolf's pet wolf, killed the man that came to check on that one. And then, it was only Jagger on the ground.

"And that's when Jagger strapped on a flamethrower and offered Wolf one option: Come out or he'd burn it down. Wolf made me turn off the electric net and he went outside. You see, it turned out that Jagger's real name was Razor - and they knew each other. Very well.

"So, Wolf taunted him, and they began to fight. Brutally. Then Wolf saw the pilot on the roof with a rifle. So, I rode the drone elevator to the roof and shot the guy to help Wolf. Which made the fight move where I was on the two-story roof locked in the TRF helicopter.

"And as Jagger tried to pull Wolf off the roof with him, Jax's team arrived in another helicopter. And in seconds, Wolf shot Jagger in the face with Jax's gun. And it was over."

She stepped closer to Hal and said, "It is over, isn't it?"

Hal's expression hadn't changed through any of it. Hate still simmered and he ignored her question.

Wolf slapped him upside the head. Hard. Blood and spit flew. Wolf snapped, "Ms. Carrington asked you a question, Hal. Answer her. And be damn glad the FBI got to you before I did."

Hal spit blood on the floor, wiping his mouth with the back of his hand. "Yeah. It's over."

The President said, "Excellent. That's it then. Cuff him. This meeting is over."

As everyone left the Oval Office, the Deputy Director of the FBI followed Velvet, Wolf, and Jax to meet Indigo in the hall. He cleared his throat to get her attention. "Ms. Carrington?"

They all turned. Velvet said, "Yes."

"I know you've had a rough few days, but it seems we have another urgent matter to address." He said after a pause, "Regarding Detective Black."

Velvet and Wolf's eyes met before she glanced back at the Director. She had to tell Jax about Dillon first, so she bought a little time, and answered, "Of course. Could we meet later this afternoon?"

He handed Velvet a card. "I'll send a car for you. Text me your location. How about four o'clock?"

Wolf nodded yes in agreement to Velvet, while holding up a hand stopping Jax's interruption. Velvet confirmed to the agent, "That's perfect. And thank you."

As the Director walked away, Jax said, "Detective Black is from the shooting in New Orleans. Why does the FBI want to question you about him?"

Brother and sister faced off, and Velvet dreaded what came next. She said, "It's complicated, Jax. This is what Wolf alluded to at Camp David. Can we go somewhere private to talk? This isn't the place."

Jax felt the edge of something ominous creep up his neck. "I'm not moving. What's complicated, Velvet?"

"Detective Black was my husband."

Chapter 23
Dillon

Jax froze. He looked at Wolf. Then Indigo. And he could tell they already knew. He looked back at Velvet. Taking her arm, he said, "You're right. We're leaving. The White House is not the place for this."

Wolf stepped in front of them. "Jax. Look at her. She's exhausted. Banged up and wearing someone else's blood. We need to get a room and at least shower first. Eat something. And get clean clothes. She was going to tell you — but there's been no time."

Jax accused, "You knew."

"Not because she offered. I found out while researching her, then got the rest of the story from her. Which is what you need to wait and do."

Jax touched Velvet's face. "I can't believe you didn't tell me."

"I didn't tell anyone, Jax. But I'll tell you everything if I can just have a shower."

Wolf said, "I'll make hotel reservations. Jax, you get us a ride."

Indigo glanced back at the Oval Office, then at Velvet as they followed behind both men talking on the phone. She said, "This has been crazy, Velvet. I have so many questions."

Velvet moaned. "Damn it, Indigo. Get in line."

A short time later, Velvet stood under the shower as hot water massaged her. She ignored the stings and twinges from cuts and bruises from the past five days and watched the last of the blood at her feet fade from pink to clear. The war was over.

She reached for the shampoo, thinking about Wolf. She missed all the intimacy they shared in Colorado. One on one. Not another soul around. With trust. Awareness. And sexual tension. The looks. The whispers and touches.

159

Their first wild time in the shower. And the last one in the treehouse. She calculated as her hand slid toward her belly.

It wouldn't be flat much longer.

And that left her L and M word issues.

Wolf already knew the L from her without the word – but he would insist on the M. She closed her eyes. Wanting him now. Not caring about any of the words.

Just him.

***

Wolf forced himself to take the connecting suite with Jax. Damn it all to hell, he'd haul Velvet down to the courthouse if he could. But she wouldn't marry him. She wouldn't even say the word.

He growled in the shower. He had no intention of staying apart from her long. He'd make her say it. Somehow. Someway. There was no question that she loved him. Even though she wouldn't say that either. But he saw it, felt it. And knew it with every ounce of his being.

Yet still, his wife to be, and his baby, were in the other suite.

All six foot three inches of him fought the circumstances he couldn't control. Hot inside and out. Both his arousal and his heart raging for her. Until suddenly, he stilled like a lion spotting prey. His blue eyes flashed as water coursed over him.

Velvet hadn't said anything about not being engaged.

***

In the hotel hall, Jax unlocked the door. He heard Wolf blow drying his hair as he carried in the clothes he'd picked up from his local flat. He didn't really live anywhere for any length of time, but having a domicile in D.C. was an actual requirement for all CIA employees. And it was convenient for his hectic schedule.

He dropped the duffel bag on the floor and hung the clothes. This would give Wolf something to wear for now. They were close to the same size though Wolf was a little taller. And he was a little slimmer – but it should work.

160

Jax ran his hand through his dark hair. It was still a little damp. He'd already showered and dressed in gunmetal gray slacks and a black button up shirt for the FBI appointment. No way was Velvet going without him.

He glanced through the open door to the girl's suite. Both showers were going strong. Heading to his kitchenette, he checked the refrigerator and grabbed a Bud Light Platinum. He popped the cap, taking a cold pull from the blue longneck. It had been days since he'd had the pleasure of an ice-cold beer without the threat of death.

Groaning in satisfaction, he carried it to the window overlooking the Gaylord National Resort. His thoughts immediately jumped to Detective Black in New Orleans – and he pulled out his phone. He searched the internet. And it didn't take long to find Black's recent death. The probable connection to Dallas and Velvet. And the manhunt for Brody Jon Grant. Fugitive.

Shit, Jax thought. Another war. This time in Dallas.

Wolf walked out of his room, bronze and barefoot with a towel wrapped around his hips revealing a wide array of scrapes and bruises. He glanced at the clothes Jax had provided, and said, "Thanks. I owe you."

Jax shook his head as Wolf headed to the refrigerator. "Hardly. What you did for Velvet in Colorado..." He paused. "You saved her life the whole time."

Wolf opened his beer and looked at Jax. "If I'd have met her earlier—"

Jax raised his hand cutting him off. "I tried for years—"

"Then now must have been the right time. And her troubles still aren't over."

Jax nodded. "I checked the internet and got the basic news on Detective Black and found out about Brody. So, they presume he's in Dallas."

"Thanks to my tip to NOPD. No one had caught the connection to Velvet."

"What tipped you off?"

"I did some deeper research after Velvet told me about her and Dillon. They had just found his body in the river." He shrugged. "It wasn't hard to piece it together. But it was painful for Velvet because he called her Wednesday night. Repeatedly. She blocked the calls."

"Damn." Jax said with a grimace. "I hate that for her. So much went down Wednesday night...the night from hell."

Wolf took a drink. "When are you going to tell me about Morocco?"

"I probably won't. Blaze's killer is dead. And Hal might be if he gets the death penalty. There isn't much else to waste breath on."

They clinked bottles in agreement and Wolf went to dress.

In the girl's suite, Jax heard Indigo's laugh and then Velvet's. They would be out soon. Good. He wanted to know about Dillon. And as callous as it sounded, it was probably a good thing that Dillon was already dead. He was sure of it.

✳✳✳

Wrapped in a towel, Velvet stood at the bathroom vanity and put the blow dryer away. Her mass of auburn waves, dry enough.

Indigo sat indignantly on the bed wrapped in her white hotel robe. Her black layered hair dry. Her make-up finished. She said, "It's appalling. You have injuries everywhere."

Velvet said, "And that's just the ones that you can see."

"It's not funny. Who beat you?"

"Well, no one actually. It was the cataclysmic result of everyone trying to kill me that left its mark."

"Don't be philosophical. I will eventually want every detail. I only heard bits and pieces at the White House. So, ok… I get that you were on the run. Why did you go to Wolf?"

"I didn't know that I was going to Wolf. Jax just told me to take Amtrak to Denver. I didn't know what I would find there. I just dressed like an old woman and packed my fake identity, a burner phone, and a gun in my backpack."

Shocked, Indigo said, "You're lying."

Velvet laughed. "I wish."

"How did you meet Wolf?"

"He pushed his way in my cabin, pressed me against the wall, and covered my mouth while I fought."

"Shit."

"So elegant."

"Shut up. What happened next?"

"He told me his name was Remington and that Jax sent him. But I didn't know the name Remington. So, he said his full name, Remington Wolf. And I knew the name Wolf. I also knew about a tattoo he was supposed to have. I challenged him to see it and he began to undo his pants."

Indigo gasped. "Where in the hell is the tattoo?"

162

Velvet smiled. "On his hip and thigh."

"And he showed you?"

"I have no doubt that he would have, but his actions proved it. And since then, he's the one that's kept me alive."

"Well, if you had to fight to survive, I'd have made him show me the tattoo. You know, as a bonus."

"Indigo, it's hard to tell a story with your side notes."

"Get over it. And you can't tell me that you haven't seen his tat. That man could eat you for three meals a day and still be hungry."

They howled in laughter. Then agreed to continue the story one wild scene at a time. It could take days. Or weeks.

***

In his room, Wolf pulled on a pair of black jeans. Zipped them. Then, stepped into clean boots. He glanced in the full-length mirror. The pants were a little tight, but he was glad to have them. And last, he pulled on a black turtleneck. Soft and warm. He ran his hands through his hair, then grabbed his watch and phone.

It would have to do.

He joined Jax in the sitting area as Indigo walked in.

Jax whistled. Indigo was barefoot in a fluffy white robe tied around her waist. Her black hair was silky. Her face, beautiful. Long lashes. Dark eyes. Eyeliner. And shiny lips.

Her eyebrows raised as she looked them over. "You two obviously didn't get the toga party invitation. Where did you get the clothes?"

Jax said, "I keep a place in D.C. and picked up a few clothes for me and Wolf. I plan on getting concierge shopping assistance for you and Velvet shortly. The shops deliver." He winked. "Though toga looks great on you."

"Toga's better than dirty clothes or nothing."

Jax drawled, "I wouldn't say that. I wouldn't say that at all."

She ignored Jax and glanced at Wolf. "You're quite a looker, Remington. What were you up to in the mountains with Velvet when you weren't keeping her alive?"

Velvet rounded the corner and met Wolf's gaze. He smiled as his blue eyes roamed her, aware that she was naked under the robe. In a few steps he kissed her, running his hands in her auburn mane and pulling her tight. Answering nothing yet answering everything about Indigo's question.

Indigo glanced at Jax. "Don't you have anything to say as your sister melts into a little puddle with him?"

Jax patted the seat next to him. "Calm down, mother hen. Come sit. What clothes do you need for a couple of days?"

She sat. Totally aware of her almost nakedness, and his…everything perfect. She said, "My luggage is at the Hilton on Stafford Street in Arlington. That's all I need."

"Ok. Give me your room key. I'll have you checked out and your things brought here."

With a bite of sarcasm, she said, "And are you going to rummage through my things, Mr. CIA?"

He smiled just a bit. "It's a thought."

But he saw something in her eyes. All the sass was a cover. She was still upset with him. Without a word, she got up, returning quickly with the room key and her credit card. He refused the credit card.

She considered him and said, "You seem… And she wanted to say, all in her space. Eager. Alpha. And damn him, sensual. But all she said was, "Different."

He locked gazes with her, wanting to touch her, but didn't. It would be a while before she went from rattlesnake to honey. He said, "Very discerning. In fact, I'd like us to talk about that."

She leaned well into his space and whispered, "In your dreams." Then sat back and said, "Now, how about food?"

He smiled. She might be mad, but she was eager to battle. And he would give her what she wanted. Total engagement.

One on one.

And it had been a long, long, time coming.

Wolf ordered room service while Jax met a driver downstairs to go get Indigo's luggage. Then they all talked about clothes along with dinner and dancing plans for tonight. And in minutes they connected with the concierge and shopped via zoom. Women first. Then the men. Clothes. Shoes. Accessories.

And finally, the doorbell rang. A male voice called politely, "Room service."

164

They dove into meals from Old Hickory. The men ate wagyu steak grilled to perfection. Rare and juicy. The women split a creamy lobster pasta dish swimming in cheese, garlic, herbs and butter. And they all shared a large bowl of Ceasar salad with homemade croutons, warm dressing, and lots of parmesan cheese.

A short time later, satisfied and content, they settled comfortably on patterned velvet sofas facing each other. Velvet and Wolf on one. Indigo and Jax on the other. And a small table on a shag rug between them.

Velvet curled up next to Wolf. He eyed her new bruises, frowning. She teased, "I'm astounded at size of a man's appetite. Each of you ate a slab of beef. Literally. I mean, someone knocked the hooves off the cow and slapped them on the grill. Together, those steaks must have weighed five pounds."

Wolf flexed his muscles. "We're big men. We work hard. And play hard. It takes a feast to keep all these muscles… Hmm, what best explains it?" He smiled and said, "I know… Hard."

Jax laughed. Velvet giggled. And Indigo rolled her eyes and raised her feet off the floor. "Eww. I'm up to my ankles in testosterone. My feet are wet."

As laughter faded, Jax noticed Indigo's wince as she lowered her legs – with scraped knees. He leaned forward and pointed. "Do you mind if I check them?"

She covered them with the robe. "They're fine."

"Indy, they are not fine. You just cracked one open. It's bleeding." He scooted over on the sofa. "I insist," and turning her, he lifted her legs across his knees.

Indigo was too surprised to stop him. He pushed her robe up her legs and her hand stopped him after a few inches. He was entirely too close to other bare skin. Jax's lip twitched. He had intentionally pushed it higher than necessary just to make a point. His gaze met hers.

And awareness played with them. Silently.

One second.

Two.

Then Indigo glanced at his lips.

And with a satisfied smile, Jax looked at her knees. And frowned. Damn, he knew her tender skin was stinging. Scrape wounds always dried, cracked and burned at a joint. He said, "I have a first aid kit in my bag."

Glancing at Velvet, he said, "We'll talk when I get back. This won't take long." And ignoring Indigo's gasp, he simply scooped her up and carried her to his bedroom.

Velvet's surprised gasp joined Indigo's.

Wolf just laughed.

Jax sat Indigo on the edge of his bed and squatted on the floor. He pulled his bag over and fished out the first aid kit. Indigo was curious at this side of Jax and watched. Forcing herself to see the real man and not the one she'd imagined all these years.

He laid out clear patches, gauze, and ointments. Then kneeling at her feet, he again slid the robe up her legs. Long tan legs. Beautifully tapered to perfection.

Indigo blocked his hand again as she met his gaze. "Nothing needs attention any higher."

There were dozens of things Jax wanted to say, or do, but instead, he silently let her comment hang in the air. The lie of it echoing in their minds. He spread her knees apart just a little – and watched as a pale pink flush rose up her neck to her face.

It could have been anger.

But it wasn't.

He asked softly, "Would you hand me the green tube?"

She reached for the tube and handed it to him. He winked. She said, "That wasn't funny."

He said, "Maybe not. But it was a whole lot of something else."

"Shut up, Jax."

He warned, "This is going to sting…"

And a flash of pain touched her knee. She yelped, "Ouch! You did that on purpose!"

He leaned low and blew on it, his lips close to her skin. Both his breath, and hands, touching her. Indigo closed her eyes. Shit. She needed to stay mad.

In the sitting area, Wolf moved Velvet to his lap.

Still surprised at the disappearance of Jax and Indigo, she said, "Jax likes Indigo."

"Like is for boys, Velvet. You're talking about Jax. I've heard him talk about Indigo for years. He wants her. You've just seen it for the first time. Now, enough about them. Are you ready to tell Jax about your secret life?"

She grimaced. "I wouldn't say that. But it's time. And Indigo doesn't know any of it either. I hate to hurt them because I didn't turn to them at the end."

He touched her cheek. "Everyone handles despair differently. It doesn't mean you didn't need them. It was just too painful to share."

She wrapped her arms around his neck, overwhelmed with everything magnificent about him. Wolf embraced her, burying his face in her hair. Smelling her and said what she couldn't, "I love you, baby."

She kissed his neck. "Wolf… I miss you already."

"So, marry me."

"Stop it."

"Then you wouldn't have to miss me. And we wouldn't have two different last names."

"Wolf—"

"Get used to it. I never said that I would quit asking."

They heard footsteps.

Catching the end of their conversation, Indigo said, "Ask her what?"

Wolf glanced at Indigo as Velvet slid off his lap. "I was asking her about the dress she ordered for tonight."

"Liar."

He laughed. "Then don't ask me."

Jax chuckled and said, "You can't win with him, Indigo. Back off."

She put her hands on her hips. "He met her Friday. It's Monday. What is wrong with you, Jax?"

Jax flared and pulled her close. "Listen to me, Indigo. Wolf saved her life more during that time than I can ever tell you. More than I can ever repay. And they're not strangers, damn it. They just had never met. I've been trying to get them together for years. Just not this way."

Shock faded from Indigo's face as he let her go. The grip from his hands, still tingling. The feel of his breath on her face, a memory that wouldn't pass anytime soon. And the up front and personal intensity of his eyes and body revealing the real worry and fear he'd felt for Velvet.

She whispered, "Jax, I'm sorry—"

He touched her arm and sighed. "There is no way you could have known. And then you got hurt today. Let's just get all this over with. The secrets and the FBI meeting – and enjoy a night out. We've all earned it."

He motioned toward the sofa. Sitting, he glanced at Velvet. "Just talk to me, Velvet. No judgment. Just tell me about Dillon."

Chapter 24
Secrets

Taking a deep breath, Velvet walked to the window and watched the courtyard as her mind sped back to New Orleans.

She said, "Everything changed for all of us after the shooting graduation night. Jax, I realize now that you were in the middle of what happened with Trevor. And Indigo, after you moved back to Texas, I buried myself in graduate studies.

"Over the next year, Dillon would stop by and check in on me as Brody's trial loomed closer. There was nothing outwardly romantic. He was professionally intense with a side note of personal. And in no time, he became a new constant in my life. Concerned. Close by. With a hint of unspoken attraction.

"Immediately after the trial we began dating, and things went fast. Sure, I had a few concerns with his dark intensity, but his attention and affection led me to romanticize it as mysterious personality quirks. Nothing alarmed or scared me."

She turned to face them. "And I chose not to tell either one of you about the relationship. Obviously, that was a terrible decision. In hindsight, a warning even. But I was living my new best life, and I knew that both of you would have taken a stand against him like closing arguments in front of a jury. Simply…because you're you."

She sighed. "Not that your concerns would have been wrong. I just didn't want the complication or interference. And after two months of dating, I skipped my master's graduation ceremony, and we flew to Las Vegas and got married.

She sat on a bar stool. "A mere two weeks after that, like I told Wolf, I knew I was in way over my head. Dillon was more than moody and intense. He drank. Not getting drunk drinking, but something darker. Maybe it was part work stress. Maybe other issues. But all I know is that it fueled what played out…intimately."

Jax got up and leaned against the wall. Watching her. Body rigid. Fury lashing him…knowing he could never change the pain that was coming.

Indigo winced. Aching. How had she not sensed any of that all the times they talked on the phone?

Velvet glanced at Wolf, sitting forward on the sofa. Watching her. Tense but supportive. She said, "And what I thought was love turned ugly. Creeping towards something that terrified me. And in less than two months I knew I had to get out.

"But he was a cop. A predator. And a smart one. All his friends were cops and I hadn't told a soul. So, I made plans to run. I got my chance a few days later when a big case came up. I knew Dillon would be occupied so I made plane reservations, got money together and packed. I was heading out of the bedroom door…and the next thing I knew, I woke up on the floor.

"A few hours later the doctor confirmed I was pregnant." A tear rolled down her face and she wiped it away. "I hurried home to gather my things and get out. I knew I couldn't tell him. Not yet anyway. He would never let me leave."

She took a deep breath. "When I got home, his car wasn't there so I ran upstairs thinking I had time. But he was sitting on the bed. Drinking. And had neatly stacked my luggage on the bed. I grabbed my bags and headed for the stairs."

Jax knew what was coming. He just did.

Velvet said, "The attack was brief, and I fought – then fell downstairs. I woke in the hospital with a concussion, stitches, a broken arm…and a miscarriage." Her voice caught. "A little girl."

Indigo covered her face and cried.

Jax walked toward Velvet, damning Dillon to hell every step of the way. Velvet put her hand on his chest, halting him, wanting to get it over with. She continued, "But in the hospital, Dillon was in tears and ashamed. He'd killed his daughter and almost killed me. But he was also scared. Because if my statement didn't match his, he would be arrested. So, I called an attorney for advice, then gave Dillon an ultimatum he couldn't turn down.

"In turn, I got a speedy divorce and his agreement to never speak to me again. And once I was healed, I left for Dallas to start over. And I did, Jax. I put Dillon behind me – and left a piece of my little one in my heart. But I learned from it and embraced starting over with a new perspective.

"Having you, Indigo, new friends, my career, and my dreams looming ahead of me, I had hope. And everything in the past was over, except for…"

169

She gave Wolf a quick glance. "A couple of things that Wolf is helping me with. And until this past Wednesday night, Dillon had kept his promise."

Jax hugged her, opening his arm to include Indigo. And the three made it through the pain of secrets.

Wolf nodded. Velvet needed this closure. This honesty. And she was another step closer to L and M.

A knock on the door interrupted the moment.

Wolf answered it. Their clothes had arrived.

∗∗∗

An hour and a half later, they turned off Pennsylvania Avenue into the Federal Bureau of Investigation. Ten miles from the hotel.

Wolf glanced at Velvet. "Are you ready?"

She nodded, her fancy ponytail swinging. She was stunningly beautiful for the meeting wearing caramel-colored high-waist pleated slacks and high heels. A long-sleeved V-neck cream silk blouse that was eye-catchingly feminine. With enough cleavage to be appreciated, but enough hidden to be elegant.

After crossing her legs, she looked at Wolf. Her green eyes now enhanced with eyeliner that had been applied by a creative hand giving her a cat-eyed look. Sultry but enchanting. She said, "I can't have that much information to offer the FBI. Surely by now they have the case facts and know all about the connection to me."

Jax answered from the back seat, "You'd be surprised at the details you can offer them about both Dillon and Brody. Your input is extremely valuable."

Wolf opened the door as the black SUV pulled to a stop. He got out and offered Velvet his hand, and said, "Agreed. And they've thought of scenarios we haven't had time to come up with. And in all honesty, they already know what they want."

Jax held out a hand for Indigo, dressed on the sassy side of lovely in a trendy dark pink pant suit and white high-heeled boots. She sighed and said, "I've had enough surprises today - tell them to hold it down."

Their chuckles faded as the entrance doors opened to the FBI.

After countless high heel clicks, one elevator, five floors, three hallways, and dozens of doors later, all four of them were ushered into a corner office.

A handful of agents in suits waited near a desk. But the desk was empty. The closest agent motioned toward four empty chairs in front of the desk.

The door opened behind them, and the Deputy Director joined them with an apology, "My apologies. I was on a call with our Dallas office. I wanted to have the latest information before we began."

He sat in the chair and leaned forward looking at Velvet. "Ms. Carrington, I don't plan to keep you long. I know that you've had a rough, few days. But... And I know we all hate that word. But...we need what you know. Your memory has all the answers to help us catch Brody."

He looked at Indigo. "Now, before I continue, Ms. Shay—"

Indigo waved her hand, "Please, Indigo."

He smiled. "Indigo. Before we begin, I would like to say how sorry I was to hear about your trouble at the CIA this morning. There was no excuse for the violence. Suffice it to say..." And the Director glanced at Jax. "I understand that bold steps were taken to avenge your assault. Isn't that right, Jax?"

Indigo glanced at Jax. "What does he mean?"

The agents in the room laughed. Wolf, Velvet, and Indigo looked at Jax.

Wolf said, "Did you kill the guy?"

Jax said, "I was tempted. I just slammed the supervisor against the wall and handcuffed him. Leaving him with a stern warning." He raised a hand. "Though I admit I was a little on the harsh side."

The women stared at Jax. Shocked. The men laughed.

One of the agents said, "Stern warning defined as: raw wrists, a broken nose, a sprained arm, and threats of a viper pit in India."

Indigo gasped as she met Jax's gaze. He shrugged. And before she could respond, the Director continued, "Now, moving on... Ms. Carrington, we have a few questions."

Velvet said, "First name, please."

He nodded. "Velvet then. Let's go back to the night of the shooting in New Orleans. Brody shot a man in front of you, correct?"

"Yes."

"Did you interfere or draw attention to yourself in any way?"

"No. I screamed. But everyone did. Then the victim fell into me."

"So, that drew Brody's attention to you."

"I would think so, yes."

"What happened then?"

"Well, we stared at each other. He was all in black with a hood so I couldn't see him. But I began to realize that his eyes were familiar – mainly because they were unusual." She paused. "And I realized who he was."

"What did he do?"

"Pointed his gun at me."

"Why?"

"I presume because he recognized me too."

"Did you say his name?"

"No. River…" She pointed at Indigo. "Her brother shot him."

"Did Brody say anything at all to you?"

"No. He just stared at me. Kind of a wild look. Intense. Like he couldn't believe he saw me. But I don't remember him saying anything."

"I see. And what was his reaction to you during the trial?"

"More of the same. He still just stared at me. A bit angrier."

"Was he angry at River for shooting him?"

"Not that I noticed." She looked at Indigo. "Did you notice anything?"

Indigo said, "Not with River. Just you."

The second agent said, "He wasn't angry with Detective Black?"

Velvet and Indigo shook their heads, no.

He confirmed with Velvet, "So, he was just angry with you. Didn't you think that was odd?"

"I didn't give it much thought. I mean, he was arrested. Anger seemed reasonable."

"Did Detective Black mention it?"

Velvet nodded. "Yes. He believed that Brody was a threat."

The Director said, "Did Brody ever say anything to you in court?"

"Not until he was sentenced. Then he ranted for a while: I'll get you. You'll pay. And a whole lot of cuss words I won't repeat." She shrugged. "They hauled him off. I just felt like it was a heat of the moment type thing."

The fourth agent said, "You dated Brody. Right?"

"Back in high school a couple of times. It was casual, not a relationship."

"High school is not pleasant for a lot of kids. They can hold grudges."

Velvet said, "I'm aware, but I can't imagine why he would hold a grudge against me. We went to the movie one time and a basketball game another. That's it. And we continued to talk casually after our last date. Then I started dating another guy."

She stopped, thinking about something, then said, "I do remember something happened in Brody's family about that time. With his sister, I think. She was younger than me. A pretty girl. I didn't know her beyond saying hi in passing. In fact, now that I think about it, his family moved after that. I'm pretty sure that the shooting was the first time I'd seen him since then."

The agent asked, "Was his sister in court during the trial?"

Velvet said, "He had a couple of rows with people there to support him. I was on the enemy's team. So, I didn't look their way or even go to court unless the prosecutor needed me. I really have no idea if she was there or not."

The Director leaned back in his chair and glanced at the agents, "Find the sister and find out what we don't know. Something turned Brody into a vigilante. We need to know what it was and how Velvet is connected. And why the shooting set him off."

He turned back to his guests. "And next, Velvet, while I'd like to tell you that I don't need you in Dallas, I do."

Jax and Wolf spoke over each other – then Jax said, "How exactly do you need her?"

The Director spread open his hands. "Brody hates Velvet. We'll find out why and take it from there. But she is the key to him being a fugitive – and we all know Dallas is where he went. The whole city is looking for her."

Velvet said quietly, "You need me to be bait."

"Yes."

Wolf said, "Then repeating Jax's question, what do you want from her?"

"I'll know more tomorrow, but the plan is to let her exposure draw him out. The media is already all over her. And there will be a White House press briefing tomorrow about Hal's arrest. After that, she won't be missing anymore. The whole world will know where she is, and Brody will find out. So, getting her to Dallas immediately means everything."

Velvet glanced at Wolf and Jax, and said, "Guys, I can't move to the next phase of my life chased by another killer. I just can't. And I refuse to believe that between you two, the FBI, the U.S. Marshalls, and the NOPD detectives, that I can't be protected from one man who isn't even a professional criminal."

Jax said, "Damn it, Velvet—"

Determined, she looked at the Director. "I'll do it. But Jax and Wolf must be in on everything. Secondly, today is still Monday - as impossible as that seems - and I need a break. Tomorrow afternoon I'm yours. Not until then. Deal?"

The Director stood and shook her hand. "You've got a deal."

***

Before long, Jax unlocked the hotel suite and all four walked in.

Jax's phone rang.

Then Indigo's.

And in a smooth move, Wolf pulled Velvet into his room and locked the door. He kissed her. Wild. And wanting more, he picked her up, groaning as she locked her legs around him.

Pressing her against the wall, he said, "I'm tired of sharing you."

Breathless, she said, "I miss you too..."

He met her gaze, giving her a hip roll. Wanting her to feel him.

Velvet whispered, "I thought you said...we weren't going to—"

"It didn't mean I wouldn't make you wish I would."

She felt the wish from head to toe. "Wolf..."

Groaning, he slid his hands under her shirt. "We've got to get out of this hotel, Green Eyes. Now. I'm not hanging out in two suites with four beds."

She moaned in frustration as he lowered her. He kissed her and said, "Go dress country casual and meet me in five minutes."

He pushed her toward the door, adjusting himself with a wince. Damn. Velvet watched him, as she backed toward the door.

He said, "Go, woman, or I'll break my own rule. Again."

Indigo was laying her phone down as Velvet walked from the guy's suite into theirs.

Velvet said, "Who called you?"

"River. Where's your lipstick?"

"On Wolf. What did you tell River? You didn't say anything, did you? I think it's still a secret—"

"I know. I just told him that I was fine and that I'd know something tomorrow. He's going to kill me for lying."

"Maybe, but he'll be grateful first that you're alive after all this comes out. Now, I've got to change."

Following Velvet as she changed, Indigo said, "Where are you going? Don't we have dinner and dancing tonight at eight?"

"We do. But Wolf is taking me somewhere now."

"Where?"

"I didn't have time to ask."

"I see that."

Velvet slipped on jeans, a turquoise turtleneck, touched up her lipstick and pulled on knee boots.

174

Wolf called out, "Velvet!"

Indigo said dryly, "Is he in a hurry or what?"

Velvet laughed. "Or what…"

Jax finished his phone call and walked into the girl's suite. Wolf and Velvet were heading out the door. He said, "Where are you two going?"

Wolf said. "Out for a while. Who called?"

Jax didn't elaborate. "The recovery plane will be here in the morning."

Wolf nodded in complete understanding. Blaze's body was being returned to the States with honors. Without any explanation about it in front of the women, Wolf looked at the clock and said, "Velvet and I are taking a ride. We'll be back in two hours and still have time to dress for dinner."

Jax glanced at Indigo as the door closed behind Wolf. He said, "Then we're going somewhere."

"Where?"

"Somewhere to talk."

"About what?"

He stepped close and met her gaze for a long silent moment. That was his answer. Butterflies exploded in Indigo's stomach. Shit. She was getting what she wanted. Was she ready for it?

***

Wolf led Velvet to a waiting taxi. He instructed, "Andrews Air Force Base, please."

The taxi driver said, "You've got it. We're on the way to Maryland."

Velvet said, "Is this the ride you were talking about?"

Wolf pulled her close, entwining his fingers with hers. "Not exactly. Do you remember your excitement flying the drone with me?"

She remembered. Especially what came after. "I'll never forget it. Are we going to fly drones?"

"No. How about a short helicopter ride? We need to get our bags from Camp David, and you've never seen me fly."

Wide-eyed she said, "You're going to fly the helicopter?"

He smiled. "I am."

She squealed. "I'm so pumped. I keep forgetting you're a pilot."

He grimaced. "That's a blow to my ego."

175

Snuggling, she said, "I doubt that."

"I'm an alpha. Those traits come with the territory."

She said softly, "I'm into your traits."

He kissed her. "And I'm into you."

And then traffic went berserk for the next 15 minutes.

Worse than Dallas.

The taxi arrived at Andrews Air Force Base, a 4,300-acre facility. The taxi driver stopped at the gate and went through the search procedure to enter the main base. Once he was cleared, Wolf pointed the way toward helicopter operations just north of the Air Force One hangar.

Velvet looked around at all the planes and helicopters. "How many of these can you fly?"

He glanced around. "All of them."

She met his gaze. "Your brilliance is everywhere I turn. I'm a little intimidated."

The taxi stopped. Wolf said, "Don't be. Our minds work as hot together as the fire between us. Now, come see another part of my world."

A jeep with two men sped toward them as Velvet climbed out behind Wolf. And she suddenly felt small and insignificant next to the size of the planes and helicopters around her. She couldn't imagine the confidence and skill it took to fly them.

The jeep skid to a stop. Wolf snapped to attention and saluted, "General."

The smiling passenger got out of the jeep and halfheartedly saluted. "How the hell are you, Wolf. I'm hearing all kind of tales about dead men on your mountain. And that you slapped Beckett till spit flew." He held out his hand. "Put it there. Damn, I hate to miss all the fun."

The General glanced at Velvet with a smile. "Excuse the language, ma'am."

Wolf said, "General, let me introduce Velvet Carrington. Jax's sister."

The General whistled. "Carrington's sister." He offered his hand to Velvet. "I'm glad to see you safe after all you've been through. Did you slap Hal too?"

She shook his hand. "No, sir. I did have to shoot his pilot though."

He howled. "Damn if you don't sound like Jax." Then he frowned. "Don't let that stay with you, little lady. A warrior does what they must. It's an honor to meet you. And hell! No one told me what a stunner you were."

He smiled at Wolf. "You'd better wear sunglasses or she'll blind you."

Wolf drew Velvet close. An indirect answer.

The General slapped his hat on his leg with a laugh. "I knew it. You're already blind as a bat - and here for one of my birds."

176

They all laughed.

Wolf said, "They flew us to Camp David this morning. I need to pick up a few things we left there since we're staying in town now. We'll only be a couple of hours."

"Help yourself and keep your eyes on the sky. Ms. Carrington, let me know if he steps out of line."

Velvet smiled. "I'll do that."

The General walked away, waving to the driver. "Out of here, soldier!"

Wolf said, "Come on, Velvet. Let's get a bird."

Fifteen minutes later, Wolf was buckling in. Putting on his helmet and flipping switches. The rotors came on.

He radioed, "Bell-niner-seven-eight. Callsign Wolf. Heading to Cactus at five thousand feet. Have fun boys."

Buckled in the front wearing her own helmet, Velvet heard wolf howls come through the helmet earpiece.

The tower said, "Roger that, Wolf. See you on the backside. High five little Carrington. Callsign Annie Oakley."

Velvet gasped, glancing at Wolf. He laughed, "Copy that. Over and out."

He flipped a switch. "We can talk without extra ears listening now."

"Did they really give me a callsign?"

The helicopter rose in the air as he said, "They did indeed."

"Does everyone know what happened with Hal?"

"Yep." Then he flew. Fast and tilted. Velvet left her stomach behind, but the rush was amazing. She screamed and held on as Wolf laughed.

***

Jax and Indigo walked the scenic route through the lush landscape of the resort toward the Potomac River. Jax pointed out various landmarks. Behind them, dusk was growing more spectacular by the moment with fanciful clouds in shades of pink, orange, and lavender.

They found a private spot under a tree where they could lounge in the grass and watch it all. Lights were coming on. At the wharf. The shops and restaurants. The hotels and streetlights. And especially the Capital Wheel – a 180-ft observation Ferris wheel in National Harbor farther down the coast.

Jax leaned against the tree with one knee propped up. Wind ruffled his dark hair as he watched Indigo settle cross-legged near him, but not close. She was gorgeous in a silver glitter top, jeans, denim jacket and boots. Her hair fluttered around her. Everything about her tantalized him. It always had.

Indigo leaned back, propped on her arms staring across the water. Inhaling the smells, including Jax's cologne, wondering if he knew that it was her favorite. She tried not to look at him. Gorgeous. Languid. And sexy as hell. Like a panther. She glanced at the Ferris wheel feeling like she was dangling from it.

They had never been together like this.

Ever.

And for the first time, she felt his eyes on her.

Jax let the tension build, waiting for the right time. He wanted *what hadn't been* to be the last thing on her mind. The past would naturally find its way into their conversations, but he wanted to shock her first – and bring all her focus to this moment.

He broke the silence and said, "I think about you all the time."

Indigo gave him a side glance. "You mean like a pet? Or a funny movie? Oh wait, or like your favorite po-boy when you're hungry?"

He laughed. "Damn, you're hot, Indy."

"Stop calling me Indy."

"I'll think about it. Are you still mad?"

She sighed. "I'm better. I was scared mainly. Worried. Being in the dark – not knowing what y'all were going through." She turned to face him. "I am truly kind of sorry."

His lips twitched trying not to smile. "Kind of sorry?"

She looked away and didn't answer him. Pissed again. How do you say I've loved you for a hundred years and you treated me like…nothing special.

He touched her hand splayed out in the grass, and said, "Do you know how old you were when I first wanted to kiss you?"

Shock ricocheted like lightning through her, leaving tingles along the way…but she played it cool. Still refusing to look at him, she said, "I doubt you ever wanted that."

He answered his own question. "You were 19."

Her eyes met his and she said, "I don't believe you."

He leaned toward her. "You were a teenager in college living with my sister. I was almost 30 and living a life of missions and secrets. The timing was wrong. Our lives were miles apart." He paused briefly. "But it doesn't mean I didn't want it."

178

"That's a lot of contemplating for just a kiss."

"I wanted more than that."

"How do you know I wanted any of that?"

"I knew."

And she saw the truth in his eyes. Her anger faded a little more as fast-moving thoughts replaced it. She frowned a bit, then said, "And yet it took 10 long years for you to find the right time?"

He pulled her close. Their legs touching. Faces, maybe a foot apart. Lights in the garden showered them in romantic ambiance. Music in the distance. He said, "I thought the time was right when you graduated. That was my plan. But Trevor happened. I missed graduation. You moved. And life got painfully complicated."

She inhaled, shock stealing her breath as she searched his eyes…his words echoing in her mind. Did he mean… He slid his hand behind her neck and said, "And I'm tired waiting."

Indigo lost all thought as his mouth covered hers, filled only with the intimate world of Jax. The taste of him. The feel. His fevered desire and the instant explosion between them. In moments he had her in his lap while the years disappeared like they had never been.

Jax groaned, lifting her higher, breathing through her thin shirt, wanting to taste all of her like he'd never wanted anything before. Indigo gasped, hanging on, hands in his hair – his name on her lips.

And then he rolled, pinning her beneath him.

It took a while for them to finally notice an airplane's roar overhead. And a ship's horn. Jax lifted his head, his eyes taking in the vision Indigo made. Her dark eyes on him, hair spread in the grass, lips moist, and her body where she always should have been.

Groaning, he sat back, drawing her on his lap for a quick hard kiss. "You are so beautiful and I'm on fire. Shit. Could I have picked a more public place to finally light us up?"

Indigo slid her hand across his chest, understanding, and feeling the evidence of his hunger under her. Breathless, she said, "Now what, CIA?"

He pulled her tighter. "You know where this leads. Where it was always going to lead."

***

179

After returning from their flight to Camp David, Velvet got ready for a night of dinner and dancing. She leaned over the bathroom counter wearing barely-there underwear and black leather boots. Her thigh muscles tightened as she leaned forward, head tilted, mouth open, to put on the last stroke of eyeliner.

An oldies groove played on her phone. Something about a brick house. Glancing down, she swapped out the eyeliner for the mascara and looked back in the mirror. She dropped the mascara.

Wolf leaned against the doorframe in black slacks, with a bare chest and eyes like blue lava. Sexual tension made it hard for her to breathe. He walked toward her and said, "I knocked. And I'm so glad you didn't hear me."

Pressing his stomach against her back, his hands slid up her body. He kissed her shoulder as they watched the encounter in the mirror. He said, "I have a question."

She whispered, "Ask."

"Will you be my fiancé?"

She gasped. He hadn't used the M word. Screaming, she threw herself in his arms. "Yes!"

He kissed her as Indigo yelled through the wall. "Velvet? Are you alright in there?"

Velvet didn't answer.

Wolf smiled. "I have something for you until you are ready to think about a ring." He took her hand.

Velvet watched as he pulled something gold and tiny from his pocket. A bow? No, a bow ring! Super fragile. She wiggled delightedly as he pulled it on her finger.

He said, "A friend made it for me. It's made of stretch silk. Something tangible for you to know we're engaged until you're ready for a real ring. And if anyone questions you, just send them to me."

She danced around looking at her hand. Half naked. A hot picture of joy as he watched. She said, "It couldn't be any more perfect, Wolf! I'll keep it forever!" And then she noticed his condition.

She touched his chest. "Oh…"

He kissed her till the fire hurt, then growling, said, "Damn it. I want you to myself," and left.

Velvet looked at her tiny bow ring as the door closed, then held it to her chest. She'd almost said she loved him.

It was coming.

∗∗∗

An hour later, all four were seated at a window table inside The Capital Grille. An establishment that promised a fine dining experience in a restaurant bar arranged in a club style setting.

Velvet and Indigo were thrilled with the social opportunity and dressed for the occasion. Velvet wore a short black satin wrap-around dress with patent leather boots. Indigo wore a bronze halter dress and suede boots. Both women were gorgeous, classy and trendy.

Wolf and Jax both wore dark slacks and jackets. Wolf had on a snug white pullover shirt that outlined his body, and Jax wore a shimmery navy button up that made his hazel eyes pop.

Wolf sat next to Velvet.

Jax and Indigo sat across from them.

Drinks were ordered. Menus delivered.

While Jax and Indigo discussed the menu, Wolf slid a hand over Velvet's thigh. She met his gaze. He leaned closer. "I'm distracted remembering your thong."

Her smile teased him. "Ahh. I thought that might be the case, so I took it off."

He felt the heat. "You didn't."

"You're right. I didn't."

"Then go take it off."

Velvet laughed, and Indigo interrupted, "Hey! Focus you two. There are four of us at the table. Would you like to share your conversation?"

Wolf said, "No. Would you two like to tell me why I found grass all over the sofa?"

Jax laughed. "Probably for the same reason we heard Velvet scream in her bedroom."

Velvet glanced between her brother and best friend. Indigo winked. Velvet said, "No way. You didn't do what you said you were going to do. Did you?"

Jax glanced at Indigo. "What were you going to do?"

Indigo shrugged with a sultry glance at him. "Throw myself at you naked."

The passing waiter dropped a glass. Wolf laughed and helped the startled man.

Jax pulled Indigo close and said in her ear, "I want that."

181

She whispered back, "That was my plan to see if you would notice me. But it wasn't necessary."

"I repeat. I want that."

Their drinks arrived interrupting the conversation. Both men tossed back their Crown and coke on ice. Civilization was difficult to slide back into after their long dry spell in missions. Velvet and Indigo choked back giggles.

After ordering their dinner, Velvet said, "How's the dancing scene in D.C.?"

Wolf said, "There are plenty of options. What do you have in mind? Entertainment? Piano bar or dance club?"

Jax laughed, already knowing their answer. Both women said, "Dance club!"

Wolf chuckled. "Dance club it is. I suggest the Black Cat. It's a mix of everything."

Velvet said, "Like what?"

"Oldies, party, country, pop, and blues. Mostly fast."

"You've been there."

Jax chuckled, "You have no idea. Our Wolf has moves."

Velvet looked Wolf over. "From what I've seen, he doesn't need music."

Wolf met her gaze and winked, remembering their dance at the cabin. He said, "It just depends. I'm not all that on the dance floor."

Jax said, "Liar. Hell, I remember—"

Wolf warned, "Easy, Carrington. I've got memories too."

Indigo said, "Well, don't stop now, Wolf. Spill it."

Jax bumped Wolf's foot, meaning shut up, and changed the subject, "Are you sure that you ladies can dance in those boots?"

Velvet laughed. "We can dance in anything."

Indigo added, "Or on it."

Someone knocked on the window.

All four turned to the blonde waving…at Wolf. Late 40s, blonde, boobs for days, all smiles and excited. Velvet, Indigo and Jax turned to Wolf as the woman headed for the door.

Wolf moaned. Jax said, "Looks like she knows you, stud."

"Shut the hell up, Jax. It's General McMillan's daughter. Marilyn."

"I've heard about her. Cougar duty calls."

Wolf glanced at Velvet as Marilyn's voice traveled up the aisle along with the clicks of her heels. Velvet raised her eyebrows and whispered, "Stud."

Marilyn reached the table with a cloud of perfume. Both Wolf and Jax politely stood. She said, "Remington Wolf. Or should I say Colonel Wolf.

Daddy told me he saw you today. It's been a while since we've run into each other, hasn't it?"

Wolf nodded respectfully, no smile, and said in greeting, "Marilyn. Good evening. It has been a while. Let me introduce you to my guests." He motioned to each, "Velvet Carrington. Her brother, Jax Carrington. And Indigo Shay. Everyone, meet Marilyn Connelly, General McMillan's daughter."

Marilyn smiled. "Oh, you must not have heard. I'm not a Connelly any longer. I'm single again."

Hiding a smile, Jax had to look away from Wolf's purposeful silence at her comment. Indigo coughed so she wouldn't laugh.

Velvet tried to cover the rudeness and said, "It's nice to meet you, Marilyn. I met your father today. It was an honor."

Marilyn frowned slightly. "Daddy didn't mention that." Then she glanced at Wolf. "So, you took her up."

Wolf said. "High and fast. A wild ride."

Jax cleared his throat and took a sip of water. Velvet bumped Wolf with a behave warning and Indigo dug her fingernails into her palm so she wouldn't totally lose it.

Marilyn got the point and looked at Velvet's left hand. She noticed the bow on her ring finger and said, "What a cute little ring. Does it mean anything?"

Wolf drew Velvet to her feet, and said, "That she's mine. We only got engaged today and haven't had time to ring shop. I'm sure you understand."

Marilyn's smile was like ice, then she turned to Jax and looked him over. "I've heard your name before. Have we met?"

Indigo looked out the window as Jax said with a straight face, "I don't believe we have. I would have remembered. I do know your father though. Please give him my regards."

Marilyn nodded, then glanced around the table. "I'll do that. Well, I need to join my dinner party down the street. Have a nice evening. And Colonel, you know how to reach me if you need anything in the future. Anything at all. And of course, congratulations on your engagement."

Goodbyes faded with her heel clicks as they sat. And then she left the restaurant. It was almost five minutes before the laughter was entirely over.

Dinner arrived at the first engagement question.

183

It was almost 2 a.m. when they returned to the hotel. Smiling from a terrific night but tired after the longest day in history. And both women's feet hurt from dancing.

By 2:30 everyone was in bed.

By 2:45 Wolf walked into Velvet's room, scooped her up, and carried her back to his bed - leaving his door open. Wrapping her in his arms, a thought flashed. Twenty-four hours ago, they were fighting for their lives on the roof of his cabin.

One villain down, one to go.

Chapter 25
The Day After

Wolf's phone rang at 6:30 the next morning. With eyes still closed, he answered curtly, "Colonel Wolf."

They opened as the Deputy Director of the FBI said, "Apologize to Velvet for me. I'm going to have to cut short her request for time off. The White House has scheduled a press briefing for 11 this morning regarding Hal's arrest and the investigation. They want you, Velvet, and Jax in the room."

Wolf said, "You'll need to call Jax. Blaze's body is being returned to Andrews Air Force Base sometime this morning. I can't commit for him."

"Understood. Meet me near the Oval Office for your press passes at 10:30. And Wolf, remember that in all probability Velvet will be caught on camera. Brody will see her."

"Got it. She'll be prepared. See you at 10:30."

As Wolf put the phone down, he heard Jax's phone ring in the other room. He got up and shut the door. Velvet mumbled as she rolled on her stomach and burrowed under the comforter, "I'm not going anywhere. You can't make me."

Wolf chuckled, getting back under the covers. He kissed her back, throwing one leg over hers. "Good morning, Green Eyes."

"Morning, Colonel Wolf, but I'm not getting out of this bed."

"You better, because what would happen if you didn't, is not happening. Your brother is next door."

She turned to face him. "Even…if…I promise to be quiet?"

He groaned, pulling her close. "You won't be."

"But…I need you—"

He groaned, doing the one thing he could do, and slid his hand beneath tiny pink lace panties to another place of warm velvet. Her breath caught.

Voice husky, he said, "Come for me…"

185

And he kissed her. His wild ache could wait. This was for her. Giving was what love was all about.

✳✳✳

After a very cold shower, Wolf talked with Jax over coffee as the women dressed.

Indigo came out first dressed in slacks and a sweater, carrying her heels. She said, "Where are we going after breakfast?"

Jax said, "I need to go to Andrews Air Force Base and meet a plane. I hoped you would come with me. Wolf and Velvet need to be at the White House by 10:30."

"I'll go with you. Who are you meeting?"

He took a sip of coffee and set the cup down. "It's a Dignified Transfer. Another paramilitary officer was with me on assignment this week. Blaze was killed in the line of duty. His remains are being returned. It's a solemn occasion where he is formally met and received home. Even the President will be there."

She swallowed the lump in her throat. "Of course I'll come. And I'm sorry. I can't imagine how difficult this is for his family…and for you."

Jax nodded, then said bluntly. "The killer died for it. Blaze's sacrifice will be remembered."

Indigo studied Jax and Wolf, and said, "There are a lot of things we as civilians don't know or grasp. We take freedom and safety for granted. I'm truly sorry."

Wolf said, "Unless it touches a family or the news, most people are not aware of the intricacies of what goes on. Not really. And that's how it should be. Those that serve and work for the United States accept the mission…and the sacrifice. It takes a lot to be a great nation."

Velvet, who'd been listening quietly at her door, asked, "How did they know where to find Blaze's body, Jax? Didn't you leave him in the desert?"

"I did. And you don't want to know all that, Velvet."

"Tell me. You did something so that he could get home. I want to know what it was."

"I buried him under a bush, then sent the text to you and Wolf. I buried my satellite phone near his body so they could follow the GPS signal. And then I went to find his killer."

Velvet walked into her brother's arms. "It's almost unfathomable. And makes dancing last night seem so frivolous. Callous even."

Wolf said, "Don't think that. It doesn't. We simply enjoyed the freedom that we fight so hard for. It's the reward. They're both powerful. Now, come on everyone. Let's get this morning behind us. They'll be sending us to Dallas soon."

∗∗∗

The CIA picked up Jax and Indigo and headed toward Andrews Air Force Base.

The FBI picked up Wolf and Velvet and turned toward the White House.

Wolf met Velvet's gaze. He winked as they both remembered this morning. He put his arm around her, and she whispered, "You keep doing that to me."

"And you keep coming."

Her cheeks flushed pink, and he entwined his fingers with hers. He said, "You look amazing in blue velvet. I think it's a new favorite of mine."

She said, "It matches your eyes."

"You like my eyes."

"You're the most gorgeous man I know, Remington Wolf. Beautiful inside and out."

He said softly, "That's the same thing as saying you love me."

"That's what I thought."

"I love you too."

She smiled. And believed him.

The White House appeared in the distance.

Thirty minutes later, an FBI agent led them through the West Wing into the back of the press briefing room. They stood quietly watching the commotion. No one paid attention to the auburn-haired beauty in a blue velvet dress or the tall sexy man in a navy-blue suit.

Before long, the press correspondents, journalists, and various media outlet reporters made it to their seats. Some assigned, some not. Network cameras were ready. It was intense. Intimidating. And tension mounted as everyone wondered what the briefing was about. They checked their notes and whispered.

Velvet leaned toward Wolf. "We don't have to talk, right?"

"I can't promise that."

"I'm nauseated."

He hid a smile, "Take a deep breath. We're in the back. No one even sees us."

She moaned, "Yet."

Wolf said, "Sometimes I get nauseated before a flight."

"Liar."

He laughed. The FBI agent did too.

She panicked. "What if he makes us talk and my zipper breaks? My heel comes off or I sneeze."

"Velvet, look at me." Her emerald eyes met his blue ones. "We've survived what they are going to talk about. You've earned the right to be here. Take the honor and don't worry. You've got this."

There was an excited flurry in the room as the front side door opened. But it wasn't the Press Secretary. President Madden walked in, and technology was the only sound you heard. All eyes were on him as the ones seated silently prepared themselves. Alert, like a race about to start. Ready to formulate the first question before they even knew anything about the subject.

The President scanned the room and said, "Someone in one of the most powerful intelligence agencies in the world put out a hit on CIA Paramilitary Operations Officer Jax Carrington, and his sister, Velvet Carrington."

As gasps rang through the room, he continued, "Over the last six days, 14 people have been killed. Several injured. Property damaged, destroyed, and dozens of crimes committed. International. Federal. And state. Horrendous acts of murder, attempted murder and conspiracy are barely the tip of the iceberg.

"The good news is that with the combined effort of Colonel Wolf, Officer Jax Carrington, and other paramilitary connections, the Carrington's survived the attacks.

"And while we celebrate that victory, our condolences go out to all the families that suffered loss. In fact, right now, Officer Carrington is at Andrews Air Force Base receiving the body of his fellow officer, Blaze Tyler, who was killed in the line of duty."

His voice rose, "And yesterday in the Oval Office, one of the most trusted members of the CIA's Special Operations Group – who himself is a Purple Heart recipient and the father of a Purple Heart recipient, was arrested by the FBI.

188

"Hal Beckett, a traitor of the United States, will be tried by a jury of his peers for all of his crimes – and be punished to the severest letter of the law."

He took a breath. "Now… Any questions?"

Hands raised as voices called throughout the room, "Mr. President!"

Pointing to a man on the front row, he said, "Jason."

"Mr. President, 'Is the death penalty on the table?'"

"It had better be. Next question?" He pointed at a woman on the second row. "Karrie."

"Mr. President, 'Will Hal lose his Purple Heart?'"

"No. He was wounded in battle and saved the lives of others. That stands. Next." He pointed at a tall, distinguished man. "Thomas."

"Mr. President, where was Blaze killed?"

"That's classified. I'll give you another question."

"Thank you, sir. Where was Velvet attacked?"

"In Dallas. Next question?" He pointed several rows back. "Janet."

"Mr. President, was your nephew, Colonel Wolf, attacked?"

"Yes. And on that note, I'd like to address everyone's attention to the back of the room. Please welcome with me, Ms. Velvet Carrington and Colonel Remington Wolf." He motioned them forward. "Please, join me."

Velvet inhaled in shock, as if on swivel sticks, all heads turned toward them. And the side aisle magically cleared of people.

Wolf whispered, "Just be yourself," as the FBI agent led them toward the podium. Voices called their names for questions already formed. And Velvet intellectually focused on one word. Shit. And after that, she let out a breath declaring to herself, I've got this. I've got this. I've got this.

That helped until the President separated her and Wolf by standing between them. She couldn't believe it. Now she would have to wing it on national television. Then she looked around the room. Why the hell not. She'd been winging it for days.

The President shook their hands and asked Wolf, "Can you handle a few questions? They're about ready to cut flips."

Wolf met Velvet's determined eyes and answered. "Absolutely."

And as the President stepped back, Wolf drew Velvet closer and took it from there.

He looked around the room and said, "We'll take a few questions. I'll go first." He pointed to a man he recognized as being a research journalist. "Jasper."

"Thank you, Colonel. Sir, how did you get involved in the situation with the Carrington's and Hal Beckett?"

"Jax and I have worked together through the years, besides being friends. He messaged me and I went for Velvet. It was that simple. Next." He pointed to a man in his 30s with a press pass.

The man smiled. "Thank you, Colonel. This is for Ms. Carrington. Ms. Carrington, where did Colonel Wolf take you?"

Wolf interrupted, "That's classified—"

The reporter interrupted and asked, "Were you alone with her —"

Wolf cut him off and said, "Look... Lance, is it? I'm not in uniform today. So, unless you want to get decked on national television, back off. And you're done. Next question."

Velvet touched Wolf's arm and pointed at a young woman in the back who looked like she was about to pee in her pants. Wolf said, "Go for it."

Velvet said, "Young lady in the back in the pink dress, what's your name?"

"Bella, Ms. Carrington."

"What's your question?"

"Thank you! Ms. Carrington, aren't you the missing woman in Dallas whose house blew up?"

"Good catch, Bella. And yes, I am."

Now everyone called out for Velvet.

Wolf said, "Last question everyone," and he looked at Velvet. "You pick."

She looked on the front row figuring they would have the toughest questions for the most press value – and decided to go for it. She pointed at a short serious man and said, "What's your name?"

"Brad, Ms. Carrington."

"What's your question?"

"What did you think of all the bloodshed?"

Velvet touched Wolf's arm as he started to interrupt. Their eyes met, and Wolf saw her anger. She said, "Let me have him."

"Go for it, Green Eyes."

Looking at the man who asked the question, Velvet left the podium and walked toward him. She said, "Seriously, Brad, blood is the best you've got? Tell me, have you ever had to fight to live? Have you had your house explode? Have you worn disguises so you weren't recognized? Have you boarded a train toward a future as unknown as a blank canvas? Have you ever had a bodyguard that saved your life, over, and over, and over?

"I want you to know that I wouldn't be here today if not for Colonel Wolf, Jax, and all the men that stood in harm's way with me. And yes, people died.

Did I see them dead? Yes. I even had to kill one myself. And hell, I didn't even know if my own brother was alive for days.

"So, to a man who has less sense than God gave a gnat, you wasted your chance to ask a question about a momentous event. Now Brad, write about that."

She spun on her heel and as she met Wolf's proud gaze, the room erupted in cheers.

***

In the Oval Office a few minutes later, the President asked, "Ms. Carrington, have you thought about running for office? That was a damn fine speech."

"Not yet, Mr. President. My diplomacy falters dreadfully at times as I'm sure you are aware. But may I say it's an honor to meet you."

He smiled. "Call me Zack, or Ace."

"Call me Velvet. And you owe me, Ace. I was terrified in there."

He laughed. "Not that I could tell. Either in the Oval Office or with the press. You remind me of Wolf...and Jax."

He glanced at Wolf. "I see a mighty big spark between you two. Do you have anything to tell me, or will you deck me for asking?"

Wolf drew Velvet to him. "We're engaged."

Velvet grinned at Ace. "I bet that scares you."

Both men laughed.

***

Jax and Indigo were quiet for the first few minutes of the ride leaving Andrews Air Force Base.

Indigo had tear tracks. Jax was thoughtful with a frown between his brows. It took him a bit to get past the solemness of the trip and see the beauty in the day again. The fall foliage. The blue sky. And the fact that Blaze was home.

He took a deep breath and glanced at Indigo. She was looking out the window. He laid his hand over hers, rubbing his thumb over her soft skin. He said, "I know that wasn't easy. Thank you for coming with me."

191

She looked at their hands together. "It wasn't easy, but it was powerful. And honestly, it scared me, Jax, to face the dangerous reality of what you do." She met his gaze. "But I am so very proud of you. You are incredible."

He kissed her. Hard, holding her face to his. And then his lips softened, and caressed. He said, "You do things to me. Deep things. With the things you say. In witnessing your passion for those you love. And your fire. You're filled with it, Indigo. And that's what I want to think about now.

"Blaze is home with those he loved. And we're about to go back to Dallas. Your home. Your future. And the reality that nothing ahead of us is a simple life. Are you ready for my kind of complicated?"

She smiled, even more beautiful with tear tracks. "Simple is overrated. Yes, life is changing…but I'm ready. In fact, with what happened to Velvet's home, I wondered if all of you would like to stay with me—"

His kiss was his answer.

Then her phone rang.

And his.

Indigo answered, "Hey, River. I was going to call—"

River said, "I just saw the news about Velvet and Jax at the White House. The White House, Indigo. What the hell did you get yourself involved in up there? Where are you?"

She knew he was upset. "River—"

"Mom and Dad are tripping. The museum is calling for you. Is your apartment going to blow up too?"

"River, listen to me. I'm ok. I'm with Jax. I had a little run in with the CIA, but he took care of it."

"Had a little run in with the CIA? I told you not to go. That's insane."

"I'll have to explain everything later. We are heading to meet Velvet and Wolf. I expect to be back in Dallas tonight or tomorrow."

River said, "And this Wolf… What a name. He looked ready to beat the crap out of that press guy on TV. Is Velvet safe with him?"

Indigo smiled. "I assure you that she is well protected. And take a breath, River. The worst part is over."

"What do you mean, worst part? There's more?"

Jax took the phone. "River. Jax here. Indigo is fine. I promise. And Velvet is totally safe as well. We'll all get together when we return. I'm sorry about all this. It was unavoidable."

"Damn, Jax. You and Velvet have been through some shit from what I heard. Are y'all hurt? Was Indigo hurt in any way?"

Jax looked at his watch – time was short. He answered, "A few scrapes. That's all. You'll see for yourself soon. Please let your parents know everything is fine. And we've got to run. Sorry to cut you off..."

And Jax ended the call.

Indigo said, "You'll pay for that. He's pissed."

"I know. But Wolf called. It looks like we'll be taking a plane ride to Dallas tonight."

In minutes, the CIA dropped them off at the FBI.

Indigo whispered as they followed directions to the office where everyone waited, "Do you think the CIA and FBI know all our secrets?"

Jax said, "You have secrets?"

"Everyone does."

"I don't."

"You live in a world of secrets."

"But they're not mine. Tell me one of yours."

"No."

"You are the one that thought the FBI was the best place to bring up this conversation. Come on. Tell me one."

"I smoked a joint on a camping trip and went skinning dipping."

He refused to smile. "When?"

"A couple of years ago."

"Did you like it?"

"We laughed like hyenas and ran out of snacks."

He choked back a laugh. "We?"

"It was a girl's trip. There were four of us."

"Are you telling me that Velvet was there?"

"Yes, but she didn't smoke the joint. She just sat in the middle of the fog."

Jax closed his eyes. "What else?"

"I drove tipsy once."

He sighed. "That's called drunk."

"Shut up. I rarely drink."

He said, "My apologies. Don't stop now. What else?"

She shrugged. "I read Fifty Shades of Grey and then bought the movie. I watched it once."

"Liar."

"Ok. I watched it a couple of times. But..."

"But what?"

193

She didn't answer.

"Indy, what?"

"I bought a condom."

He stopped walking. "When?"

She looked away. "Six months ago."

His gut tightened. "Indigo…"

She looked back at him. "But it's still in my purse."

He leaned close, "You need supervision. And we are going to have a long discussion about your passionate propensity for the wild side." He backed her against the wall. "And then I'm going to give you what I have waited way too long to give you – and you won't need a damn movie."

She smiled.

He narrowed his eyes. "Did you get the reaction you wanted?"

"Should I keep the condom?"

He kissed her.

Hard.

After walking down two more hallways, they knocked on a double door. "Come in!"

Eight people sat at a large table. Two massive monitors were on the wall. One with a picture of a man they recognized. And the other a city map of Dallas.

The Director said, "Jax and Indigo, join us. We are all aware of the somberness of your morning. Blaze was an excellent officer."

Jax nodded. "Indeed."

As they settled next to Velvet, the Director said, "Agent Williams is the Special Agent in charge in Dallas." He waved his arm. "Agent Williams, the meeting is all yours."

A man in a dark gray suit about Jax and Wolf's age walked to the nearest screen. The man on the screen had long light brown hair a little on the wavy side. Extremely light blue eyes. Sun-tanned skin. And a beard. Muscular and intense. And except for the prison jumpsuit, he looked like someone you'd find in a gym.

Williams said, "This is the parole release picture of Brody Jon Grant. He is now 29 years old. Of course, that doesn't mean he hasn't changed his appearance since then, but it gives us the basics. And you can easily see that he has matured and toughened a great deal since going to prison.

194

"Unfortunately, since the discovery of Detective Black's body, there has only been one video capture of him outside a store in Alexandria, Louisiana. After which, he vanished. No internet footprint. No phone connection. No family contact. No credit card usage. Nothing. Except a tip from the New Orleans Police Department."

He said, "Colonel Wolf, I understand we have you to thank for that."

Wolf said, "It was my only option to get the FBI and U.S. Marshalls headed in the right direction."

"It did. Dallas."

Jax said, "Ok, so we all presume he's in Dallas. Do we know why he is all in a rage for Velvet after two dates?"

Williams said, "We've learned a great deal. So, let's start with history. We followed Velvet's mention of Brody's little sister's mystery back in high school. Her name is Lori Grant. At the time she was 15. And we think she's the key to all of it."

He looked at Velvet and asked, "What was the boy's name that you dated after Brody, and how old was he?"

"Spencer Moore. And he was older than me. Eighteen I think." And she noticed the quick spread of excitement through the agents and asked, "Why?"

"You confirmed our projection. Let me give you the timeline we've put together. Spencer had a secret relationship with Lori Grant for a month or so. Secret, because she was only 15. And near the end of their time together, you dated her brother Brody. After which, you began to date Spencer."

Velvet winced and covered her face. This was not going to be good.

Williams continued, "It was a summer of teenage hormones. We've all been there. But this one left Lori desperate and pregnant while everyone else moved on. In a perfect world, Spencer would have landed in jail and Lori would have had support and guidance. But neither happened, and that's why the family moved. Lori wouldn't tell them who got her pregnant and her life fell apart. She lost the baby through the trauma. And only a few months before the shooting in New Orleans, she died in an accident."

He paused and glanced at Velvet. "After that accident is when Brody found her journal. And then a few weeks later, filled with her young truths and grief, new vigilante Brody sees you while trying to kill a man who raped a young girl. The timing must have been traumatic for him. The memories making him focus on you."

Velvet moaned, "I don't know what to think, much less say. Lori was a beautiful girl. Kind and gentle. It's all just awful. And Brody...I get it. Seeing me at that time, no wonder he snapped."

195

She looked at Wolf. "Which means, we presume that since he killed Dillon, prison didn't change his focus. He's not going to stop coming after me."

Wolf said, "Only when we catch or kill him. Grieving because of the loss of one innocent girl doesn't excuse the killing of another. That's insanity from Hal Beckett's point of view."

Jax said, "So, we trap him using Velvet to draw him in. Do you have any evidence that Brody is in Dallas?"

Williams said, "There are approximately 20 murders in Dallas each month. Two in the last few days had Brody's DNA on them. He's there."

Velvet asked, "Why were the two people killed?"

"One was a carjacking. And the other, a robbery home invasion."

Wolf said, "He's escalating to survive. What's your plan?"

Williams said, "We have a special news bulletin set to air in Dallas tomorrow to follow up on the White House press briefing today. We'll celebrate Velvet's safe return and thank the city for searching for her. We'll publicize it and draw him out."

Wolf said, "To where?"

Williams said, "The logical place would be Velvet's house. It puts less people in danger and provides a higher emotional content. Are you good with that, Velvet?"

She nodded. "I can do that."

The Director asked, "Jax? Wolf?"

They both agreed.

He said, "Excellent. Then everyone needs to head south this afternoon. Anyone need a ride to Texas?"

Wolf glanced at Velvet, "I'll fly us in. I need to stop at my place in North Carolina."

Jax said, "The CIA will fly Indigo and I down."

Velvet said, "Do we need a hotel room since my house is—"

Indigo cut in, "No. Stay with me. And be prepared, River will show up. Cranky."

Chapter 26
Brody

Brody sat quietly in the grass outside a garage apartment north of Dallas. It was mostly country with a touch of suburb. Peaceful. A cool wind blew. He was alone except for an old golden retriever curled up next to him. Its golden hair now sprinkled heavily with gray. Frisky playfulness long gone. His tail wagged when he noticed Brody's glance. Brody rubbed a hand across his back in response.

The old man who'd hired him to watch his house, property and dog, left today for a couple of weeks on vacation with his brother. The old guy was 87. His brother, 89. They bickered. Laughed. And grazed continually in the kitchen telling stories and farting. Brody smiled. It would take them a day to reach their Toledo Bend cabin with all the bathroom stops they'd make.

And he was jealous of them. They'd lived a lifetime to earn those crazy antique tales, with homes and bodies just as old. But not him. He wouldn't have that. A wife. Or kids. No old tales or homes. He'd crossed that line after he found Lori's journal.

And his education, his character, and his family's hope washed away the first time he pulled the trigger. The second. And almost a third. Velvet had been lucky. But not her ex-husband. Or the two men here in Dallas.

Brody sighed and thought back to the White House press briefing he'd watched before noon. And then he'd pulled it up on the internet and watched it again, and again. Velvet knew pain now. He believed that. She'd killed a man too. And for some reason those truths changed everything. The driving rage to watch her suffer like his sister, flickered and died. Poof. Gone like fall leaves in the wind.

And now something else stirred to take its place.

He touched Velvet's body on the phone screen from head to toe.

Velvet was a gorgeous woman.

Chapter 27
Dallas Bound

Wolf and Velvet were about 10 miles from Andrews Air Force Base. They were borrowing Ace's personal plane for the trip to North Carolina and then on to Dallas.

Velvet met his gaze in the backseat of the FBI SUV. "Which beach do you live on?"

"It's on Emerald Isle. You'll love it."

She sighed dreamily, "One of the barrier islands… How long is the trip?"

"A little over an hour. Not long at all."

She looked at the time on the car dash. Three-thirty in the afternoon. She wondered how much of a hurry they were in to get to Dallas. "How long—"

He squeezed her and said, "We'll have a couple of hours to ourselves before we need to get back in the air. I aim to land in Dallas by midnight. So…" He kissed her softly. "How does some down time on the beach with your fiancé sound?"

"Please tell me no one else will be there."

"No one will be in the house, or on my dry sand. The wet sand and water are public."

"Really. So, what if they have one foot on wet sand and one foot on dry? Does it become a legal matter or a boxing match?"

He laughed. "You would come up with that scenario. Why don't we just think about no one else being in the house."

She laid her head against his shoulder and said softly, "And what do you plan to do in the house?"

"As much as I possibly can."

The FBI driver stopped at Andrews main gate.

It didn't take long, and Velvet watched Wolf prepare for take-off in the plane. This time no helmet. Just a headpiece.

He winked. "Go look around. They're going to top off the fuel. You'll even find a bathroom."

The President's personal plane was a Beechcraft King Air 350i. White with navy and turquoise stripes down the side and up the tail. Twin props. Round porthole style windows. And an elevated interior fitted with heated ivory leather seats. Two pull-out tables. A refreshment center. And excellent noise cancellation technology with Wi-Fi.

Velvet shook her head at the small amount of luggage they brought on board. Two well-worn backpacks and duffel bags that looked like they'd been run over. Twice. And a brand-new hanging bag for the new clothes they'd bought yesterday.

She thought of her destroyed home and winced, then decided she'd think about that tomorrow when she was standing in front of it. But for now, she was relieved that her Jeep was literally packed full of her things. Valuable. Favorite. And personal. Things she'd never have chosen to leave behind.

But survival mode had changed that.

And Wolf changed everything else.

Glancing out the window, she watched the men drive the fuel truck away. Wolf called out, "Hey, Green Eyes, are you ready for another rush?"

An hour passed in a flash going 350 mph at 32,000 feet. It seemed like they'd just leveled off and Wolf was beginning the descent.

Velvet watched North Carolina and the Atlantic Ocean get closer, and closer. The beauty of the layout of the land amazed her. All the waterways. The beaches. The houses. And the tiny dot people playing in extraordinarily green water. Hmm. It was cold green water. Maybe those were sharks.

She decided not to think about that and said, "How much longer?"

He held up a finger and called the tower at Bogue Field on the North Carolina mainland for permission to land. The Marines were well familiar with the President's personal plane.

Then Wolf glanced at Velvet and said, "We'll be landing shortly. And it's only about a 15-minute drive to my house."

"I can't wait! Now, let's talk about sharks. I see black dots in the water."

He chuckled. "They do swim by, from time to time. It comes with the territory."

She sounded out the creepy Jaws movie soundtrack.

"Cute. Now, hang on, we're going down. And don't worry about sharks, we won't be swimming today."

199

They landed and were escorted to the Bogue Field gate. A bright yellow souped up dune buggy style jeep was waiting for them. It had a windshield. Roll bars. Seating for four and headlights. *Purple Rain* was playing on the radio.

A man in his 50s wearing jeans and a sweatshirt high fived Wolf. "Damn glad to see you are all-in-one piece Wolf-man." He shook Velvet's hand. "You too, Ms. Carrington. That was quite a press briefing."

Wolf said, "Thanks, Hoot. You can say that again. I appreciate you picking us up. We'll only be here for a couple of hours. Is everything quiet?"

"The beach is like a windy sleeping baby. Quiet. And your place is open and ready. Food on the stove and something to drink in the fridge. Just drop me back at the office and take Lightning." Hoot pointed to his Jeep and smiled as Velvet climbed into the driver's seat.

Velvet smiled at Hoot and said, "I like your wheels." She pointed at the passenger seat when she looked at Wolf. "You flew us here. My turn."

The men laughed and climbed in. Wolf pointed the way.

Velvet turned down the music and said over the wind, "Why do they call you Hoot?"

Seventeen minutes later, Velvet pulled up behind a rental shop beach house and dropped Hoot off. And from there, Wolf motioned to the sand road that led through the white grass-topped sand dunes down to the beach. He turned off the music and said, "Drive on down. Let's ride along the beach."

As Velvet turned onto the beach, she stopped and sighed as it washed over her. Emerald water. White sand. A few people riding horses along the water. Totally gorgeous. And quiet. The tourist areas and beach houses didn't seem to be busy at all. But then again, it was October.

A mile down the beach, Wolf pointed at the next beach house. "Park right here." She stopped at the stairs and looked up.

His home was a large, sturdy, but cozy two-story house above the dunes. It was green. A soft green somewhere between pale green and moss green. And it had at impressive number of windows – all with shutters. A wrap-around porch on the ground floor had a boardwalk staircase that made its way by multiple levels down to the beach. And a wolf was painted on both entry posts.

Velvet got out and said softly, "Oh, Wolf…"

He joined her. "Do you like it?"

"It's perfect. I love the style, the color, the staircase, and the wolves. It's magical."

200

Smiling, he said, "That will win you some brownie points. Come on, I'll race you up."

She laughed. "Like that's fair."

He threw her over his shoulder and ran up the stairs leaving echoes of her squeals and laughter in the breeze. He opened the door and carried her in, locking it.

Velvet was still smiling when he kissed her. Like he had waited as long as he could. He backed her against the wall, wild, sliding her up higher for the rest of her. He raised her shirt, kissing her stomach. Then, slid her even higher, so he could rub his lips along her zipper.

Passion exploded in Velvet at the speed of his desire. Her breath, lost between groans and gasps. Wolf met her gaze as he unzipped her jeans. He said, "I can't wait."

Before she could even respond, his phone rang. He froze. Letting her slide down, he said, "Damn it!" And answered the phone growling, "What."

It was Hoot. "Sorry Wolf-man. But listen, your brothers called for me to go pick them up. They'll be here with their families in 20 minutes. Tops. I just thought I'd warn you."

All Wolf said was, "I owe you, Hoot."

He chunked the phone on the sofa and turned to Velvet. "My brothers and their families are on their way. How's that for timing. Son of a—"

Velvet pushed him against the wall, surprising him. Meeting his gaze, she unzipped his pants and knelt as he breathed her name.

✳✳✳

Half an hour later, down the hall, Wolf heard the bathroom door open and close. About that time, his oldest nephew jumped on his back. Again. He met Velvet's amused gaze as she rounded the corner, smiling at two other boys latched on to his legs.

And girls were everywhere. The twins in lavender. Three in pink. One in red. And the last one in jeans and a ball cap, dismissing her sissy sisters.

Unnoticed by the others, Velvet leaned against the snack bar and smiled at Wolf. She said, "It looks like you need some help."

Thirteen new faces turned to stare at her, and she felt like the perpetual deer in the headlights.

The boys scrambled off Wolf, yelling, "Get her!"

Velvet screamed, laughing, and ran out the back door, across the porch, and down the stairs. Three boys and six girls, all under the age of 10, were in hot pursuit. Laughing, Wolf followed the herd running down the boardwalk.

The boys were gaining on Velvet.

Velvet vaulted over the rail and landed running. The boys screamed with delight and flew off the boardwalk like flying squirrels landing in the sand. The pink, lavender and red girls turned their noses up at getting dirty and continued down the stairs with Wolf trying to get around them. The tomboy simply bailed off the boardwalk after her brothers.

In an awkward run in loose sand, Velvet contemplated her options. She was getting close to wet sand, which meant the green waves were close and cold. She could smell the salt. Hearing footsteps and victory yells, she spun to hold them off. Wolf scooped her up just before the boys slammed into them. Screams and laughter were loud as the girls danced around them like a princess war party.

Wolf's eyes locked on Velvet's swollen lips, remembering the hot feel of them not long ago. He said huskily, "I'm going to love making babies with you."

She whispered in his ear, and he kissed her. The kids quickly retreated, fussing about kisses and yucky stuff.

Back in the house, Velvet formally met everyone.

Wolf was the middle brother.

Thorn was the oldest. He was married to Meg, short for Megan. And all six girls were theirs. They had decided to stop trying for a boy.

Sterling was the youngest brother and married to Adele. The three boys were theirs. And they were still trying for a girl.

For a long while the talk jumped back and forth between the press briefing and Hal, to what happened in Colorado. But then they moved onto what they really wanted to know. Specifics about Wolf and Velvet. Already knowing they were a thing but wanting answers from the family bachelor.

Wolf caught Thorn's demanding eye and Sterling's knowing one. Both looked at Velvet. Hint. Wolf glanced at the clock, ignoring them, and said, "Why don't all of you take this food. It will spoil since we're about to leave."

Meg shook her head in pretend exasperation. "Damn, Wolf. There was nothing subtle at all about that shove out the door. I almost tripped."

Wolf winked. "Damn, Meg. You're quick. Let me help you and Adele pack everything."

Velvet bit her lip to keep from laughing and turned, only to find Thorn and Sterling in front of her. Sterling said, "What's on your ring finger?"

Velvet glanced at her finger with the bow and smiled. "Darn. A ring."

Sterling came back, "Sassy. I can tell you're Jax's sister."

Velvet said, "And I can tell you're Ace's nephew. Mr. Ambush. You know, put me on the spot in front of the entire world."

Everyone laughed and Wolf pointed toward the door. "Please. Don't make me be rude."

Meg laughed on the way out with a bag of food. "That comes naturally for you."

Wolf kissed her cheek. "I love you, Meg."

"Eat dirt, Wolf. I love you too."

Wolf watched Hoot's van disappear with his siblings as Velvet walked back to the kitchen. Grabbing a rag, she leaned over to wipe the table and said, "Don't we still have a few min—"

Wolf pressed her from behind as his mouth trailed from her shoulder to her neck. He unzipped her jeans and leaned her forward. "I've got something for you..."

Velvet grabbed both sides of the table. And hung on.

Twenty minutes later they prepared to leave the beach house.

Wolf pulled the table back in place. Velvet touched the gouges on the wall and glanced at the scratches on the floor. She looked at Wolf. "We need a rug and bumper pads."

He winked and joined her. Touching the gouge, he said, "I'll never forget where that mark came from."

"You might need to keep a repair kit handy."

"That wasn't what you said a few minutes ago."

"I didn't say anything a few minutes ago. I couldn't."

He smiled, touching her lips. "I heard a lot."

She kissed his finger. "Indeed." Then rubbing his chest she said, "Thank you for not mentioning the M word today. I know how much it means to you."

"It didn't mean I didn't think about it." He hugged her, then led her to the door. "We'll have a lot to talk about after Brody is behind us."

She nodded. "Do you think Brody saw us on the news?"

"With news alerts on our phones, absolutely. There's no doubt he's got a burner phone. Are you ready for what's ahead?"

She walked out on the back porch with him. The moon was shining on the water. Waves breaking along the beach. So peaceful. She said, "I never thought I'd have to forget him once, much less three times. I want him behind me, Wolf."

"Tomorrow could be the day."

"Do you think Jax and Indigo are in Dallas yet?"

Wolf checked his watch. Almost 6 p.m. "They are probably just getting there."

∗∗∗

Twenty-three hundred miles from Emerald Isle, Jax and Indigo got off on the 9th floor of The Gabriella apartments in Dallas, Texas.

Having been several times to Indigo's place with Velvet, Jax held out his hand for her key when they reached #957. "Let me clear it first since Brody is in Dallas. No doubt he knows where you live."

Indigo should have been creeped out at the thought. But they were about to be alone after 10 years, and a lot of hot making out for 24 hours. Including some intense teasing on the CIA flight from D.C. She met his gaze and handed him the key. They both knew what was coming. He pulled her against him and kissed her as he unlocked the door.

Pulling his gun, he searched through the entire four-bedroom apartment. Indigo waited where her foyer opened into the artsy living area. Spacious with a wall of windows. Totally contemporary, with splashes of color. Varnished floors. A glass-encased fireplace in the wall. And a large white velvet sectional sofa in the corner with pillows in red, purple, and black sequin.

Three large pictures hung prominently on the wall behind the sofa. A horse and cowboy – both sweaty. A waterfall. And a bride wearing nothing but her veil and sparkly heels, looking back over her shoulder at someone.

Indigo laid her purse and jacket on the snack bar. Anticipation high. But not about Brody. She looked down at her sexy dress and boots. Hearing Jax cuss, she looked up as he took long strides out of her bedroom – taking off his holster and tossing his shirt. He headed straight for her with a bare chest and hungry eyes.

He shook his head. "I could smell you in there. I can't wait."

She ran and jumped. He caught her, kissing her. Possessive. Hot. And bold. There would be no more holding back. Ever. And Indigo met him wild for wild, locking her legs behind his back as fire filled the room.

Groaning, Jax met her gaze as he found only bare skin under her dress. Everything he was dying for and nothing in the way. Hoarsely he said, "You've seriously been naked the whole trip?"

No answer was required as his hand found the fire underneath the ruffles. He captured his name on her lips. Her fingernails raked his back as he held on to her, sending her flying toward the edge of something…

She gasped, "Hurry, Jax—"

And he took her right where he stood in the hall. She screamed sharply when he tore through the barrier. He stopped, aware, as he met her gaze. His breath ragged, he breathed, Indigo…"

Wild and breathless, she shook her head, "Don't stop—"

And then love exploded after waiting too damn long.

Both, still breathless, he carried her to the bedroom afterwards. He lifted her for another kiss. "Indy…I'm a little late telling you I love you."

She smiled. "There wasn't much time for conversation. So, you really love me?"

"Since I was 34 - without ever kissing you once."

She hung on as he lowered her to the bed. "That's incredibly beautiful, Jax. I forgive you. You already know I love you."

Snuggling with her in pink and white striped sheets, he said, "I do." Then he frowned and drew her against him. "I was too rough. Your scream of pain—"

"You weren't rough. You were magnificently hard. And it hurt for an instant."

He growled hungrily. Ready again. "Why didn't you tell me you were a virgin?"

"Why did you presume I wasn't? Because I have a passionate propensity for the wild side?"

He rolled on top of her. "Maybe because of the joint smoking confession, or the skinny dipping, or the Forty Shades of Gray, the condom you bought, or the fact that you were nearly naked on a CIA plane."

She whispered as his hands made it hard to focus on words, "But…I didn't use the condom."

He whispered against her lips, "But I didn't know it was the first time you bought one. But I do know I was your first, and your last."

Several hours later, Jax winked at Indigo as they collected clothes off the floor. He wore jeans but still wouldn't let her get dressed.

Indigo glanced at the clock. "Jax Carrington, River could show up at any moment. I need clothes and you need a shirt."

He caught her as she ran to the bedroom, and said, "And what if I'm not done?"

"You can always pull me in a closet later."

The doorbell rang as he laughed.

Indigo squealed and ran to the bedroom. She threw Jax a shirt. "Hurry, he's here!"

Jax pulled on the shirt and said, "Take a few minutes to catch your breath. I've got this."

"Don't forget that he's rude when he's stressed."

He kissed her. "I know River. He just needs to see that you're in one piece."

"Right. Naked in the room with you."

He smiled and shut her door.

Running his hands through his hair, Jax glanced around the room on the way to River yelling through the door, "What the hell, Indigo! Are you in there?"

Jax dropped a button he found on the floor in his pocket as he opened the door. Shocking her brother, he said, "Hey, River. Come on in. I was busy and Indigo's in her room. We've had some crazy days. Sorry about scaring everyone."

River shook his hand. "It's good to see you. The press briefing blew my mind. It's hard to believe you and Velvet were targeted like that. And what happened with Indigo at the CIA? I told her not to go." He looked around. "Where are Velvet and the Wolf guy?"

Jax glanced at the time. "They should be here any minute. Wolf was flying them in."

"Flying, as in he's a pilot?"

"Yep. He's a colonel in the Air Force."

"Then you and Indigo are here alone." He studied Jax. "That's unusual. Velvet is usually with Indigo."

"It's been an unusual time." Jax walked toward the kitchen. "How about something to drink?"

River sat on a stool at the counter still full of questions. "And what about the CIA thing?"

Jax said, "It was a mix-up about protocol. I took care of it."

"And what's your job at the CIA that you could just take care of it?"

"I kind of fill in where I'm needed. I'm handy to have around."

"Don't bullshit me, Jax."

"Then don't ask questions that I can't answer. You saw the briefing. Let it go. A whole lot of shit went down. You'll see that Indigo is fine." He paused. "Now, moving on. Indigo has water, Dr. Pepper, tea and something pink. Take your pick."

The doorbell rang.

River said, "I'll get it."

He opened the door. Velvet screamed and hugged him. "River!"

River squeezed her and took in the Wolf man without a smile. Then he lifted Velvet's chin to check her out. "You've been through hell. Are you ok?"

"I am! All my bruises are healing. And I want you to meet Wolf. Remington Wolf. And Wolf, meet River. And be nice, guys. No macho stuff. We've all been through hell."

Jax called from the kitchen, "Velvet, Wolf, what's your poison? Water, Dr. Pepper, tea or pink stuff?"

Wolf said, "I'll give you a hand."

Wolf watched the big handsome cowboy with Velvet as Jax put ice in the glasses.

Jax noticed. "Remember, Wolf, he's the one that shot Brody. He's the good guy. No need to harm him."

"Right. Where's Indigo?"

"Dressing. She'll be out in a minute. What do you want to drink?"

"Anything but pink stuff. And why was she undressed?"

Jax ignored Wolf's question and carried the glasses to the sitting area.

Moments later they heard Indigo coming down the hall. She rounded the corner with a smile, and only a brief widening of her eyes when she glanced at the floor showed alarm. Jax and Wolf both caught her expression and looked at the floor. A black bra was right next to River's foot.

Wolf was closest and kicked it under a chair.

Jax winked at Indigo as she blushed, hugging her brother.

Velvet caught the look on Jax and Wolf's face. What had she just missed?

It was almost midnight when River left. The two couples walked out on the balcony. It was chilly nine floors up with the breeze.

Wolf said, "Agent Williams texted. We meet at 10 in the morning at their office."

207

Jax asked, "What time is the news bulletin?"

"Noon."

Velvet said, "Do I need to practice a speech?"

"No. He said your sincerity is better than any speech, considering what he saw at the White House. Just talk from the heart."

Indigo said, "Well, I don't know about you, but I just want to know that all the people with guns are going to be there."

Jax said, "There will be undercover all around us. Brody's a federal fugitive with three kills under his belt and one victim, plus Velvet. They'll be watching for him."

Wolf said, "And Jax and I are there. Visible and armed. Just be sure that both of you stay close to us."

✳✳✳

Velvet was sound asleep in Wolf's arms later that night. The door to her room open and respectful. Her breath softly touched his chest as he thought about all the variables affecting tomorrow's trap.

Brody hadn't been born with killer tendencies that terrified everyone as he grew up. He'd been on the right path in life, socially and emotionally, with intelligence and compassion. But grief and pain had tossed him a curve he'd never recovered from. Now he was like a criminal bloodhound on the hunt.

Wolf sighed. Brody wasn't a soldier with strategic plans instilled in him that you could project he might try. The man was capable of anything. Anytime. Anywhere. Like creatively unstable dynamite.

Revenge could still be his motive. Or it could have transformed into something else. Regardless, it looked like spilled blood would be the only way to stop him.

✳✳✳

Brody sat in the old man's Honda, diagonally across from Indigo's apartment complex. Finding an address was as simple as the internet these days. Anyone's. So, this afternoon he waited for them to show up. And tonight watched the five of them through a glass wall with binoculars. Easily, since most apartments were dark early.

Jax and Indigo arrived before dark.

208

River showed up later. Good ole River. Brody rubbed the scar the cowboy shooter had left on him in New Orleans. He wouldn't forget him anytime soon. That had been an impressive shot in the heat of the moment.

Then last, Velvet arrived with the colonel from the press briefing. He noticed the man's hand close to her ass and knew that he'd had some of that. Not that he blamed him. Velvet was extraordinary. Though it might make the colonel more aggressive when the time came for him to make his move.

That meant, stealth or death.

Brody stayed until Indigo's lights went out. He knew two things for sure. One, as star of the hour, Velvet would have plenty of protection here in Dallas. And two, he'd have to kill Jax and the colonel to get her.

He started the car and headed back to the old man's house.

In twenty-five minutes, he turned onto a rural road. And in exactly a mile, he pulled in the driveway of a yellow Victorian house. He parked next to his garage apartment and got out. Turning, he smiled looking across Velvet's back yard.

At some point Velvet would come home.

And vanish with him.

Chapter 28
Full Circle

Early the next morning, Velvet stirred under the covers, waking up. And stretched. She reached for Wolf, but the bed was empty. She rolled over and looked in the hall. She could hear Jax singing in the kitchen.

She laid back on her pillow realizing today was Wednesday. Seven days since quitting her job. Seven days since packing her belongings in the Jeep for an adventure in Oklahoma. Seven days since setting out to search for her alpha warrior. And late tonight would be seven days since Jax had texted her from Africa. Around the country and back in only seven days. And she'd found her alpha.

Speaking of, where was Wolf?

Sliding out of bed wearing Indigo's Dallas Cowboy tank top and skimpy pajama shorts, she walked down the hall to the spare bedroom. She heard Wolf humming and water running in the bathroom. Indigo joined her in the hall, scaring her on purpose, and with silent giggles, they stalked Wolf.

Wolf stood in front of the mirror in unbuttoned jeans. He finished the last pass of the razor on his stubble beard and laid it down. Then, splashed water on his face.

Standing, he dried it and hung the towel, looking in the mirror only to see his young, beautiful, half-dressed, sneaky audience. His grin was slight, but sexy, as he met Velvet's gaze. Then Indigo's. He said, "What can I do for you ladies? You out hunting this morning?"

Velvet smiled in appreciation. "You were missing. I found you."

Indigo said, "We found you." She looked at Velvet. "Do you think he'll let me see it?"

Velvet giggled at the quick frown on Wolf's face. She explained, "Your tattoo. I told her no."

Indigo walked closer looking at his side. "I see part of it—"

Wolf stepped aside and said, "Forget it and back slowly out of the room."

Indigo huffed, "Come on, Wolf. I just want to see it."

Jax heard voices from the kitchen and walked in wearing shorts with a rag thrown over his shoulder. He took in the scene. "See what?"

Velvet said, "She wants to see Wolf's tattoo. I told her no."

Jax laughed, "Indigo, you would see a whole lot more than a tattoo. Leave him alone." He looked at Wolf. "See what I've put up with all these years? Two half-naked women. Fledgling vultures. It takes a saint to survive."

Wolf leaned back against the counter and drawled, "They are far from fledglings, and I had brothers. This is a hell of a lot different."

Velvet smiled. "See what you missed?"

Wolf pointed at Indigo and Jax. "Out." He caught Velvet's arm. "You stay."

Indigo argued as Jax pulled her out of the room and shut the door.

Wolf sat Velvet on the counter, pressing between her legs and cupping her butt for a tight fit. "Indigo is wild."

Velvet slid her hands up his chest. "She's curious. And yes, on the wild side. But she's harmless. And a virgin I have you know."

He doubted that at this point, but lowered his mouth, "Too much information." And kissed her. Slow and deep like a caress that intended to go somewhere.

Velvet whispered, "I know what you want."

He picked her off the counter, holding her against him. "I don't like restrictions with you. I want us in our own home. Taking showers. Dancing without music. And making babies hanging on the porch rail."

She soothed the beast. "I know. I want the same thing. Maybe it will all be over today."

"It damn well better be. You're mine, Green Eyes. I don't intend to love you from afar. It's a pain in my ass."

"You are direct." She kissed him. "And such a tasty alpha."

Jax hollered down the hall. "Breakfast is ready! You snooze, you lose, and the bacon is mine!"

Sitting in the breakfast nook by the windows overlooking Dallas, they ate fried French toast drizzled with maple syrup and a tower of crispy bacon. High carb, high calorie, and a major sugar rush.

Velvet said, "I'm shocked you had this type of food in your house, Indigo."

With an amused glance at Jax, Indigo said, "I didn't. We stopped at the store."

Jax said, "A man would starve with the type of food both of you keep in your houses."

Wolf smiled at Velvet remembering their conversations at the cabin about meat.

Indigo said, "Should we dress up for the news announcement today?"

Jax picked up the last piece of bacon and instructed, "Wear pants. And no heels in case you need to run."

Indigo looked at Velvet. "Seriously, would you have thought of that?"

"Yes. But then, I've had to run."

***

Wolf joined Jax on the balcony while the women finished dressing. Both wore black military cargo pants, a polo shirt, and were armed. Two tough, tall, good-looking men. Wolf, more rugged with his longer brown hair and electric blue eyes. Jax, more military with short dark hair and hazel eyes.

Leaning on the rail looking out over early morning Texas, Wolf said, "What's next for you after Brody?"

"The CIA is going to offer me Hal's job."

"It's about time. You're a great leader, and you won't have to be in the field as much. You'll have more time for a wife."

Jax nodded in typical man style without any discussion whatsoever. "Yep."

Wolf said, "You're not going to like this, but Velvet will end up living with me. She won't marry me."

Jax turned. "She loves you. You're engaged. What the hell—"

Wolf held up a hand. "Easy. I'm working on it. Dillon did a number on her. She needs time. That's what the engagement is for."

"Damn it to hell. I failed her. I was out fighting—"

"Let it go, man. We can't know when those things will happen."

After a long pause, Jax said, "I'll only shoot Brody three times instead of four for taking care of Dillon for me."

Wolf said, "After I kill him."

Inside the apartment, dressed and ready to go, Velvet and Indigo both took a sip of coffee. Velvet dressed for the broadcast in a fall-colored boho top, gold jeans that matched, and knee boots. Indigo dressed on the gothic side in a black lace turtleneck, black jeans, and lace up boots.

They watched their men.

Velvet said, "I'm going to live with Wolf when all this is over."

Indigo faced her with a frown. "Live? You mean like shack up? Why? When is the wedding?"

"I can't set a date."

"That makes no sense. You love him, and he could burst into flames just looking at you. Isn't he good in bed?"

Velvet looked at Wolf outside. "Look at him. Good is a pitiful description for Wolf."

Indigo laughed. "Ok. He's hotter than hell."

"Better."

"Then why can't you set a date to get married?"

Velvet glanced at her cup. "I can't even say the damn word."

Indigo moaned. "I'm confused. What word?"

"The M word." She turned to Indigo. "Dillon was a nightmare, Indy. The vows I made to him showered me in ashes. I'm... Well, I know it sounds ridiculous, but I'm terrified to say them again."

Indigo's eyes watered. She touched Velvet's arm. "Oh, honey. I'm so sorry...for all of it. Does Wolf—"

"He knows. And he's helping me get there." She touched her belly.

Indigo gasped, "Oh shit. You're pregnant."

Velvet half-giggled, half-snorted at her comment. "That was sweet."

They both laughed. Velvet continued, "But if I'm not pregnant, I will be."

"Then Wolf needs to work his magic and get you legal."

Velvet quietly watched Indigo. Waiting.

Indigo said, "What? What did I say now?"

"It's what you haven't said, isn't it?"

Indigo blushed in answer.

Velvet smiled. "I take it you didn't need to strip to get Jax's attention."

Indigo glanced outside at him. "I didn't even have time."

The men walked in.

∗∗∗

Just before ten o'clock, Jax turned Indigo's cream-colored BMW into the FBI facility. Known as the J. Gordon Shanklin Building, it was named after the longest-serving Special Agent in Charge of Dallas. It wasn't gigantic, but big enough on 15 acres.

Velvet said, "The FBI and CIA are intimidating."

213

Wolf said, "They're good at what they do, and they earn the vibe they give off. It has its benefits."

Indigo said, "Do you think Brody has any idea that the feds are onto him?"

"If he's evaded them this long, I say yes." Jax said. "A fugitive crossing state lines is in for a world of hurt. And while he's lost it, he's not stupid."

They parked.

The men unfolded out of the smaller sports car and Indigo said, "Sorry guys, I think I need a bigger car. River hates it."

Wolf said, "At least you save gas if he drives."

They laughed. Only Wolf.

A blonde in a tailored suit escorted them to the third floor. Second hallway to the right. Double doors. She didn't talk much but her one glance at Wolf and Jax said a great deal. Indigo wanted to make a snarky remark, but Velvet nudged her, pointing at the woman's gun.

Indigo rolled her eyes.

The men acted like they didn't notice any of it but didn't miss a thing.

The woman knocked on the double doors and left with only a nod. Following instructions to enter, Wolf leaned close to Jax as the women walked ahead of them, He said quietly, "You better keep handcuffs nearby. You're going to need them with Indigo."

Nodding politely at the ten people in the room, Jax whispered back, "And Velvet needs a fire extinguisher for you."

Special Agent in Charge Williams said, "Good Morning. Have a seat." He motioned to four empty chairs at the table. He looked at Velvet. "Do you have any questions about today?"

She said, "I do. How big of a crowd is usual for this type of thing? I'd like a picture in my mind of what to expect."

Without hesitation, he said, "With six major news stations…I'd estimate two dozen crew members - or more. And they'll all want an exclusive bite for themselves so, expect several questions. Plus, podcasters. They might try to throw you a curve question to increase viewing. And that's all happening directly in front of you.

"Then there are always neighbors, bystanders, thrill seekers, weirdos, the mail lady, delivery drivers, kids on bikes, screaming babies, and pets. There could be well over 100 people around the entire area. Not necessarily close to you. But close enough to watch and listen.

"Lastly, we've asked for a fire engine, the fire chief, and firemen around your damaged home to guard it. Along with the two detectives from Dallas

PD." He paused. "And that's not including the undercover U.S. Marshals and FBI that will be everywhere. Plus, the four of you."

Velvet said, "Wow. Thank you. Is anyone else talking to the media but me?"

"The mayor insisted on opening remarks. The lead detective will say a few words to you, shake your hand - that kind of thing. The fire chief will briefly reference the explosion of your house. And then the mic is all yours."

"So, I wing it."

"Any way you want." He looked at the other three. "Do you have any questions?"

Jax asked, "Do you have any new leads on Brody?"

"No." Williams said.

Jax continued, "What about the DNA on the two Dallas victims. Was any of the blood Brody's? Is it possible he was injured in the attacks?"

"A little of the blood was his. Nothing substantial, and not near enough to suggest he was incapacitated in any way."

Wolf said, "About the Dallas murders, where did they take place? No one mentioned the location."

Williams said, "Near Amtrak station."

Wolf nodded. Then asked, "So, just to hear you confirm it, was the area around Velvet's place outside McKinney thoroughly searched for Brody?"

"Twice since we were notified Saturday. Door to door. Everyone knew everyone and everything. Nothing was suspicious."

Wolf said, "That's it from me then."

Williams said, "Anyone else?"

Indigo said, "May I ask a question?"

"Certainly."

"What do we do if something happens? I don't know, shooting, screaming, or more explosions."

Agent Williams said, "You do whatever Jax and Wolf tell you to do. Instantly." He looked at Velvet and said, "I have one last thing to tell you."

Velvet sighed. "Please don't. It's been a rough week."

He smiled. "It's not that bad. We decided to go for the emotional drama to draw Brody to your house. We'll have the news crews prepared ahead of you to broadcast every move you make. Your arrival. The first time you see your house. Everything in real time. Real emotion. Before any speeches even start.

"Can you do that? No one will interfere. And it'll be your decision when to go to the podium. If Brody's watching, hook him. We'll all be waiting."

215

Velvet looked at Brody's picture on the large screen. She nodded. "I'm good with that."

***

Forty minutes later, Velvet watched as Jax turned down her country lane. Cars were lining the street. They rounded a few curves and saw the fire truck in the distance and people walking toward her house. Or what was left of it. News vans were there. And a crowd had gathered.

Velvet and Indigo looked at each other in the backseat. Velvet's expression was tense, remembering the explosion. Indigo's eyes welled, remembering the fight to find her. They reached for each other's hand.

Wolf glanced back at Velvet. "We can stop if you want more time."

She shook her head. "It's ok. Let's do this. And then it's over."

Jax said, "We'll give you the lead when we get out of the car, but we'll be right behind you. Ignore the reporters if they shout questions. You're the boss." Then he glanced at Indigo. "This isn't your first rodeo with all of this."

Indigo said, "No. I spent a great deal of time in front of the camera pleading for help to find Velvet. I needed them to spread the word."

Wolf said, "They might ask you questions as well."

"That's ok. I owe them."

Cops motioned Jax to pull into Velvet's driveway. A few firemen stood around the remains of the house. The news podium was set up in her front yard, and reporters and cameras were already lined in front of it – all focused on the arriving car. People were literally everywhere.

The car stopped.

Jax and Wolf were out of the car, opening the back doors in a flash. Velvet and Indigo's names were being called as they stepped out. Velvet with Wolf. Indigo with Jax. Questions were yelled as Velvet led the way toward the house.

"What was it like to run for your life?"

"Was Colonel Wolf really your bodyguard?"

"How did you kill the man?"

Velvet didn't answer as she silently made her way closer to the house. Where she stopped suddenly, throat locked with sudden emotion. There were handmade signs. Balloons. Flowers. Missing posters with her picture. Gifts. Yellow ribbons. And her name was everywhere. Tears dripped as she knelt to

216

pick up a stuffed kitten…and turned to hug Indigo as she cried. Indigo cried with her. Some things you just couldn't prepare for.

Wolf felt Velvet's emotion - moved himself at the blackened ashes of her home, and the love of a city for one of their own. Shaking it off to focus, he scanned 360 degrees. Seeking the next round of danger after her. Thinking… Where the hell are you, Brody? I just need half a second with you. If that.

Jax's experienced eyes looked, and found, the authoritative posture of the marshals around the scene. And the stealth of FBI agents eyeing everyone but Velvet. Then he glanced at the rooftops for the sniper.

Brody was a dead man today. One way or the other.

Brody Jon Grant, dressed in jeans, tennis shoes, and a greasy Bon Jovi T-shirt, knelt barely an acre behind Velvet's destroyed house. His long hair was gone. Now it was shaved on the sides and thick on top, with a goatee instead of a beard. He wore sunglasses and earbuds as he listened to the broadcast, while he deceptively tinkered with a lawnmower - and watched it live on his phone.

Only one little acre separated him from Velvet. One.

He glanced across her backyard but couldn't see her through the crowd. He was pumped though. When he woke up this morning, he thought today would be a regular day. Nothing special. Until he received the news alert. Velvet was coming right to him with a whole lot of fanfare.

He listened to the reporter elaborate on Velvet's crying. He sighed. Not because she was crying, but because it would take a miracle to get to her in the middle of all those eyes…and guns. He snorted…pretty sure God was fresh out of miracles on his behalf.

Instead, he thought of his options and stood, looking behind the old man's house, beyond the property line to undeveloped wilderness. Woods, thick with brush. A creek. A boat. A four-wheeler. And an interstate three miles away.

So many possibilities.

He used the silent dog whistle and the retriever waggled around the corner. He rubbed his head, "Come on, Duke. Let's take a short hike."

They disappeared into the woods.

Velvet didn't take much time looking at her house after the tears passed. She'd do that later. It was harder to ignore the acrid smell of burned plastic, wires, wood and so many other things in the ruins at her feet. She waved at the firemen. Then all the people in the yard. They waved back, smiling. Most of the women wiped tears.

She turned and met Wolf's gaze, then nodded at Jax and Indigo. Then headed to the podium.

Mayor Walker clasped Velvet's hands in his and faced the media. He called in triumph like they were announcing the winner of a boxing match, "Dallas, Texas, welcome with me, Velvet Carrington! She is home!"

Cheers rang loudly and the media captured it all.

Next, Fire Chief Tramonte shook her hand and added his welcome before briefly discussing the explosion.

Lastly, the two detectives that worked on her case drove her Jeep home and gave her the keys.

And then the podium was Velvet's.

Wolf stood a step behind on her right. Jax and Indigo, a step behind on her left. The press moved closer, calling her name. Excitement and anticipation high. Velvet understood that it was exciting to have a case like this in their hometown. Big time stuff like traitors. Murders. The CIA. The FBI. A colonel. A paramilitary officer…and her. And even better, it all came to a head in the White House on national television.

Velvet raised her hand asking for silence.

Gorgeous, even with tear streaks and a tiny smudge of soot on her face, she said, "Before I begin, I would like to introduce to you the incredible people who made it possible for me to be here today."

She touched Jax. "My brother, Jax Carrington, was the one who discovered the plot against us and set in motion the plan for our protection. And then discovered the identity of the man responsible."

She turned to Wolf. "And Air Force pilot, Colonel Remington Wolf. The only man Jax trusted to be my bodyguard. Incredibly skilled, he saved my life for days."

Then looking at Indigo, she said, "And most of you may recognize Indigo from her media mission here in Dallas to find me. Beautiful, bold and loyal, she's a friend like no other.

"So, on behalf of all of us, I say thank you Dallas, for your amazing support and kindness when I was missing."

She blew them a kiss. "I'll never forget a heart like yours…the size of Texas."

Everyone cheered, then questions broke through.

"Jax! Can I ask…"

"Velvet…"

"Colonel Wolf, is it true…"

Velvet pointed to a reporter she recognized. He said, "Velvet, when and how did Jax let you know that you were in danger?"

"He texted me Wednesday night."

"What was the first thing you did?"

"Disappear."

She pointed to a woman podcaster. The woman said, "This is for the Colonel." Wolf nodded. She asked, "Where did you take Velvet to keep her safe?"

"That's classified."

"Because you're the President's nephew?"

"Because it's classified."

Velvet hid a smile and said, "Next question." She pointed at a tall serious man in the back. The man said, "Velvet, did you know Colonel Wolf before this threat?"

"No. I knew a man named Wolf was a friend of Jax's. That's all."

"So, how did you meet?"

She glanced at Wolf. "He captured me in an Amtrak sleeper car."

"Where?"

Velvet smiled. "Sneaky…but no comment."

Another reporter called out, "I have a question for Indigo."

Indigo nodded. The reporter asked, "When did you finally see Velvet?"

"Monday in Washington D.C."

"Why were you in D.C.?"

Indigo paused. "Well—"

Jax interrupted, "No comment."

The reporter tried again, "But…"

Jax said, "I repeat. No comment."

Velvet said, "One more question."

A teenage boy standing at the edge of the crowd called out, "I have one!"

Velvet said, "Sure, Jess."

He said, "Did you find out who blew up your house?"

"I did. A female mercenary did it." She didn't tell him the woman was dead.

"Were you in the house when it blew up?"

"Close. I was running across the yard."

"Were you scared?"

"I was terrified."

An hour later, the media was gone, the firemen, detectives and spectators. Basically, everyone except two U.S. Marshals and two FBI agents. They slipped away and watched as Velvet visited with the neighbors.

Six neighbors had collected a few things they tried to save after the explosion. Velvet took the time and looked through some of the boxes, grateful that they had even tried. Her grandmother's iron skillets survived. Some of the patio items. And a few things from the garage that had flown into the yard. Her bike. An ice chest. A girly tool kit for household use. A few gardening tools. And that was only the first three houses.

An hour later, Velvet changed into jeans and a T-shirt out of her vacation luggage in the Jeep. Then she pulled on borrowed rubber boots from a neighbor and stepped into her house. She stood in, what had once been, her foyer and watched as Wolf followed Jax's directions to her bedroom. Jax headed to the kitchen. And Indigo worked in the driveway, boxing everything that was salvaged.

Only one FBI agent remained.

And the country neighborhood had returned to normal. From the distance she could hear kids playing. Cats fighting. Dogs barking. Laughter. Arguments. Someone mowing. A baby crying. Music. And the aroma of bar-b-que, which for some reason, made her want to cry.

She just stood there. Silently. In the remains of another life that wasn't quite over.

Wolf watched her, then said, "Velvet, you need a break. You don't have to do all this in one day."

She met his gaze across the debris field, "I don't want it to go another day. What if Brody didn't see the news?"

Jax and Wolf glanced at each other. That was possible. Unlikely, but possible.

Jax said, "Let Wolf and I look through all this. We'll stack what we think you might want to look at. Walk around the yard. Get a coke. Grab your blanket and pillow and lay out back. We're right here and the agent is watching you."

"Brody is not here and I'm fine."

220

Wolf walked toward her. "You are not fine. I'll get the blanket and come with you. We'll just chill."

Velvet shook her head. "No. Don't stop. I need you and Jax to do what you're doing. Because when we leave here today, I don't want to ever come back. I don't want to rebuild my house, and I don't want the property."

They all knew she had reached her emotional limit. Indigo said, "Why don't you and I go lay out and let the guy's sort through this."

Velvet sighed. "That's just it, Indy. I don't think I want to talk. I don't want anything. I just need to be still and quiet. I'm tired of blood. Of soot. Of destruction. And of Brody."

Wolf stopped in front of her. "Of course you are. So, do what you need to do – just don't leave the yard. Not for any reason. We still need to play it safe. I've got to be closer to you than anyone else."

In moments, Velvet let her hair down and kicked off the rubber boots. She pulled a thin red quilt out of the Jeep that her grandmother had made and a pillow. And after grabbing a Sunkist, she walked barefoot across the yard to her favorite spot under the willow tree.

Laying out the blanket, she settled on her back, auburn hair spread around her. The willow tree was just beginning to lose some fall leaves, so the filtered sun played peek-a-boo among the long, graceful branches. The clouds played chase in the sky. And the pressure choking her slowly faded away.

She closed her eyes.

***

Maybe a miracle wasn't impossible, Brody thought, as he watched Velvet laid out like an offering in her back yard. She was at the most 40 feet from the road in front of the old man's house. And another 70 feet from him in the garage.

He picked up the binoculars. Her arms were over her head. Breasts bulging showing deep cleavage. Her body was lean but curved in tight jeans and her legs were bent at the knees. Propped up and spread apart.

He groaned at the swelling in his jeans. Tight became tighter. Harder. And he adjusted himself, adding a few strokes for good measure. He hadn't felt this hot in a long, long time. He laid down the binoculars and picked up the rifle.

Looking through the scope, he scanned the only men he saw around her house. The colonel. Her brother. And at the neighbor's house, he was pretty sure the man in the lawn chair on the back patio didn't live there. He was armed. Alert. Stern looking. And he hadn't talked to a soul for at least an hour.

He put the rifle down and screwed the silencer on. He had two options. Either Velvet came to him, or he'd go get her. Either way, men would die. But he would get what he'd wanted since he was 17, having wet dreams about her.

Only this time he wasn't dreaming.

And then he watched in surprise as the retriever wagged his tail and walked down the driveway. Crossed the road. And joined Velvet, licking her face and laying by her. Velvet squealed in delight and wrapped her arms around him. Through the open window, he heard her voice, "Oh, Duke, hey boy... What are you doing out here by yourself? Where's TJ?"

In minutes, Brody had the rifle propped through the window. He could still hear Velvet. He zeroed in on his target and waited. One minute. Two. Then he heard it coming. And when the UPS truck sped by, he pulled the trigger.

Chapter 29
Attack

Wolf stood in the middle of Velvet's burned bedroom and smiled, watching and listening to her laughing with the golden retriever. The dog rolled on his back, biting at her hair flying around them as she scratched his belly.

Jax shoveled a pile of debris out of the way and said to Wolf, "Old man TJ lives back there. He's ancient and cranky but he loves Velvet and that dog. She doesn't cook Cajun much but when she does, she brings him and his older brother some. I'm surprised he didn't walk over with all the commotion. Maybe he's having an arthritic day."

Wolf asked, "Does he live alone? I saw someone working on a lawnmower in the garage earlier."

"His brother visits, and he rents his garage apartment to guys from time to time for help around the place. He's particular about the men too. They have got to pass his triple L test."

"And that is…"

"The dog has got to like the guy. His brother has to like the guy. And then TJ must like - that they both liked the guy."

Wolf laughed as he dug in the closet. "That's what you call old-time logic."

Indigo called out, "Hey, Jax. Come help me load this."

Jax stepped over the blackened kitchen sink to the grass. "Coming."

Wolf frowned at the sound of a vehicle speeding down the road not far from Velvet. It drew closer fast and his hand moved to his gun. Flap up. But a UPS truck tore by like a bat out of hell, slinging rocks and making a racket.

He turned back to the closet. Damn idiot. He was probably delivering color books or toilet paper.

On the neighbor's patio, Agent Barrow watched the UPS truck fly by. Then his head popped back against the chair. Hard. A hole in his forehead. His eyes were still open as blood pooled in his lap.

✳✳✳

Brody propped the rifle in the window. Tucked a pistol in his pants and backed into the shadows. He blew the silent dog whistle. Once. Twice. Three times.

Velvet startled when the retriever lumbered to his feet and hurried home without a backward glance. How odd. Then she heard a noise. Was that a faint cry?

She got up and walked toward the edge of the road to see down TJ's driveway. Duke disappeared into the old two-door garage that reminded her of a barn. Something fell. She glanced back toward her house. Wolf was carrying a large box out of the remnants of her bedroom, ashes falling everywhere, as he talked on the phone. Jax and Indigo were loading boxes into the bed of a truck they'd borrowed.

She looked over at the agent behind her neighbor's house. He didn't seem concerned about where she was or attempt to stop her. She walked across the road and followed the gravel driveway to the garage.

What if TJ was hurt?

Nearing the door to the garage, Velvet called out, "TJ? Are you in there?"

No answer.

She stepped inside, glancing right, and found herself staring at the end of a pistol. Her mouth went dry, and she knew before she even met the eyes behind the gun, who it was.

She whispered, "Brody."

He twisted her hair around his hand, pulling her toward him. Smiling, he said, "I've missed you."

Velvet pushed away from him, and he popped her on the head with the gun. Pain radiated and she moaned as he jerked her back. He said, "Listen closely, hot stuff. You'll want to be very quiet. Look at the window."

She glanced next to him and saw a rifle pointed toward her house. She inhaled to scream, but his mouth covered hers. Rough. And at that point she realized that the man who went to prison was not the same one before her.

224

She didn't know this Brody at all.

Grabbing her by the hips, he ground himself into her. Velvet panicked and fought. He pulled her hair – yanking her head back brutally, and she cried out.

Duke growled, interrupting the struggle.

Brody said, "Don't make me kill the dog."

Velvet's bottom lip burned from a split. She tasted blood and said, "What did you do to TJ?"

"Not a damn thing. He's at Toledo Bend with his brother. I live here now. Isn't that a kick in the ass? It worked out perfectly."

Feeling blood trickle down her temple, she asked, "Why won't you leave me alone? We both know I had nothing to do with what happened to Lori or the shooting in New Orleans."

"That's just your excuse. You put yourself between her and Spencer. And in New Orleans, you were in the wrong place again. Always beautiful. Always soaring high. While I was drowning in rage and grief."

His voice softened, "At least until I saw you during the press briefing in D.C." He studied her face. "You've experienced pain now. I respect that. And you've killed a man to survive. I respect that too. So now… I don't feel the hate anymore."

Incredulous, she said, "Then why are you here?"

He pulled her tight. "Because you forget… I've been in prison. And I haven't had a piece of ass as fine as you in years. But I will today…and tomorrow…and the next day. Which means, I'm going to kill the colonel and your brother if you even open your mouth. You're coming with me."

Velvet felt the blood drain from her face. He was going to kidnap her. Would this nightmare ever end? And then anger replaced her fear. She wasn't going anywhere. Out of the corner of her eye, she saw metal tools hanging on the wall. And with a quick move, she headbutt him - shoving him back.

He stumbled against the rifle, sending it sideways through the window as glass shattered. Growling, he reached for her as she grabbed the tool, but he slapped her before she could use it. She hit the ground and the dog lunged for his leg. Growling, biting, and shaking his head furiously.

Face stinging, Velvet crawled away, then climbed to her feet. But before she could run, Brody threw her over his shoulder, then headed out the back door in a run toward the woods. Duke, still attacking him.

She screamed.

Back at Velvet's house, Wolf set the sooty metal box by the water hose and listened to Agent Williams' summation of the day over the phone. He glanced back at Velvet on the blanket. She wasn't there. He hung up on Williams and scanned the yard. No Velvet. He jogged toward the agent next door.

Hearing breaking glass, he looked at the old man's house across the street. Then, turned to the agent as he stepped on the patio. And in an instant, the dead agent told him all he needed to know.

Spinning on his heel, he yelled for Jax and took off across the yard toward the old yellow house.

Jax yelled at Indigo as he ran after Wolf, "Lock yourself in the Jeep and call 911! Stay there!"

Wolf could hear a commotion in the old garage as he ran. A dog was fighting. He jumped the ditch as Jax whistled. Loud. Wolf spun to a stop, rocks flying. Jax motioned for him to circle around to the back. He would take the front.

And then they heard Velvet's scream.

Velvet fought furiously as she screamed in rage. She yanked Brody's hair and scratched him anywhere she could reach. He yelled and yanked her hair so hard he pulled her off his shoulder. She landed on the dog and they both yelped.

Brody jerked her off the ground and slapped her again, while kicking the dog. He put the gun to Velvet's head and said, "I can rape you dead or alive. Do you understand me?"

Jax's voice was deadly as his voice carried across the yard, "Let her go, Brody."

Brody looked up as Jax approached, tall and lethal, one step at a time with his arms outstretched, his pistol aimed right at him. He pulled Velvet higher as a shield. His pistol still aimed at her head. He backed up and said, "You better back off, Jax. It won't work. She's going with me. I've earned her."

Jax said, "Velvet. Look at me."

Velvet dangled in front of Brody. Hair wild. Blood dripping down her face. Eyes wide with anger and fear as she locked eyes with Jax.

He said, "That's it. Just look at me. Don't listen to him. He's not taking you anywhere."

Brody said, "If you don't stop, I'm going to shoot the dog first. Then I'll shoot her in the leg. Then the head."

Jax stopped.

Wolf approached from behind Brody and Velvet.

His rage was wild. He could smell it. Taste it as he neared Brody's back. He tucked the gun in his waistband and pulled his knife. With a glance at Jax, he reached for the pistol barrel aimed at Velvet's head and yanked up. The shot went wild as she fell to the ground.

At the same time, Wolf jerked Brody's head back exposing his throat and stabbed him in the neck. Blood ran in crimson rivers down his chest and back as his knees slowly buckled. He collapsed gracefully onto his back. Eyes on Wolf. Mouth moving without a sound. No air reaching his lungs. But still he clawed the grass to reach Velvet.

Wolf stepped on his hand, then leaned down and pulled out the knife. "Die, you crazy bastard."

And without another thought for the dying man, Wolf scooped up Velvet and carried her to the blanket under the willow tree. He held her on his lap as she sobbed, her hands gripping his shirt. Soothing her, he talked softly, smoothing her hair as he watched Jax jog toward the cop cars screeching to a halt.

He said, "I've got you, Green Eyes. I've got you. It's over. I promise."

Between sobs she said, "You told me...not to leave...the yard."

"This is not your fault."

She tried to explain. "Duke...the retriever, ran away. I thought something...was wrong with TJ. But TJ...wasn't there. Brody...was living there."

He said, "Damn. He slipped right in. He killed the agent next door."

She sat back, blood and tears on her face. "When? The agent saw me leaving the yard. He looked at me. I know he did."

He shook his head. "He wasn't looking at anyone, honey. He was shot in the head."

She moaned. "Brody had a rifle in the window. He threatened to shoot you and Jax if I screamed. So..."

"So, what happened?"

"We fought and Duke tried to protect me." She looked around. "Where is Duke?"

"He limped behind the house. We'll check on him."

The sirens broke the silence as multiple ambulances arrived. The coroner's van. The FBI. The U.S. Marshals. The CIA. And the news. Again. One road over.

A short time later, Indigo brushed Velvet's matted hair as she sat on the ambulance stretcher. They watched as two black body bags were loaded into a white van.

Indigo said, "I wanted to help but Jax made me hide in the Jeep. I hid like a coward while two men were killed, and you were attacked. There's something wrong with that picture."

Velvet said, "A man was shot and killed on the patio just feet from where you were loading things in the truck. Of course, Jax wanted you safe. He couldn't be in two places at once."

"Don't be logical. I hate that. And look at you, your top lip is busted, your nose is bloody, and you have bruises on your face. You might end up with a shiner and what is that knot on your head? Is that blood?"

"Brody hit me."

"With what?"

"His pistol."

Indigo snarled, "That asshole."

Velvet laughed, then grimaced as her lip burned. She said, "You never say that."

"Well, it fits. I'm just glad Wolf killed him." She frowned. "And how exactly did Wolf kill him?"

"He stabbed him in the throat."

Indigo's face paled. "That's extreme."

Velvet shrugged. "Brody was going to shoot me in the head and rape me dead or alive. I call that extreme."

"Shit. I'm glad I was in the Jeep."

They laughed in the middle of it all. Some conversations help put things into perspective.

***

Wolf rode with Velvet to the Medical City Dallas Hospital emergency room. Service was prompt with the FBI arrival. And a news bulletin was playing on the waiting room television. Everyone knew who she was.

A nurse hustled them to the back, then motioned Velvet to the bed. "Have a seat. The doctor will be in shortly." Then she took her blood pressure, temperature, and asked a few questions before she left the room.

Velvet sighed. "I didn't need to come to the hospital. I didn't get treatment after the explosion, the wreck or almost freezing. Why now? I'm fine. A mess, but fine."

"Hitmen were after you. We didn't have much of a choice then. But today I insist. He beat you. Then you fell off his shoulder and hit the ground. You need x-rays."

"The bleeding stopped and everything works."

He leaned over her, forcing her to lay back, then kissed her softly. "Hush, woman. I won't take no for an answer."

She whispered, "What's next, Wolf? Is everything really, really, over?"

"Yes, Green Eyes. It's over."

"It was seven whole days."

He winked. "But I was there for five and a half."

***

Jax crawled under TJ's house filled with spider webs and a dank musty odor. Duke whimpered and scooted farther back in the shadows. Jax saw blood in the dirt. The dog was hurt, and terrified.

He coaxed gently, "Come on, boy. It's all over. The bad guy is long gone. Come on. Come on, Duke. You know me, boy. I've got a treat for you."

Dragging his arm through the dirt, Jax held out a hunk of ham from the neighbor. Duke's tail thumped in the black dirt. Jax drug himself a little closer. The dog's eyes went from Jax to the ham. He whimpered.

Jax continued talking gently though he was madder than hell, "Here, boy... You can trust me. And since the bad man bled all over your back yard, as a reward you can piss all over his scent every day. He earned it."

Duke inched closer to the ham.

Jax scooted back toward the light.

And so it went, until he'd coaxed the dog out with three hunks of ham. Indigo ran for a bowl of water.

She returned with fresh water and set it near the dog, whose eyes followed Jax's every move. Jax gently smoothed the aged golden fur on his side, seeing the jagged cut. Not deep apparently, but long. And the dog wouldn't let anyone touch his hip.

He searched on his phone for TJ's cell number and called him.

No answer. He called again knowing that TJ couldn't move fast.

TJ answered, "Jax? That you? Where have you and Velvet been? Someone blew up her house."

"Hey, TJ. It's me. Yeah. We know. A lot is going on and something's happened at your house today. Where are you?"

"Me and Chester are at Toledo Bend. Is it Duke? Or the new guy, Andy? Are they ok?"

"That's why I called. Duke has a few injuries. Who's his vet and I'll get him taken care of."

"Doc Green. He's not too far from the house. Just give him a call and he'll run right over. What about Andy?"

He sighed. "Damn TJ, I hate to tell you this, but Andy was a fugitive from Louisiana that was after Velvet. His real name was Brody Grant. He was killed in your yard today."

"Killed! Son of a... Why? Did he hurt Velvet?"

"Yeah, TJ. He did. But she's going to be just fine."

"I'm coming home. You tell Ms. Velvet I'm so sorry. I didn't know he was a bad guy."

"Stay there, TJ. Let all this calm down. The reporters have been all over the neighborhood. And it's all over the news. We'll keep in touch. I promise. And I'll call Doc Green right now."

TJ was already telling Chester about it before the call even disconnected.

Indigo pet Duke while Jax called the vet. His old, tired eyes had closed with a full belly, and he was sound asleep. She met Jax's gaze when the call ended.

He said, "Doc will be here in five minutes. He's bringing a tranquilizer to put him to sleep in case the hip or leg is broken. He'll keep him at the clinic until TJ gets back."

She said, "You were amazing with Duke. I love the way you totally immersed yourself in him." He reached out and touched her lips. "You're talking about last night."

"I... I guess I am. You have quite a powerful way about you, Jax."

He leaned over Duke and kissed her, then smiled. Not just a private smile. It was more a, I remember every sound and move you made while I was in you last night, smile. And I want it again.

She closed her eyes at the pure rush of memory that hit her, then she met his knowing gaze. She whispered, "Make a baby with me, Jax. Please."

He grabbed her face with both hands as he kissed her. Wild and deep. Voice ragged, he said, "I'm powerful? Indy, I'm hard as a rock after 11 words from you. And since that condom is still in your purse, a baby's coming."

She said, "Eleven words? Seriously, you counted them?"

Doc Green drove up.

And River right behind him.

***

Back at the hospital, Wolf waited for Velvet to finish the list of x-rays the doctor required. Someone knocked on the door. Wolf said, "Come in," and turned.

A handsome man with a long blonde ponytail stepped in and glanced at the empty bed.

Wolf held out his hand. "Dominic."

Dominic recognized the man from the news and shook his hand. "Colonel Wolf, I believe. I'm surprised that you know me."

"Research was required. I needed to know who was in Velvet's life. You stood out."

"I can't imagine why."

Wolf smiled. "Of course you can."

Dominic nodded. "Ok then. So, you know that we're close friends."

"And I appreciate that. She needed you."

"I see. And now, she has you."

The door opened and the nurse wheeled in Velvet, who squealed with delight, "Dominic!" and launched herself out of the chair.

Dominic caught her. Laughing. But Wolf saw the truth flash across the man's face. He loved her enough to only be her friend.

Velvet smiled, "Oh, Dominic, it is so good to see you... Did you meet Wolf?"

The nurse pointed at the bed and Velvet backed up to sit on the side and continued, "I'm so sorry I couldn't tell anyone that I was safe. Wolf..." She glanced at Wolf. "Is extraordinary. He saved me—"

Dominic stepped close to the bed and lifted her chin. "Look at your face. How many times have you been injured – or in danger through all this?"

She said, "Well, mostly Wednesday night, Friday all day, Saturday there was a helicopter loaded with killers and later there was a crazy bear, Sunday two more killers, Sunday night the home invasion with five killers...and today with Brody. So, a few times. If not for Wolf, I wouldn't be here."

Dominic looked at Wolf. Reality was sharp. Dominic's eyes said one thing - thank you.

Velvet said, "Did you bring Chantel?"

He smiled. "She has a gig tonight and sent a hug. We will catch up with you another time. And I need to go. I just wanted to see you myself. I'll be glad when you are safe and not in the news anymore." He kissed her on the head. "Take care on your new adventures, Velvet."

He turned to Wolf and held out a hand, "I owe you, Colonel."

And after a handshake, he was gone.

Velvet stared at Wolf. "Did I miss something? He was not himself."

Wolf leaned against the wall. "You are in the hospital. And, well, that was quite a list of horror you gave him. He probably left to throw up."

She winced. "I guess that was a bit much. I got carried away."

"I'm kidding. He's relieved you're safe." Then he said directly, "He's in love with you."

Sorrow crossed her face. "I didn't want to hurt him, Wolf. Honestly."

"You didn't. Life happens. You, of all people, know that. He's a good man. I respect that."

She smiled and rubbed the bed.

"Just say it, Green Eyes. You want me in your bed."

The doctor walked in with a chuckle. "Well, good thing I didn't wait a few more minutes. Things might have been way more interesting."

✳✳✳

Dusk was fading into darkness as the FBI dropped Wolf and Velvet in front of Indigo's building.

The aroma of Italian made their stomachs growl as they walked into the apartment. Jax was setting the table and said, "Hurry with your shower. We have meat lover's lasagna, fried chicken alfredo over angel hair pasta, stuffed mushrooms, breadsticks, alfredo dip, and cheesecake for dessert."

Indigo said from the kitchen, "Plus Caesar salad. And we're starving...so if you shower in 10 minutes, we'll do the dishes too." She glanced at the clock. "Now you have 9 minutes and 50 seconds!"

Velvet glanced at Wolf as they turned down the hallway. She said, "I don't feel like washing all those dishes."

After 11 minutes and 29 seconds, they sat down for dinner. Barely dry and dressed in lounge wear, Velvet was squeaky clean, but her face looked...painful.

Indigo moaned and put her fork down. "Velvet, I can't eat. You look like someone beat the hell out of you."

There was stunned silence for two seconds as the men stared at Indigo. Had she lost her mind? Velvet burst out laughing. And as expected, they followed suit…after Wolf pulled Indigo's hair.

Once the initial wave of hunger was satisfied, catch-up conversation began.

Jax said, "Velvet, I half expected the hospital to keep you overnight because of the blow to your head. What did the doctor say?"

"The cat scan was good. Nothing but skin damage from getting smacked with the gun. He put in one liquid stitch so I can brush my hair without opening the wound."

"What about the rest of you? Like Indigo pointed out, the blows you took left a story of their own."

"I'm sore, but nothing is broken. Just scrapes and minor cuts. I certainly added to my collection of bruises. So, other than being colorful, I should be back to normal in a couple of weeks. He suggested a long hot bath."

Indigo said, "Then why did you take a shower?"

Velvet rolled her eyes. "I didn't feel like washing dishes."

Indigo laughed. "You believed that?"

Once the laughter faded, Wolf said, "How's Duke?"

Jax said, "I had to crawl under the house and coax him out with chucks of ham. I didn't rush him. Poor guy was terrified and bleeding. I called TJ to get the vet information. To make a long story short, I advised TJ to stay at Toledo Bend and Duke will stay at the vet until he returns."

Velvet moaned. "Brody beat him, and then I fell on him. Was he hurt bad?"

"He's old, but he's tough. Wood and rust were found in a long, but shallow, tear across his side. And a tendon tore in his leg. He'll undergo surgery tomorrow and heal up just fine for an old fella."

Velvet said, "He growled at Brody when I cried out. But he attacked him when he knocked me down. It was shocking how ferocious he became. I had never even seen him growl before."

Wolf said, "He loves you. We'll make sure and get him a special treat."

Jax said, "Hey, that reminds me. Velvet, I put the things we salvaged from the fire in the storage unit. And you'll never guess what Wolf found, covered in soot but intact in your closet."

She squealed, "The safe actually survived!"

"Indeed, it did. Your purse, driver's license, wallet, jewelry and pictures of Mom and Dad. Your important papers and even your phone." He pointed to a suitcase by the wall. "I brought what you might need for now."

Velvet headed for the case and knelt. Opening it, her eyes welled with tears. She cleared her throat and said, "You know, it's not just the big things one loses that's hard. It's also the little pieces of life that we bring along the way - beyond what we carry in our hearts. There's something about being able to touch a memory. Like these. And the things in my Jeep. Grandmother's quilt. Mom's hiking hat. And Dad's whistle."

She held up a cotton candy pink tutu from when she was six. "I am totally grateful to start anew with what I have."

Indigo knelt by her, and they explored the contents. Velvet picked up a black satin drawstring bag with a bunny on it, and with a grin, set it aside.

Indigo recognized the bunny and looked at Velvet. "You really bought one. I thought you were kidding about that. Let me see it…" And she pulled out a very skimpy bikini. Black with a Playboy Bunny logo in strategic places.

Velvet laughed. "I wasn't kidding."

Jax said, "Damn, Velvet. That's a string. Did you wear that?"

Wolf drawled, "And she can wear it again. Toss it here…"

But his phone rang.

Jax's too.

And both men headed to the balcony with phones to their ears.

✱✱✱

It was late when Wolf drew a bath for Velvet. He threw in a tan scoop of salt from a jar she handed him. The heat of the tub filled the room with a scent that smelled like…

Glancing at Velvet, he asked, "What's in the jar? It smells like you."

She dropped her robe, and taking his hand, stepped into the large square tub. Her body was covered in bruises. Old and new. Shades of purple, gold, and red. Even green. And her beautiful face was marked again with violence from today.

Her green eyes met his blue ones. "I make a custom bath salt."

Wolf watched her body sink below water that had a shimmer to it. Auburn tendrils hung from her messy bun, and her full breasts formed an inlet to her chest. She maneuvered her legs to hide the rest of her. Part tease. Part modesty.

234

Sitting on the edge of the tub, he touched her face, "I'm going to need a cold shower after this."

Smiling, she said, "I heard that men are turned on by scent."

"I'm turned on by everything about you. Including scent. What's in the jar?"

"I was told that my body chemistry reacts best with jasmine and gardenia. So, I mix that lotion with a touch of sandalwood, a sprinkle of fairy dust, a hint of vanilla, and a drop of honey to bath salts. Come on, get in with me."

"I don't think that's a good idea. You've been through enough today."

"You can soak with me."

"We'd do a lot more than soak if I get in that water, Velvet."

She looked solemnly at the water, and said, "Maybe that's exactly what I need."

He said softly, "I'm not saying it isn't. But my gut tells me it's too soon. You're holding something back. What aren't you telling me?"

She gracefully skimmed the surface of the water with her arms. She didn't want to tell him. "What makes you think that?"

He said softly, "What happened when you were in the garage with Brody?"

She avoided looking at him and held up her arm to let water run all the way down to her shoulder. Buying time.

"You need to tell me, Green Eyes. For your benefit – not mine. Nothing he said or did changes anything between us. You know that."

"I'll think about it."

He went another route, "Was Brody worse than you expected he might be?"

Her laugh was short and cynical. "He wasn't what I expected at all. Except for the gun. I expected that."

"Tell me how he was different."

Looking in the water, she ignored his direct question and started from the beginning instead. "My concern was for TJ when I stepped in the garage. I looked to the right when I didn't see anyone, and a gun was pointed at my face. I knew it was Brody, and my only expectation was to be shot."

Looking at Wolf, she said, "But he was a Brody I didn't know. In look and demeanor. He tangled his hand in my hair, pulling me toward him. I struggled and he hit me on the head. He threatened me with a rifle pointed at you and Jax, and I tried to scream." She hesitated. It was as hard as she thought it would be to tell him.

Wolf repeated, "What do you mean, tried?"

235

And then she just said it, "He kissed me, covering the scream. He was rough and getting wilder. Manhandling me." She paused. "And I panicked. We struggled and Duke growled. And with Duke's interruption…we had a brief conversation."

Wolf brushed a tendril out of her face and said, "About what?"

"I asked about TJ, thinking he'd hurt him. And then found out Brody lived with TJ. Then I asked why he was still after me when he'd learned that I didn't know about Lori and Spencer's relationship. And do you know what he said?"

Clearly not expecting Wolf to answer, she continued, "He said that was my excuse. That I was responsible for putting myself in the middle of it. Making it worse for Lori. And that even in New Orleans I was in the wrong place again – staying entangled in his rage."

She paused, "Well, at least until the briefing in D.C. yesterday."

"What does that mean?"

"Things changed for him. He respected that I had suffered. Had killed a man even. So now it wasn't about hate for him. It was…"

Wolf knew what it was about but coaxed her, "What was it about now?"

She hugged her knees to her chest and met his gaze. "Sex. After being cooped up in prison. And not just rape. He…was kidnapping me. He threatened to kill you and Jax if I screamed."

Wolf hid fury for a man he'd already killed. "And what happened next?"

"We fought. The rifle fell. The window shattered. And he hit me. When I fell, Duke attacked him, and it was quite a commotion. I tried to get away, but he threw me over his shoulder and took off out the back. But…"

She slid close, water splashing as she touched Wolf's thigh. Her body tense as she locked eyes with his. "He didn't rape me, Wolf. I promise. He mauled me through my clothes but there hadn't been time—"

Wolf lifted her out of the water to his lap. He held her face. "Don't you dare feel shame or guilt. You did nothing wrong…and you survived. He ambushed you – and that he even managed to do that - kills me. But I am proud of what you've done, your bravery, and the fight in you.

"I will always be there for you, Velvet. In good times and bad. In every today and tomorrow. I'm in love with you. Nothing changes that. And damn sure not Brody."

Velvet kissed him for his ferociousness and his tenderness. How she loved him. And how she ached to say it.

Chapter 30
14 Days

The phone call came early the next morning.

Velvet and Wolf met in the hall with their luggage. Wolf kissed her and said, "Are you sure this is what you want?"

"Can I imagine being without you for two weeks? No. But if you're going to be running back and forth between repairing the cabin, preparing the beach house, and senate hearings in D.C., then yes, I'm sure."

She touched his chest. "But you don't have to drive me to Oklahoma. That was part of my original adventure."

"I'm driving you there. I want to check it out and get you set up before I fly back east. I also talked to the real estate office and added a few requests of my own. One, for a policeman to drive by once a day. And two, permission for you to bring a firearm."

"But if you drive me, won't you have to rent a car to get back to Dallas?"

"They'll have one waiting on me when we arrive. I'll make it back to Dallas in plenty of time to fly out at ten. No problem."

She nodded - then frowned. "Why am I not allowed to help plan the party you're throwing on Emerald Isle?"

"Maybe because it's a surprise and I don't want you to lift a finger. Your only job is to let those bruises heal and get back to your adventure vacation. You need that time, Green Eyes. Get all this behind you. Hike. Nap in the hammock. Daydream around the campfire. Wear that Playboy bikini. Read. And soak in the hot tub.

"You also need to think about changes you want to make to the beach house and cabin. When I come for you in two weeks, we are going to hit the ground running."

He glanced at her belly. "A lot of changes are coming."

She touched her stomach. "That reminds me, I need the address to the beach house in case I do some shopping."

He touched the phone in her back pocket. "You missed your phone."

"That's easy for you to say, you had yours."

Jax came out of the other bedroom with his luggage. "You're causing a traffic jam."

Indigo sighed when all the luggage was stacked in her foyer. She said, "I can't believe all of you are leaving at the same time. The men, I understand. But Velvet, I can't believe you're still going to Oklahoma by yourself. You found your man, why bother?"

"Indigo, it's my adventure vacation. Away with the old... A new beginning. Besides, the place is already rented. Only now, my mountain man will come get me. And you are going to be occupied anyway since you have Jax now."

Jax said, "Hey, easy there. She's always had me."

Indigo said, "Yeah, as I pined from afar and stared jealously at the wedding portrait of the almost naked bride on my wall."

They laughed, and Velvet corrected, "She is naked, not almost naked. I don't think the veil counts as clothes."

Jax kissed Indigo and said, "The veil works for me as a dress."

Velvet asked, "And when is the wedding?"

Jax whispered in Indigo's ear and she blushed crimson. He said, "Pretty damn soon. When is yours?"

Velvet glanced at Wolf and the M word stuck in her throat. Wolf moved her toward the door. "Alright people. We are out of here."

And they were gone.

Indigo stared at the closed door, the silence, suddenly loud. She didn't want to think about Jax leaving. Without looking at him, she said, "Why can't I go with you? At least Velvet had a choice."

He stepped behind her, embracing her. "I don't know my schedule yet – but all that will change by the time I come back."

"How will it change?"

Turning her around, he wrapped arms around her bare waist and said softly, "When I first saw the picture of the naked bride on the wall, I thought it was you. I did a double take to be sure."

Her frown eased, and she smiled. "You thought I hung a naked picture of myself in my living room."

He winked, sliding his fingers under the waistband of her lounge pants. "Don't act like that's such a far-fetched idea. If it's wild, you're willing. So, tell me, why is it on your wall?"

She glanced at the picture and said, "It's the look on her face as she looks back at her groom. I love that look."

He kissed her. "The next time I see you, I want that picture with you in it."

She whispered, "I can make that happen. Now, how come you haven't asked me what the sweaty horse and cowboy picture mean to me?"

"I already know."

"Then what is it?"

He pulled her tight. "You like to ride me."

***

In the Kiamichi Mountains of southeastern Oklahoma, Wolf followed the directions toward a cabin perched above Eagle Fork Creek. They wound through the roads and pulled to the top of a ridge. An impressive cabin overlooked a mountain range dotted with fall colors.

He pulled Velvet's Jeep to a stop next to his rental Silverado pickup and they were out of the Jeep in moments. Velvet pulled him to the overlook. She smiled and said, "It's not the Rocky Mountains, but for a Louisiana girl, this seemed adventuresome to me. Well… It did a week ago."

Wolf said, "It's a perfect choice…and great for hiking. You have a beautiful creek and no blizzards."

She said, "And no hitmen."

"Exactly. But still, where is your gun?"

She laughed and they raced to the Jeep.

It took six trips to unload.

Clothes went to the master bedroom with a fabulous view and a king-size bed.

They set up her mini desk on an impressive black granite U-shaped counter in the kitchen.

Fresh food went in the fridge and pantry.

Her grandmother's quilt and pillow were tossed on the leather sofa in front of the gas fireplace.

The pistol was snug in its holster on the snack bar.

And her phone was in her pocket.

Then it was time for Wolf to leave. Velvet felt tears and looked out windows that were now a watery blur. She couldn't see the hot tub on the deck, the Adirondack chairs around the firepit in the distance, or the hammock under the trees.

She couldn't tell him goodbye. She couldn't.

Wolf took her hand and said, "Walk with me."

He led her outside, and down a trail that led to the creek. They sat on a moss-covered rock and watched blueish green rapids. The breeze was gentle. And everything was peaceful.

Wolf said, "Do you remember telling me that things with Dillon went too fast?"

Velvet hadn't expected that and met his gaze with a frown. He drew her on his lap. "It's important for you to have this time, Velvet. To rest your mind from the past and embrace everything ahead of us. I get your issues with the L word and the M word. I do. And if you aren't ready to marry me, then we'll wait until you are. I mean that."

Worry in her eyes, she said, "That's what your party is about, isn't it? A wedding reception."

"I hope so."

"But if I'm not ready yet?"

"Then we'll dance the night away at the best engagement party Emerald Isle has ever seen."

A tear trickled down her face. She said, "Say it for me, Wolf. Please."

He cupped her face. "You love me."

She kissed him. "With all my heart."

He crushed her against him, wanting to take her here and now. But he couldn't. She'd been through too much, and that wasn't always the answer. She needed time and he would make sure she had it. Even though it separated them.

He glanced at his watch. Damn it.

Velvet sighed. "I know. It's time."

Wolf said, "I'll keep an eye on you."

Her eyes widened. "With a drone?"

He smiled. "No. But I'm tracking your phone. I'll always know where you are."

"You hacked me."

"And you're surprised?"

She laughed. "Hardly."

He slid off the rock. "Stay here. Don't watch me leave. And I'll be back in two weeks. I love you, Green Eyes."

And she watched him walk away. Aching before he was even gone.

He called over his shoulder, "Go for a hike. Your vacation just started."

Chapter 31
Three Days Later

Wolf circled the cabin and landed the helicopter on the mountain at two in the afternoon. A snowplow had cleared the entire area and was parked close in case it snowed again. He walked across the yard bundled in his parka and snow boots. It was 10 degrees and on the windy side as usual.

A military contractor had men removing bullet rounds out of the logs, the porch, the door and the shutters. The rest of the team came behind them and filled in the holes. And after that, an electrical team would arrive to repair any damage to the electric barrier.

Two vans were backed up to the porch. One for intelligence and security. The other to install the new bunker door. They were waiting for him to let them in.

He stomped snow off his boots and keyed in the code. When he opened the door and stepped into the room, images of Velvet flashed across his mind. He looked at the fireplace. The kitchen. The stairs going up to the bedroom. He saw her everywhere…and knew he'd smell her in the bed.

They normally talked or videoed in the evening. And texted off and on with his wild schedule. The rest of the time he debated on going to get her.

Eleven more days was too damn long.

The sound of men clomping across the floor in boots and hauling equipment demanded his attention. He pointed out the damaged bunker door.

Three hours later, stew simmered on the stove for the workers as he worked on his laptop. His phone dinged with a text.

Velvet: Hey, mountain man. I couldn't get a call to go through. Are you at the cabin?
Wolf: I am. And I see you everywhere.
Velvet smiled: I like that.

Wolf: Well, it makes it hard.

Velvet didn't miss the innuendo: How hard?

Wolf smiled: I was checking to see if you were paying attention.

Velvet: I have an image now.

Wolf sighed: I have a houseful of men. I picked the wrong time for where this conversation is headed.

Velvet: Where's it headed?

Wolf: Phone sex. So, change the subject and tell me about your hike today.

Velvet: It was fabulous. I hiked along the creek then dozed in a bed of fall leaves. And woke to a little fur ball with teeth and claws snuggled next to me.

Wolf frowned: What was it?

Velvet: A bobcat kitten. I figured the mother was near, so I took off. But he followed, crying.

Wolf: Did you have your gun?

Velvet: Of course. And bear spray. But the mother never showed up.

Wolf: How close were you to the cabin?

Velvet: Not close at all. So, I brought him home.

Wolf: To the cabin? She could trail you. A 40-inch bobcat is nothing to take lightly. I'm coming to pick you up.

Velvet: Wait, I was prepared. I called the Department of Wildlife. It turns out that a nursing bobcat was hit by a car not too far from here. They thought they had found all her kittens – but missed one. They came and picked it up. I miss it already.

Wolf shook his head: It's going to be like this all the time, isn't it?

Velvet: Like what?

Wolf: Adventure everywhere you turn.

Velvet smiled: What do you expect. I'm going to live with a Wolf.

Wolf: That's for damn sure.

Chapter 32
Day Nine

Indigo got off the plane at Ronald Reagan Washington National Airport and headed toward baggage pickup. She knew that Jax was at Trevor's funeral today and she wanted to be there for him when he got home. Well, surprise him actually. Though she wasn't quite sure how she was going to accomplish that. All she had was an address to an apartment complex. No apartment number. No key. And she certainly wasn't going to show up at the CIA gate again.

After getting her single suitcase, she headed for the nearest coffee shop. There was no way that she could eat a thing. Her stomach already felt like it was on a roller coaster.

Wildness kept getting her into trouble.

Her only consolation was that Jax like wild.

A lot.

After ordering a caramel Frappuccino, she settled at a lone table overlooking the Potomac River. Taking a deep breath, she decided to call the only person she could. Wolf. He was the President's nephew and Jax's best friend. If anyone could get her in Jax's apartment, he could. Hell, he probably had a key.

Steeling herself for a healthy dose of his teasing, she picked up the phone and counted to three…then hit dial.

✳✳✳

At Arlington National Cemetery, Wolf stood next to the car waiting for Jax to give his final condolences to Trevor's mother. It had been an extraordinary military funeral. A casket team, a firing party, a bugler, and of course a flag

244

folding presentation. Moving. Powerful. A true honor for the man who'd given so much.

Wolf glanced beyond the grave to a lone man in handcuffs and four federal agents that stood at a distance. Hal was there. But that was all. He was not allowed to participate or be referenced in any fashion. It was only fitting. He'd made his choice to dishonor the choices for which his son had lived and died.

Jax turned toward Wolf and raised an open hand. Five more minutes. Wolf nodded at the same time his phone vibrated. Smiling, thinking it was Velvet checking on them, he was surprised to see Indigo Shay flash across caller ID.

He answered, "Indigo, everything alright?"

A nervous Indigo said, "Yes. Well, no. I need something fast, Wolf. And don't mess with me. I mean it. I can't ask Jax."

Wolf frowned. "What did you do, Indigo?"

"I need you to get me inside Jax's apartment. I only know which building it is."

"You're in D.C. again."

"Obviously. Now, you know people – so you can get me in there before he gets home."

Wolf's mind went to work. "Where are you?"

"The Ronald Reagan Airport. Where are you and Jax?"

"Arlington National Cemetery."

She moaned. "I have horrendous timing."

Wolf said, "I disagree." He glanced at Jax. "I think your timing is perfect. Now, take a cab to 7th Flats, 1825 7th St. NW in D.C. It'll take you 30 minutes. Someone will be waiting for you. What do you have on?"

"A red dress and heels."

"Well, they won't miss that."

She breathed a sigh of relief. "I owe you, Wolf."

"Damn right you do," he laughed. "And I always collect."

"You're such a smart ass. A handsome one, but still a smart ass."

"It takes one to know one. Now, get going…"

He hung up as Jax walked to the car. Getting in the driver's seat, he started the engine.

Jax took off his jacket and tossed it in the back before getting into the front. He was quiet on the drive out of the cemetery, then glanced at Wolf. "Did Hal say anything to you?"

"Not a word. Just glared. Did he say anything to you?"

"He tried, but the agents stopped him."

245

Wolf asked, "Is Mrs. Beckett going to be alright?"

Jax nodded. "This was a double blow to her, but yeah, she's too smart not to let go and move on." He paused. "Talking to her was like talking to Trevor. At least part of him will still be alive and helping people."

"You were the best kind of friend to him, Jax. He's finally where he should have been all those years ago."

"That's the truth, Wolf. It feels right." He let out a deep breath and the weight was gone. He checked his phone. No messages. He looked at Wolf. "I saw you on the phone. Anything come up?"

"Actually, it did. I need to run a couple of errands. Can I drop you at your flat?"

Jax looked out the window. "Yep. I'll head down to the wharf later. We can meet up there."

Wolf smiled. That certainly wouldn't be happening anytime soon. But he said, "Sure, sounds good to me."

∗∗∗

The manager silently unlocked Jax's door and let Indigo into the flat, then promptly left. Indigo's heart was pounding as she glanced at the time. Jax would be here any minute. Now what should she do? She'd scratched every scenario she'd thought of, so now she would have to wing it. She groaned. How could she surprise him fresh from a funeral without looking insensitive. She looked down at her clothes and red suddenly seemed entirely too brash.

She raced to the bedroom and threw open the suitcase. Rifling under her dress clothes, she pulled out a pair of well-worn jean shorts and a long sleeve LSU T-shirt. It was perfect. Soft and sweet with memories, as good as a hug. She kicked off her heels. It wasn't about her. She wanted to be comforting for Jax.

As she wiped off lipstick, she heard the key in the door.

Before Jax even shut the door, he knew someone was in the apartment. He felt it. Unsnapping his holster, he tossed his jacket on a chair and walked softly toward the hall. He smelled her before he saw her.

Indigo stood at the large window on the side of his bed overlooking the city. Bathed in sunlight. Young. Gorgeous. And unusually shy as her loving eyes locked with his. In a few long strides he had her in his arms. His mouth

246

on hers. He didn't even realize he'd whispered her name. But she'd heard it as her bare feet left the floor.

Jax turned with her astride him. Caressing. Absorbing her essence and inhaling her scent as he kissed her…starving…unable to get enough. He pressed her against the wall. Their eyes met. He said, "I love you, Indigo. How did you know I needed you?"

"I love you…and I just knew. I had to come."

Desire raged in Jax. Wild, he ground his hips against her, and groaned, "I don't want you to think it's just the sex."

She smiled, gasping between kisses hot enough to burn, "Of…course not."

He unsnapped her shorts, growling hungrily at the hot softness he found underneath. "Though," he said hoarsely, "In all honesty…sex between us is…killer, baby."

And in one quick motion, his zipper was down.

Later, still breathless, Jax kissed her softly as he slid her arms up the wall, their fingers entwined.

He said, "Do you want a small wedding or a large one?"

"Any wedding considering our current position."

His grin flashed. Sexy. "Marry me right now."

Her eyes widened. "You mean—"

"I mean, get dressed and let's go. There are wedding shops along the way, jewelry stores, and we'll find a witness. And there are judges everywhere."

Her legs tightened around him. "My answers always been yes, Jax."

"Then let's do this. Just us."

At that, she frowned just a little. He said, "What?"

"I…I have a secret."

"And…"

"Well, Velvet may be surprised when she finds out, but Wolf won't be."

Jax's mind flashed to the amused grin on the manager's face when he walked in. He said, "Wolf got you in."

"Less than 10 minutes before you. And he said I owe him."

Jax laughed. "And he'll collect. But not today."

Chapter 33
Day Eleven

In the Kiamichi Mountains of Oklahoma, Velvet lay in the hammock as the breeze rocked her. Red and gold leaves trickled down around her. An eagle soared overhead as clouds performed ballet moves across the sky. A black bear watched her for a few minutes before ambling down to the creek.

But Velvet didn't see any of it.

Her eyes were focused on the wedding dress on her phone.

She'd started shopping after Jax left the first day. All she'd been able to do was pull up the website at first. Then the next day she looked at three dresses. The next, she looked at twenty. And by the fourth day, she'd found one that she couldn't stop looking at. So, she bought it.

Touching the screen, she imagined the feel of the creamy satin, wondering if… No, when… She would be able to put it on. It had shipped three days ago and would be in Emerald Isle no later than tomorrow.

Wolf would be there by then getting ready for the party, but he wouldn't open it. She'd shipped dozens of things, and it would simply be one more package. One that was a little longer maybe. Larger, but not heavy, with do not bend labels all over it. But nothing that would hint as to what was inside.

She'd bought a party dress too. Similar style, but short, the exact blue of his eyes - just in case she couldn't open the other one. She also bought beach clothes. More mountain clothes. And lingerie. Classy and naughty. Lots of high heels and some new body jewelry she'd found most alluring for another sparkly lap dance over the Rockies.

And then she scrolled to the baby pages she'd marked. She picked out a couple of her favorites for Wolf to look at. Woodland baby animal decor for the cabin including fake trees and a huge stuffed wolf. And a sea life theme for the beach house with starfish, sea horses, turtles, octopus, whales, and a lighthouse pole lamp that played ocean sounds.

She touched her stomach. She was late. It had been over a month since her last period. And 15 days since their first time in the shower. Then several times during that timeframe. And once more at the beach house before they left for Dallas.

She'd tell him after the party.

Closing her eyes, she tried to say the words, *I love you*.

They almost came out.

∗∗∗

In Washington D.C., the senate hearings on Hal ended early. The witnesses had spoken, and the evidence presented. That meant the internal investigation was now in the hands of the Attorney General of the United States.

Grateful for the extra time, Wolf packed and drove from D.C. to Emerald Isle in just under five hours. It was almost dark when he backed his truck in the garage. Hoot had party furniture already stacked against the wall.

And inside, an impressive pile of packages waited in the foyer, most addressed to Velvet. He hauled her packages upstairs. Then he carried things he'd bought for them upstairs. They'd decided on a new comforter and pillows. A few bathroom enhancements for the shower, tub and vanity. And a few things for the balcony deck. This would at least get them started.

Opening the closet, he hung a heavy zipper bag of custom ordered outfits for Velvet – including two evening gowns. One black. The other green. His family's social holiday season would hit in a couple of weeks. He knew Velvet was shopping too, but he wanted to surprise her.

Lastly, he unlocked the safe and left four velvet boxes inside. Two for formal wear. An emerald earring and necklace set and a diamond set. And two small black velvet boxes for their wedding. Whenever it may be.

An hour later, he was on the beach, breathing in clean air and feeling the chilly breeze. He dropped the towel and walked naked through cold waves capped with moonlight…thinking of Velvet.

∗∗∗

Back in the Oklahoma mountains a light snow was falling. Velvet sat in front of the fireplace with her box of keepsakes. She glanced through it and pulled out a long pair of black satin gloves. She smiled sliding them on. Gloves were so elegant. She stood and waltzed around the room.

249

Sitting back down, she repacked the gloves and looked for the Playboy bikini. It was such a tiny bit of nothing that erotically said so much about the wearer. She found it under the jewelry box.

She stripped right there in front of the fire and stepped into the black string bottom. It was a mix between a thong and a G-string, with a metallic gold Playboy logo on the only strip of material that covered something. Which wasn't much.

She walked through the cabin to the bedroom mirror and posed. Then danced – though nothing like she would ever do in public. Wolf would love this. Slowly she turned, checking her body in the mirror. No more bruises. Just smooth skin.

Wolf had never seen her without bruises.

Back in the den, she slipped on the itty-bitty top with gold Playboy logos that didn't cover much more than her nipples. Her breasts dwarfed the bunnies dying for extracurricular activities.

She wondered what Wolf was doing.

And for the next half hour she practiced saying *I love you*. But it wasn't happening, which was ridiculous. Three little words should not be hard to say - especially to Wolf. She'd wildly given him everything else. Why deny him that when it damn sure was true?

He wasn't anything like Dillon. Nothing about their relationship was like Dillon. Wolf was hard, and tender, a bonfire, a windstorm, and a cresting wave all at once. His love took her places, and he deserved those words.

Then she had the silliest idea. And in a second, she felt 13 years old as she practiced writing the words – glad no one would ever know.

Velvet loves Wolf.

Velvet loves Remington.

Velvet Carrington loves Remington Wolf.

I love you, Wolf. I love you. I love you. I love you.

She drew little hearts and contemplated her next move. Then, screamed and ran for her phone. She opened the text app and typed: I love you, Wolf.

She stared at it for a while. Erased it, then typed it back. Added a heart emoji. And erased it again. Shit.

Maybe if she had a little something to drink to loosen her up. She opened the fridge and looked at Wolf's two bottles of beer. She touched her stomach. Shit. She couldn't.

She took out her drawing tablet and drew an image of Wolf in the shower. Including the wolf tattoo…and a few more defining facts.

Feeling the ache it caused, she grabbed the phone and typed: I love you, Wolf.

And hit send.

***

Twelve hundred miles away, Wolf was in the shower washing the ocean off. His phone dinged with a text. He leaned over and read Velvet's message. Smiling, he turned off the water, then tapped video call.

Velvet screamed when the video call rang. Hiding her racing heart, she accepted the call. Smiling at his wet face, she said, "You got my message."

Water dripping from his eyelashes, he smiled. "I did. And I wish I was there to read it in person. I love you too, beautiful." Then noticing black straps on her shoulders, he asked, "What do you have on?"

She played it casual, "Just a bathing suit. And it looks like I caught you in the shower."

"I took a dip in the ocean and jumped in the shower to wash off." He knew, but asked anyway, "Which bathing suit?"

She gave him a teasing look. "A black one. Wasn't the ocean cold?"

He snapped his phone into the wall holder while watching her. Things were about to get interesting. He ran both hands through wet hair. "It was damn cold. Now back to the bathing suit. Does it have bunnies on it by chance?"

She licked her lips. Flat out, hot and sexy, then answered, "Three actually. Tell me, Wolf… Does the cold water affect your body?"

He stepped back, totally naked and dripping wet. Aroused. He said, "See for yourself. Now… Prop that camera up and let me see you."

Breathless at his quick dive into phone sex, her hands shook somewhat as she propped her phone in the stand next to her computer. She took a couple of steps back and hoped no one had hacked their phones.

He could see all the way to her waist and touched her barely covered breasts through the phone. His eyes met hers. "Take it off."

Her top landed on the floor. And the Playboy bunnies were gone. Velvet heard his growl and cupped her breasts for him.

Wolf said, "Damn, baby…yes… Now, back up."

And Velvet gave him what he wanted. Skin. Suggestive positions. Teasing. Views from all angles. And then she licked the phone screen. All six foot three inches of him looked ready to jump through the screen.

Wolf slid his hand down his body…lower…and lower, until he held what he had for her. He said, "Reach behind that last bunny for me."

Velvet's gaze moved from what his hand was doing, back to his eyes. She ached for him and whispered, "Wolf…"

His voice was husky as he said, "That's it, Green Eyes… Do it for me…"

And her hand slid beneath the bunny.

Chapter 34
Last Day

It was a chilly morning in Oklahoma as Velvet took her last hike along the Kiamichi trails. Wolf was supposed to be here in about an hour, and she was ready. Packed. And thrilled to finally be face to face with him after two long weeks.

But he had been right – this time had been good for her. She had found her way back to the thrill and excitement of the adventure that was supposed to begin that Wednesday night three weeks ago. Before life exploded.

She felt it singing through her veins again. Something new. Something wild. Something hotter than hot. Something with...

Wolf.

It had always been about Wolf.

How destiny must have laughed when she scheduled her vacation in the Kiamichi Mountains when Wolf was in the Rockies. And how God must have roared instructions to the heavens as He led her and Wolf every step of the way. Crushing what the enemy meant for harm and turning it around until she was right here, right now...with battle ravaged angels.

Glancing up at the morning sky, she smiled. Grateful for the peace that returned while hiking the trails. Running along the creek. And gazing out over the mountain range. Leaving ashes of Dillon, her house, Ziva, the two poachers, Jagger with his team, and Hal forever behind.

A noise interrupted her reflections, and she stepped out of the trees at the bottom of the hill. She heard it getting louder. Walking toward the creek she looked around but couldn't see anything. That's when she realized she'd heard it before and looked up. Rotors.

Her phone rang.

She screamed, then answered, "I hear you! Where are you?"

Wolf laughed, "Coming up the creek behind you. Turn around."

She spun and the helicopter rounded the bend, coming up the creek toward her. She screamed and danced as it swooped by, his smiling face looking through the glass.

He said, "I'll land at the cabin and meet you on the trail!"

Heart pounding, Velvet took off running wearing shorts and an old Air Force sweatshirt of Wolf's, her ponytail flying behind her. The sound of the rotors faded up ahead, but she never slowed down. She had two more bends in the creek before she was back at the cabin.

She rounded the next bend and saw Wolf running toward her dressed in his Air Force uniform. In moments, he caught her mid-air, and their lips met. Starving. Wild. And then came the smiles. Quick kisses. And the reunion.

Wolf drank her in. "You are gorgeous." He rubbed her legs, "And your skin...you feel so good. No more marks or bruises. You are sexy as hell. I can't believe I agreed to leave you here—"

Velvet blurted breathlessly, "I love you, Wolf." Then, covered her mouth in total surprise.

Wolf kissed her. "Say it again."

She held his face. "I love you."

"And I love you, Green Eyes."

She ran fingers through his shorter hair. "You rarely call me, Velvet."

"The same way you rarely call me Remington?"

She grinned and spread her hands across the medals on his chest. "Look at you… You are so fine in uniform."

He winked. "And here I thought you had determined I was hot in anything."

She said softly, "Or nothing."

He cupped the back of her neck. A masculine move. Possessive. "I missed you, Velvet Carrington. Let's not do this again. My life echoes with emptiness without you."

And she melted. Literally. Her heart sent a wave of hot honey through her. She whispered, "Then marry me, Remington Wolf."

His lips lowered, "It's about damn time," and kissed her. Then, stopped abruptly as he locked eyes with her. "When?"

"I thought tonight—"

And he pulled her behind him as they ran to the cabin.

Before long, they moved her luggage to the deck. Wolf stepped inside to set the alarm and noticed a couple of sheets of paper under a bar stool. He was looking at them when Velvet walked around the corner. She gasped and snatched them out of his hand.

He followed as she backed up with them behind her back. Holding out his hand, he said, "I wasn't through looking at those."

Pink cheeked she said, "Wolf... No. They're mine."

He tilted his head with a grin. "I wouldn't say that. What I saw before you rudely snatched them, was clearly all mine."

She crumpled them in her hand and backed out on the deck. He followed and she said, "They weren't meant to be seen, Wolf. They were..." She moaned. "Personal. I'd been practicing I love you—"

He hooked fingers in her belt loops and tugged her toward him. "I call that creative. But I'm so much better than a picture."

Reaching for him in agreement, Velvet bumped the papers out of her hand. And watched, shocked, as they rose higher, and higher in the mountain breeze. They wedged in the biggest holly tree she'd ever seen.

Velvet stared at the tree in dismay. "Wolf, you have got to get them."

He laughed. "Now you want me to see them."

She grabbed his shirt and pleaded, "Wolf, our names are on them. Our full names! You are naked and you're related to the President." She paused and stepped back. "I'm going to throw up. I bet some ladies on a bible retreat are going to show up here and those papers are going to flutter down—"

He laughed. "And be a dream come true. Let's face it, a bible group is better than a reporter's convention."

She closed her eyes with a groan. "Reporters. Please don't say that."

He grabbed hold of the overhead door frame with both hands. Beautifully masculine. Leaning close, muscles bulging, he said, "I guess this is a good time to fess up about a secret that I have."

"Like what?"

"I'm considering a run for the senate."

Her eyes widened and she waited for him to tell her he was joking. He didn't. She said, "I think you are more than considering it."

He lifted her chin for a kiss. "I am. In North Carolina. Ace is pushing me to do it now since he is finishing his second term. The new inauguration is in January. The time is right."

Velvet screamed and wrapped her arms around him. "You will be the perfect champion for the people! The people's bodyguard. I can see it now!"

Then she groaned. "You have got to at least get the drawing out of the tree, Wolf. Seriously. Shoot it down or something. It looks just like you."

He slid his hands deep in her back pockets and pressed her against him, dancing a slow hot groove without music. He whispered, "That ink will fade and be gone in days. The real thing goes with you. So, let's get a move on… We've got a wedding waiting in Emerald Isle."

A tow truck honked, pulling into the clearing. The driver parked next to her Jeep.

Wolf said, "That's our cue. I'll load your luggage in the bird while you give him your keys."

Chapter 35
Emerald Isle

It was mid-afternoon when Wolf landed in North Carolina. And in minutes, they were headed to Emerald Isle in his truck. Velvet was on the phone with Indigo.

Wolf glanced at her. She had turned her nose up at food all morning yet had been starving all afternoon. She cried during three phone conversations. And touched her stomach dozens of times during the trip.

Back in New Orleans, she hadn't been pregnant long enough to experience the symptoms. But he had nine nieces and nephews and knew the early signs. Velvet was pregnant.

He smiled as he merged into traffic. They would be having a conversation as soon as they arrived home. Glancing at the clock, it was a little after three and the wedding was at six on the dot.

Velvet hung up and turned to Wolf. "Indigo is hiding something. All her phone calls with me have been... I don't know, like talking to Jax. Saying something without saying anything. Did she join the CIA while I was finding bobcats and drawing you? What is she up to?"

Wolf laughed and deftly evaded admitting anything either. He said, "Who knows with Indigo. Her and Jax are probably making up for lost time. And let's face it, everyone is busy with the new normal. Right?"

She paused and repeated, "Right." But she studied him. That wasn't a Wolf comment at all. So, there was something she didn't know about Indigo. Well, she had a secret too...only she needed a pregnancy test to be sure.

After reaching the beach house and unloading, they had a few precious minutes before others began to arrive. Wolf shut the door to the master suite upstairs and locked it. Then backed Velvet toward the king-size bed and followed her down.

He rolled on his side and draped his leg over hers. Kissing her, he slid his hand down her body. His fingers teasing the sensitive skin of her inner thighs at the frayed edges of her shorts. Sexual tension sparked.

Watching her, he whispered, "Are you going to show me your wedding dress?"

She squirmed at the tease of his touch. "No…and your hand is distracting me, considering I will be wearing it in less than three hours."

His fingers slid under the edge of her shorts…much closer to the fire. He said, "Do you know how bad I want you right this minute? Two weeks was an excruciatingly long time."

She glanced at his proof, and up at him. "You're not exactly hiding it."

"Then you know how *hard* it is for me to wait till after the wedding."

She smiled as her hand covered his exploring one. "Then what are you stirring up down here?"

"I'm making sure you think about this every time you look at me tonight. Because it's damn sure what I'm going to be thinking about."

He moved his hand from where it was causing trouble and covered her belly. "Now let's talk about you being pregnant."

Not expecting the sudden switch of conversation, she said, "But I haven't even taken—"

"Aren't you late?"

"Yes, but…"

He kissed her. "Come with me…" and led her to the bathroom. A pregnancy test was on the counter. He said, "I bought it yesterday…for right now."

He opened the door to the toilet and leaned against the wall. She looked at the toilet and at him and said, "You seriously think you're going to watch me?" And without waiting for his response, she said, "Out."

"It's nothing that I haven't seen before. You pee in the snow."

Her mouth opened in shock. "I can't believe you said that."

"It was survival. It's not like you watched out for mountain lions, bears, wolves, or badgers with your pants down. That was my job."

Grabbing his shirt, she pulled him to her. "But we aren't in the mountains, Remington."

He winked. "But we will be tomorrow."

She shook her head with a smile and pointed. He stepped aside and she shut the door. Wolf waited. And heard her start crying. Smiling with a fist pump, he opened the door.

And by 4 o'clock, Velvet and Wolf were in separate bedrooms getting ready.

✳✳✳

Wolf's sisters-in-law, Meg and Adele, arrived at 4:15 to finalize caterer and decoration setup. Workers had set up fairy lights everywhere, bathing everything in a soft romantic glow. Inside. Out on the deck. As well as lining the entire boardwalk down to the beach.

And for the intimate wedding of 35 guests, six round tables with chairs were set up and spaced throughout the den. And a few more on the deck. All with crushed velvet tablecloths in various shades of green. Sparkling lanterns. And designer place settings.

The wedding dinner would be formally served with lump crab meat over filet mignon. Wedge salad. Stuffed artichoke. And lobster bisque with seasoned crusty bread.

Dessert was the wedding cake. Simple, yet elegant with three small tiers of champagne cake with lace frosting and a bottle of champagne on ice.

And the wedding itself would be a fireside ceremony, with the family preacher, and blues rock music by *Kaleo*.

Wolf had powerful family and friends to make all this happen in a few hours.

✳✳✳

Later, Wolf finished drying his hair wearing black tuxedo slacks with a silken sheen. He ran hands through hair the color of whiskey streaked with sunlight. Shorter now, since he'd had to wear his uniform for the senate hearings.

He smiled putting on cologne, his blue eyes creasing at the edges. Bangs falling close to his left eye. Velvet barely knew him as suave and sophisticated Remington. A man who knew well how to maneuver in polite society and elite social circles...as well as in the wild.

He looked forward to meeting her at the altar.

Or...before.

Walking into the spare bedroom, he pulled on a white silk shirt and buttoned it up. Tucked it in, then added a black bow tie that was a little larger and a lot sexier. And last, the cummerbund, enhancing his firm ripped skin.

He glanced in the mirror, then at his watch. It was 4:45. Slipping on the tuxedo jacket, he slid the wedding license in the side pocket with the rings.

He was ready.

The doorbell rang as he left the room.

***

A smiling Meg welcomed Jax and Indigo at the door. She took one look at Jax in a black-on-black suit and motioned her cheek. "Plant one right here, pretty boy, and then introduce this beauty with you."

Jax smiled and kissed Meg's cheek, then said, "Meg Wolf, meet Indigo. Velvet's BFF since they were teenagers. And Indigo, this is Thorn's wife, Meg. Thorn is Wolf's oldest brother."

Meg took in the stunning brunette with eyes like ebony and full red lips, wearing a green halter dress, and said, "Indigo, if you leave here single tonight, something is wrong with the men I know." She rolled her eyes to Jax.

Jax said, "Nothing's wrong with me - she's taken. And what is with the silence? Where are your princesses? I don't hear giggles or see flashes of glitter."

Meg laughed. "Thorn and Sterling will arrive closer to the wedding with the kids – and they won't stay long."

Indigo smiled. "You are the one with six girls. Five princesses and one tomboy, right?"

"Absolutely," Meg laughed. "She wants to be like Uncle Remington."

Jax waved at Remington, who appeared and saluted, heading upstairs. Jax said, "I presume Velvet is upstairs."

Meg said, "Yes," and caught sight of Wolf.

Indigo said, "Wow…good Lord a mercy, who was that, and what happened to Wolf?"

Jax laughed. "He cleans up good. And maid of honor or not, I think you better wait until he comes back down before you go up to see Velvet."

Adele rounded the corner, hands on her hips, and said, "He's going to mess up everything she's done to get ready."

Laughter filled the room. That was true enough.

✳✳✳

Velvet was naked in the middle of the room, except for a pair of sexy bridal heels she was bending over to tie. They were almost four inches tall. Ivory. With a classy net bow across each toe strap, and satin ribbons that tied around her ankles. Feminine hot.

She pulled the last bow tight as the door opened behind her.

Stunned, Wolf dropped the box in his hand at the sight before him.

Velvet's surprised eyes met his hungry ones. She sensually stood, turning to face him wearing a satisfied smile all brides want to wear on their wedding day. One, because of the gorgeous adonis in her room. And two, because of his most excellent response.

She covered her two most private areas and said, "You are a couple of hours early."

Wolf headed toward her. "The hell I am. I'm right on time."

She backed up teasingly, "So, you like my shoes?"

He caught her arm. "What shoes?" And his mouth covered hers. Velvet's eyes closed as his fire touched her. Everywhere.

In moments, Wolf forced the lava down and held Velvet's face. She was absolute perfection. Makeup to entice. Her auburn hair in a decorative braid draped over one shoulder…causing one nipple to play hide and seek. And she smelled incredible.

He said, "You are everything beautiful, I've ever seen, all rolled into one."

She touched his face. "Have you looked in the mirror, Wolf?"

"Today isn't about me, Green Eyes. It's all about you."

She kissed him softly. "Which reminds me, I've got to get my dress on before Indigo gets here. I heard the doorbell —"

"They're here – and saw me come upstairs. They'll wait. I have something for you."

She slipped on a silk robe as he went for the small gift box he had dropped on the floor. They stood on the deck as she opened it. With a soft gasp, she picked up a tiny band with two rows of diamonds surrounding it. Possibly vintage, but certainly valuable. "Wolf… this is gorgeous…and so tiny. The entire ring is diamonds."

"It's an heirloom. Mom gave it to me years ago for my bride. It's a pinky ring, she called it. Dad gave it to her on their honeymoon. She wore it for years. It's yours now – to wear or save. I wasn't sure if women still did the something old, something new, something borrowed—"

Velvet reached up and kissed him, and finished, "Something blue." She stared into his amazing blue eyes and said, "It's the perfect gift." She held out her hand. "Let's see if it fits."

And it slid on her right-hand little finger like it was made for her.

She smiled, raising her hand in the late afternoon sunlight. "How beautiful." And then she glanced at him with a mischievous glint in her eye. "I have a gift for you too. Though it's not anything like the ring, I think it's perfect for you."

He touched her belly. "I'm surrounded by gifts."

"I think mine will surprise you." She paused. "Hmm, how can I say this? It's a rush."

Wolf looked at her and frowned at what immediately came to mind. She laughed at his expression, and he said half question, half comment, "You want to fly."

"I want you to train me to be a pilot."

Scooping her up, he whooped and spun her around. "Damn right I will!"

Wolf's phone beeped.

Jax texted: Get out of there.

***

Wolf jogged downstairs, passing Indigo heading up.

Indigo said, "Did you tell her?"

"Of course not. I didn't want a black eye from Jax on my wedding day."

She laughed, then said, "Speaking of wedding day, that shade of lipstick won't look good in your pictures."

He laughed and wiped it off, heading down to see his future brother-in-law. They had a wedding in 45 minutes.

The Secret Service arrived five minutes later in two black SUVs. Four agents searched the surrounding area and swapped shifts with the agents that had been on the premises for hours.

The preacher and photographer arrived 10 minutes after that.

Then family and guests began arriving – with Hoot serving as valet, and Meg as hostess for:

Wolf's parents from North Carolina, Mr. & Mrs. Xavier Wolf.

Indigo's brother and fiancé from Dallas, River & Miranda.

Velvet's friends from Dallas, Dominic & Chantel.

And next was Thorn with his and Meg's six daughters in floral dresses, and Sterling with his and Adele's three sons in suits. (The girls would lead the procession as giggling flower princesses, and the boys would stand in as ring bearers by the fireplace. Where they could be watched continuously…and threatened visually.)

Adele was the event coordinator with eyes on all things. She met Wolf's gaze and nodded. It was a go.

Jax and Indigo headed upstairs with Meg and the flower girls.

Wolf waited at the bottom of the staircase and looked at the door to the master suite. Then at his watch. Ten minutes to go.

They were waiting for one more thing.

Flashing lights from escorting police on the road lit the darkening sky. Coast Guard lights lit the shoreline. And a flurry of activity from the Secret Service indicated that the President & First Lady had arrived. Uncle Zack and Aunt Caroline.

✳✳✳

Velvet ignored the commotion downstairs as she looked in the mirror – suddenly, a bundle of nerves. Had she picked the right dress? Even though she looked elegant, her cleavage was full and the dress snug as satin skin. She almost panicked…then closed her eyes. Wolf would love it and that's all that mattered.

She took a deep breath and glanced down at her fabulous heels peeking out from under the small train of her dress. They were perfect. And then she smiled. She could do this…and get used to the bright lights of society events. She'd have to. Wolf was going to be a senator.

After he was hers.

She turned as the music started. A sensual yet haunting blues melody that she loved carried on the air…*I Can't Go on Without You.*

Jax knocked, then opened the door. "Come on, beautiful. It's time. He's waiting for you. Impatiently, I add. You know he's going to kick us out after an hour, right?"

She laughed. "Maybe two."

And Jax joined Indigo in line.

Out of sight, Velvet watched the procession.

Meg ushered her two youngest daughters to the stairs and whispered, "Throw flowers and go meet Daddy."

Everyone laughed as they threw petals singing *Let it Go* all the way down. Stumbling on the next to last step - while Uncle Remington caught them.

The next two – the twins, were mad at each other and threw petals much harder than necessary…ignoring the warning looks from their father.

And the last two sisters walked one at a time. Graceful. Smiling. And tossing flowers like mini models. Even the tomboy.

Meg sighed in relief. There was hope for the other four.

Indigo and Jax, as maid of honor and best man, glanced at Velvet behind them in the doorway, then descended the staircase. Indigo squeezed Jax's arm hoping her smile didn't show her stomach's desire to misbehave. The President was looking at them and she could see the Secret Service through the window – with a gun.

Wolf grinned at Indigo as they passed by him. He could tell.

And then all eyes rose to the double doors on the balcony.

With each step, Velvet could see more, and more of Wolf…until she stopped at the top of the stairs. He was unbelievably handsome. Wild and sexy in the tux. And the expression of love on his face would last her a lifetime. As well as the desire, when his eyes lowered to take in the rest of her.

Wolf stared at Velvet and smiled. She looked like an exotic princess in an ivory satin sheath with a diamond tiara. Gorgeous, yet alluring, with a deep cleavage held up by narrow straps. His eyes lingered there, then traveled down a body he knew so well. He noted the dip in her waist. The smooth slide of material over her belly. The tight hug over her hips and the hint of her V as the tightness moved down her thighs.

She took a step down and he met her gaze. He stepped up. She smiled and took another step down. He took two up - and winked. She laughed and stepped down again. He took the remaining three steps and wrapped his arms

264

around her thighs and carried her down. All the way to the fireplace before letting her slide down.

Everyone clapped, delighted, at the vibrant display of romance - and Velvet's pink cheeks. Wolf tucked her arm in his and glanced at the preacher he'd known since he was a boy. He said, "The bulleted version, Reverend."

Velvet turned shocked eyes to Wolf and everyone laughed, especially Jax.

And the wedding was beautiful. Beyond the twinkling lights, the fireplace, and fabulous oceanside atmosphere, it was personal, direct, and holy under God within 20 minutes. Including the ring ceremony and blessing.

And then Wolf kissed his bride. Her neck first. Then her ear. And leaning her back so far that he literally held her up, he captured her lips. And then led her to the deck for their dance.

An instant later, an Air Force jet flew over.

And the Coast Guard cutter set off fireworks.

Inside, Adele nodded to the caterer like this happened every day, and dinner was served.

Velvet was entranced as Wolf danced with smooth moves, and perfect rhythm under stars and fairy lights. With dips, lifts, and spins until the song slowly faded.

He kissed her and whispered, "You look breathtaking tonight. I could hardly restrain myself."

She smiled, touching his chest. "You didn't. And I don't care. That was the most romantic bride and groom entrance I've ever seen."

"If they only knew what I was thinking."

She laughed. "Wolf, everyone knew what you were thinking."

He glanced through the open doors at his mother with a chuckle. "I shall no doubt hear about it."

She smiled at the guests having a good time as music played softly, but she could still hear the ocean. "Wolf, I won't forget a minute of this. It's perfect. Absolutely perfect."

Sliding his arm around her, they walked toward the doors. He said with absolute sincerity, "Let's get this party started so our fine guests can go home."

***

After dinner, Thorn and Sterling took the kids home.

The adults socialized. A couple of cocktails. More music. And a few couples danced on the deck. It was October chilly - but not winter cold. And it was too beautiful to be anything but spectacular.

Jax and Indigo walked down the boardwalk with their wedding rings on their fingers now. Jax pulled her in the shadows as his hands held her hips. Possessively. Familiar with her body, and legal. He pressed against her and said, "I want to see you naked in the moonlight."

She trailed her hand down his side teasingly. "I don't know that tonight's a good night for that, CIA. What with the President, the Secret Service—"

A man cleared his throat somewhere in the dunes.

Indigo giggled. Point made.

Not caring in the least, Jax ran his hand through her hair and pulled her mouth to his. Deep. Hungry. And too damn quick. He groaned. "We haven't even been married a week. I need more than random time with you."

Indigo soothed the beast, "I know, baby. Me too." She paused, hoping for good news. "I saw you on the phone earlier. Was it them?"

His lips turned up on the corner. Pleased. "They offered me the position. I'll be full-time at Langley and part-time...well, anywhere else I need to be. Which means, I want you with me in D.C., Indigo. Permanently. Now. We'll find a place."

Wanting to scream but not wanting the problems a scream would undoubtedly cause with security, Indigo jumped in his arms. "Congratulations! I'll leave for Dallas tomorrow to pack. And I'll come as fast as I can..."

His mouth covered hers. She would be coming as soon as they left from here.

＊＊＊

Dominic hugged Velvet as he met Wolf's gaze a couple of steps behind her. Wolf's look was direct, but calm, and Dominic was grateful. It took a confident man to trust a man that loved his wife in a special way. But those special feelings were quickly settling into memories that they could all live with. Honorably.

He glanced at Chantel as her and Velvet hugged. Velvet had been right about Chantel. She was the one for him. Just like Velvet was the one for Wolf.

266

Wolf stepped up. As they shook hands, Wolf said, "Thank you, Dominic. I'm glad that you both could make it. I know it means everything to Velvet. And me. True friends are incredibly valuable."

Dominic smiled. "Amen to that. And congratulations. It was a gorgeous wedding. Not that it could be anything else with the two of you." He laughed. "And an excitingly fast and eager one. A photographer's dream."

Wolf chuckled. "I hope you took some shots. I'd love to see your work."

"You have. At Indigo's."

"You're kidding. You took the naked bride?"

"And the sweaty horse and cowboy – who is her husband. He was the one she was looking back at in the picture. And the waterfall in the middle was their honeymoon."

"Damn. He didn't mind her baring it all?"

Dominic said with clear double meaning, "It appears that when you're confident in what you have…"

Wolf saluted him. Indeed.

✳✳✳

River and Miranda met Jax and Indigo walking back up the boardwalk. River looked at Indigo's manhandled dress, then rolled his eyes to his new brother-in-law. "Do you and Wolf always have trouble with self-control?"

Jax stepped closer and said, "Excuse me, Miranda. But kiss my ass, River. You're probably wilder than a bucking stallion on the ranch when no one's looking. I'll bet Miranda has got to lasso your ass for a break."

Miranda and Indigo gasped, then burst out laughing from the shocking image.

River wanted to deck Jax. They all knew it. But Jax said, "Come on River. Lighten up. Indigo and Velvet are our wives now and not your responsibility. Take a break."

Turning the corner on the boardwalk at that very moment, Wolf winced at Jax's announcement, and said, "Shit."

Velvet froze. Looking at Jax, she said incredulously, "What did you say?"

Jax moaned to himself and met Velvet's disbelieving gaze. She looked at their hands. Wedding rings. But they hadn't been there earlier. She glanced at Indigo, trying not to be hurt – since she'd done the very same thing to them.

Velvet said, "When?"

Indigo pleaded at the hurt in Velvet's eyes, and said, "It was supposed to be a surprise."

"It was." Velvet said softly, "Again, when?"

Jax took Velvet's hand. "She came to D.C. and surprised me after Trevor's funeral. We got married that afternoon. No one was there, Velvet. And almost no one knew until today. We were on our way to tell you now."

Velvet glanced at Wolf. "You knew."

"I did. I had the means to help her get into Jax's apartment. And it was their surprise to share. Not mine."

She smiled. "You're an amazing friend, Wolf. Like when you came to me for Jax."

He touched her face gently. "And here we are. All married. Except bucking stallion, River, and Miranda."

And it was hard to say who laughed the loudest.

Maybe the Secret Service agent in the dunes who'd heard it all. Certainly Jax. Eventually River. And Wolf, as he held up a hysterical Velvet. Indigo almost wet her pants. And Miranda…she just laughed knowing that she'd never tell them what all River could do on a stallion.

✷✷✷

And within 45 minutes, everyone had left.

Looking across the patio at the moonlight on the water, Velvet heard the last car drive away. The front door closed. And then she heard his footsteps. It had been a long, two weeks apart and they were finally alone. Husband and wife. Tingles raced through her body as she turned.

Wolf was coming.

His blue eyes were locked on her with every step he took. The smell of the hunt filled the air and an image of Brave running through the forest in the mountains crossed her mind. That was the look he had.

Wild and hungry.

Wind blew her auburn hair. It was loose now. Floating wildly around her. Her dress lay in a satin puddle on the deck. Her heels, next to it. Naked, she smiled and danced in the wind like a fire-haired gypsy.

His jacket hit the floor. His tie. Velvet cupped her breasts, squeezing them as his cummerbund disappeared over the side of a chair. Wolf responded to her move, sliding his hand down his body and squeezed what was ready for her.

Breathless at his boldness, Velvet took a teasing step backward down the boardwalk.

Wolf pulled his shirt from his pants and didn't bother with buttons. He ripped it open. It fluttered to the floor as buttons rolled under the table. Wearing only black silk pants, he kicked off his shoes and said, "You're incredibly hot, Velvet Wolf. And I'm going to make you come so many times…"

Velvet gasped as her muscles reacted deep inside, and she flushed with desire. He smiled. Knowing. She backed down the boardwalk as he stepped out of the house onto the patio. Then she turned and ran. Wild. Beautiful. And sexy as hell, flying naked down the boardwalk toward the ocean.

The chase was instinctive for Wolf. He darted, muscles tight with masculine speed and beauty as he scooped her up. Their kiss was wild. Ravishing, as her legs locked around him. And fast was the only way to go. As she reached for his zipper, he reached inside her, and they both cried out.

Powerful, hot, and hard, Wolf carried her into the ocean until waves lapped his legs. Then covering Velvet's mouth with his, he dove deep into her, forever capturing the woman he'd waited a lifetime for.

The End

Epilogue

Wolf and Velvet's love flourished for decades.
Both as pilots.
They had seven children.
Fifty-eight grandchildren.
Colonel Wolf served five terms as a North Carolina Senator.
Two terms as a North Carolina Governor.
And two terms as the President of the United States, Bodyguard for the People.

Books by Patti Corbello Archer

WOLF
A CIA romantic suspense thriller

Louisiana Secrets Series
FBI romantic suspense thrillers with brother heroes:
Bloodline – Book One
Obsession – Book Two
Killer Dance – Book Three
Masquerade – Book Four

Double Target
A modern-day western romantic suspense thriller

Amazon Author Page:
Amazon.com/author/patticorbelloarcher.cajun.lady.com

Author website:
PattiArcher.com

About the Author

An avid reader, writer, and blogger, Patti Corbello Archer is from southwest Louisiana. A place where nature influences everything. Surrounded by lakes, rivers, bayous, swamps, fabulous Cajun food, and intriguing history, creating a tale isn't difficult. Secrets are everywhere.

Romantic Suspense Thrillers are her genre of choice simply because you get it all. Passionate love and romance. Thrills. Mystery. Action. Adventure. And always the magnificent hero. Each story lights the characters and plot in a way that draws you in – bringing you along for every breathtaking step.

Patti has published 6 books on Amazon to date. Paperback and eBooks. Audiobooks are coming in 2026.

You can follow her on her Amazon author page for all new releases or find her on most social media. Her website is Patti Archer.com.

And remember… A perfect story is about a world where love's beauty always reigns. Always thrills…and is always flaming hot!